DESTINIES

Shaping the future that was...

By
HAG HUGHES

Pen Press

Published in 2009 by Pen Press

First Edition

The author asserts the moral right under the copyright, designs and patents act 1988 to be identified as the author of this work.

Cover design and photography copyright Hag Hughes.

Printed and bound by Thomson Litho, East Kilbride

For Susan Hughes,

'May the value of your achievements, be reflected in the loving smiles that adorn the faces of those to whom you mean the most. You have done for us more than you could possibly imagine.'

thank you, thank you, you're far too kind...

I would like to thank the following people for their help
and guidance in making this all possible...

Cassie Gledhill.
As always, and more than ever.

Paul McKenna.
The greatest teacher.

Dr. Richard Bandler.
Genius.

John Sheldon.
Knowledge, advice, and great teeth!

Geoff Lloyd.
Unending inspiration.

Hag Hughes

A colourful chap, with an equally colourful final school report, 'Don't come back next term' was the general gist.

Since then the lure of sex, drugs and rock 'n' roll was a little too tempting, so a couple of decades and a couple of rather curious hangover remedies later, he finds himself in this rather strange new place called reality.

His experience is drawn not only from a mis-spent youth, but a continued fascination with the workings of the human mind; how to learn from it, how to adapt it, and ultimately how to control the programs we run internally as easily as those upon the computer screens we find ourselves increasingly dependent upon. As you will see from the author's note, he has dipped a proverbial toe into an entire pool of human resources that seem to be largely ignored by the so-called experts in today's psychological studies.

Hag has been both tutored and certified by Paul McKenna (yes, certified, not sectioned) as both a hypnotist and master neuro-linguistic programmer, so now extends his studies of the various aspects of psychology, physiology and behaviour. (Although usually amongst the female species in various bars around south London.)

Having lived in Surrey since birth, he continues to do

so with his two little angels Bradley and Lara. He has no plans to disappear off to anywhere warmer yet, not till the inland revenue catch up, anyway…

Destinies is Hag Hughes' second novel. His third book, *Mr. Right*, delves deeply into those bar room interviews and beyond, offering a proven system that girls can use to meet, attract, vet for suitability and then capture the heart their perfect man. It's due to be released in mid 2009, so for advanced notification, please register at; www.haghughes.com

Thank you and good night.
(He exits, stage left, bowing to a standing ovation.)

Author's Note

Have you ever met a stranger with whom you truly connected, chatted for hours with little care for anything else in the world, only to meet them another time shortly afterwards and struggle for words, leaving shortly afterwards, disappointed and confused? Let me clarify this phenomenon for you...

In the field of psychology, it's widely accepted that humans make sense of their world by three primary representational systems; auditory (what we hear), visual (what we see) and kinaesthetic (what we feel). Each of us has a primary representational (rep) system that we use, which is clearly evident in our language. For example, three people talking about the same event might sound something like this:

> A. 'Wow, there was such a good vibe as we entered; I felt it was going to be an awesome party and I positively tingled with anticipation.'
> B. 'Yeah, the party sounded great, the music rocked and as soon as we arrived I caught up on all the gossip.'
> C. 'Totally, I've been looking forward to it for weeks, and the sight of all those girls, well, the pictures in my head were...'

You get the idea, although this is obviously a massively over simplified example. We all use a blend of all of the three rep systems in everyday contact, but we each lean towards one of these three as a primary system.

In my own personal studies of psychology, physiology and sociology, I have identified a further three systems, which I believe blend seamlessly with the already established traditional three rep systems. These are simply; optimist, realist and pessimist, which combined with visual, auditory and kinaesthetic, gives each of us nine different operating modes at any given time. Again, let me give you a simplified outline of how this works.

Three men meet in a bar, they decide to each stake £100 in a few games of cards. Each man enters the game a realist, after all, it's only a game of cards. One man loses all his money, and has now become the pessimist. He also entered the game a visual, seeing what the coming week might hold, but he leaves a kinaesthetic, as he feels bad about losing. The second man leaves with the £100 with which he entered, therefore remaining a realist; after all, it was just a game of cards wasn't it? He arrived a kinaesthetic, feeling okay about the game, and left fairly unchanged. The third player however, left with double his original stake, therefore he leaves an optimist. He had arrived an auditory, with a nagging voice of doubt that the game was not such a good idea, but leaves a visual, dreaming of what to do with the winnings. From a physiological angle, player one leaves quietly with slumped shoulders, player two level headed with a knowing smile, and player three stays in the bar with his smiling head held high to buy a round of drinks and chat happily to the beautiful girl at the bar, who also is currently an optimistic visual. After all, she's talking to a confident winner whose future looks bright.

But in the cold light of morning, the optimist has blown his money, and reverts back to a realist, as he needs to get to work. His bright visual rep system has now returned to his default auditory as he hears his boss' voice reprimand him for being late, and the girl has morphed into a kinaesthetic because she feels cheap for allowing herself to be drawn in by a gambler. She then blends from her previous optimistic state to one of a pessimist as she feels she has been taken for a fool. So now we have an auditory realist trying to make conversation with a kinaesthetic pessimist, it's no wonder there's little to talk about over the breakfast table!

The scary thing is, we are all three players at any given moment in our lives. They are just representations of our subconscious mind and the way we react to our immediate surroundings. The player we choose to be at any moment could well set us off at such a tangent, that we will hardly recognize the person that we were, once we arrive where we weren't meant to be.

This book is truly unique, as most authors are indeed human and only write in their primary representational system, therefore only appealing to those that share that view of the world (this is why we each have our own favourite authors, that seem far less appealing to others). I, however have consciously written *Destinies* in all nine representational systems, and it is indeed the ultimate story of *'what if...'*

I hope you enjoy the ride!

DESTINIES

shaping the future that was...

1. Give me a ring…

I nose my inconspicuous blue B.M.W. convertible into a discreet corner of the Pizza Express car park. It's a Saturday, four in the afternoon, and a bright, clear day. After a little deliberation I decide to leave my coat in the car, despite the chill in the autumnal air, and walk briskly towards the bar on the other side of the road.

Once safely across the four surging lanes of people sat trapped in their tombs of steel and rubber, I notice that the outside tables are strangely vacant. It seems like only hours ago that they were filled with the vibrancy of youth and animated conversation from the summer so recently deceased. A lone stark tree stands naked, embedded in the momentary earthy break in the expanse of dull grey pavement, its leaves shed like lovers' clothes about the floor. I pause before entering, to check my phone for messages, then continue on inside.

I approach the desolate bar that had served as many a night's entertainment with some trepidation. *'Should I really be having a drink before going on'* I ask myself.

'Probably not' is the resounding yet ignored answer that springs immediately to mind.

'Hello, mate, get us a pint of Stella could you, I'm parched.'

'So the wanderer returns, thought you'd been abducted by aliens,' retorts Giles the young barman, sporting a crisp black collar and his usual Cheshire cat grin. I throw my eyes up and survey the area. The flat screen that occupies the back wall shows muted football players, moving to the sound system's dominance of Fatboy Slim's 'Bird of Prey'. I slide my pint off of the bar, then saunter back outside.

I sit in the orange sunlight as it hovers above the shops opposite, falling almost hypnotically towards their roofs. I take in the view, noticing a small girl, probably only five or so years old, playing hopscotch on the pavement opposite. Her mum and dad are just the other side of the shop's plate glass window, wrestling with both their desires and bank balances over the new Magnaflex kitchen they are about to order. The balding salesman though, appears to have far more interest in trying to sneak a peek down the wife's cleavage, than closing the deal by way of a shaken hand or a signed contract. I observe them for a time, sipping my beer, then close my eyes to quietly enjoy the sun's weak rays gently warm my regularly pampered face.

At twenty-eight years old, I have certainly seen a great deal of the good times, and very little of the bad ones. I present a TV show called *Bully Boys*, where people have a chance to get back at all the guys that picked on them at school, transmitted to the nation through the black plasma slab that adorns every living room wall in the land. There hasn't been a punch-up on set as of yet, but I feel it's only a matter of time.

BANG!

As I look up swiftly, those rays that had served as such a relaxing glow now penetrate my retinas with the fiercest of bites. I struggle to balance the vivid colours before me in order to witness the limp body sent skywards over firstly the bonnet, then the roof of the green Ford Focus. The car screeches crookedly to a halt some yards from its victim, and then out of the driver's door flies a hysterical woman.

The victim, a man wearing a long black leather coat, lies motionless in the road. His long, dark, lightly curled hair is splayed out around his down turned head. A pool of crimson blood then slowly fans from it.

I am stunned, unable to move. What seems like an hour passes as people around me are frozen in inaction, the shock has rendered them incapable of movement. Then, the strangest thing I have ever witnessed happens, he begins to move.

At first it is just a jerk, a quiver of his head, followed by a slight rolling of his torso. Slowly he becomes more animated, and after a few failed attempts manages to roll fully over, onto his back. He rests for a moment, then suddenly his arms begin to move. Within seconds he struggles, quivering and convulsing, to bring his two hands together over his head. They touch, and he simply disappears, only to re-appear a few feet from where he was previously, face down in a pool of blood. I shake my head to clear my thoughts of what I have just witnessed. I am truly astonished. He then moves again, slowly rising to his feet, staggering with all the effort and concentration required in his obviously fragile state.

He looks around, disoriented, and heads in my direction. He barges past those that have mobilized to help him, eyes fixed on mine, locked in trance. Stumbling up the curb, he then staggers, blood pouring from his mouth, as he makes his determined way towards me. I sit in absolute shock as I watch him approach. He eventually reaches my table and collapses across it, his flailing arm sending my beer to the harsh stone floor with a crash.

'Take this and follow its power, it will save your life,' he gravely rasps, thrusting something metallic into my hand. His eyes roll back into their sockets as he vomits a wave of crimson life onto the floor, before appearing to deflate and roll from the table, choking and gagging on the blood that slowly fills his lungs.

Once on the pavement, he curls into the foetal position and sobs as his convulsions expel the last remains of life from his broken body. He dies at my feet before the ambulance arrives.

I'm caught up in the flurry of activity and eternal questions that ensue. It's not for a good hour or so, do I open my hand to see the gift the recently departed stranger has given me. Once open though, my hand reveals the most beautiful ring I have ever seen…

2. 'Mornin' Officer'

Four months later.

Tuesday, another drab miserable Tuesday. I guess spring is only just around the corner, so it can't be all bad, but it's still a drab miserable bloody Tuesday though. I pad my way to the bathroom wearing my silk boxers from the night before, Wendy is a fabulous girl, but *so* naughty that she usually gets me well and truly hot under the collar before we've even left the restaurant, let alone driven home (we rarely get that far before the urge overcomes us though). She lies asleep; in the perfection of a dream world so vivid it could lull her into eternal peace. As I make my way down the creaky seventies staircase of our neo-geo insular paradise, with its nice, square, *'enough room for two point two children and a Labrador'* garden, visible out of the double glazed plastic faux sash windows, I notice a letter upon the doormat. Not unusual, you may be forgiven for thinking, but this particular letter is emblazoned with the crest of the local constabulary. Worrying.

I pluck it from the harsh bristle mat and hold it up to the light in order to inspect it. No clues from the outside, so I continue into the kitchen and flick the red glowing switch on the polished stainless steel, and I must say extremely overpriced, spherical designer kettle.

Moments later I am enthused by the fact that a

perfect pair of cups containing Twinning's English Breakfast, accompanied by three slices of apricot jam smothered wholemeal are making their way back up the stairs with the help of a butler's tray, that was once given to me by my late dad's butler, accompanied by the letter in question.

I rest the tray at the end of the bed, on the side I have recently vacated, as Wendy begins to stir.

Her beautiful blue eyes burst into life as she greets the morning with her unquestionably fabulous smile. She sits immediately upright, allowing the bed clothes to slip provocatively under the line of her perfect breasts.

What on earth is a boy to do, I ask you!

We breakfast on the thrill of love and passion, followed by some cold tea and toast before we greet the morning proper. Wendy takes to the shower, and as I fight the urge to join her, I notice the unopened letter still resting on the butler's tray.

I reach over to it just as she re-appears from the bathroom, naked of course. About an hour later I finally manage to open the envelope in question. It contains a letter from the Chief Superintendent of Guildford C.I.D.

My presence is summoned by a certain Mr. Ian Montgomery, to clarify, *yet* again, the circumstances around the gift of the ring they hold as evidence, given to me by the dying leather-clad man.

I arrive at Guildford nick some hours later. Officer Beale is stood behind the desk, and relays my details into the grey seventies looking telephone.

'Take a seat over there, Mister Todd, Chief Superintendent Montgomery will be down in a moment.'

Beale gestures to a row of dilapidated blue chairs that sit by the yellowing plate glass window.

The first five minutes pass at the rate that a herd of three-legged elephants might move, the next five at the reduced speed of a herd of two-legged, and the following ten minutes positively drag by. Just as I begin summoning the energy required to stand and leave, the door is thrust open. A tall, thin and rather flustered looking man in a charcoal pinstripe suit enters, offering me his hand at arm's length. We shake, and after a brief but evasive apology we head upstairs to his generous but cluttered and tired office.

The leather chair sighs as I drop my full weight on its creaking carcass, I imagine the infinite variety of crimes that had been picked over with a well worn grooming device from this very chair. Murder, rape, arson and slavery to name but a snippet. This chair could tell some stories, and that's exactly what Montgomery wanted to hear; another story.

'So, Mister Todd, can you run through for me the exact sequence of events that led to your possession of this rather ornate ring on Saturday, twenty-eighth of October, two thousand and seven.'

I relay the story again, for the record, and leave Mister Montgomery as puzzled as I, as to why I am now the owner of such an obviously extremely valuable item.

The value, I would later learn was an unfathomable wealth beyond any man's dreams, and I'm not talking monetary, but I'll get to that in good time, so read on.

I sit at the traffic lights of the one-way system, and observe the impeccably intricate nature of this perfect piece of jewellery I now possess. The ring appears to be made of a single highly polished silver coloured band, the centre of which is set with three quite chunky sapphires, evenly spaced around its circumference. The stretch of metal between these stones is slightly bevelled towards the edge, and each section has a word set deep into it, but a little difficult to decipher as it is appears to be hand engraved. I squint to reduce the now clear sky's glare to read; Daz, Aparip, Aka. I slip it onto the middle finger of my right hand, and although a little tight, feels at home. I decide to leave it there.

A sharp blast of the car's horn behind wakes me to the green light ahead. I throw the B.M.W. into gear and lift the clutch as the now bright amber glow turns to red, halting all but my own progress. I lurch across the junction, flicking the indicator left, and head out of town towards home.

3. Holiday!

'What time's our flight again, dear?'

'Midday, Christ you men are all the same.'

'Love you too, sweetie!'

'Come show me then, Rambo!'

An hour passes and we are now seriously late for our flight. The airbus to Malaga had probably been revving its engines with anticipation before we'd even hit the check-in desk, but we make it, just!

On board and buckled up, Wendy grips my hand with stellar enthusiasm as the lumbering bird chugs its way skyward. Her nails leaving fierce indentations in my wrist. I'll get her to kiss my wounds better later on though, no doubt.

The flight follows the usual form, by way of a flood of drinks followed by a plastic, shrink wrapped *something* on rice. This then followed by a brief display of the duty free goods, that are cheaper in Tescos these days, before the (probably half-cut) captain announces the ground temperature is a favourable thirty degrees, and we will be on it within ten minutes.

Once through the laughable attempt at European immigration control, we set about the search for our 'Dolphin Tours' rep.

Wendy spots the twenty-something-year-old lad, wearing a bandanna and cut-off sleeved tee shirt next to the two tone blue coach, emblazoned with the dolphin logo.

We're each handed a bottle of mineral water from a large plastic cooler as we board, and secretly hope this isn't an admission on the tour operator's behalf that we are indeed going to be stuck on this coach for hours on end. I had never been to Morocco before, so wait in my seat with a tingling sense of anticipation as the coach slowly loads to capacity.

With a hiss and a lurch we're off, on our way into the great unknown. The light is fading fast by the time we hit the coast road, but the rising moon illuminates the sea to our left perfectly. The gentle rippling of a peaceful night's incoming tide dances with a sparkle as it washes its way up onto the beaches that stretch out invitingly. I close my eyes and drift into a light sleep, dreaming... dreaming... dreaming...

It's dark and I stand alone on the beach, but the moon is full and I can just make out a figure in the distance. The silvery grey light brings life to her perfect hair, blown gently by the incoming sea breeze. She walks towards me, slowly and rhythmically, swinging her fabulous hips at a perfectly hypnotic rate, mesmerizing my vision as I sink deeply into a state of total relaxed anticipation. I begin to walk towards her as she slowly unbuttons her tight cashmere top, then flicks her head back to clear the blonde ringlets that were partially obscuring her perfect and achingly beautiful face. She's smiling.

As the distance between us closes, my anticipation

heightens. I feel my jeans tighten as the blood pumps its way to my growing manhood. I tear open my shirt and drop it to the wayside as we close in on each other's stare. Our eyes are locked now, as if an invisible beam of light draws us together. She's closer; I can see the shadow of her erect nipples protruding through her tight, white tee shirt. She crosses her arms over her chest and pulls it over her head to reveal her plump aroused breasts, held in a delicately laced bra. I unbutton my jeans in anticipation, as the distance between us diminishes by the second. I can see her features clearly now, the sparkle of her eyes grows stronger and stronger as we meet, crashing into a passionate embrace. Our open mouths compress together with tongues outstretched like jousters' lances, bursting into a frenzy of unbridled emotion, the raw passion of our bodies groping, licking and biting in a frenzy of lovemaking. I yank at her jeans, bursting the buttons open and sink to my knees as I take them to the ground, her hands find the back of my head, pulling me closer...

'Jack! Jack! You're snoring.'

I awake with a start to find the moonlit beach has vanished, and Wendy is shaking me by the shoulder to rouse me from my slumber. I yawn deeply after a swift shake of the swede, then nestle back into my seat with a contented smile as I observe the girl of my dreams sitting next to me. She returns the gesture, smiling cutely and our fingers entwine in a lock of love as the coach grumbles its way to one of Britain's last outposts, the great rock of Gibraltar.

*****

Sunday morning greets us with a ray of much needed sunshine. I step from the pine bed, and cross the pine floor into the pine-clad shower room, in order to have a swift pine-scented splash. Wendy rouses from her monochrome fantasy world as I re-enter the room. We lie and cuddle for a while, discussing sporadically our dreams of slumber, mixed with our expectations of the next seven days. We are set to take the eleven o'clock ferry to Tangiers, so leave the room at nine on the dot.

We arrive at the ferry terminal, or should I say the pre-war hut that serves as a ferry terminal, in plenty of time to take in the local scenery. Unfortunately this comprises only of a few cafés and tourist shops selling a range of tat from yesterday's papers or a selection of yellowing Mills and Boon novels, to rubber spiders and inflatable dolphins. Typical Euro tourist junk.

Whilst on the subject of junks, I feel we may be better off aboard one, than the rusty relic of a floating shipwreck we are about to enter, that bears its name proudly on the orange streaked bough, in what appears to be Russian.

'Oh dear,' I think, 'we may have been better off paying the extra few quid to go from the main ferry terminus, but I guess it's a bit late for plan revisions now.'

We board. There is a large central room that appears to be a main lounge, polished wooden floorboards abound, and the adequate, if not luxurious, seating is screwed to the floor in neat lines around its perimeter. The centre is left open, as if a dance floor, but I doubt a boogie is on the cards for today's voyage to northern Africa.

Wendy and I mooch around on deck, playing the fool and flirting, before settling down on a pair of loungers that rest in the sun on the port side. I close my eyes and imagine in vivid detail, as I melt into my subconscious world, the fun ahead of us in the coming week. I have no idea what to expect from this strange and new part of the globe that we are about to set foot upon, but I feel a tingling sense of anticipation grow inside me, as we drift off, out into the unknown.

4. Tangiers

My God, What a culture shock! After clearing the non-existent border control, as three hundred locals storm past the lone trestle table that houses a solitary overwhelmed official, we make our way out into the baking hot sun. Not a moment is wasted though, by the mob of local taxi drivers who immediately descend, engulfing us with promises of the best value for money and the most comfortable cars. Without a blink of hesitation, I grab the seemingly least pushy of the crowd and head towards his cab. Even as we drive away, the competing drivers are running alongside our chosen steed, trying to shamelessly out sell the victor.

'Could you take us to the nearest Hertz please, mate.'

'Hertz, no, no, no. My brother have rent a car that much better than Hertz, we go there.'

I glance over to Wendy, who simply shrugs with a smile.

'Okay, mate, take us to your brother.'

We sink back into the plastic seats of the ancient beige Merc, as it weaves its way through the worryingly narrow back streets en-route to said brother's rental lot.

We arrive, in what would only be described back in Blighty, as a dump, both some twenty minutes later, and twenty quid lighter. Taxi man disappears into a small room that wafts cigarette smoke from its doorless opening. A moment later, brother of Taxi man appears. He is sporting a tache like Borat's, and a vest that was fit for the bin some years ago.

'You special customer, you want American limo?'

'Er… no, mate, the Peugeot 205 will be just great, how much will that be?'

'No, no. You want American limo, it comes with TV and mini bar. The price is good, so you can be cool in our country.'

'No mate, I really don't want the limo, how much for the Peugeot?'

'The Peugeot not cool like American limo though, I can do really good deal for limo.'

'Listen pal, great though the limo is, I just want something small and inconspicuous, so please, how much for the small car?'

'What, my limo no good? It not big enough for your English ass to sit in? Our country not good enough for you to want to look good in?'

'Bugger this. Oi! taxi man, can you just take us to Hertz as I asked please. Your brother is great, but he and I are not really firing on the same number of cylinders, comprehende?'

Taxi man then reappears, frowning heavily and shaking his head.

'I cannot understand why you insult us like this, we bring you welcome to my home of family and all you are doing is insults, why is this?'

'Listen mate, all we want is to go to Hertz. Are you going to take us or what?'

Graaathhhh, thpufffff. Taxi man spits on the floor in front of me, then looks up menacingly. I hadn't noticed his rather muscular physique until now, but it becomes painfully obvious that I might yet get to sample the result of his many years of lifting small donkeys, or whatever other equipment the local gym may have to offer. Two more men then appear from the smoking room, and stand menacingly near its doorway. I decide it's time to scarper.

'Come on, Wendy, let's get out of here.' I clasp her hand and march towards the street outside.

'Hey Englander, you have forgotten something!' Taxi man shouts after us, but neither of us wait to find out. Truth be known, we're so shit scared it could be a ton of gold, but survival instincts have taken over and we're not stopping for anything.

The *anything* we later learned at the Hertz check-in desk, found not more than half a mile away, was our entire complement of luggage. I was certainly not going back for it though.

*****

With Tangiers fading fast in the rear view mirror of the predictably crisp and clean Hertz Peugeot 205, my buzzing sense of anticipation returns. We pass an inconspicuous road sign after only a few moments, informing us that our destination of a coastal town that goes by the name of Asilah is a pleasingly close 45 kilometres away. I tap my toe to the tightly woven chord carpet and pick up to a perfect 110 kilometres per hour.

Wendy and I arrive at the imposing forty foot high walls an hour or so later, the twisting potholed roads proving that the 45 kilometre distance the sign promised was only relevant to those with a helicopter. A tarmaced break in the white-washed stone fortress' walls offers us passage to the hotel we had booked, that bears the most indescribable name imaginable. Once unloaded and freshened, we mooch our way to the hotel pool, set in the small, but high walled garden that stretches to only about 30 foot square. We sink into the steaming water, and the warmth it brings is a welcome release for the tension that my muscles were unwittingly holding. Then, after twenty minutes or so, I manage to relax enough to finally acknowledge the hunger that has been constantly growing inside my neglected stomach.

'I need food, let's go tidy ourselves up and see what this town has to offer.'

Wendy smiles with her usual seductiveness, and we retire to our room. Two hours later we emerge, refreshed but still chlorinated, and make our way into the town for some grub.

There are sunsets to amaze, sunsets to impress, and then there are the most colourfully evocative sinkings of Earth's illumination to simply stop you dead in your tracks, in total awe of the absolute power, beauty and wonder of the world we are so fortunate to live in. This, is one of those no holds barred type of sunsets.

Even the locals have stopped work to migrate to the city walls in order to catch the last hints of this splendorous display of colourful emotion as it dips its way down past the ocean's horizon. I stand with my arm around Wendy for quite some time after witnessing such a spectacle, first numbed with emotion, but then shiver as the evening's comparative chill finds its way beneath my flimsy short-sleeved shirt. We decide to move on, before we are indeed numbed also by the cascading temperature. We mooch arm in arm along the promenade, taking in the local culture and idly discussing our restaurant of choice for the evening. Swordfish drizzled in a herb butter, set on a bed of zesty lemon infused rice and coarse chopped peppers is the description that most draws saliva, so we sit with fingers entwined on a wooden topped table in anticipation. The food is fabulous, the view spectacular and the beer, okay I suppose. I daren't check the sell by date, but it its aroma is somewhat pungent... Hmm. The locals don't drink, so we are advised by our Norwegian restaurateur to remain discreet, as drunken behaviour will likely end up in a rather uncomfortable bedroom, with bars on the windows and a uniformed host. Point taken, we amble back to the hotel sedately and take mint tea in the lounge before retiring for a night of passion.

We breakfast alone at an entirely respectable nine thirty, in the ornately decorated yet coolly calming dining room. The absolute diversity of colour that is overpoweringly evident in the mosaic patterns spread intricately around its walls is so impressive it renders me silent for the entire meal. Once fed with fruits and breads, Wendy disappears back upstairs for a mo whilst I wait downstairs in the reception. A Fez hatted chap appears almost immediately with another urn of minted refreshment, and I sink back into the camel skinned sofa with a '*Rif Tours*' brochure in my hand. As the tea bleeds into my veins, I feel a growing affection for the country we find ourselves guests in. I slouch, engrossed in the pictorial guide of the mountain city of Cefchaouen. The stark white walls contrasted with their trademark bright blue doors is a sight to behold, that and the now derelict ruin of a marble clad mountain-side paradise hotel that was apparently once home to the Beatles now seals it. As a great fan of the fab four I simply can't pass by the opportunity to sample a slice of their history, no matter how contrived or exaggerated it may be. Suddenly drawn into the hope that they may have once visited, I decide we should take the tour, commencing every morning at ten thirty apparently, from the main square.

5. St. Peter

The Tour guide ushers us towards the relic of a coach we're due to call home for the next few hours. The waft of stale sixties air envelops me as the doors whoosh open inches from my nose. I place a trusting palm onto the tubular chrome hand rail, but feel it flex just a little too much for my liking. The rust around the welds serves as a warning for any who put even the lightest faith in its ability to do its simple job. I open my grip and use the door frame for leverage instead. The driver turns his head towards me with a mixed gold and gapped smile as his teeth show their varying stages of disrepair.

'Welcome aboard, my friend, follow your ways to back of coach and make comfortable, okay?'

'Thanks, mate,' I return with an amused face as I climb the couple of steps into this retro time machine, then make my way along the passageway past the filthy seats that shamefully wear an acid casualty designed swirl of burgundy and green paisley velvet. Wendy and I opt for a place three quarters of the way down, and sit in hopeful anticipation as to what the day might hold.

The coach fills quickly, and after a short welcoming speech through the diabolically inadequate audio system by Raymond, our effeminate tour guide, we chug our way out of the city walls and into the open countryside.

After only a few minutes of driving, I notice how rapidly the scenery changes from city to suburb, then outskirted scattered buildings blend into desolate wasteland just moments later. The empty road ahead of us has neither junctions nor road markings, the few random points of reference marking the gaps between sandy expanses are simply the odd burst of marijuana plants or a few stork nests set in the occasional dehydrated tree.

'Sod breaking down out here,' I mutter to myself as the relentless sun beats through the grimy window, before returning to the *Perfect Home* magazine I had bought in a newsagent whilst we were still in Gibraltar.

After half an hour I begin to feel a touch light headed. The combination of dodgy Moroccan roads, dodgy Moroccan fare, and reading whilst on the move have conspired against my brain and sent it swimming. I note, however, with amusement how the roles in the modern world have truly been gripped by sexual polarity. Whilst I sit studying colour combinations for our hallway, and kitchen styles for the refurb we plan to begin some time in the near future, Wendy sits reading a book whose cover features a strapping lad with a pair of taut buttocks clad in nowt but a pair of elastic white jodhpurs. Boys choosing wallpaper whilst girls read pornography, how did that happen with nobody noticing? Closing my eyes, I try to ignore the discomfort of the glass that serves as my head's harsh pillow.

I rouse some time later with a fuzzy swede. The heat of the midday sun has taken its toll now, and my swollen tongue gasps for a drop or two of crystal cool water. Delving into my rucksack, I retrieve a bottle of disappointingly lukewarm refreshment that serves as merely adequate at best, although my parched throat welcomes the re-hydration and softens in response.

'Jeez, what time is it?' I ask Wendy. She grabs my wrist, and in an over dramatic way brings my arm to within an inch of my nose, saying;

'I don't know Mr. Wolf, let's find out shall we? Oooh! The big hand is almost at the twelve, and the intsy wincy little pinky is looking straight at the two, so I'd guess it must be around two in the morning, wouldn't you say? No! Scrap that, it's blaringly hot and the sun is above us, make that two in the afternoon.'

'Thanks love, two would have been sufficient.'

'So look at your own watch next time, Romeo.'

'Yeah, okay, point taken. Man do I feel fuzzy, how much longer do we have to endure this manky rat den for?'

'Probably only another hour or so, we're just reaching the base of the mountain now.' I look longingly at the thin dress, draped across her perfect shoulders as my eyes wander down further to her full...

'Stop staring at my tits will you, I'm horny enough as it is, without you eyeing me up at every opportunity, you're like a bloody rabbit.' Wendy shoots me one of her heart melting grins, and right on cue, my heart melts. I quietly skulk back to my interior design journal, with a smile to my face that truly ignites the soul. Christ, I am so lucky!

The coach unexpectedly veers to the right, I lollop onto Wendy's shoulder.

'Hey tiger, thought we were going to wait till later,' she whispers enticingly. I rouse, and glance up to meet those vivid eyes, that draw me in for a deep, deep kiss.

BANG! The rear of the coach clips a rocky outcrop in the road, that sends the back end hopping abruptly across the narrow mountain path. I instantly draw my attention to the window, and note for the first time that we have indeed climbed some way up, and are now threading our way along a seemingly treacherous stretch of road. The twists and turns fall ever tighter, yet the driver's speed appears ever constant. I begin to feel the root of deep concern growing in the pit of my stomach.

With the coach slewing and sliding beneath us, I stare out of the window with growing anxiety, and watch as the dust and shards of grey rock spill over the cliff edge from the worn and overworked tyres. The drop is increasing, and the jagged rocks seem ever more deadly as the road width depletes to almost a single track. Wendy's face pales as a growing look of concern spreads across it. Her freckled brow furrows as a grimace appears with every twist and turn, the driver's control becomes increasingly reckless as the passengers become more and more agitated. I start to sweat, then notice that I've begun to turn the ring on my right hand with the first three fingers of my left hand. The greater the increase in speed of the coach, the faster the ring is spun on my finger.

Then, a sense of relief spreads throughout the interior. The road opens up again, and everyone takes a deep breath before relaxing back into their previously paused conversations. I close my eyes once more and loll onto Wendy's shoulder.

'Bugger off will you, I'm reading.' She pushes me away forcefully, so I take the hint and find the familiar, if somewhat uncomfortable window my pillow once again.

*****

Crack! I'm awoken with an explosion of pain from the front of my face, as my nose impacts with the back of the seat I have been thrown against at great velocity. A lunge to the left followed by one to the right has my head thumping into the window, leaving a smear of blood. I cannot decipher what is happening; the world is just in a spin around me, set to the terrified screams of all inside. We are mid crash, but the sequence of events appear to be happening in such slow motion. The wail of car horns outside, the screech of burning tyres that frantically fight for grip, and my realisation that with the coach sliding sideways at our current speed and trajectory, we will tip over the edge of the cliff in a fraction of a second's time. I grasp my hands together in a moment of panicked prayer, only to find the world dramatically slowing to a stop.

I open my eyes, I hadn't even realised that I had closed them, but must have done in the sheer panic, and look in awe at the frozen world around me. Glancing down at my tightly clenched hands, the thumb, fore and second fingers of my left hand are all clasped tightly around the ring on my right, squeezing the three sapphires simultaneously. I release my grip, and then notice the tension I am also carrying in both my shoulders and jaw. One by one I slowly release the pressure from my taut, aching muscles. Curiosity invades my mind like never before, I notice that everything around me is held in a state of suspended animation yet I alone am free to move. How can this be? I wonder. The dust particles hang in the air in front of my face, and I look to my side, jumping with fright as I see Wendy's face is fixed in a tortured scream. I reach out to touch it, still soft skinned, but the muscles of her face have contracted into hard sub-skin knots, just as mine were only a moment ago. I stroke her hair, it moves with the softest of touches, but reacts like an astronaut's might, bobbing and floating in a vacuum without the aid of gravity to keep it in check. This disturbs the dust particles in the air around me, and I begin to wonder what else I can affect in this surreal world.

'Everything,' comes the bold reply. Startled, I look around for the source of the voice. Shocked, I see none other than an aged Michael Caine standing in the aisle wearing a blue boiler suit. I blink my eyes and shake my head in an effort to clear my mind enough fathom what the hell is going on.

'You're about to die, old son, but I guess you knew that when the coach tipped its arse end over a three hundred foot cliff edge.'

'I don't understand,' I pathetically offer.

'No, you lot never do. That's where I come in though, to act as a sort of guide to help explain a few things, get you on the right track so to speak.'

'But…' Caine holds his hand up in an open palmed stop sign.

'Let me introduce myself, you've probably heard of me; Guardian of the Gate is my official title, and one I quite like actually, but most just call me by my more popular name, Saint Peter.'

'So I'm dead?'

'Well, not yet. Given a couple more seconds and you certainly would have been. Smashed, crushed and then burned alive in the wreckage. A horrible way to go I must admit, I hate it when we get the burned alive ones, they stink the place out for weeks.'

'Heaven?'

'Yes of course it's bloody Heaven, where else do you think I'm Guardian of the Gate, down there with… *Him*?'

'You swore!'

'Yes of course I bloody swore, I swear all the bloody time. I'm Michael bloody Caine, haven't you seen any of my films? And no *"Only meant to blow the bloody gates off"* jokes whilst I'm on the subject either!'

'I thought you said you were Saint Peter, are you lying as well?'

'No I'm not bloody lying. It's all a matter of perception.'

'Perception?'

'Yes, perception. Let me explain: Suppose you were walking along a pavement, the sun was out for the first time that March, and you came across a half eaten burger, in a half opened wrapper sat directly in the middle of the path in front of you. What would you do? My guess is that you would cuss at the kids that had discarded it and walk on without a second thought. Now imagine that same half eaten burger sat innocently in the path of ten starving and shivering men who had slept rough for five days, running towards the only form of nutrition they have seen in almost a week. Imagine, as they fight and jostle over such a precious source of food. It's obviously of a far higher value now, therefore their perception of it is somewhat different to yours wouldn't you say?'

'Yeah, I suppose so, but what the hell has this got to do with you being both a famous seventies actor and the guardian of the gate?'

'Perception, my old fruit. The thing is, once you get up here, you can't take your body with you, so everyone sees you the way that their mind perceives that they *should* see you, be it litter or nutrition, warm or cold, Michael Caine or Saddam Hussain. You are

27

seeing me as I was in that old film with the Minis in Italy, where the coach tips over the edge of a cliff at the end. You obviously identify that character with the saviour who is going to dig you out of this shit hole you seem to be firmly wedged in. It's your own personal perception of who's going to save you. Comprende?'

'Er… yeah I suppose so, but how are you going to save me though?'

'I'm not.'

'You're not?'

'No, I'm not, my old son.'

'Fuck.'

'Now look who's swearing.'

'Do you fucking blame me? I'm just about to plummet down a three hundred foot cliff, smashing, crushing and burning myself to a hellish oblivion, and you have the audacity to berate me for my fucking language!'

'A hellish oblivion can be arranged, my old son, but from what I've seen of it, I certainly wouldn't recommend it. Let me help you out a little here, take a deep breath and listen a moment, 'cos I think this could be important to you:

'You have on your finger a ring, and yes, ornate though it might be, innocent it most certainly isn't. On your hand is the power to change the world, the destiny of all around you and possibly the future of the planet you lot call home. It has graced the hand of many before you, and will also be passed to many after you, provided you don't really fuck up and lose it or something. It cannot be destroyed, it cannot be replaced, and it certainly cannot be imitated. It is the original eternity ring.'

'Eternity?' I question.

'Yes, Jack, eternity. However that doesn't mean the bearer lives forever, it just means the ring will, so don't go getting your hopes up.'

'Oh. So what happens now?'

'Oh yes, sorry, where was I? The ring bearer, that's you by the way, will have it passed to him, or her, you've got to be so fucking P.C. these days it dries me up, by the previous ring bearer once his or *her* ninety second privileges have been exhausted.'

'What the Hell are you talking about?' I interject.

'Are you going to shut up and let me bloody finish or what?'

'Yes, sorry, continue.'

'Anyway, your ninety second privileges start now, as you have used the ring to summon them by depressing all three stones at once. This is the signal to the universe that you need time to halt. What this also means, is you have been given three time slots in which to reverse time and re-assess your decisions or actions. Time in the real world stands still, you can take as long as you like to suss the situation and do whatever you need to, to put it right. Some tossers have taken weeks, months or even bloody years to decide what to do. The downside to this is that time doesn't stop for the bearer, you'll age at your normal rate. You must have heard of people that seemingly deteriorate or go grey overnight, they aren't freaks, they're just previous ring bearers who've agonised for years in their frozen world for the right decision to make, only to return, seemingly only thirty seconds earlier, as the old men they had become during their indecision. My only advice to you is this; make your decisions with your gut, it is usually right. Agonising over your options in the consciousness of your mind has never worked, so don't be tempted to prove the exception. It doesn't work, believe me.'

'So let me get this right, I have eternity to decide what happened thirty seconds ago?'

'No, you have the rest of your natural life span to decide what you would be better doing thirty seconds ago than you already did, but best not die of old age before you make a decision.'

'Right, so how do you propose I get myself out of this shithole then?' And with that, Michael Caine smiles and simply fades into the ether.

Great.

I run through the words I've just heard over and over again, still making little sense of them. I can't even remember my own name with the mess that my brain is in, let alone what happened thirty seconds ago. *Get out*, is my first instinct. A wise one at that, me thinks. Trust your gut he said, and as I have no desire for my guts to be sprawled down the side of a rockface, so see this as a good option. I draw my knees up, place them on the seat, and hop over Wendy into the aisle. Upon reaching the front, I try to open the doors, but they are stuck fast. *'Ahh, pneumatic,'* I finally deduce. I find the release switch on the dashboard a moment later, wincing at the vile stench coming from the inanimate driver that I have to lean across in order to depress it. Nothing, I press it again, still nothing. No power, I conclude. Damn. I make my way back down the coach, looking for the emergency exit. Relieved, I see it about three quarters of the way down on the right-hand side. There is a mother and child obscuring my access to it, so thinking quickly I gently lift the child into another seat, then return for the mother. She, it transpires, has never heard of Weight Watchers. I tug and heave at her grossly overweight carcass, her light floral dress tearing with the effort as she slumps and slips from my grasp. I eventually get her into a headlock and drag her, face first, into the aisle.

The window whooshes as it glides up out of my way by its horizontal overhead hinge. I leap from the coach, finding the dry ground a little farther than I anticipate, and jar my back in the process. After a moment of discomfort I jog over to the safety of the undamaged Armco barrier a little way back down the road. I glance over its edge to remind myself of just how lucky I truly am. I turn, face the coach, and clasp my ring in my three fingers, ready to apply the required pressure for the spectacle I am about to begin.

I stop, overwhelmed at my own selfishness. Surely

there's something I could do for the rest of the passengers. My thoughts then spring to the overweight woman I had so much trouble shifting. Wouldn't want to try and oik her out of the window. Hmm, this presents a problem. I shake my head in an effort to stimulate its contents. I can see what Caine meant now, I could vacillate on this for hours, getting older in the process. What are the implications, I wonder, of saving a group of tourists to continue their lives as normal, albeit with altered destinies, as opposed to me *not* intervening with the natural order and allowing them to plummet to their graves? There could be a mass murderer on board, and my interrupting this chain of events could have catastrophic consequences. I recall reading of the doctor who saved a rather famous patient of his from the affliction of peritonitis, deadly if left untreated, only to have a guilt and remorse filled existence a few years later, once his patient recovered to become one of the most powerful men in history. Adolph Hitler was just another cut and stitch job to the surgeon at the time. I decide to let the coach plummet.

Wendy, what about Wendy? I can't let her perish aboard the coach, now can I? My hands fall to my side as I walk back to the stricken vehicle.

Once back inside, after a rather awkward climb through the exit, I look around at all the faces. There are plenty of children, a good spread of pink-skinned tourists and the odd few Saga louts. I feel an overwhelming sense of guilt at leaving them here. I sit for a moment in a vacant seat and contemplate both mine and their fate. I honestly don't think I could live with myself if I just let the coach go, killing everybody on board, when all that's required is a little effort on my behalf. I look at the overweight lump still slumped in the aisle, then the open exit window above her, then decide I need a better plan.

*****

Bingo! It comes to me almost immediately. Caine said that I have thirty seconds of history to play with. Thirty seconds before the world ceased to function we were happily trundling along the mountain road. It wasn't until we happened across this deceptively sharp bend that we got ourselves into all sorts of trouble. Therefore, if I can halt the coach before the corner, we will all get round safely, everyone gets saved and I won't have to lug old fatty chops there out of the window. Brilliant! I rise from my seat and make my way again to the front of the coach. I take a good look at the location of the brake pedal, and check that I can reach it easily when the time comes. I also check where the air brake is, just to make sure. Back at my seat, I push Wendy back into the backrest and perch, muscles taut like a sprinter, with my feet up on the seat, ready to hop over her and dash to the front. I'm presuming all goes back to where it was previously once time is resumed, so leave old fatty on the floor.

Trembling, I grasp the ring in my three fingers as before, but begin to have second thoughts. What if the ring just resumes time as it is happening and we all tip over the cliff anyway, I'd bitterly regret hopping back on board to save everyone, that's for sure. But then what if it does exactly as Michael Caine said it would and I save everyone. Hmm, what a decision.

'Fuck it,' I think as I squeeze the Sapphires with all my might. There is a flicker to my vision, like on a duff old TV set, and in an instant we are back up the road, rapidly approaching the deadly corner. I leap from my seat and sprint towards the front, flying into a mid-air Karate kick as I land on the polished and worn lino floor, sliding along at high speed before crashing into the dashboard and pummelling the brake pedal into the bulkhead, causing the wheels to instantly lock. The coach slides and veers violently to the right, then the left whilst the screams can be heard from both the tyres and the passengers as we rebound off the rocky wall on the inside edge of the mountain and lunge towards the Armco barrier that shields us from the deadly drop. After a teetering moment of imbalance the coach rights itself and thankfully remains on the road, as it is now only a glancing blow, not as full an impact as we would have had, should I have allowed fate to take its path a little further up the road. The sound and motion relents somewhat as the coach eventually grinds to a stuttered halt at forty-five degrees to the direction of travel, blocking the road entirely. A car appears from around the blind corner ahead and swerves and slews as the driver fights to keep control of his wayward vehicle in the looming

presence of the completely blocked road.

There is a dull thud and the coach lurches to one side as he smashes into the middle of our vehicle, the impact lighter than it could have been but still enough to compress the front of his car, bursting the radiator and breaking his rather Roman looking nose on the steering wheel. He, it must be said, is not impressed. I look back up the aisle for a little moral support, but the faces only bear hate and anger. All of a sudden there's a barrage of insults flooding my way, 'why had I done this?' 'Am I drunk, mentally unstable, or simply a lunatic?' The onslaught of abuse from the passengers is relentless for over five minutes, eventually subsiding once I hold my hands in mock surrender and begin to explain;

'We were all going to turn the next corner and plummet down the cliff, I saw it, honestly, when Saint Peter came to take us and he offered me the chance, you know, to save us all.' This just fuels a fresh wave of insults, people begin throwing stuff at me and telling me to get off the coach. I'm beat, even without a decent fight. I know I'll never win against the logic of those who hadn't seen it for themselves. I mooch back to my seat with a stooped posture and dropped shoulders. The most annoying part is that I had saved most of these sorry bastards' lives and they don't even realise it.

'What the hell was that little performance all about then?' Wendy questions as I sink back into the warm velour seat. 'I thumped my face on the bloody chair in front thanks to you, I feel like I've broken my nose, and my neck is killing me. Just what the fuck do you think you're playing at, Jack?'

'We were all going to die,' I explain vigorously, 'I saw it with my own two eyes. The next corner coming up is deceptively sharp, and we would have plummeted over the edge to our deaths had I not intervened. Honestly, it all unfolded in front of me in slow motion before time ceased and I was able to rewind the moments leading up to it. I know it sounds crazy but you've got to believe me, I saw St. Peter before me in the aisle and he told me what to do.'

'Jack, much as I love you *sweetie*,' she starts sarcastically, 'this is all just a little bizarre. I suggest you don't fall asleep in the sun again without a hat on. The rays have obviously softened what few brain cells the beer didn't totally kill last night. Anyway, I think the driver of that car might want a little word with you.'

I look up to see a red faced Moroccan coming my way...

A palm crossed with silver and a shaken hand later we are back on the road. We arrive at the local (if you can call a 37 mile detour *local*) hospital over an hour later. There had been so many complaints of back and face injuries that Raymond the effeminate tour guide had decided that a pit-stop was in order. I was public enemy number one, so endured a constant barrage of snide comments and barbed remarks as the tourists were tended to one by one over the ensuing three hours.

I feel like I need a cigarette, so mooch outside to see if there is anyone partaking. I recognise a couple from the coach, but they turn their backs as I come within conversational striking distance. Bollocks. I have never smoked, never before have I had even the slightest urge, never really seen the point in it, but here and now, that's all I crave. Then, the most surreal moment of my life strikes me with a hammered ferocity. I see my first ghost.

The watery translucent image of the approaching ambulance is somehow far more frightening than the events on the coach. I immediately rush inside to drag Wendy from her waiting room chair to witness this curious spectacle.

'What on earth are you talking about, Jack, there's nothing there but concrete and sand. I think you need to see someone, did you hit your head or is it just the sun?'

'No! Don't you see the ambulance, look! The crew are taking the bodies off now. My God, it's the mother I dragged into the aisle, she's dead, dead don't you see, look at her! They're taking her in through those doors over there, can't you see it, don't you believe me?' Wendy frowns as she shakes her head, 'You're fucked up, Jack, totally fucked up. Go and get sedated then lie down for a couple of hours, you're really beginning to annoy me.'

I stand aghast at the scene only I seem to be privy

to. The ambulance doors slam and it speeds back up the dusty road, out of sight. Could it just be the sun? I'm starting to question my own sanity. Did the world stop? Did I save everyone? Is it all just a trick of my mind? It all seems too real, too vivid. I draw a chair up to a table in the shade and sit in quiet contemplation.

6. Bully

The rest of the trip had been a little strange, to say the least. Wendy would hear no more of the events I'm sure I had witnessed and I also remain somewhat confused. What had *really* happened aboard that coach? Was it all just a dream, a previously dormant psychosis rearing its ugly head, or did I really halt time and save everyone's life? Best '*Google*' it and find out...

After numerous searches I am still a little flummoxed as to what's really going on. There seems to be no constant theme as to what 'a three sapphired ring with the ability to alter time' is all about. The usual searches for 'time distortion' bring a plethora of narcotics adverts, a couple of clairvoyants and a few religious ones to boot, all that the 'ring' searches bring up is adverts for shops and wholesalers, whilst a search for 'St. Peter freezing time' just roots the nutters out of the woodwork. I remain at a loss as to where to look next, other than depressing the three stones again to summon St. Peter, therefore using the second of my three time slots for no good reason other than curiosity. I then notice I am running a little late for work, so kill the computer, grab my keys and charge out of Weybridge town, towards Shepperton studios.

*****

I roll into my usual parking slot outside studio twelve and pause a moment to survey the area. A platoon of bloodied infantrymen wander past in high spirits on their way to a dismally depressing World War One trench scene, whilst a green fish with legs waves cheerily to them as she passes in the opposite direction. My friend Tess then appears from the special effects building where she works, cigarette in hand, with a stranger at her side. I wave as I exit the car, and she acknowledges with the curtest of nods. I head into studio twelve.

'Jack, where on earth have you been? We're due to go out to the nation at six, and it's gone five now. Get your arse through make-up and into that studio within thirty minutes, or I'll tear *your* bloody hair out as well.'

That was Brendan, bless him, tearing his hair out. He always gets a little edgy before a live show, and flaps around the set like a mother goose. Brendan is a good old boy though, a late forty-something tubby man who stands five foot five on a good day, and four foot three when he's bent forward with his head in his hands on a bad one. Originally from Dublin, he is never without his uniform of a creased suit and colourful tie, set at half mast, with wildly unkempt hair of grey with white highlights. He blames it on the stress of working with me.

After a pamper and a polish I find myself standing in the wings, glancing at the stage and the generous brown leather sofas upon which I will shortly be sitting, as they glow under the intense glare of the studio lamps. I look to the wings on the opposite side of the stage, and see Melvin, the unfortunate dweeb that is the first of several stars of this week's show, receiving a last minute pep talk from Sally, the show dolly bird, before his five minutes of fame.

The now relaxed and smiling face of the portly Dubliner commands for silence whilst gesturing for the cameras to roll. 'And on in 5... 4... 3...' he mimes the final two digits with his, er... digits, and the studio audience are prompted into a wave of applause by the scruffy oik waving the 'clap now' placard in front of them. The music explodes, the intro is running, and 'Heeeeeeeere's Jack!'

I bound onto the stage full of smiles and enthusiasm, cracking a couple of well received, but scripted jokes before calling for hush.

'Ladies and gentlemen, welcome once again to *Bully Boys*, the show that puts the boot into bullying. And for all you oiks out there who feel the need to pick on someone at work, in class, or just randomly on the street, here is a sure fire lesson for you to learn: What goes around, comes around.' The camera then zooms in close on my extremely well practised yet sardonic smile, pauses for a moment, then upon my cue of an extremely theatrical wink into the lens, retreats to a three quarter body shot. 'Sally, could we have our first guest please.'

A wave of cheers, whistles and applause sweeps from the audience as Sally glides to the wings in order to chaperone our first guest of the show. Melvin sheepishly walks onto the stage, staring furtively from his feet to the audience, then back to his feet as Sally's arm helps him along his traumatic path to centre stage. I greet him with a firm handshake before guiding him to the sofa, as he sinks gratefully into the one at ninety degrees to mine.

'So, Melvin, tell us a little about yourself.'

'Well, I grew up in Brierley Hill, West Midlands, where I was picked on at school because of my large ears and hooked nose. I then went to work at the steel works in Sheffield before, er… being made redundant. I was picked on there as well because I was too short to reach the top two racks in the workshop, so everybody called me the Stumpy Goblin.'

'Yes,' it hadn't struck me until now, but this drip really does look like a goblin, 'so, go on, Malcolm.'

'Melvin, my name's Melvin.'

'Yes, sorry Melvin. So what happened next?' I glance to Brendan who is now four foot three, gently shaking his head in his hands, and swear I can see another one of his hairs turn white. Melvin then drones on for another couple of minutes, finally realising I had been trying to prompt him back to the script he was supposed to be following on the autocue screen, and no, I wasn't really that interested in his Aunt Mildred's blue and green parrot from Malta.

'So here, *Melvin*, we have the footage of how you well and truly got your own back on Billy Black, the ringleader of the guys that bullied you at the steel works.' I glance to the overly made up blonde sporting a black and blue sequinned evening dress, then ask; 'Sally, can we have the film please.'

Sally smiles inanely at the camera as she pushes down, with both hands, on a large, theatrical, but disconnected red button upon the table she stands behind. A screen then lowers from the ceiling so as the studio audience can view this priceless piece of revenge we had plotted on Malcolm, sorry *Melvin's* behalf.

The scene opens in a builder's yard, the footage is of a CCTV camera showing a white transit van pulling up outside the site office. A slightly overweight Billy Black is then seen exiting the van and walking up to the door of the trade counter. The scene then switches to the interior of the office where Billy makes himself busy with selecting the nails, screws and other assorted fixings he needs for the job in hand. The camera even catches him pocketing a few products, but this is glossed over by my running commentary of the unfolding scene. A member of staff (an actor in costume, of course) then challenges him on the products he had placed in his pockets. This, is a masterstroke, the actor was only meant to be pretending to take a survey as a distraction to Black, but upon noticing his criminal activity the actor had decided to confront him as a more avid distraction. Meanwhile, the screen then splits into two and we see his van being lifted carefully out of the way by an enormous fork-lift-truck type of vehicle. A replacement van is then put in its place, with identical signage on the sides so as to replicate Black's vehicle perfectly. Once given the nod, the actor retreats, leaving Black to think he has got away with his petty crime. He then joins the sizeable queue to pay for the timber he needs from the yard. He waits patiently until he nears the front, at which point another actor, also clothed as an employee, enters the room demanding the owner of the Black's liveried van to move it, as a delivery of slabs is due at any moment. Black predictably ignores this request, as he is now near the front of the queue. A second request is then made as he arrives at the head of the queue, next to be served. Again, he ignores it. The actor then leaves to the cry of 'I warned you,' and disappears out of the trade counter's front doors.

Black then pays for his timber, collects his pink slip and returns outside to load his van, only to be stunned into momentary silence as a 4 ton bucket fronted earthmover smashes into the side of his van, lifting it eight feet into the air, before charging up the yard with it and dumping it into an industrial sized skip. Black, as expected, goes completely mental. The bleep bleeep bleeeeps from the censor's swear button invade the studio as if it's a form of full volume Morse code. Black runs to the earthmover, banging the side with his fists and shouting at the driver in a fit of rage. The driver wisely stays put, only swinging the vehicle around in an effort to try and fend off Black's attack, sending him reeling backwards. This further enrages the builder who now starts throwing paving slabs at the cabin of the enormous vehicle. The situation is clearly growing out of control. Black then retreats, collects up an eighteen foot long scaffold pole and curls one arm around it, the other hand cupped on top, a couple of foot in front. He then runs at the digger as if in a modern day jousting match, screaming at the top of his voice. The digger driver, thinking quickly, swings the bucket around to swipe the incoming weapon from Black's grasp. The metallic 'Dong!' from the pole's vibration numbs his whole upper body immediately, and he falls to his knees hugging his chest. Brendan is then seen in the corner of the screen frantically waving a clipboard at anyone in sight, to bring a close to this David and Goliath spectacle. I rush over to Black whilst he remains on his knees, microphone in hand and camera crew at my side forming an invisibly impenetrable defence against any further attack. He knows, I'm sure, he's been had, so I approach with little trepidation as I'm eager to dissolve the situation.

'So, Billy,' I start, as he scowls at me with pure venom in his eyes, 'How does it feel to be live to the nation right now? Tell the *Bully Boys* audience what it's like to have the boot on the other foot, so to speak.'

The explosion of expletives leaves little pause for thought, as the censor's swear button seems to have been taped to the desk. The camera then pans away, the volume fades to mute and the screen bleaches to white.

'So, Marvin, what do you think of our little jape then?'

'Melvin, I've told you my name's Melvin.'

'That's what I said, Melvin, you must have misheard.' I glance briefly at Brendan, who is now crouched to just over three foot tall with his hands wrapped firmly around his shaking head.

'Quite good actually,' Melvin retorts, 'that bugger has been asking for it for years. Ooh, sorry, am I allowed to say bugger?'

'Yes, Melvin, that's fine. So after years of abuse do you finally feel your demons have been laid to rest?'

'Oh yes, Jack, they really have. That Billy Black is just a blip in my past now, I'm ready to move on and face the world a stronger man.'

The audience erupt again into applause and whistles. I wave my hands up and down in a calming motion with a smile comforting enough to placate even Satan, as the off camera oik walks back and forth with the placard that says 'keep clapping'. He then retires, allowing the applause to peter out.

'So Melvin,' I see Brendan, arms outstretched, thanking the Lord, 'we have a very special guest for you tonight. Sally, would you bring on for us, Mr. Billy Black.'

Applause returns, mixed with boos and jeers, although quiet is called for rather swiftly this time by the placard wielding oik. I stand to meet Black as he enters, but Melvin seems to be already squirming in his seat as the builder approaches. Sally beams her radiantly polished smile to the audience as she accompanies Black on his short trip across the brightly lit stage towards the two right-angled sofas, but finds it a struggle in her precarious stilettos as Black's pace steadily increases from a stroll to a march, then he bursts into a sprint. The grimace of anger his face wears gives all the clues Melvin needs to leap from his sofa and hide behind me, in the vein hope I will shield him from the imminent attack. I stand with deer in headlights shock to the speed of my incoming aggressor.

Bam! Black takes a flying punch at my nose, bursting with blood upon impact, the startling reality strikes me as I pitch rearward, floating at least ten feet horizontally, on my way to the wooden floor. Melvin then jumps onto the sofa screeching and flapping like a startled macaw, then bounces his way from one end to the other, avoiding the violently swinging fists of the livid builder, retreating eventually over the back and off to the rear of the set. Black outsmarts the goblin though, and hurls the other sofa after him, expelling a roar of rage as he goes Neanderthal in his efforts to hurl the heavy piece of furniture at his victim. The sofa floats momentarily, before bringing Melvin awkwardly to the ground. The rear wall of the set then crumples with the ensuing impact as Melvin and the heavy sofa slide the last few feet as one, bringing it all crashing loudly to the floor. I turn my head to see Brendan waving frantically with his arms over his head shouting;

'Kill it, kill it, go to the adverts for Christ's sake,' his face now as white as his hair. Black has caught up with Melvin, and is pounding his fists into the nerd's face, causing an explosion of blood and tears from the defenceless victim. It's absolute carnage. The audience are in uproar, Brendan's in pieces, I'm still in shock, and Melvin will be in A&E any minute. Best go to the next chapter, this one's getting a little out of hand!

7. Bollocking

We sit alone in Charles Hess' plate glass office, waiting nervously for the big man to arrive.

'It was your fault, you made too much of a meal of it, we should have just given him a fucking parking ticket or something.'

'Oh shut up, Brendan, what do you honestly think that would do for the ratings? *"Ooh, a horrid man gets upset over thirty fucking quid,"* c'mon, Brendan, get real.'

'It's bollocks, Jack, if I go down it won't be alone, I can assure you of that.'

'Brendan, nobody is going...' Bang! The glass door swings open, shuddering on its doorstop before returning half closed as Charles, sorry, Mr. Hess, enters the room. He turns to close the door precisely behind him, then strides purposefully to his desk. He stands six foot six, with shoulders that carry the strength of three men. His tailored suit triangulates his powerful Swedish muscles into an overpoweringly daunting figure, and his voice has a presence to match that of his physique.

'What the fuck are you two clowns trying to do to me?' Hess sweeps his fingers through his shoulder-length blond hair, placing it precisely behind his left ear, then continues as he puts his ceramically encased espresso onto the polished steel rimmed glass desk; 'I've had a fucking meteor hit me from above because you pair of idiots are incapable of performing a simple risk assessment. This fucking Black guy was a liability from the start, you saw how he overreacted in the builder's yard, so what on earth possessed you to put a fucking idiot like that on live national television?'

Hess leans forward, scowling at the pair of us, looking for answers. I side glance Brendan, who looks as flummoxed as I do.

'Well?'

'Charles, we, er... fucked up, I admit it,' Brendan starts, 'but on the budget we are working with, to research and find another nerd and re-shoot the scene in under a week is just impossible. It's live TV for God's sake, there's bound to be a fuck up now and then, surely?

'Not on my fucking watch there isn't. Now get out of my sight and come up with a better show, consider *Bully Boys* shut down with immediate effect. Now fuck off before I get really annoyed.'

8. Snow joke

It's Thursday lunchtime, and with the plug well and truly pulled on *Bully Boys* I find myself a little short of employment, so I decide to meet Wendy for lunch. She and I discuss the merits of an impromptu snowboarding weekend in Tignes over a rather disappointing ham and cheese croissant in 'Costapacket Coffee', located dead centre of Weybridge High Street. Throwing caution to the wind, we decide to head to the Alps immediately. After all, I have a little something up my sleeve... A swift pit stop home to retrieve the bare essentials, and we are on our way south, clouds in the rear view mirror, and spring sunshine accompanied by fresh white powder on the horizon, perfect.

The Eurostar terminal is its usual disappointingly grey self, such a contrast to the colourful hope we have waiting at the end of the Eurotunnel of dreams. We board our train by nosing the Beemer into our shared coach seven. A sllliiide clunk to shut the door followed by a lazy dunkedy-dum-dunkedy-do-dunkedy-dum dunkedy-do for a couple of hours and we find ourselves in sunny Franglaterre. We stumble upon the road south quite easily, as the road north would have required a snorkel, and head towards Dijon on our big adventure.

The docks fade backwards to a blur as suburb and countryside blend favourably at a pleasing rate, bringing the familiar and welcoming large brown pictorial signs denoting places of local and historical interest, offering an insight to the diversity of culture the country has to offer. The road peaks and troughs as we eat our way south, and the true rural nature of the French land glows invitingly around us.

In less than an hour outside of Calais, we find ourselves surrounded by a wealth of spring colour. The fields of gold and green spread to the horizon, blanketing the hills with life, the yellow daffodils that streak past in the central reservation take their last gasp as they give way to the vibrant colour that the fresh tulips offer with their later bloom. Mile upon mile, hour upon hour, the endless stream of motorway monotony eventually ekes into both our veins and our brains like a numbing virus. My excitement of the new world around us has all but disappeared and my focus on the car in front intensifies to a form of tunnel vision that worries me. My concentration dwindles and my eyes are beginning to sting and close on their own accord. I blink repeatedly to try and stimulate some life into them, whilst noticing the conversation has now petered out. I glance over to see Wendy reclined in her seat with sealed lids. I lean over and squeeze her thigh;

'Wake me up when you see the snow, Babe, I'm pooped,' is her only response, and with that, the only invasion to the silence is the roar of the road and Vivaldi gently pouring from the speakers.

Our aim of arriving in Tignes today seems a little

impractical now, with the impending evening darkness only an hour or so away. The tiredness of driving solidly for the last six hours is taking its toll. The only breaks we've had were for fuel, for both ourselves and the car. I'm knackered, plain and simple. We arrive at the landmark town of Dijon some three hundred and sixty miles from Calais and decide to make an overnight stop. The sun takes a dive for the horizon as we are greeted by the town's quirky streets, and we watch the last glints of the day sink dimly behind the rooftops, slightly out of reach, disappearing forever.

Surprisingly, the first hotel we come across is both reasonably priced and vacant to the tune of one double suite.

Once upstairs, we shower and change, then decide on steak *avec frites* by way of room service, washed down with a bottle of red on the balcony. With muscles diminished and brain cells depleted, we're both snoring by ten.

*****

The 7 a.m. sunshine greets us through the lazily left open curtains, bringing warmth to the overly decorated bedroom. The dark mahogany four poster we lie upon is intricately carved, and draped with swags and tails of cream cotton lined deep red velvet. The crisp white bed sheets scrunch with their over starched stiffness as I peel the covers back and head to the bathroom.

Room service is right on cue at eight, with its usual array of poached egg and streaky bacon, accompanied by a large selection of curiously sweetened breads and pastries. We munch our way through more than our fair share of Francois' farmyard before a swift shower and a long overdue lovemaking on the rug that lays before the open but unlit fireplace.

The nearby church steeple's chime of ten o'clock invades the bedroom unrelentingly, I wonder how I had missed the past eleven, but feel thankful all the same. Wendy positively glows in her perfect slumber as her blonde hair fans across the heavily varnished wooden floor like a halo. She rouses as I rise, and begs me to take her back to bed. Tempting though it is, I think of the slopes ahead of us and my gift that has to be presented in just the right way, so resist and continue to the bathroom for my second shower of the day.

With a swipe and a pin number in the past, we head out of town, roof down, with the promise of fresh white powder paramount in our minds. Tignes is less than half a day's drive in the most adverse of conditions, so today with the sun making a dash for centre stage, I'm confident we'll be there it in time for lunch.

We join the main A31 again, which blends seamlessly into the A6, taking us south to Lyon. I'm a little concerned with the lack of snow, and the fact that the temperature is swiftly rising. I feel we are more likely to need shorts than snowboards when we arrive, but hey, a little sun never hurt anyone, except those with skin cancer that is.

Grenoble comes and goes in a flash, then it's a steady climb up the mountain. The greater the altitude, the thinner and colder the air becomes. The damp roads are beginning to show signs of slush, this in turn becomes whiter and whiter as the road winds its way up. The greenery around us bleaches to the coat of stale snow it wears and my fears of snowlessness melt like the icicles that line the road, hung from branches of otherwise naked trees and rocky ledges. The gently flowing turns are leading us to Bourg St. Maurice, our next target town, yet it seems to take forever to appear. When it eventually does, Wendy and I decide the chill of the mountain air has more than replaced the fresh *'wind in your hair'* style of the decapitated Beemer. We halt outside the railway station and I press the button wearing the icon of what looks like my car with a giant lightning bolt striking it midway, only to hear the sound of silence. I press it again, still nothing. Damn.

'What's up, sugar?'

'The hood seems stuck, maybe it's frozen or something, it just won't budge.'

'Are you sure you're doing it right, hun, you know what you're like with techno stuff.'

'Wendy, after owning an array of B.M.W.s for almost a decade, I think I know what the poxy buttons are for, okay?'

She raises her eyebrows in the most sarcastic way possible, then sinks back in her seat to absorb some more rays. I begin jabbing the switch with increasing ferocity.

'It's probably just the fuse.' Mmm, good point, hadn't thought of that. I reach over to the passenger side and slump on Wendy's lap as I wrestle with the glovebox latch. She wriggles her hips and thrusts them upwards;

'Oh, baby! Here and now, you brave boy, with all these people watching, you're just *so* naughty!'

I laugh, a well needed pause to my steadily increasing anger at mechanical inadequacy. We find the manual, locate the fuse box and identify the offending article. It was indeed a blown fuse, no doubt from the chill of mountain air stiffening the roof mechanism, and making its task of closing the lid just a little too much for the little blue translucent plastic encased strip of foil to handle. I check the array of replacements, only to find an empty slot where the spare used to be. Great. I scan the rest of the fuse box for one of the same colour and therefore a similar rating, then pluck it from its nest. My thoughts being to use it to close the roof, and then return it back to its original home, enabling my car to be fully functional again. I slide the little blue piece of plastic home in slot twelve, then get back into the driver's seat and gently press the button. Nothing.

'Ignition, Babe?' Wendy then crosses her eyes and rolls her tongue over her lower teeth to push out her lip and mumbles; 'Durrr, spaz, owned Bee emms for how long?' then laughs with me at my own stupidity. I flick the ignition switch and press the button once more. Click. The fuse has blown again, and the smile is swiped from my face immediately.

I lean across out of my seat and pop the glovebox lid to investigate. The fuse is hot, and I burn the tips of my fingers as I try to retrieve it. A moment later I have the offending article in my grubby mitts. I discard it over my shoulder and search for a further replacement. This, it transpires, is not as easy as it may seem. The slot I had removed the previous fuse from was the heating system, this means we have now forfeit the luxury of heat in the quest for cover. I scan the fuse box for the next victim. Lights and windscreen wipers seem basic essentials, the horn and indicator fuses are too light an ampage, so it's down to a battle of the electric windows versus the stereo. The stereo has to go, so I withdraw the fuse from slot number six, and press it into the vacant slot twelve. Again I turn the ignition key, thumb the switch and 'Ping!' another life lost. Bollocks.

'I'm no expert, Babe, but I think you need to try something different.'

'No shit, tell you what, I'll change the fuse again and this time, when *you* depress the button, I will pull the hood up manually, therefore easing its task and saving the last fuse. I can then return said last fuse to the heating system and we can head for Tignes unperturbed.' I lean over yet again, withdraw the fuse from the electric window circuit, then slide it home into slot twelve for the third and final time. Wendy then walks the long way around to the driver's seat and sits waiting for my command. I straddle the rear seats, grinding slushy grit into the charcoal grey leather upholstery, bracing myself for the imminent effort. I grasp the hood with both hands and give the command, 'Now!'

'Ping!' Last life lost, Game over. The effort I use to pull the hood is in vain as it fails to budge a millimetre. I lose both my grip and my balance, pirouetting backwards over the headrest, only to land in Wendy's lap.

'What the fuck are you doing, Jack, I'm getting bloody tired of all this larking around and I'm beginning to feel the cold.'

'Sorry, Babe, I'm trying my best, but the damned thing just won't budge.'

'Just forget about it then. Put the windows up, the heating on maximum and let's just get going.'

'Er…'

Thirty minutes from Bourg St. Maurice and the snow is piling higher and higher. Any semblance of greenery has been well and truly obliterated, The intermittent swipe then shudder of the windscreen wipers, though annoying, is less of an issue than the open roof, windows and inoperable heating system. Wendy is shivering heavily, and I notice the light flurry of snow we had been enjoying has now well and truly turned into a blizzard. I pause our progress for a moment in order to retrieve a blanket from the boot of the car. 'Only twenty minutes to go, love, and we'll be there.'

Wendy cracks a small but meaningful smile, I carry

on up the mountain through twist and turn with my frozen fingers welded to the leather steering wheel by a heavy glaze of ice, until the great Tignes dam is upon us. We drive across this awesome spectacle of human engineering and arrive in the main town some ten minutes later. 'Le Grande Chalet Van Duc' is relatively easy to find, although parking poses a bit of a problem as the roads are absolutely chocker. I stop outside the spruce structure and painfully unload our bags, then nose the Beemer into a rather narrow parking slot about one hundred metres away. The walk back to the chalet is somewhat fraught; leather soled brogues are not really intended for skating, and I find little confidence in their ability to grip sheet ice. My whole body has become completely numb, so the fall I suffer from walking head first into a roof hanging icicle the size of a small child that I fail to notice has little effect on me in the way of pain, for now anyway.

I open the chalet door with my elbow, as my hands are now both extremely painful and completely stiff, moulded into the curvature of the steering wheel, only to be greeted by a spectacular open fire and an attractive but rather serious looking French woman behind the reception desk.

'Bonjour.'

I return with as near to a smile as my face can muster without fear of cracking the skin, whilst my stiff jaw mumbles an inaudible response. Wendy is perched on a nearby sofa, glowing in the radiant heat of the open flames. I sit with her in order to defrost a while, as my tired mind selects neutral and glides slowly down the hill to oblivion.

*****

The hypnosis of the flickered flame had induced a deep trance in both of us. We sit, now thankfully thawed, on the sofa and begin to fully take in our new surroundings. My eyes drift up, to the vast beam structure that pulls the walls together and provides enough rigidity to support both the floors above us and the snow-laden roof. The wood must be twelve inches square, and runs diagonally, horizontally and seemingly randomly at various angles across the entire span of the reception area. The architect must certainly have had a vivid imagination and a great sense of humour when he came up with the design that hangs above our heads. Either that, or he had a personal grudge against the poor builders who had to construct this amazing maze of timber. The traditional circular suspended stag horn style light fittings are also present, but primarily for show, as the real illumination is by way of the sporadically placed spotlights that bear down on us, giving harsh shadows and highlights in sharp contrast to the flickering orange glow that the fire emits. I wake Wendy with a warm kiss to the lips and head over to the frosty receptionist.

'*Bonjour*, the name is Jack Todd, we have a luxury chalet booked for two, see voo play.'
'Yez, Mister Todd, Maxwell ere will show you to

your reum.' I glance down at the receptionist's desk to note that everything upon it is precisely laid out. The paperclips are all filed neatly, the same way up at two millimetre intervals on a magnetic block. The pens are set in a line, again all uniform and level, the reservations book looks as if it has been ironed and the pages bleached. Even the 'post it' notes appear to have been stuck on the wall with the aid of a spirit level. Anal would be an understatement. I almost ask if I should wash my hands before scrawling my moniker on the book, but decide to rebel, and just smudge the ink a little instead. She breathes out sharply with disgust through her pointy little nose at my apparent carelessness, I smirk at the thought that she probably won't sleep until the end of the page is reached now, and the leaf is turned to a crisp fresh white one. Maxwell then appears at my side. Tall, muscular and cropped hair, he wears a deep emerald waistcoat over a white collared shirt, tucked neatly into a pair of dark pinstriped pleats that drape over black suede loafers. He gathers up the bags, gesturing for us to follow. I presume he doesn't speak English.

'Help, Babe, I'm stuck!' Wendy pathetically stretches out her hands from the sofa with a cheeky grin. I trundle over and pull her from the clutches of the soft furnishings.

We follow Maxwell out of a door to the rear of the building and shockingly find ourselves in the most beautifully colourful garden. It takes a moment to fully absorb what surrounds us, as I am somewhat taken aback at the sudden shattering of monochrome we have grown accustomed to whilst outside for the last couple of hours.

We are in a courtyard, probably thirty metres wide by forty metres long. The wooden walls are punctuated by brass numbered apartment doors, and bordered by a broad wooden deck on all four sides. Bright green grass coats the ground that sits half a metre or so below, broken only by the occasional flower bed or tree. Teak sun loungers and tables rest randomly throughout the garden, occupied by people chatting, reading or just relaxing. In the centre is sunk a large and inviting, but dormant, circular hot tub that must be five metres across. My eyes follow the steam up and up, past the balconies of the second floor apartments and on to the pitched steelwork that holds the enormous glass roof in place. This architect *really* had a sense of humour I mumble as Maxwell gestures for us to follow him once again. At the far end there is a small but fully stocked bar, the similarly attired green waistcoat wearing barman smiles a greeting whilst nodding his head to one side as we approach. Maxwell exchanges a few words in French before leading us through a wooden archway, into a slightly narrower covered walkway. This time, we are out of the main building and into the open, although protected from the elements in a fully enclosed glass tunnel, that threads its way to the half a dozen log cabin chalets that are spread throughout the grounds. The contrast back to the snow blanketed surroundings seems just as alien as the colourful courtyard we were in only a moment ago.

'Wow, this is going to take some getting used to,' I voice to Wendy, who looks as bemused as I feel. Our glass tube delivers us safely to door number six, placed squarely in the middle of our home for the next couple of nights.

From the outside it resembles an extremely large garden shed, but once inside, elegance is more of a five star luxury hotel. The entrance porch opens up into a vast living room, complete with roaring fire, generous leather sofas, large plasma TV and intricately woven rugs that spread themselves out upon the deeply piled cream carpet.

Maxwell silently waves us in, throwing open the doors to the bathroom, bedroom and kitchen. I am stunned at the sheer luxury of the place, black granite worktops in the kitchen accompany the solid oak fronted Poggenpohl units and Smeg appliances. The bedroom boasts a thermostatically heated super king-size bed and an en-suite bathroom, complete with inbuilt Jacuzzi, Champagne fridge and an array of flowers that wouldn't look out of place at the Hampton Court Flower Show. With our bags placed upon the rack in the bedroom, Maxwell hangs around just long enough for me to suss he wants a tip, so I stuff a five Euro note into his bulky mitt before he disappears out of the front door.

'Oh my god, Jack, this is just *sooo* out of this world!' Wendy leaps at me, arms outstretched, knocking me flat onto my back on the bed. We kiss and cuddle, then progress a little further. A deft flick of the bedside array of switches has the electric curtains gliding silently closed to seal off the outside world, as the bedroom lights automatically dim to a nicely romantic flicker. We enjoy the warmth of each other's bodies, eager flesh pressed upon waiting lips, rolling and play fighting, pinching and biting. Our passion takes us from bed to floor, then bedroom to lounge.

We dose quietly some hours later, depleted and spent, upon a natural deep fur rug in front of the roaring fire.

'I guess snowboarding's off the menu for today then,' I observe, as we gaze to the now inky black sky through the large bay window. 'Let's grab a shower and see if we can't have some fabulous food and a boogie.' Wendy opens her heavy eyes and gazes deeply into mine. 'We could always get room service...' I offer with a raised eyebrow.

'Race you to the shower!' she replies, as she springs into life off of the rug, and is gone before the words even register.

*****

We find 'Collette's' off the main drag, down a rather poorly lit side street. Despite its location, it seems to boast an overflowing popularity. The building itself is roughly made from unfinished stone and dark wooden beams. Lighting is by way of some fake flickering lamps that set the mood perfectly. We order a beer and a wine respectively, then take residence in a booth set into an alcove. Celebrations are taking place at the bar as a group of German skiers enjoy their last night before returning home. Within the hour they have progressed from half litre glasses of frothy headed beer to an array of shots, both flaming and colourful. I order steak hot rocks, which arrives thankfully after only twenty minutes of waiting. A slab of red hot slate is placed upon the table, served with an array of uncooked slices of onion, peppers and courgette. This is accompanied by three plates; two empty for serving our food onto, and one bearing slices of raw spiced beef. A bowl of chips follows, then a bottle of wine appears in hot pursuit. I brave the first slice, and place the meat onto the red hot stone. It bursts into a sizzling steaming life of its own immediately, and is cooked in seconds. Wendy goes next, piling vegetables around her beef in order to fully test her palate. A waitress arrives shortly afterwards with a selection of dips and sauces, but the food tastes so good I fear they would only detract from our enjoyment. We eat in a frenzy, famished from the day's exertions both inside and outside the chalet, then order a custard topped bread and fruit pudding for desert, delicious!

An hour or so later, we build the strength to rise back to our feet. Standing at the bar, we are inevitably drawn into a conversation with the homebound Germans.

'My name is Peter, and this is my two elder

brothers Hans and Christian. My father's name was Anders, so before I was born my mother would always say, "Here are Hans and Christian, Ander's sons." It made her laugh I guess, until I came along, then it, how you say, petered out.'

I smile at the drunken man's humour, but feel the growing urge to leave as soon as possible. He grabs a hold of me around my shoulders and starts swaying and singing to the accordion music I had previously been selectively deaf to.

'Let's get out of here!' I shout to Wendy over the din, she acknowledges with a nod and a smile, then leads me out of the bar by the hand, down the road and back to our nice warm bed.

9. The slippery slope

Morning greets us with a burst of brilliant sunshine. I mooch into the kitchen to see if there's any hunting or gathering to be done before breakfast. The full height retro refrigerator door swings open on its polished ball bearing hinges to reveal an absolutely stuffed interior. There are several types of cheeses, meats and vegetables, two bottles of white wine, butter, milk, eggs, the lot. I turn my attention next to the cupboards, finding various forms of bread, croissants, cereal, biscuits, both choccy and plain, tea, coffee and hot chocolate amongst a sea of other foods and drinks. Wow!

I carry the tray laden with our morning feast through the living room and out onto the veranda. The view down the mountain to my left is spectacular, and with the time a little after nine, the slopes further up the mountain to my right are already teaming with skiers and boarders alike, snaking their way around each other only inches apart, occasionally unsuccessfully. With a drained cafetière and only prune jam and croissant shrapnel left on our plates, we decide to head into town in order to rent a couple of snowboards.

*****

Panting heavily, and damp inside our waterproof clothes from the effort of lugging our equipment to the base of the lift, we pause for breath. Wendy looks at me with those fabulous wounded puppy dog eyes.

'Jackiiieee, this is meant to be a romantic weekend, not an army training exercise.'

'I know, darling,' I reply soothingly, 'we're here now though, should be plain sailing for the rest of the day.'

'It looks really easy, but are you sure we'll pick it up by just watching the others?'

'Of course, my dear, just follow the master,' I josh, pulling a size ten cheesy grin. A moment's recuperation, and we hop onto the nearest lift.

'Are you sure this one just takes us to the top of the nursery slopes?' Wendy enquires, as the shuddering chairlift seems to be gaining altitude a lot quicker than it ought to for the hundred yard hop to the top of the shallow slope.

'Er… yes I think so…' I reply unconvincingly. We look at each other in dread as the chairlift climbs higher, over the top of the nursery slope and heads relentlessly up the daunting mountain ahead.

High above the town, we finally see the tower which houses the large wheel that reverses the progress of the lift. We approach it with some trepidation.

'So, Jack, you just put your weight on the board and glide gracefully off do you?'

'Seems to be the way to do it, how hard can it be, I mean *honestly*?'

We land in a pile, causing the lift to be halted as we crawl like wounded animals from the path of danger.

'See, piece of cake!' I offer. We both laugh at ourselves for ages, no doubt from a mix of embarrassment and a fear of how we are to descend the mountain in one piece. We then set about clamping our feet onto the polished and professional looking boards we had acquired at the hire shop. Once bolted firmly to mine, I crouch, somewhat unsteadily, with my new found imbalance and offer;

'Right, race you to the bottom. Last one down makes the tea for a whole week!' And with that I lurch forwards and begin to glide. Easy.

As momentum increases, the speed becomes quite hair-raising. I lean back to keep the nose of the board from digging in, but this renders me incapable of steering in any direction. Faster and faster I traverse the mountain, I'm totally out of control but it feels so exhilarating, daring, and really rather good. A group of ski school learners were to be my downfall though, literally. With great bowling forward motion, I plough into their group, sending them flying in all directions. The shock they experience from this incoming projectile is expressed with shouts and curses in several languages quite foreign to me, some throw snow at me, and a rather overweight woman even whacks my leg with her pole. They move away and resume their lesson a little further down.

I look up to Wendy, her progress is slower, but more controlled than mine, gliding short distances, but falling upon initiating a turn. I wait for her to reach within a couple of feet of me, then rise back to my feet and glide away again, out of her reach. 'That's two sugars, Babe, and a dash of milk. It's good to be a meanie every now and then,' I shout.

'You bugger!' she hollers after me, I turn to beam a conceited smile back to her, but this only causes further imbalance. I catch the edge of my board in a rut as I frantically wave my hands to steady myself. The edge digs in and flings me backwards at such a rate that my goggles fly off down the mountain before I thump heavily into the frozen ground. Dazed, I lift my head, surprised to see Wendy already sat next to me. 'Have a nice little sleep did we, Rambo?' I force a smile.

'Remember, no sugar, sweetie, and I'd like biscuits with mine please.' She rubs my nose affectionately with her index finger, then BOSH! Plants a great big snowball in my face.

'Race is still on, Babe,' she cries as she wobbles away, falling every few yards.

By the time I reach the café at the base of the run, Wendy has finished her cappuccino and is sunning herself in a recliner.

'Couldn't wait, Babe, you can make the next one.' She grins at me with the sun glinting off the mirrored lenses of her Prada sunglasses. Time for a plan.

'I've been thinking, Babe, why don't we book a lesson for this afternoon?' Wendy's grin becomes a full on smile.

*****

Later that evening we take a bath and a hot tub together. The muscles in my back are so stretched and sore, I feel like I've been tied to the back of a car and used to tow a caravan. Our afternoon lesson had been enlightening, and we both had taken the time to learn how to read a piste map in order to find the correct lift next time we journey up the mountain. All in all we're rather pleased with our efforts, and sit at the dinner table in the restaurant's bay window, watching the swirling blizzard outside and the map spread between us, planning tomorrow's big adventure.

*****

Sunday dawns in our chalet at around ten o'clock. I shower and dress, then leave to get the morning papers whilst Wendy snores. Out through the hotel reception, noting the new crisp new white visitors' book on the desk as I pass, and out into the late morning sunshine. I see evidence of the massive dump of snow we must have had during the night all around, cars have almost disappeared beneath a candyfloss coating of white. The implication of this doesn't quite reach my brain until I spot something odd about my own car; the roof – or lack of it to be precise. The interior of my car is filled to the point of overflowing with snow. Bummer.

I return to the chalet a little disheartened, but after a

few stretches and a couple of runs down the nursery slope, we are ready for the big adventure. Chairlift after chairlift we thread our way up the mountain and far, far away. We are dumped at what I can see is the highest point within easy access. We hop off the lift and glide with our new found skill to the edge of the descent.

Once buckled up, a swift *'Tally Ho!'* and we chase each other down the mountain with increasing velocity and skill. We return to the café we craved so much yesterday with vigorous excitement. We jabber animatedly over a late lunch, then decide to make our way even further afield, embracing the fresh sport we've so recently learned. Not realising how late it had become, we hopped onto the lift to begin the journey that would change our lives forever.

The usual lurch catapults us up the piste as we settle into our seat for the steady rise to the top once again. We have chosen a slightly more adventurous route this time, as our ability continues to grow with our confidence. When we reach the second chairlift station however, the attendant is turning people away, saying the lifts are now closed for the day. Thinking quickly, I turn to Wendy and whisper; 'Play along okay, I'll get us up to the top.'

'Fermé,' the attendant announces as we approach.

'You speak English?' I enquire, *'Oui,* a little, er… Closed,' he replies.

I smile at him, then offer; 'My girlfriend and I were up near the top having a little fun in the woods,' I gesture something crude with my hands whilst winking, 'and I left my rucksack behind up there by accident, with our passports inside.'

He thinks a moment, then Wendy pushes out her bottom lip in a show of disappointment.

'Be quick, we are closed.' He unhooks the chain barrier allowing us to hop aboard the last lift skywards for the day. We cuddle, kiss and giggle our way up the mountain, mile upon mile, as it seems to take forever. Then, suddenly, with the turnpoint in the near distance, the lift groans to a halt. We sway back and forth for a few moments, waiting for the ride to resume. It doesn't. We sit for a while waiting, twenty feet above the soft snow that lines the piste, and look around. We are truly alone, there is no visible life for as far as the eye can see, just white below us and a fading blue above, I notice for the first time the complete silence that invades my paranoiac sense of desolation. The town is so far below us it isn't even a spec in the distance. The orange planet that dominates the sky is sinking at a steady rate and I'm beginning to think we're in some trouble here.

'What are we going to do, Jack?'

'Well, this isn't quite how I had planned it, but no time like the present I guess.' I remove one of my gloves, but accidentally drop it down to the powder below.

'Planned it, planned what? What on earth are you going on about, Jack?' I reach into my pocket and press a small blue crushed velvet covered box into her hand. With my un-gloved hand I open the lid.

'It's a little difficult to get down on one knee up here, but Wendy, will you marry me?'

I see her eyebrows rise above the line of her sunglasses as a tear rolls down each of her perfect cheeks. I can only see my own face in the reflection of her glasses, but imagine her captivating blue eyes flood with emotion as she pulls me towards her, for the longest and most perfect kiss of my entire life. It's only when we break our embrace that we notice the box has disappeared. After a quick and frantic search, we both lean over the front of the chairlift to spy firstly my glove, then a tiny blue dot in the snow next to it. I only hope the ring hasn't fallen out on its journey to the floor. We turn to face each other with tight-lipped smiles, 'Only one thing for it,' I say, 'we'll have to jump.'

'Okay, how are we going to do that with this safety bar in front of us though? Hang on a minute, I've just realised what you said. Jump, are you absolutely crazy, we must be twenty feet up, we're sure to die from this height.'

'No, Wendy darling, don't worry, it's light powdery snow, like falling onto a feather mattress, I promise. Besides which, if you strap your snowboard onto both of your feet, the resulting displacement of snow will cushion the landing even more.' Wendy thinks a moment, then replies;

'You and me amigo, till death do us part.'

I lean behind and press the release catch that allows

the safety bar to rise out of our way. We buckle our rear boots into their bindings and stare at the distance below. It seems both an awfully long way and an awfully bad idea. We shuffle our bums to the very edge of the seat. I glance over to Wendy and give her a reassuring nod, if only she knew how absolutely shit scared I was.

'Wait, wait, stop. I don't think I can do this, Babe,' pleads Wendy.

'We'll be fine, promise,' I lie. 'On the count of three. One... Two...' and with that a mechanical groan rings out as the chairlift lurches into life, tipping us off balance and sending us both flailing through the air to the ground below.

Thud! Thud! We hit the mountain like a couple of coal sacks. The impact, although heavy, was not fatal. I look above us to see the chairs glide by on their way back down the mountain, smile in irony, then turn to check Wendy is still breathing. After a moment's rest, we locate both my glove and the diamond studded ring, thankfully still in its dark blue box. A kiss and a cuddle later and we turn to head back down the mountain.

'Last one down buys the Champagne!' I shout as I make a slightly swifter start than Wendy. She does, however beat me to the bottom, so I'm lumbered again. Hmmm.

With a hot bath and a celebratory meal at the best restaurant in town on the agenda, the only thing to dampen my spirits is brought home when we limp and hobble our broken way past my car en route to the chalet, I shudder at the thought of digging out all the snow the following morning before our dreaded open top return journey.

10. Amber coloured inspiration

Brendan sits in a corner of The Crown sipping his pint of Bombardier.

'Sorry I'm late, couldn't get away from the house, D.I.Y. duties,' I pathetically offer whilst turning my head towards the bar in order to acquire a pint.

'Pint of Becks please, Dave, and a bombardier for the old Irish git in the corner.'

Dave the landlord pulls the pints as I wait in anticipation of my first glug of chilled heaven this week. I spot a familiar face a little further along the bar, so take a couple of paces towards him. 'Do I know you from somewhere?' I enquire.

'Yeah, You're Jack Todd aren't you, the gameshow host?'

'Yes, but I'm sure we've met before.'

'The name's Hazy, Paul Hayes to be precise, but Hazy will do. You know my friend Tess, from the special effects department at the studios.'

'Ahh yes. Now I remember, you were both talking outside the fire exit of her building a couple of weeks ago. So who are you here with?'

'Just me at the mo, I'm waiting for my mate Beaker to return so we can go and play a prank on one of our buddies. Should be a laugh, I'm sure you'll hear about it if it all goes to plan.'

'Things rarely do, my friend, enjoy the rest of your evening.' I slide the two pints off the bar after a jangle of change makes its way to my pocket, and return to Brendan's table.

'What the Hell are we to do, Jack? I've not got an idea left in me.'

'Rob the poor, and the rich, then retire somewhere tropical.'

'C'mon, Jack, I'm being serious, we're fucked I tells ya.'

'It's a good job I have a plan then, isn't it? What, my dear Brendan, drives every human being to distraction, what was the original sin, the temptation, the absolute desire to do wrong in every human being?'

'What on earth are you talking about, Jack, did you bump your head when you were away skiing or something?'

'Yes, rather hard actually, but that's not what I'm talking about. I'm talking about the basest human emotion that evokes abnormal behaviour, that turns men into animals and women into, into, er... I don't know, but something equally as, er... you know what I mean.'

'No, Jack, stop talking in riddles will you and just spit it out why don't you.'

'Lust, Brendan. Lust is the root of all unreasonable behaviour. You can see it every night in any given pub, two blokes who both fancy their chances with a member of the local female bar hopping talent, would rather step outside and punch seven shades of shit out of each other than discuss a rational solution to the two fellas and one girl situation. The same two fellas with the girl removed from the picture, would happily spend the evening's drinking in the same pub without even the slightest hint of a murmur.'

'Okay,' Brendan concedes warily, 'but where does this tie in with a television show?'

'Easy,' I reply, 'all we have to do is put a punter into a compromising position that may induce the emotion of lust, and let him dig his own grave as the camera witnesses it.'

'We've had our fill of punch-ups this month I think, any more and we really will be flogging the *Big Issue* at Waterloo station.

'Don't be ridiculous, Brendan, let me give you the full low-down…'

I relay my fabulous idea over the next couple of pints, Brendan gets itchy feet, so we decide to head back to his place near Shepperton, to form a cunning plan as to how we are going to pitch this to Charles Hess.

*****

I leave Brendan's place and head home. It's almost five in the morning, and the merest hint of dawn is showing promise of waking the skyline, either that, or I'm so tired I'm seeing things. My numb head buzzes from the lack of sleep and one too many scotches at Brendan's kitchen table. I'm happy though, because in the back of my car I have the storyboards that we've been working on all night. I just hope Hess goes for it, or I'll be fresh out of both ideas and a paycheck. I cross Walton Bridge, and turn right down the road that runs parallel to the river, towards Weybridge. I glance to my right catching the late moon's reflection in the fast moving water, and look on ahead to the bridge over the Thames, that leads onto Desborough Island.

On the bridge sits a battered white Volvo estate with only one headlight working, and what appears to be a fan of blood from the front wing. Also, a couple of people seem to be bundling something that looks suspiciously like a dead body over the side of the bridge, and a third man stands by the section of road I am rapidly approaching. The third man turns to look into my headlights, then immediately returns his attention to his two colleagues. He then sprints back, shouting at the other two guys, only to leap onto the railings on the side of the bridge and dive head first into the water. I know my eyes are playing tricks on me due to my tiredness, but I could have sworn it was the guy I met in the pub earlier, Hazy, that leapt off the bridge in a panic. I feel the urge to stop and offer some help, then think better of it. Whatever's going on, I don't want to be the next body in the river, thank you very much. My fears are quickly allayed though, as sat upon the next bridge along is a police car occupied by two officers watching the goings on. I breathe a sigh of relief as my conscience is let off the hook for not stopping, and continue wearily on my journey home.

11. The sales pitch

We sit again in the glass torture chamber that is Charles Hess' office.

'Right, Brendan, remember to keep your mouth shut and let me do the punt, you're far too nervous to sell him the idea cleanly.'

'But it's a shit idea and it's full of holes. If anything goes wrong we'll never work in the industry again.'

'If we cancel this meeting with only two minutes notice, Hess will make sure we never work in this industry again anyhow. So unless you have a better plan I suggest you clam up and let me get on with it.'

'Too fucking right, Jack,' booms Hess as he enters the room. 'You won't even be able to get a job cleaning portaloos at Glastonbury if you cause me an embarrassment like *that* ever again. This had better be good, or I'll have you two clowns for breakfast.'

Hess strides around to the far side of his desk and drops down into the leather chair. He reclines, knitting his fingers together behind his head and lifts his leather soled Church shoes onto the desk, crossing his legs at the ankle.

'Come on then, Jack, I haven't got all day.'

'Well, Charles,' Hess raises an eyebrow, 'Mister Hess, I mean.' Brendan closes his eyes and starts shaking his head again, 'Brendan and I…'

'You,' Brendan interjects, '*you* have had this fookin' plan.'

'Okay, *"I, Jack Todd"* have formulated this fabulous new show to truly capture the attention of the public like nothing else that has ever gone before. The title of the show gives a little away, insomuch as *Dangling the Apple* plays on both the traditional *"dangled carrot of enticement"* theory that any donkey being led to walk is blissfully unaware of, and the enticement of the sexually symbolic apple that Adam took from the tree of temptation, admittedly only after a little encouragement from a rather devilish snake. As red blooded males, it's all too easy to be led astray by the flash of some taboo flesh, an unexpectedly lewd comment by a particularly attractive member of the opposite sex, or maybe just a little flirtatious behaviour from the local barmaid or page three model wannabe on the paying side of the bar. This failing in all men is a route for exploitation, for interest, and for the further study of human behaviour. My new show will not only display how weak man can be when presented with the hope of carnal knowledge, but reflect a true insight into the patterns of thought within the male mind. The morals versus desire tug of war, if you will.'

'Okay,' Hess returns with a pensive look, 'So how are you going to portray this in a way that is both mild enough to be acceptable to the viewing public, without the inevitable outcries of public decency, and yet interesting enough that they don't just zone out and search for the *Eastenders* omnibus on their remotes?'

'Easy,' I retort, 'the good old tried and trusted path of points make prizes. What we will need to do, is run an advert in one of the national papers that reads something like this: "Do you have the perfect relationship? All rosy at home? Large cash prizes for the wife or girlfriend who knows her husband or boyfriend extremely well, and can answer a few simple *'yes or no'* questions." That should get them flooding in by the boatload!'

'Okay, so you have your innocent wife or girlfriend, your potential adulterer, and the planted bimbo for a temptation, what next? How are you going to sustain a captive audience week in, week out, with a show like that? I can see the initial euphoria of something different, but four or five weeks in, and all you have is a little CCTV footage of a bloke having a bit of a letch, and a pissed off wife. Hardly cutting edge now is it?'

'Well Char...ister Hess, this is where my big idea comes into play. As I previously said, points make prizes. Not only that, but everybody loves a bit of a gamble. The girlfriend, or wife, is brought into the studio prior to the game in order to have a filmed interview. During that interview, several questions are posed to her with regard to her husband's behaviour. The usual *"is he honest? Can you trust him? Will he run off with the twenty-year-old au-pair?"* type of questions would run throughout the interview, then a more general background of her relationship with him might follow. The reason for this would be to get a kind of grounding as to where she sees their relationship, and what kind of a guy she envisages him to be. We then follow the target for a week or so, learning his habits and routines. Once familiar, we plant both the cameras and the bimbo ready for action. On an agreed night, with everything in place, the game begins.'

'What game? Come on, Jack, get to the point, you're eroding away my morning.'

'The game of life, the battle of the sexes, the push and pull of attraction versus flirtation, the dangling of the apple.' I reach down and grab the roughly sketched storyboards. 'Okay, Charles, here we have a workable scenario that Brendan and I thrashed out last night; The show opens in much the same way as *Bully Boys*, it's a tried and tested formula and we all know what does and doesn't work with the set-up. The contestant will come onto the stage, and join me on the sofa.' I wrestle to swap to storyboard number two. 'After the usual niceties I will pry for some "*live to the audience*" information about how well their relationship is going, a couple of scenarios would be presented to her with regard to the target's loyalty, and it will basically be a re-run of the interview we have already performed a week earlier, so she will be well rehearsed in the answers she needs to give, and more than happy to defend him. A screen will then lower from the ceiling, as on *Bully*, and begin to show the carefully edited film that we have surreptitiously recorded of the target's activity, the target being her husband or boyfriend of course. In the example I am using here, the target wanders into his local for his usual couple of pints after work. He is then brought into contact with the *"apple,"* on this particular occasion being the new barmaid he hasn't previously met.'

I reach for storyboard number three that shows a busty barmaid wearing a loose fitting top with just one too many buttons undone, bending down to retrieve something from a low-level shelf. The target sits on the other side of the bar, and is seen to be nursing a pint whilst observing her activity.

'At this point,' I continue, 'with the film paused, the contestant is offered four scenarios as to what happens next. They appear on the screen over the faded image of the bar.' I scrabble for the next board, and written roughly upon it are her four options:

He carries on drinking without noticing the obvious distraction.
He becomes embarrassed, and looks away.
He tries to take a sneaky look down her blouse without her noticing.
He makes an obvious play at staring, adding a lewd or flirtatious comment in the process.

'The contestant is then asked to make a decision as to the most likely action her partner will take. At this entry level of the game, we can offer her five points for a correct answer, and obviously nil for an incorrect one. Once her decision is made, we re-run a suitably relevant comment from the previously recorded interview, to corroborate her answer. The film then returns to the bar, where the target's behaviour is then shown. If the contestant's answer was incorrect, we now have our interest. As the scenes get more and more risqué, and the points rise higher, the reactions from the contestant will increase accordingly. Imagine the contestant's reaction, when on the fourth or fifth question, the apple asks him to come upstairs for a coffee after the pub closes and he accepts. The reaction live in the studio will be electrifying when we show the original recorded interview of her outrightly dismissing the thought, yet with the prospect of bigger points, and therefore more money, she sees that her perfect partner is all too easily led astray, and she actually bets he will say yes! She will be betting her potential winnings on his rapidly depleting morals. It's a sure fire winner, Charles, top of the ratings within a month I'll bet you.'

'Okay, I admit you are on to something here, Jack, you've got me hooked. But how are you going to guarantee a series of wrong answers, and therefore a colourful reaction?'

'We will be able to gauge how well the show will go from the collected footage and previous interview, so we can choose the couples that will cause the biggest surprises. I don't even think we need to go for the most volatile reactions. Imagine if the game runs completely the opposite of how it's anticipated. A target that is seen as a real ladies' man, you know the type, fake tan and Ferrari key ring, who everyone assumes is a bit of a player is then to be seen on screen full of self doubt and false bravado, or totally loyal to his current girlfriend who sits watching in the studio, when confronted with the prospect of a beautiful, yet overly forward temptation in a cocktail dress. It will be a revelation to break down the preconceived assumptions the public make about the stereotypical man. We can also use the agency to supply some really stunning girls to get both the reactions and the ratings truly flying.'

'Okay, Jack, you've convinced me. Sammy's putting together the programme schedules for next month, so hook up with her and get her to let me know the time slot you decide upon. I want it to be prime time, I think this is going to be big.'

Hess cracks a smile for the first time in history, but then I have to go and open my big mouth again.

'Er... Mister Hess,' I continue, 'I proposed to Wendy, my girlfriend, last weekend, and whilst I'm really looking forward to cracking on with the new show, I think it's an ideal opportunity to zip off and get the whole marriage thing sorted and done as swiftly as possible. After all, there will be nothing for me to do for a couple of weeks whilst Brendan sets up the potential players.' The blood rises to Hess' face as he nears boiling point.

'Does my fucking office door have a Butlins holiday camp logo upon it?' Hess blasts, 'Are you seriously taking the piss to that enth degree? I have only *just* allowed you to work on my shift again after the embarrassing debacle that graced the nation's screens two weeks ago, and you have the audacity to ask for a fucking holiday!'

'I, I...'

'Get out, the pair of you and take your fucking holiday if you must,' Hess then lowers his voice to a more controlled but no less menacing one, 'but be warned; the show had better run as smooth as greased rails when it hits the screens or the pair of you cannot even begin to comprehend how miserable I will make the rest of your lives.'

'Yes, Mister Hess, thank you Mister Hess...' We back out of his office with stooped shoulders and dropped heads, closing the glass door securely as we go.

'Bejayzus, you have such a nerve, I cannot believe you asked him that!'

I shrug, 'Good job he didn't know I've just been to the Alps or he would have really lost it.' Brendan chuckles away at the nervous prospect of putting together the show that will save our careers. I just hope he does a good job or we'll both be in hiding for at least ten years.

12. Reservations

I leave Brendan with Sammy, scheduling when my meteoric rise to the top of the ratings will commence, and head out to the car park. It's raining, bugger. Having not had time to fix the Beemer's roof, I've resorted to stretching a silver coloured heavy duty wheelie bin liner over the front seats in order to stop the damp soaking into my trousers. Wendy thinks it's far from stylish, and has been hassling me to ditch the silver for a far more sophisticated black bin liner, but I assure her it's just fine in silver, more space-age I tell her, although with the wind rustling the cheap thin plastic, it's even beginning to bug me.

I head out of Shepperton, over Walton Bridge again, remembering momentarily the scene I had witnessed near here only a few hours ago. I dismiss it from my mind and head towards town in order to secure a couple of plane tickets to somewhere exotic.

*****

After a struggle with the pay and display machine in the High Street, that robs me of at least a pound more than it should do, I head into 'Sunsets Travel Services,' where apparently *your dreams become a reality,* according to the slogan scrawled across the door in a rather modern but abstract looking orange typeface.

The crisply decorated, yet traditionally tasteful interior wears light cream walls, split midway by darkly aged beams that compliment the four vast mahogany desks, of which only two appear to have occupants. The girl to my right looks as if she is straight out of college, and can't be more than eighteen. The other salesperson however, appears to be closer to what I'm looking for; tall and slim, his head sports a thick but neatly trimmed coat of grey hair, speckled with black flashes that are set off perfectly by his short goatee beard. His nose has a narrow pair of rectangular frameless glasses perched upon it, and he wears a dark suit with a contrasting white shirt and red tie. The man stands as I approach, offering a welcoming hand. I take it, shake once, and then relax into the seat that he gestures towards in front of his desk.

'Good morning, sir, my name is Graham Hobbs, and how can we be of service to you today?'

'Er… I'd like to book a wedding, somewhere exotic, something different with a bit of culture and a taste of adventure I guess.'

'Fabulous, sir, will it be a large party?'

'No, just a few drinks afterwards, why do you ask?'

'Sorry, sir.'

'Jack, you can call me Jack,' I interject.

'Sorry, *Jack*, I was referring to the number of travellers, not the celebration arrangements.'

'Ahh, gotcha. Sorry, not enough sleep I guess. It will only be the two of us though, me and my fiancée

Wendy. We were thinking of something luxurious, but with jungles, beaches, mountains and jet-skis, that kind of thing.'

'Right, okay, I presume a weekend in Droitwich isn't where we're heading on this one then is it, sir. When are you looking to travel?'

'Anytime tomorrow,' I answer, 'for a couple of weeks I guess.'

'Yes, sir.' Graham smiles, then pauses for an uncomfortable length of time whilst holding my stare. 'Oh, you really do mean tomorrow,' he says surprised, 'I thought you were joking. Best get the old whip cracking then and see what we can find you. Holly, search your database can you, dear, for thrilling wedding venues with a bit of punch.'

He smiles at me again, then frantically stabs his keyboard as an array of colourful pages flash past on his large computer screen.

'Have you thought of something *extremely* different, we are offering great deals on the North Pole. You are taken to the Russian Naval base of Murmansk where you board an icebreaker ship and head North. From there, you join a dog sled team and continue on skis to the pole itself, marrying literally on the top of the world if you will.'

'No, I don't think so. We've just been snowboarding and that was adventurous enough thanks. Besides, Clarkson had the right idea, going in a 4x4 truck and even he had a load of hassle.

Somewhere hot I think is in order, with definitely no penguins.'

'Okaaayyy, how about this; two weeks in New Zealand, staying on a fruit farm and working as a helper at a bungee jumping site. It says all jumps are included.'

'No, I don't think you quite heard me. We are going to get married, so something romantic, five star, with a beach and some sun will be fine. I'm sure we can find our own entertainment whilst we are there, so please, no more dog sleds or bungees.'

'How about this, Mr. Hobbs?' chirps Holly, 'A scuba diving holiday in South America, staying in a 5 star luxury hotel for one week, complete with spa, seven swimming pools, tennis club, glass-bottomed boat excursions, jet-skis, deep sea fishing and a choice of six restaurants. There's a party held every Saturday for all the residents on the rooftop garden of the hotel's eighteen storey tower that overlooks the magnificent coastline. Then, the following afternoon you move to an island paradise for the second week. The island is called Shambhala, and it's here you have a beachfront pavilion with its own infinity edged plunge pool, wooden deck, marble floored bathroom and all the luxuries you can imagine. This includes use of the exclusive complex's facilities of bars, restaurants, hot tubs, masseuses and diving instructors. The wedding takes place on the Wednesday, at the specially constructed palm tree platform that juts out into the sea almost quarter of a mile at high tide. It also says here, that of the estimated three thousand shipwrecks around the Brazilian coastline, only about half have been discovered and registered, so there is plenty of exploration to be done either by guided underwater tours or in a more laizzes fare style. There's also a new underwater sculpture park that has just opened, that was created by the apparently famous artist Ben Lowe, whoever he is when he's at home. Sounds fab though, Mr. Hobbs, doesn't it!'

'Certainly does, Holly, thank you. Could you email me the details across so I can show Mr…'

'Todd, Jack Todd.' I imagine the ridiculous world we live in today, as the images fly off of Holly's computer screen and into cyberspace a million miles away, only to land safely onto the screen of another computer not six feet away from it.

'Here we are, Mister Todd,' as Graham swivels the large flat screen towards me, I am taken aback at the sheer beauty of the resort; palm trees, white sand, empty beaches, an array of swimming pools draped in scantily clad models and edged with colourful bars and outdoor restaurants. Heaven.

'I'll take it, how much?'

'Ahem, let me just see, three thousand eight hundred and twenty seven pounds.'

'Crickey, that's quite a lot.'

'Each.'

'Ouch!'

'Plus flights.'

'Ooooooo,' I wince.

'And taxes.'

…I wait, but that really is it, 'I take it that includes breakfast?'

'Yes, Jack, I believe it covers breakfast.'

Ten grand on a couple of weeks in the sun, bargain. Wendy will be thrilled to pieces. Best stop at the super expensive lingerie shop in Weybridge on the way home so she can show me *exactly* how thrilled she is later this evening.

*****

'Hi, Honey, I'm home,' I holler as I step over the threshold of suburbia at just gone five.

'In the conservatory, Babe,' comes the distant reply. I mooch down the hallway through both the lounge and dining room to arrive in the pleasantly warm but airy greenhouse that's welded to the back of the building. I momentarily muse that I have just spent half the cost of said greenhouse on a two-week jolly, but best keep that under my hat.

'Perfect timing, Babe, I'm just about ready to serve up.' Wendy rises from the nest of wicker corner sofas, dropping her *Weybridge Society* magazine to the floor and pecks me on the lips before disappearing into the kitchen in order to retrieve a home-made ham and three cheese pasta bake from the oven.

'How did your show proposal go?' her muffled voice asks from the kitchen.

'Great, I'll tell you in a mo,' I reply, as I lay her naughty little present on the large glass topped table, with a fresh rose I had pinched from the old biddy at number twelve's front garden.

'Wow, you sexy man!' Wendy comments with widened eyes as she re-enters the conservatory, 'Best try them off immediately.' She grins like the happiest Cheshire cat on a nose full of cocaine.

'That's just the icing, Babe, look what I have just arranged for us to do tomorrow.' And with that I spread the printed sheets from the travel agent's booking confirmation, complete with pictures and descriptions all over the table.

'Our flight leaves at eleven o'clock tomorrow morning, Babe.' My smile is so enormous it hurts my face. Wendy almost drops the pasta to the wooden floor in surprise. Carefully she slides it onto a placemat, then wraps firstly her arms, and then her legs around me as we lock in a passionate kiss. I turn and walk to the stairs with her clinging to me like a Koala bear.

At 7 p.m. we make it back downstairs for our neglected pasta. After ten minutes in the oven it's hot and crispy again, so we sit in the conservatory as the sun fades, enjoying the buzz of fresh love, fresh pasta and our imminent wedding.

'You look knackered, Jack, didn't you sleep very well last night? You were gone by the time I woke, so it must have been early.'

'Late and early, love, I got in at gone five, and was back out the door by seven thirty, so yes, I'm absolutely shot.'

'Poor Jacky babe, I'll pack our stuff whilst you go sleep. You deserve it, Babe, you're the best.'

'Christ, I haven't told you what happened last night!' I exclaim as the thought just floats back through my tired mind. 'I was on my way back from Brendan's down the river road, and as I drew up to the bridge that goes over to Desborough Island I saw three men throwing a body into the Thames. Then one-Hazy was his name, jumped in after it.'

'What? What on earth are you talking about, Jack, you're not going to start all that rubbish about ghosts and bodies again are you?' Wendy, now looking serious, 'It's not funny if this is a joke, and if it isn't, I thought you had got over all these hallucinations. How much had you drunk by then?'

'No, Babe, it's not a joke, and I wasn't drunk. I saw Hazy and his friends bundle a body into the Thames, I promise. He said to me in the pub it was a prank, but I didn't expect him to kill someone.'

'Jack, stop it! What are you talking about *kill someone*, this Hazy character, is he another one of your ghosts or something?'

I am bereft of words, I expected some support, not a barrage of denial.

'You're just tired, Jack, you've hardly slept a wink and with the stress of going to see Charles Hess today it's just brought all this back again. I don't want to hear another word about it, now go and lie down.'

For once, I do as I am told.

13. Getting a Brazilian

The plane touches down in Recife after what seems like an entire week of travelling. I'm pleased to see that the shanty towns that surround Rio are less prevalent in Recife from the air, but as the heat of the late afternoon sun hits us upon exiting the airport, the beggars and stray dogs are just as plentiful. It seems that not only are the streets littered with mangy animals and decaying cars, but Children of all ages run, play and fight around us. Men and women wander aimlessly amongst the hooting cars and swerving mopeds, it's like a diluted Calcutta, a city of abandoned people. I grab a handful of Wendy's bum and steal a long lingering kiss on her perfect lips as we take in the sensory assault that invades us.

Moments later, a taxi speeds us to our hotel. A magnificently ostentatious landmark, located a mile or so south of the Bo Viagem beach. I cannot believe the massive contrast in lifestyle a short cab journey can offer. We approach the hotel down a palm lined driveway, through perfectly manicured gardens that sprout a Technicolor explosion of tropical beauty from every flowerbed. A tall ornate fountain is the centrepiece of the turning circle in front of the large gold framed glass doors that welcome us into the five star reception. An African looking man in a crisply starched white uniform, complete with a safari style hard hat, also in white, immediately springs to our attention, opening our doors and instructing two other men to retrieve our bags from the boot.

Wendy and I gasp as we enter the vast marble floored reception. The large and imposing gloss white desk has three smartly uniformed attendants, all in matching uniforms of dark turquoise shirts, fastened by gold cufflinks at the wrist.

'Welcome to Hotel Paradisio,' the tallest of the three says with a smile. 'I trust you have had a good journey and would welcome some refreshments before checking in. If you could just swipe this credit style card we have produced for you through the slot of the machine on the desk, and select a four digit pin number, I will print all the relative paperwork and bring it over to you in the bar. Tell Henry, who is tending the bar today that you are checking in, and he will prepare for you our customary welcome drink. It does contain alcohol, so if you would prefer, a non alcoholic version can be specified.'

'Great, can I have the alcohol from the last guy that turned it down added to mine then?' Wendy jabs me in the ribs.

'Sorry sir, I don't follow.' The African chap then appears at my side and gestures towards the bar. 'Naboo here will show you the way.' I smile, swipe, stab the keyboard four times, then head in search of my complementary glass of Brazilian brain numb. We walk through the vast reception area as over ten feet above us the slowly rotating fans move the cooler air around to level out the temperature. We progress from the reception to a spaciously laid out and lightly decorated lounge. The sheer quality and style of the place is truly breathtaking.

A row of floor to ceiling length light net curtains flow in the breeze as they partially obscure the enormous open French doors, leading to just one of the many swimming pool areas. We exit the building to be confronted by the warmth of the air once again. A myriad of palm trees and other exotic flowers and plants lay sporadically throughout this leisure area, a lifeguard sits atop his umbrella-shaded highchair like a big kid, sipping a drink through a straw from a hollowed out pineapple. At one end of the kidney shaped pool sits a sunken bar, where a couple sit on their submerged stools whilst chatting to the dry and smartly dressed employee on the other side of the watertight bar. Its roof is a spread of palms and large bamboo tubes, its walls all white render except the one that serves as the side of the pool, this is tiled in a multitude of light, mid and dark blue mosaic tiles to match the rest of the pool's inner coating. The depiction of a large shark on the pool's floor prompts a comment from Naboo, our guide:

'We have several names for the city here in Recife, some call it "Little Venice" due to the number of bridges and waterways, the River Bebaribe meets here with the River Capibaribe. They mix their way together before flowing out to the Atlantic, we have mimicked this here with our complex of seven interconnected swimming pools that you see all around you. All of these pools have their own theme, yet one can swim from one to the other without the discomfort of getting out.' I notice that this pool does indeed have a tributary leading off from it to connect to another pool just the other side of a row of palm trees. 'This is the Dive Pool, we name it this because of all the tourists that come to our beautiful city to dive with the sharks. Our ocean just outside the city has such an enormous shark population, many call this *"Shark Town."* That is why this pool depicts a mosaic shark on the bottom.'

'This is paradise, Babe, I love you sooo much I could just explode!' Wendy pulls me in for a swift bit of lip to lip massage, then ruffles my hair with a big cheeky grin upon her face.

'Best not do that, Babe, your blood might make a hell of a mess on the floor.'

'Haw, haw, you're so funny.'

Naboo then takes us over a bridge and down to another pool area that has water cascading into it from a six metre high waterfall.

'This is the Rainforest Pool,' he states proudly. The pool itself is completely surrounded by a jungle of trees and palms, leaving most of the area in shade except the pool itself. A small monkey swings from a tree, and lands on the roof of the bamboo shack bar that sits to one side of the pool.

'People love to come here and relax when the sun gets a little too intense, the shade cools nicely and the kids love playing and climbing in the trees.'

I see a monkey puzzle tree wind its way into all sorts of directions and imagine it brimming with eager kids, daring to go ever higher before being reprimanded by their parents.

'The pool is not busy today, as we have a fancy dress parade for the children at four o'clock, so they are all at the clubhouse getting ready. It is usually quite a spectacle if you want to come and watch. They all congregate for a fresh fish barbecue afterwards at the Funtime pool, you'll know it by the bright colours and childish decor.' Naboo leads us to the bar, where another Black African stands wiping glasses.

'This is Henry, he will prepare your welcome drinks, then I will return when your bags are in your rooms and your booking forms have been printed. Please, enjoy the surroundings and I will return in half an hour.' Naboo then tips his hat and leaves before I can reach into my pocket for his tip.

'Don't worry, sir, in this resort we are not allowed to accept tips, rules of the management. I am Henry, your barman for the afternoon, would you like alcoholic or non-alcoholic welcome drinks?'

'Alcoholic, and make them doubles please.'

'With pleasure, sir, take a seat and I'll bring them over to you.'

Our drinks arrive in tall glasses that have pear shaped bottoms perched upon short stems. The drink itself is a multitude of spirits infused with a crushed ice fruit juice blend, with sliced fruit and the obligatory naff two inch high umbrella.

Naboo then returns in a topless golf buggy twenty minutes later, just as we slurp loudly at the last remains of slush in the bottoms of our glasses.

'Hop in,' he cries, and we do as instructed. 'I would like to take you on a brief tour of the resort, and presumed you would rather ride than walk after your journey. Then, you will have your bearings for later on, when you are deciding whereabouts you would like to dine.' Naboo's English is almost perfect, his accent a mix of Native African with strong Oxford overtones. The buggy lurches forward with instant inertia, as all electric vehicles seem to, and we commence our tour. The Shipwreck pool is the next around the corner, and it features an enormous fibreglass moulding of the back end of a Spanish galleon protruding at forty-five degrees from the centre. Upon closer inspection, it houses a small barbecue servery for those who want a swift tuna steak panini whilst bobbing around in the refreshing pool. It also sports a fresh orange juicer that cascades its liquid down like a chocolate fountain for anyone to collect a small cup and fill it at will.

From there we move past the Tropicana restaurant that serves a variety of local style dishes blended with the sophistication of Wedgewood and Sheffield's finest, then on past Freddy Frog's Tropical Pizzaria as we descend into the Funtime area. Large cartoon characters and fun slides abound, the fancy dress parade is nearing its final preparations and an enormous table drenched with all the food a child could desire runs along a two metre high wall that is covered in extremely artistic New York subway style graffiti. The hubbub of busy mums and expectant children is electrifying, so much emotion in just one tiny corner of the world is so beautiful to see.

'Next along is the Holiday Pool, the largest of all, and most popular. There is no theme to it, just interesting shapes.'

We look at the pool ahead of us, its form has no regularity or symmetry, and I doubt there's a straight edge anywhere. The floor is made of a multitude of randomly spread coloured tiles that all glisten metallically in the sunshine. The complex shape weaves and works its way back and forth, and there must be at least a dozen bridges crossing from one section to another, the whole thing must be over an acre in size. It's certainly the most spectacular pool I've ever seen. The hundred or so bathers that remain in or around it certainly seem to be enjoying it, and a great number of people are also enjoying food from the two large outdoor restaurants that flank either side of it. I think it might well be the place for us to spend tomorrow morning, I wonder if they'll knock me up a swift egg and bacon.

'Finally for your tour, sir, we have the Health Pool, this brings us back to where we started as it connects with the Dive Pool.' The Health pool is truly fabulous. Completely circular with Aphrodite's image on the bottom, Around approximately a quarter of the circumference lie ten massage tables, three of which are occupied, a mud pool set on a wooden deck, that resides next to a hot tub that could seat at least ten people sits a little further around, and a couple of rows of static exercise bikes finish the semi circle. The rest of the outlying area is littered with sun loungers, tables and chairs. There is a wooden building to the far side which probably occupies the same footprint as my house, but compared to the eighteen storey hotel in its background, a quaint chalet is how it appears.

'Inside the chalet, sir and madam, we have several rooms for acupuncture, aromatherapy, reiki and other treatments. There is also a sauna and steam room. The refreshments bar is closed today, but will re-open at six tomorrow morning, it serves fresh fruit juices, smoothies and salads. I trust you have enjoyed our little tour, but please step down as we must now continue on foot.'

Naboo then guides us back through the lounge doors we had left the hotel by, via a narrow but ornate wooden bridge. Once back through both the lounge and the reception areas, we find ourselves at the lifts. Floor twelve is punched by Naboo's finger and we glide effortlessly up to our level.

Naboo then leads us down the dimly lit corridors to our room. The door to room twelve thirty-seven opens smoothly to reveal a panoramic view of the ocean through the floor to ceiling plate glass windows, a ridiculously sized super double king-sized bed dominates the room, that is also decorated with loungers, bean bags and two low level coffee tables.

We mooch inside, drinking in the luxury of our surroundings as Naboo demonstrates the functions of the room's remote control device. Curtains swish, lights fade then brighten, even the bath begins to fill at the touch of a button. I take the remote from Naboo and point it at Wendy.

'Which button is the mute then?' I ask, as Wendy gives me an amused frown. Naboo seems mystified at my question, and I dismiss it before he pays it too much thought.

'Dinner is served from seven in all the restaurants, and the dress code for tonight is smart casual, so a jacket must be worn, but a tie is not required.'

I thank Naboo for his help, and he leaves after a curt bow.

'Mute, I'll show you the way to mute *me*, young man.' Wendy wraps her arms around me and we make passionate love on the floor right next to the large window, it feels strange to be naked, frolicking right on the edge of a forty metre drop, but the glass will certainly prevent us from rolling over the edge.

Dinner is a fabulous blend of lobster to start followed by seared sea bass, set on a bed of shredded vegetables and topped with a rather pokey Thai chilli glaze. Desert is a simple scoop of vanilla, followed by a couple of Irish coffees on the patio, as we relax for a while, allowing the rigours of travel melt slowly from our peacefully reclined limbs. After almost an hour, we decide to return upstairs, and find sleep is only a blink away once our bodies are one with the sheets.

*****

We rise early, and with the time difference between our surroundings and our bodies a half a dozen hours I'm surprised we sleep in as late as seven, but thankful all the same. We enjoy the pleasures of each other's flesh once again before a shower and a shave, then take the smooth riding elevator to the eighteenth floor for a much needed breakfast on the roof terrace.

'Oh my god, Babe, am I really seeing this?' Wendy asks as the lift doors glide open. The scene in front of us is absolutely breathtaking. The entire roof of the hotel is laid to lawn, not the usual tropical species of harsh dry grass, but the far gentler type that adorns the gardens of our proud England's home counties. There seems to be no barrier to the edge, as if one could walk clean off of it into oblivion, but I notice after a moment that there is, in fact, a two metre high glass wall that runs seemingly seamlessly around the entire perimeter, giving the transparent illusion of freedom. There is a central serving station where the staff congregate, waiting for the orders to arrive inside the high speed dumb waiter, straight from the basement kitchens nineteen stories below. It is built as a circular bar might be, with a central pillar housing the food lifts, and a range of staff placing the plates onto the heated bar for the waiters to distribute to the eagerly waiting diners. Spread from this central serving station, a plethora of tables stand, with staccato spacing throughout the entire roof garden. These are interspersed with abundant flowerbeds and half a dozen palm trees that must be over six metres in height. Amazing is such an understatement, it's almost an insult. Edward shows us to our table, and hands us a narrow card with the breakfast options on, also sporting a breakfast Champagne list on the reverse. I muse it must just be the extremely wealthy and the extremely poor that consider alcohol a viable breakfast option, the only real difference being a burst of bubbles in a roof garden or a brown paper bag on a park bench. Is it really just the middle class who have got it so wrong?

'Wow,' I say, 'scrambled eggs with smoked salmon, a dash of Earl Grey and crisply tanned wholemeal seems to be the order of the day.' A waiter appears with a large basket of oranges and a strange looking contraption slung over his shoulder. 'Oranjuice please sirmadam?' he enquires. We both nod, and then watch as he swings the bright chrome contraption from his shoulder, kicking its legs out to form a tripod. He then flicks a switch on its side after hanging a glass jug to its underbelly from a hook. A buzzing, grinding noise then follows as he slices a whole orange on a circular blade, only to impale it onto the rotating cone atop the three-legged machine. Moments later a jug of freshly squeezed orange juice is placed upon the table.

Our tea and toast arrive immediately, our eggs fifteen minutes later.

'They really have got this place just right,' I think out loud,

'Mmm, best come back every year then Rambo,' is Miss W's answer.

'Best get yourself an executive job to cover it then, my angel,' I retort, but without a following comment from its recipient. A dull thudding enters the airspace, a noise that slowly grows in both intensity and volume. I cannot place it. Moments later a speck on the horizon morphs into a shape, one that soon becomes familiar as a helicopter. Its course is straight for us, its height dead level to ours. I chat further with Wendy about our week's expectations, hopes and desires. We speak of the fabulous diving ahead of us and just absorb the breathtaking view around us. All of a sudden, I realise that the helicopter's path remains unaltered. It approaches unrelentingly towards our breakfast terrace, and flashes of 9/11 thread swiftly through my grey stuff as my concern grows. The chopper must be less than a hundred yards away, yet still it persists on its course. Fifty yards away and I'm now scared, the iridium coated windscreen of the Bell Jet Ranger is so close I can almost read the pilot's name tag.

'Wendy,' I bark, 'I think we should make a dash for the lift, we're all going to die!'

'Oh for Christ's sake, Jack, will you knock it off,' she replies, agitated, I reach over the table, grab her head with both hands and spin her face around into the direction of the incoming projectile.

'Jesus Christ, Jack, let's get out of here.' She stands ready to run, but as she does so, the chopper banks right within ten of metres of the glass perimeter screens to show a pictorial image of a volcano between two palm trees and the 'Shambhala Tropical Resort' logo painted on its underbelly. The helicopter then drops from view, towards a landing pad that hides behind a screen of palm trees near the complex of pools.

'We were on the brink of running too,' the man at the adjoining table offers, 'it certainly looked as if we were all done for there for a moment.' I turn in my chair to be greeted by a lean looking man, black spiked hair and Ralph Lauren polo shirt. His partner is slim, brunette with a hint of auburn, and extremely pretty. I shake his hand. 'Jack, Jack Todd, and this is the fabulous Wendy. We're here to get married, all a bit last minute really, only booked it on Friday.'

'That's a coincidence, so did I. My name is Richard, and this is my fiancée Victoria, we're due to be wed on the island that bears the same name of that chopper that had us all somewhat concerned.'

'Wow,' I reply, 'us too, next Wednesday morning.'

'And us in the afternoon, cheers.' Richard raises a toast of freshly squeezed, and we all chink glasses. We turn to resume our meal, then leave via the stairwell in order to walk off a few of the freshly imbibed calories.

After a quick pit-stop at the room to douse ourselves in lotions and potions to keep both the sun and the mozzies at bay, we're set for a stroll into town in order to find the famous Sao Jose market and absorb some local culture. Our stroll to the market, however, seems a little impractical, as the desk clerk estimates it to be a fifteen minute cab journey at least, and given the speed the local cab drivers hurtle along at, that could be about sixty miles. A taxi sits in waiting outside the front doors of the reception, so we find ourselves under way immediately.

As our perfect paradise surroundings fall behind us, the harsh reality of local poverty and brutal lifestyle return to all sides of the car. As we enter the city, I look curiously at the ornate and once beautiful, yet now depressed and decomposing architecture. I'm saddened as the intricate and ornate iron balconies with hours and hours of skilled labour in their history of creation now weep tears in rusty streaks down the buildings they were once proud to adorn. The obvious expense of a previous wave of cash-rich developers has now fallen prey to the decay and demise of the environments, both financial and natural. The once white paint now peels and cracks, falling away with chunks of plaster and brick. Unfortunately this town needs more than just a plaster to heal it though. Our taxi driver drops us at the Pont Boa Vista, but from the view, I think the Boa more likely refers to a snake, than the Portuguese term for beautiful.

We find the market inside an enormous hangar-style building, a large entrance probably fifteen metres in height greets us, the sheet steel to the face of it is painted a pattern of green and turquoise concentric arches, surrounded by ornately cast beams and supports that rise to a peak at the top of the pitched roof. It reminds me of a more colourful version of London's Smithfield market. We enter the relative coolness this vastly high ceilinged structure has to offer, and spend an hour larking and flirting among the stalls, Wendy buying a couple of bits for cousins and nieces, whilst I just drink in the colour and energy of the stimulating atmosphere.

Next on the list is Bom Jesus Street, the main drag in Recife. The place to see, and the place to *be* seen *in*. The street is lined with more tall, iron balconied buildings, although these, by contrast are in impeccable condition, resembling the style of the French quarter in New Orleans. I notice the large number of African faces, and cultural ingress from that vast continent that has arrived here through the pain and degradation of the slave trade. Now the faces show welcoming smiles, and their culture offers such a diversity of cuisine, art and fashion. Something their forefathers would have thought an impossible dream just a couple of generations ago. We stop and take in the paintings of a local street artist, his work is mostly of the city, painting it in a favourable light, catching the slices of a world too easily missed by the rush of life that carries us all too swiftly to its end. One piece I love instantly is a simple acrylic work of a crushed Coke can lying on the white sand, half in the shadow of a palm leaf, the sun glinting off the silver end cap reflects the beach upon which it has been discarded. A blemish in paradise if you will, it sums the sadder parts of this city up so perfectly I buy it immediately.

Bemused, the artist returns me my change, and it's only after I see this expression upon his face I realise I have broken with tradition by paying the full asking price. I almost feel guilty that I've robbed him of ten minutes negotiation, the feeling of outwitting a dumb tourist of his easily found funds, which he probably finds just as stimulating as the painting itself. He folds a coarse and loosely woven grey cloth carefully around his work, securing it with a criss-crossed loop of green hairy string. It gets everywhere that stuff, I wonder if I can buy shares in it?

'Hey, Babe, waddaya think?' Wendy is draping a narrow cut dress over her front by the hanger, it's a deep purple with a thin tapering flash of silver from one hip to the armpit, it looks sensational.

'Nah, might be alright on a fit bird, but a fat minger like you would just look like a petrol station in it.' She sticks her tongue out at my obvious humour, and disappears back into the shop to try it on, only to reappear a moment later with a brown cardboard bag.

'They only had size eight, Babe, so I guess it'll be a little loose around the tum, but just right everywhere else.' I smile at the thought of her wearing it to dinner this evening, and look forward to peeling it off her shortly afterwards. We take in a coffee with the view from the table fronted café in Bom Jesus Street, then head back to our pampered five star seclusion aboard another well worn Merc taxi.

*****

'Good afternoon sir, madam.' Naboo nods his head as he greets us at the hotel doors. 'Did you both enjoy the splendour of the city?'

'Yes, Naboo, a true diversity of tastes and experiences,' I gloss.

'Wonderful, Mister Todd, and could I enquire if you would like me to arrange any activities for after lunch; Jet skiing and wake boarding are popular at our private beach, or possibly an all over body massage for you both at the spa?'

'Brilliant, I'll take the lot. Thanks, Naboo, you're a star.' I shake his hand and move swiftly inside.

'Miste…'

'You sod,' Wendy whispers, 'you know he meant either or, don't you.'

'Yes, yes. Got to get my money's worth though.' Wendy leans in for a kiss. I reciprocate as we walk, but become startled as we bump headlong into Richard and Victoria.

'Wow, sorry about that. We should look where we're going.'

'No, don't worry, Jack,' replies Richard with a smile, 'I can see you were otherwise engaged. Listen, what have you got booked for tomorrow? We're chartering a boat to go diving. With some luck we're bound to find some reefs to explore. Do you both dive?'

'Yeah, we were thinking of getting a dive or two in before we head over to the main sites around Shambhala Island, so that sounds great.' I turn to

Wendy who nods, with eyes almost as wide as her grin.

The day pans out as expected, and we find ourselves in a beach front restaurant, watching the shadows stretch further and further down the beach as the sun goes down.

'My body's killing me,' I complain, the Jet Ski's pounding on the waves has compressed my spine, leaving me about two thirds the height I was this morning, the wakeboarding stretched my arms to the length of 'Mr. Tickle's' and the deep tissue massage has thinned me to the point where I feel like I have been fed through a mangle. An hour or so by the pool helped me return a little nearer normal again, but I still feel like I need more pampering.

'Why don't we take a hot tub when we return to the hotel then, Babe?' Wendy suggests, it sounds like Heaven, but then anything with her at my side feels like Heaven. Our long lip to lip welding is then interrupted by the arrival of a freshly pinked lobster, set on a bed of roasted vegetable, cous-cous and a side salad of diced tomato, cucumber and raw carrot. A fruit-based ice cream desert finishes off a perfect meal, and we wander along the beach back to our hotel as the curtain of darkness gently falls from the sky.

14. Reef encounter

'Come on, Babe, I said we'd meet them in reception by nine.'

'Keep your pants on, Rambo, I'm just doing my legs.'

I open the bedroom door and glance down the corridor, the room next door also has the door open, so out of curiosity I glance around the doorframe inside, only to be greeted by Victoria who is just walking out, bag in hand and the arm of her sunglasses poked between her breasts. My brain sends me a sharp jolt, and my eyes revert to hers, a foot higher.

'Hi, Jack, how did you know this was our room?'

'I didn't, we're next door, I was just hurrying Wendy along and thought I'd see what was going on outside when I bumped into you. Coincidence I guess.'

'We seem to be having a few of those,' she observes, then disappears down the corridor in search of her fella. Wendy then appears with a smile, and we head downstairs.

Richard is at the reception desk, discussing a trip they were arranging for him tomorrow, and once sorted he comes over to greet us on the sofas we're waiting on.

'Right, I've been down to the jetty earlier this morning and everything's sorted. All the kit is there, and we've got ourselves a nice little thirty foot dive boat, complete with a platform at the back, to zip us out to the reefs.'

We all four hop into the waiting cab, Richard in the front whilst Wendy occupies the middle seat in the back. We head south, away from the city and out into the suburbs that then deplete to dusty fields, jagged rocks and overgrown bursts of greenery.

Richard turns in his seat, 'As I said, I came down here this morning to sort everything out, so we should be set for a great day's diving, the water here is clearer than out of the taps at home.'

'Sounds great,' replies Victoria, 'Jack and Wendy have the room next to us, dear.'

'Wow, that's certainly quite a coincidence, you're going to tell me they live in Weybridge now, and booked the day before the flight.'

'Er... you're not going to believe this...' I reply, and ten minutes later we find ourselves amazed that we haven't bumped into each other at home.

After an hour or so a small fishing village comes into view. The cluster of brightly coloured buildings comes closer, and I ponder on the fact that these houses and shops were built on a much tighter budget than those in the city, yet remain well looked after and simplistically beautiful on their own. As we enter the village the residents seem far prouder than their city counterparts so close by. Well kept flowers hang from baskets and flood from troughs that line the tidy streets. Everybody seems to have a purpose, the aimlessly wandering unemployed of Recife are replaced with a vibrant populous of hard working locals who welcome us with a genuine smile. The narrow streets guide us to the sea front, where a pontoon extends out into the water with a dozen or so boats tethered to its cleats. We find ours about halfway down, a cheery chap leans over its windscreen, polishing it with a cloth.

'*Obrigado*, my friends, I am Carl. Your first time dive in the Brazil?'

'Hi, Richard, and this is Victoria, Jack and Wendy,' one by one we all shake his hand, 'and yes, it is the first time we've dived here, I understand it is very beautiful, some even say the best diving in the world so we're really looking forward to seeing the fabulous colours and natural splendour down there.'

'Yes, my friend, but the reason I ask is not for the beauty, it is for the danger. Do you know that Recife has more than one nickname, they probably only told you it is called Little Venice because of the bridges, but it is also called Shark Town by those who dive. There are more sharks here than anywhere else in the world, so if you think you might panic, it may be best to stick to the hotel swimming pool.'

I gulp, and Wendy grabs my shoulder. 'Jack, what does he mean? I'm worried.'

'So, Carl, what is the likelihood of us being attacked by a shark today?' Richard asks in a very pragmatic way, as if he'd just asked if decaff was an option at his local Starbucks.

'Small, we have hundreds of tourists dive every

season, they all go home with their arms and legs. There has only been forty-seven attacks here in the last fifteen years, and only ten of those killed the diver.' He laughs, but I sense he is the only one who finds this amusing. 'Honestly, you are more likely to be kissed by a dolphin, than nibbled by a Bull shark, but it's good to be aware. If you see one, just chill out and it will pass. If you panic and flap around, it's more likely to think of you as lunch, so just remember, and keep your eyes open.' He points his fingers at his eyes, then winks at the girls. 'Have fun, amigos.' He hops from the boat and begins to untie it before we have even set foot aboard.

Carl pushes us off with a bare foot to the bough, and then waves with a smiling face as I spark the engine into life. We chug slowly from the cove, then glide up onto the plane as soon as we reach the open sea. The smooth water still produces the familiar pounding up and down as we make progress out into the Atlantic, but we level off once the depth sounder tells us we have ten metres below us to the bed.

'Okay, boys and girls, time to go aquatic. Richard, could you drop the anchor and we'll call this home for a while.' Richard heads to the front of the boat and operates the lever to send the weighted metal chain whirring and jangling as it falls beneath us. Wendy then turns to me with a genuine look of concern.

'Babe, I don't want to get eaten, that man has really scared me.'

'Don't worry, my love. Richard and I will drop down first and take a look around. It'll be okay, I promise.' Richard and I pull on our shortie suits and start to check through our kit. We help each other with our buoyancy control devices, or B.C.s for short, that carry the tanks on our backs, giving them a quick couple of puffs from the tank to inflate them a little. I check the display on my dive computer that I strap to my wrist, and a flick of the switch confirms that my flashlight is as flashy as it looks. We're almost ready, the weights belt goes on next, and Wendy then plants a smacker of a kiss on my lips before I sit on the edge of the boat to pull on my fins.

'I'm gonna go real easy, two or three metres at a time,' I call to Richard. He nods absently, and is lost in his own preparation ritual. I cough up something slimy and use it to lube the glass of my mask before a swift splash in the water to clear it. I then push the mask onto my face whilst stretching the rubber strap over my head. My heart rate is higher than it should be, the anticipation of my first dive of the season mixed with the unwanted comments from our host has me unusually stressed. I feel a tension between my temples as if an invisible elastic is pulling them together, into my throbbing head. The higher the tension, the heavier I will breathe, the heavier I breathe, the less time I will get down below. I close my eyes and try to release the negative thoughts from my mind.

'Jack, are you with me?' I jerk my eyes open, Richard is sat next to me with a raised eyebrow of expectation.

'Yes, sorry I was miles away.' We plug our regulators into our mouths simultaneously and take a couple of breaths of reassurance. With one hand over my mask and the other on my regulator, I lean backwards and anticipate the plunge.

Spadoosh! It takes a second to orient myself to the boat again, but once done I head over to the anchor chain, my guide for the next ten metres. Richard appears to my right, also finning towards the chain, and we meet there one after the other. I give the 'O' sign with my thumb and forefinger and Richard returns the signal, followed by a thumbs down sign to signify the start of our descent. I depress the valve to allow some air to bleed from the B.C. and we glide gracefully down. As we descend I can feel the pressure slowly building in my ears, I pause at three metres to equalise, then hover a moment before continuing. This cycle means repeating the process twice more before reaching the bottom. Once there, I glide around for a couple of minutes before catching sight of Richard again. Another 'O' followed by a thumbs up, and we make our way back to the chain that leads us up to the boat on the surface, stopping once again on the way up to allow our bodies to acclimatise to this alien environment.

'Cool, Babe, you'd love it down here, there's so much wildlife, and colour. The water's crystal clear and you can see for thirty metres at least. Get hooked up, Babe, and I'll *really* show you a good time.' I clamber onto the rear deck of the boat and struggle my way back over the stern. Dropping my cylinder to the floor, I then race to help Wendy get kitted up. I'm buzzing with such a massive dose of excitement I find it hard to contain. Wendy and Victoria have both exchanged bikinis for shortie wet suits whilst we were below, and also swapped trepidation for exhilaration at our animated return. Richard is jabbering like a ten year old at his first cup final as we all rush to return to our underwater adventure.

My second dive at the reef starts off with a bang, my first sight upon entering the water is the curved beak of a very large loggerhead turtle crashing into my mask. He carelessly flaps away like a slow moving spacecraft and I decide fall in close behind. He leads me into a magnificent coral maze, like the white rabbit leading Alice into Wonderland. I glance back up at the girls, the familiar stop start descent repeating itself, although unnecessary for the boys, as we are now attuned to the depth at which we are diving.

Once on the sea bed, we go in search of stimulation, Wendy and I lead, Richard and Victoria in the close, but not immediate vicinity. The reef we have found is absolutely teaming with life, fish of such colour and beauty that an artist would struggle to depict. Florescent blue queen trigger fish dart ahead of us, skittishly changing direction at will, whilst every hidey-hole I peer into conceals a cheeky looking red squirrel fish trying to get some sleep. I am hypnotized with the splendour and every turn of my head astonishes me. The colours, the shapes, everything is so surreal. A short distance from the reef we find a half buried tug boat, and dropping down into it we enjoy the thrill of exploration coursing through our veins immediately, although this simple vessel holds little of interest, so we leave it in our wake after a brief inspection, in search of more stimulating finds.

We both enjoy the next twenty minutes or so at the bed, gazing, frolicking and generally exploring before the flashing yellow light on my dive computer has us rising back to the surface once more. A stop halfway up to keep the bends at bay has me scanning in disbelief at what must have been above us for our entire dive. Adrenalin is pumping through my veins as a six-foot reef shark heads straight for us. There are three or four other sharks gliding close by, but this one seems intent on swimming straight at me. The features of his face are becoming clearer, his dead eyes, his emotionless mouth and, of course, his frightening rows of viciously sharp teeth. He's getting closer and closer, this feels very wrong. Am I about to become the next victim for the headlines? I take the finger that bears my ring of destiny into my other hand and place three fingers over the stones. The sweat that pours into my eyes from my forehead proves distracting as the mask begins to fog, my brain races with all scenarios and solutions, but it runs at a speed that I cannot keep pace with. Suddenly, an answer becomes clear. If an attack is instigated by the shark I can depress the stones and halt the passage of time once more. This will allow me to swim up to the boat, grab the flare gun, and attach it to my B.C. therefore allowing me to fire it into his open jaws. This flashes through my grey matter in a split second, but I feel sure of a plan now. My instincts, however, take over and my body prepares for an attack. I quickly draw in a breath and my entire body tightens. My fingers poised on the gems ready to depress them in an instant, I am frozen solid, but the graceful predator merely swims within two metres of my face, before a rapid change in altitude has it pass safely overhead.

Wendy is alongside me, clutching onto my arm with both her hands. Her nails digging deeply in as I think to myself; *'please don't bleed, please don't bleed.'* I glance around to find Richard, but he's nowhere to be seen. We have to remain at the stop for at least a couple of minutes, but the time drags like hours. I cling to Wendy in a state of tensed nervousness, preventing her from surfacing too soon, I pray to all the Gods that will listen, and will my dive computer to show me a green l.e.d. when the time to surface arrives. It's the longest two minutes of my life, ever. I think Wendy is in mental shutdown, she hasn't struggled or fought to be free since the sharks appeared, it's funny how an absolute threat of death can affect you in ways you wouldn't normally conceive. Had I been asked the question theoretically, *'what would I do if surrounded by sharks with very little air in my tank?'* The answer; *'breathe calmly for two minutes then rise slowly,'* would be so far off the agenda it would be in a different stratosphere.

Once on the surface, we fin our way to the platform as swiftly as possible whilst not attracting unwanted attention from those below. I help Wendy up first, then freeze as a dorsal fin smoothly slices through the water not two metres from my head. It's time to get out of here. I clamber as quickly as I can back onto the safety of the platform, then stand to see Richard and Victoria sat in the boat, already stripped of their gear.

'Christ, Jack! Have you two got a death-wish or something?' Victoria asks, 'We saw the sharks as soon as we reached the bottom, but you and Wendy swam out of range too quickly for us to warn you. We thought you'd notice them soon after us, but you've been down there, oblivious, for half an hour. We've been fretting about what to do, we didn't want to get back in the water so we've just had to wait up here for what seemed like hours.'

Wendy is calm but obviously in a state of mild shock. She removes her kit methodically and in silence, as I do likewise. I cuddle her for all I'm worth, but her eyes seem fixed somewhere my words couldn't possibly reach. Richard thumbs the boat into life and we slowly make our way back to the comparative security of the rickety wooden pontoon.

15. Shambhala

We sit with a relaxed sense of anticipation as to what our next slice of paradise will contain. With packed bags, we wait in the lounge area for our helicopter to arrive, reflecting and discussing the past week's events. Richard and Victoria relax into the deep white cushions of the luxurious sofa that sits opposite ours. Wendy and I melt together as only true lovers can, at peace with each other in a state of complete subconscious yet un-self-conscious harmony. I cannot believe how the last few days have evaporated without trace, as only distant memories of massage, dining and swimming seem accessible in this state of numbed relaxation. The fruit laden departure drink of 98 proof alcohol probably hasn't helped either, but I feel at one with the plump cushions, never to move again.

'I'm so chilled, a terrorist could run in with a bomb now and it wouldn't bother me in the slightest,' offers Richard. I've learnt in the past week of his quirks and idiosyncrasies, so now know how to take him. The cool and laid-back exterior is prone to snapping without warning once a misplaced comment or action comes in his direction. Caution and diplomacy is the way to work with Richard. I bet his employees have to keep plenty of Savlon in their desks, ready for the next time they need to bite their tongue.

Victoria by contrast is so laid-back she's past

horizontal. More a spiritual type with a heart of gold, though certainly not the beads and kaftans type. She always dresses flawlessly with clothes that show her size eight figure perfectly. She's not as neat and regimented as her partner, who I've noticed even straightens the cutlery when we sit down for a meal, but I sense that she usually gets her own way. I silently wonder how they ever became lovers.

Naboo enters the room, impeccably dressed as usual. 'Sirs and madams, we have had a call from the inbound pilot, your carriage will await in a few minutes from the pad behind the Rainforest Pool. Your bags will be taken by my staff, so if you could make your way out, we can have you on the island for lunch.'

I look at Naboo, and for all his starched white clothes and highly professional appearance, I know deep down that he probably lives in a tiny bedroom somewhere on the complex, earning an embarrassingly low wage for adding that special personal touch that makes a place like this come alive. I silently wish that the board of directors who own these large concrete money generators realize the true worth of the people imprisoned within them, and reward them accordingly. I have seen the catering trade from all sides, and it can be as grim as a heroin addict's flat. I doubt Naboo will ever leave, for he's part of the furniture. His psychological shackles will hold him here until his breath is too shallow to be of use to the company, then he will be discarded like a sour milk carton, out into the heat of the harsh world without the support or structure that has nurtured his entire adult life. Yes, I pity Naboo, as I see what he has in store for his future, even if he doesn't yet realise it himself. As we stand to leave, I break the rules and slip a fifty into his pocket without him realising. I know a man like Naboo is too proud to take a tip when the invisible empire he works for would frown upon it, but he really deserves it, and more.

I see the chopper approaching out of the tall French windows, and I suddenly feel sad to leave. We follow Naboo's white hat out into the morning sunshine one last time, through the complex of pools, restaurants and bars that have been our home for too short a time, over the bridges that connect them and finally to the helicopter pad where our Bell Jet Ranger sits expectantly with its blades turning at a now reduced pace, kicking dust into the air as it waits. We all shake Naboo's hand as we leave, he bows slightly at every shake, and there is a slightly awkward moment when he returns a banknote that Richard tries to pass him in the handshake. I cannot hear the conversation over the noise of the aircraft, but Naboo appears not to be accepting the gift. Richard simply shrugs and turns towards the helicopter. We all give one last smile as we enter the Bell, and buckle up for our next instalment of living in paradise.

The engine revs rise and the blades increase their velocity as we bobble for a moment before lifting clear of the pad. Wendy's grip on my arm increasing with the revs of the engine, refreshing the marks from our one and only dive this past week. The nose of the chopper dips slightly and we swoop around, before we know it the trees are below us and the bathers on the sandy beach shrink to a gathering of dots as we head out over the ocean, gaining altitude as we go.

The light turquoise shallows fade to a deeper inky blue as we leave the mainland behind, our journey taking just an hour and a half, before the pilot drops our altitude once again as the island of Shambhala comes into view.

'Wow, Babe, look down there!' Wendy points at the jumping dolphins that play in the water, arcing in formation as they excitedly follow our flight path. The colour of the sea lightens again as we approach the shallows of the island, our pilot dropping to just ten metres, exaggerating the speed we're travelling at.

'Let me take you on a quick tour around the island before we land, so you can savour the beauty of our wonderful home,' the pilot announces as he banks left, and our only view is of sky or water for a few moments, until we level out to see the splendour of our awaiting paradise. We chase along the perfectly white deserted beaches that are lined by palm trees and the occasional shack. It seems that the only inhabitants are a few locals and a dozen holidaymakers. After exploring the north side of the island we then climb a little higher as we turn inland, over the forest that covers the central part of the island. Two dormant volcanoes dominate the skyline ahead, and our pilot drops to within a few metres of the treetops to give us the most spectacular view. Further south we head, following a river that cascades over rocks and waterfalls, making pools and tributaries on its journey through the lush green trees. A clearing shows a small village, with half a dozen basic houses arranged in a circle. A group of children play in front of one of the homes and all wave as we pass overhead, the mother beating the dust from a rug that hangs from a line. It reminds me of *Tom and Jerry*, I wait to see a cartoon grey cat scamper from the house, knocking her off her feet, but we pass over before my imagination runs too wild.

Rising slightly higher now, to clear a ridge of grey rock that juts from the trees, we see the coast beneath us once again. The pilot banks right and we head west along the southern edge of the island, past a fishing village where small boats are casting their nets in the beautifully clear waters only half a mile or so from shore. Moments later the pilot takes us slightly inland again, this time over a few buildings and immaculate gardens that will be our home for the coming week. I can see the Atlantic to our left, and notice the 'W' shaped cove our residence is built in. The pilot circles the vast wooden stage that serves as a landing pad once, then sets us gently on the ground, instantly winding down the engines. As the noise reduces I become acutely aware of the volume we had been tolerating on our journey here, a contrast I hope to the tranquillity our new surroundings will offer. We step from the helicopter and make the dash to safety under the rotating blades that slowly decelerate above our lowered heads and flailing hair. At the edge of the platform stands three English looking faces; two men and a woman, all wearing crisply ironed Hawaiian shirts that bear light and dark blue floral print upon a white background, the Shambhala logo embroidered on the breast of each one.

'Good afternoon, ladies and gentlemen, welcome to The Shambhala Island Resort. My name is Emma, I am the resort manager, and these are my close assistants; Robert, who is in charge of leisure and entertainment and Peter who is accommodation and catering manager.' They both nod their heads when introduced, then a small local girl of about twelve appears to hand us all a freshly cut flower each.

'And this is Bounty, she always loves to welcome new guests to the island she has called home her entire life.' Bounty smiles as she places the flower in one of each of our hands, kissing it before she does so, then bows after welcoming us to the island. She then retreats, back down the wooden steps, out of view.

'Let me guide you to the reception, so we can get you settled in as soon as possible.' She gestures to an islander wearing a similarly patterned, but orange and brown flowered shirt, who immediately runs towards the chopper to retrieve our bags. We follow our hosts down the wooden stairs, and then along a walkway suspended a couple of metres from the jungle floor, to the cawing of tropical birds that sit amongst the trees around us. I feel as if we are on our way to meet a tall man in a grey suit, bearing an eye patch and a shaven head, to a greeting of; 'So, Mr. Bond, you find me at last.'

The Bond villain doesn't materialise though, and we find ourselves sitting once again next to a pool surrounded by palm trees. Our checking in forms are spread on a low level table in front of us, so we all take a seat on the cream cushioned wicker sofas that surround the inviting pool and await further instruction. The barman pours four flutes of Champagne from the draught tap, infuses them with a dash of pomegranate juice, before plunging several pomegranate berries into the glass, that sink slowly to the bottom. Peter then appears with a silver tray, upon which four credit style cards sit bearing the volcano and palm tree logo embossed in gold, two with a 7 on, and two with an 8. I look to Richard, 'Guess we're neighbours again then.'

'Fabulous, let's settle in, then meet Victoria and me back here in an hour.'

'Sounds good to me.' I glance at Wendy who gives a slightly lopsided grin in response, though I take it as positive nonetheless. We follow Peter along a short paved path through the maze of palms, which eventually open out onto another wooden walkway that runs parallel to the golden sand of the most perfect beach I have ever seen. The surge of the ocean rolls in and out with the hypnotic rhythm of a slowly swung pocket watch, as we stride left then right towards our accommodation.

A short while later we arrive at number 7. A wonderful eight hundred square foot, deeply toned wooden pavilion that sits proudly on stilts that plunge deep into the sand, its large floor to ceiling windows draped in white linen curtains that flow invitingly with a wave of animated splendour. The dark timber floors invite us over the threshold into a simply decorated yet seductively enticing living area, boasting more cream coloured sofas and loungers, punctuated by bright orange and rust coloured cushions, whose backs are draped in hunters' trophies of skin and fur. The ceiling is alive with the rotation of several fans, circulating the perfectly thermostatted air gently around the room. I glance to Wendy with a knowing smile, and feel the upcoming week will certainly be a good one.

Peter fades into the background, as Wendy and I seek to explore our new world in every detail. The kitchen is predictably well appointed, and the bedroom as fantastic as any man's dreams. Wendy and I predictably spend most of the hour's preparation time enjoying the pleasures of the each other's flesh in these fabulously romantic new surroundings, stopping early to avoid incurring a raised eyebrow from Richard upon our return to the world outside.

An hour and fifteen minutes later we find ourselves sitting back around a low level table at the poolside bar, buzzing with endorphins yet only slightly refreshed due to the swift wash that replaced the much needed shower. The Champagne flutes find their way into our hands once again, and we begin discussing the week's activities with both Richard and Victoria.

A return to exploring the fabulous undersea world that Brazil offers seems to be the theme of the afternoon. Richard leads the conversation by speaking of the *'Ben Lowe underwater sculpture park'* that I'd also been told of whilst booking the trip.

'Honestly, mate, it's a must see attraction. Apparently they have such a massive selection of sculptures down there on the seabed it will truly blow your mind. I've heard that there's a 25 foot dolphin made purely from barbed wire, a group of bronze characters, twice life sized, all holding hands in a circle on the sand, a one-third scale model of the Eiffel tower, lying on its side as if it has been melted to the ground and all sorts of other crazy stuff. Mate, we've just got to get down there and see it all.' Richard speaks animatedly as Wendy's clasp around my forearm tightens yet again with every word.

'But, Babe, what about the sharks? I really don't like the idea of swimming with those horrible creatures again, they scared the living daylights out of me,' she pleads.

'Don't worry, my darling, I'm sure there won't be any sharks around this island, it's only near Recife that they congregate, that's why they call it Shark Town. Just to put your mind at rest, I'll ask the staff when we go to book the boat. I'm sure they're fully aware of the local wildlife. Besides, I'm sure we've had our close shave for the holiday, so it'll be plain sailing from now on.'

'Now there's an idea.' Wendy answers, wearing one of her super confident smiles, 'You boys can go and get eaten by sharks tomorrow whilst we take a sail boat out to the horizon and back.'

'Sounds perfect, boys, don't you think?' adds Victoria, now beaming like a cheeky Cheshire sofa scratcher.

'Sorted,' Richard concurs. 'Right, I'm famished. Let's see what this town has to offer.' He stands immediately and walks purposefully to the bar. A glance to his leather strapped Breitling confirms that it's neither lunch nor dinner time. The barman offers a plate of olives, followed by some more drinks and a couple of menus for our perusal. A plate of vegetable kebabs is ordered with a side of crunchy deep fried calamari to keep us going till dinner time, and with another flute in my hand, I'm beginning to feel a little sozzled. The afternoon fades slowly as Wendy and I take a stroll barefoot along the beach, hand in hand, joking, flirting, kissing and laughing with every couple of steps taken.

We dine on beef Wellington and Champagne by room service, sat, immersed in the gentle bubbling of the infinity edged pool that is sunk into the deck of our wonderful pavilion. If life could possibly be any better than this, I think I would just explode with delight.

*****

The banging on the patio door is Richard, it's a little after nine in the morning, and I'm still asleep.

'Come on, get up. There's fish to fly with and treasure to be found, Ooo Arr!' he tries in a diabolical pirate voice. My brain struggles to keep up with my momentum as my feet stagger their way beneath me to the door.

'Be with you in a minute, I'm just... er...'

'Incapable of finishing the sentence?'

'Yeah, incapable of finishing the sentence.' Richard comes in through the lounge and heads straight for the kitchen fridge.

'Not been shopping yet, dear?' He asks with sarcastic amusement. I smile by return and disappear into the bedroom to prepare for the dive ahead. Wendy beckons me back to bed, but like a good boy I continue to the shower and scrub the stale scent of last night's passion from my body, watching the foam swirl and dance as it disappears gently down the inefficient plug hole.

Once cleansed and clothed we make our way out into the rising heat of the day.

'Phew, gonna be a hot one,' I comment to Richard, who just nods and looks ahead through his dark tinted Armani eyewear. We reach the jetty after ten minutes of walking, and true to form Richard has already been down here this morning to ensure all the correct kit was prepared for our day's adventure.

'I've arranged for the girls to take out a fourteen

135

foot Taurus this morning, and a twenty-two foot Sea Line this afternoon. Victoria is a great sailor, and extremely competent. She certainly knows her jib from her rudder, I can tell you.' Richard's face breaks a smile for the first time this morning, and I feel it's going to be a good day. We walk down the jetty together, and hop into the bright orange Rib at the end. All our gear is ready to go, and we cast off immediately. Richard fires up the outboard with a stab of the electric start, and we set off into the great unknown once more.

'Right, Jack, look in the top of my dive bag, and you'll see a brochure bearing the co-ordinates for the sculpture park, punch them into my G.P.S. and we'll plot a course, so to speak.'

I do as instructed, and with a couple of bleeps, the digital arrow shows us the way. Twenty minutes out and we are nearing the dive site, the bleeping director tells us we are only two kilometres from our destination, and begins a blip, blip, blip countdown.

Bleeeeeeep, we've arrived. A red bell buoy rocks back and forth lazily in the water, hardly dinging the brass audio marker as it bobs. *'Welcome to the Ben Lowe sub aqua sculpture park'* is emblazoned across the main body in a plain *'Man Ray'* blue coloured serif text.

'Drop a line then, my son, and let's go exploring,' commands Richard, wearing an enormous grin at the pure adrenalin of a fresh dive.

We suit up and throw on our B.C.s in a flash. Then

with feet finned and eyes agoggled we plunge backwards into the crystal clear abyss. Down we fall, further and further towards the sea bed. I stop momentarily to equalise my ears once again, just to remind my body that we have indeed been this deep only days before, then see Richard do likewise a little further down. We plunge gracefully towards the art, taking in once again the absolute beauty of our surroundings. A shoal of probably five hundred silver and yellow finned fish, no more than six inches in length, scurry past. These are followed by a large lolloping drum fish that's uncharacteristically dull in colouring; brown, speckled and austere in its lazy animation. Some orange and red snapper looking chaps then fly past at an important rate, wiggling their tail fins with such dramatic fury that they disappear in an instant, obviously off to somewhere far more important. Only now, as we near the twelve metre deep bed, does the beauty and splendour of the sculpture park become fully apparent. I float in what seems like thin air, as the slowly reducing buoyancy of my B.C. allows me to hover slowly down amongst these perfect works of art, submerged beyond the dreams of all but the most adventurous eyes that sit, behind the glass masks that dare to brave the depths of the Atlantic Ocean. I, Jack Todd, feel so totally and utterly ALIVE!

I feel almost naughty as I reach out to touch the rigid arm of a three metre high steel casting of Adolph Hitler's bust, in full Nazi salute. This is opposed by a rival, but no less powerful bust of Sir Winston Churchill, showing his equally famous victory sign. I float back a little to grasp the full picture, and conclude that scissors did indeed beat paper, hands down.

Richard appears to my left, signalling for me to follow. I do so without question, trailing his deep blue fins across the sea bed lowers me into a surreal trance, from which I only break when the true magnitude of what he's showing me becomes apparent. I am absolutely gobsmacked at the spectacle that is laid out before me; a twenty metre round model of London has been laid in cut and welded steel on the bottom of the Atlantic Ocean almost half way around the world from the city it mimics. Awesome! I drop down to inspect it further, and marvel at the intricate detail that abounds; St. Paul's dome is there in all its glory, as is Tower Bridge and the Natural History museum. Such attention to detail must have taken years to achieve. I float, in abstract awe of the creator of all of this. I will hunt down Ben Lowe upon my return to London and shake him firmly by the hand, of that I am sure. Moments become like hours as we drift from artwork to artwork, sculpture to sculpture, the absolute presence this place holds could humble to silence even Plato or Socrates. I mooch between the sculptures like a spoilt kid, touching, wondering and feeling my way into a state of complete nirvana. Sadly though, my dive computer gives me the yellow light all too soon, of which I must obey. I begin to rise to the surface in a slow and deliberate manner, signalling Richard with a 'thumbs up' as I go. He joins me at the five metre station to chill for a few moments before returning all the way to the surface.

We break into the fresh air of the normal world around us with such a burst of enthusiasm.

'Jeez, did you see the dolphin, it was the most awesome thing I have ever seen, it just went on forever, and the three dimensional London was just incredible,' Richard bursts enthusiastically, his regulator tossed to the side.

A surge of water then rolls over his head, encompassing him entirely, but only to re-appear a moment later, coughing and choking for a few seconds, as he had been caught by the saline swell with his mouth open. We clamber aboard the Rib once again, and begin to remove our kit.

'Richard, my God, that was absolutely amazing! We've just got to get the girls down here to see this.'

'Absolutely mind blowing, Jack, did you see the enormous Hitler and Churchill busts?'

'Yeah, mate, it was awesome. But something's just struck me, as dive buddies we drifted a little far away from each other down there. Bit dangerous that, in case anything happened that is.'

'Mmm, see your point, I guess we'll just pay a little more attention to that next time. We've got a couple of hours to wait before our bodies are stable enough to dive again, so do you fancy buzzing out a bit to see if we can find ourselves an undiscovered wreck?' The smile on my face is all the answer Richard needs, so with a push of the starter, we find ourselves up on the plane and in search of our next adventure.

A couple of hours pass quickly, the sun is perfect, and we are treated to a cooler of sandwiches and fresh mineral water for lunch, compliments of the Shambhala Resort. Then, suddenly the sonar picks up an irregular shape on the bed. We appear to be over a ridge, that plummets to a deeper depth quite quickly. The chop is quite bad here, and the water throws our static Rib around a fair bit. I'm beginning to feel queasy.

'Let's get in the water,' I tell Richard, 'I'll bet some old galleon came a cropper on this a few hundred years ago, must be worth a look.'

'You and me both, drop a line, and let's see what we have down below. From the sonar pattern, we should at least have some interesting landscape to explore.'

'Cool.' I set about switching tanks, then get my clobber on as soon as possible.

Spadoosh! I hit the ocean backwards and drop a few metres to calmer water. Richard follows, then gives the okay and thumbs down signals for our descent to begin. We reach the rocky ridge quickly, and then fin along it, taking in the beauty of the vivid colours around us. More tropical fish flurry through the coral and plant life. I begin to wonder if we are truly clear of shark territory.

Then, after ten minutes exploration, we amazingly

come across the fatally wounded carcass of a World War Two cargo plane. The wings are missing, although evidence of the impact is spread to our left and right, an engine sits attached to a section of wing and the tail is mostly there but the front has been completely destroyed. As we drift closer, I notice it sits below a ledge that overhangs from the ridge. I guess the plane must have actually crashed into the ridge after plunging into the water at high speed, killing all that thought they had survived the first impact, sometimes life is just not fair. The closer we get, the more my anticipation builds. We may well have discovered an unknown crash site. After all, it wasn't in the guide I was perusing on the way out here, so fame and fortune could be ours at last!

I glance to Richard, he seems as excited as I do as we reach the aluminium skin of the stricken aircraft. I run my bare hand across the outer surface, it's rough with the growth of sea life of fifty years submerged, and draw a deep breath as we penetrate the aircraft via the gaping hole in the front.

The interior of the plane is incredibly spooky, it's dark and empty, except for some flight cases buckled down to the floor of the cargo hold. Each case is about four feet long by three feet wide and three feet tall. There must be thirty or so of these cases in here, I grab my flashlight to inspect, but they are all locked tight with large padlocks. I gesture to Richard, but he just shrugs, pointing to the rear section of the plane as he floats away. I fin with him, and although interesting, I find nothing worth a second look. The cases hold my curiosity though, I return to inspect one more closely. After a few minutes scraping the surface from the top of one of them, I am shocked at what I uncover. A metal swastika logo is embossed into the top of the flight case. It sets my brain reeling, what could they possibly contain that would have them in an unmarked plane off the Brazilian coastline? I wave Richard over to inspect, but I think what we really need to do is get one of these up into the boat.

A raised pair of eyebrows and some indecipherable hand signals later, we're trying to break a case free. I find a large steel jemmy bar in the mid section of the plane, and set to work with Richard to loosen the buckles that hold one of them down. After five minutes of wrestling we finally break one free. The weight of it is incredible, and we struggle to move it at all. After a further ten minutes of us pushing and levering it with the large bar, we finally have one near the gaping hole at the front of the plane. I gesture to Richard that we should both hold on to the case, and inflate our B.C.s fully in order to lift both it and us to the surface. This, was pure fantasy on my behalf, as even two fully inflated vests had absolutely no hope whatsoever of shifting it. I glance down, to see my dive computer's flashing light is telling me we need to surface, probably all the heavy breathing whilst manhandling the box has used my gas up far quicker than expected. I *'thumbs up'* to Richard, and we glide serenely back up to the five metre stop, allowing our blood to recover before the final rise to the surface.

*****

Back in the boat we begin to run through what we
have seen.

'Wow, I didn't see that on your wreck map. I know
there's loads of undiscovered stuff out here, do you
think we might have stumbled across something
important?' Richard retrieves the map from his dive
bag for a closer inspection. We check the co-ordinates
on his hand-held G.P.S. and program an index mark,
so as we can plot a course for the exact same spot next
time we're out. The chop has reduced slightly, but we
decide to head away from the ridge in order to find
some more tranquil water. Besides, two dives and
empty tanks means we need to head home anyhow.

Richard stands at the wheel, occasionally referring
to the G.P.S. as we make steady progress back to
Shambhala Island. No matter how carefully I read the
map, checking and double checking the co-ordinates,
there seems to be no evidence of a crash there.

'I think we can lay claim to a discovery, mate,' I
tell Richard triumphantly, with an inane grin washing
over my elated face. 'I'll check the records on-line
when we get back to the resort, but from the look of
this map, it's ours.'

'Cool, best keep it to ourselves until we can have
the discovery confirmed officially, wouldn't want
anyone else taking the glory.'

'Yeah, too right, wow what an unbelievable day

this has been. The sculpture park was awesome, and now with the hope that this is going to put our names into the history books, well what more can I say!'

I sit in quiet contemplation as to what we may have found, a few things bug me though, that don't seem to be adding up.

16. Wrecking the marriage

We return to the jetty from where we had departed what seems like a decade ago. Richard and I had experienced such a magnitude of sights and emotions since we left this morning I wondered what could possibly top it. Then I see Wendy, sipping a cocktail with Victoria in the ocean front bar, and I knew my day was about to get even better. I muse momentarily of how life could have been so much different. I thought I had lived a full and happy life when we were careering towards the cliff edge aboard that coach in Morocco, but now, more than ever I realise that life just keeps getting better and better, if you let it.

We make our way to the bar, and join the girls at their table.

'Hey, Rambo, d'ya wrestle any sharks today?' Wendy asks with a hint of smirkasm.

'No, but shook hands with some of the greatest characters in history, then flew like Peter Pan over London before discovering a new wreck that'll prove to be the greatest find of the century. How did you two get on?'

'Ha, ha. We had an absolutely fab time, didn't we Victoria. We sailed for miles and found the most incredible group of dolphins that insisted on jumping and playing around the boat for ages. It was incredible, Jack, honestly.'

'Two beers please, mate.' Richard interjects as a

passing waiter comes within striking distance. 'And Victoria…' Richard asks with a tilted head.

'Not for me, this is my second already, and we haven't eaten yet.'

'Wendy?' he continues, but she simply places her flat palm over the half full glass in front of her.

'Just two beers then, sir,' the waiter confirms, before retreating back to the bar. We stay for the duration of the drink, then head off as couples to our individual timber castles to prepare for dinner.

There are only three restaurants inside the complex, and a journey outside it seems inadvisable after our aerial tour in the helicopter showed us little in the way of civilisation outside the chain linked security of the Shambhala Resort. We opt for the bar that furnished us with our drinks, overlooking the jetty for our meal, and take our seats around a highly polished circular wooden table, just inside the enormous drawn back glass doors that lead out to the patio area.

With our respective girlfriends all clued up as to the find today, we talk further about what it is we may have discovered.

'What on earth is an unmarked Nazi plane doing off the coast of Brazil, and what about its strange cargo? Unlikely to be weapons, after all why would they be flown to somewhere that was in sympathy with the allies, and more to the point, why would they be in locked cases that weighed a ton? There's more to this than meets the eye, I'm sure of it,' I begin.

'I know, mate, I've been thinking along the same

lines since we got back, so I flicked on my laptop and did a search for *"strange cargo and wrecked planes in South America."* The results were disappointing to say the least, I also checked the on-line aviation records but the plane doesn't seem to have been reported missing, so I tried being a little more specific, and began searching for *"Nazi Brazil,"* and look what I found; a BBC article dated Wednesday, November 26, 1997 that reports the following.'

Richard then dictates from the notes he has made concerning the article that transfixes us all immediately.

A bank vault containing more than $4 million worth of property allegedly stolen from victims of the holocaust has been opened in the Brazilian city of Sao Paulo. The contents – including cash, gold bars and jewellery – are thought to have been brought to Brazil by Nazis who fled Germany at the end of the Second World War. The hoard was deposited in the name of Albert Blume, a German who came to Brazil before the beginning of the war. He is alleged to have acted as a banker for other Nazis who fled to South America later. That is the opinion of the special commission set up by the Brazilian Government to investigate the Nazi presence in the country after 1945. Despite the fact that Brazil sent troops to fight alongside the Allies in Europe, the commission has concluded that the government also allowed eight fleeing Nazis to settle in the country.

Albert Blume died some time ago. But his family

147

denies that he had anything to do with the Nazi party after his arrival in Brazil. They say the money in the vault is not the property of Holocaust victims. The government commission says it will run chemical tests on the hoard to try to establish exactly who the property belongs to. It is also hoping that Mr. Blume's diary, also recovered from the vault, will shed some light on the situation.

Richard then re-folds his notes, and continues, 'I then made extensive searches for any further information, but the story just disappears into ten years' worth of ether. No follow-up report, no investigation, no results from the tests. It's a cover-up, and I think, ladies and gentlemen, we have just uncovered a few million pounds' worth of Nazi gold. It makes perfect sense, there was never a report of the missing aircraft, and it was miles from where one would expect to find a Nazi cargo plane to be flying either during or just after the war. It's also unmarked, so therefore not an official military mission; there are dozens of extremely heavy and securely locked flight cases down there, and there's no evidence of any troops. There must be at least ten times the amount of gold that the picture on the BBC website showed, so I think it is irrefutable evidence that we have on our hands one of the greatest hauls in history.'

We all sit in shocked silence for a few moments, trying to fathom the magnitude of what has just been said.

'Oh my God,' says Victoria, 'all those poor Jewish

people's teeth and family heirlooms, it gives me the creeps.'

'Forty million four ways is ten million a head,' Richard answers, 'don't tell me your conscience is *that* strong, darling. If you feel so passionately about it that you can't take it for yourself, then you can always spend your share searching for the victim's families and returning their teeth, but I think you'd be wasting your time, and recovering a lot of repressed memories that are better left entombed in the backs of people's minds, not brought back to the forefront. These people have lived the horror far too often in their history, do you really think they would thank you for turning up on their doorstep with their great uncle George's gold capped molars and pocket watch that might have been a distant relative's two generations removed? Come on, angel, get realistic. Anyway, whatever we do about this is bound to be better than leaving it on the sea bed to slowly rot away. Let's get a couple of cases up and see exactly what we're dealing with, after all, it could just be Hitler's laundry.'

'I'll agree with that,' I concur, 'Babe?'

'Sure, Jacky babe, Richard's right, there's no point in leaving it down there for somebody else to find, is there?'

'No, I suppose not,' concedes Victoria, but she doesn't look convinced. 'I think we should all go down tomorrow and see what's really there before we get too engrossed on the moral issues here. Let's sleep on it and see what tomorrow brings.'

The three of us all agree with her and decide to talk further tomorrow, when we have a little more accurate an idea of what we are really dealing with here. Dinner passes pleasantly, and the girls head back to the rooms as Richard and I enjoy a nightcap on the jetty, discussing the plan for tomorrow.

'You do know,' I say to Richard, 'we mustn't breathe a word of this to a living soul, you know how people have a habit of disappearing in South America, and I certainly don't want to be one of them.'

'Couldn't agree more, mate, I just can't stop thinking about the prospect of all that gold down there though, just for the taking. It seems too easy.'

'Well,' I chuckle, 'they do say the best things in life are free!'

We high five, down our Rums and head back to our adorable fiancées.

*****

The eight o'clock sunshine welcomes me back to the full colour of reality in paradise. The swirling bulges in Wendy's eyelids tell me she's still with the shiny, happy people in dreamland, so I head to the bathroom for a splash and a shave alone. Richard is predictably knocking on the patio door by half past, and also as predicted he has already been down to sort the gear for our exploration. We take coffee on the patio, and sit a while to discuss tactics.

'I spoke to the guys, and told them we were meeting another two couples who were going to join us on jet skis, so couldn't carry any gear. That way, at two tanks each we were able to secure sixteen tanks without raising any suspicion. I also asked for a parachute and some rope as we would be trying our hand at parasailing, the guy said he knew someone a couple of k's away from whom he could borrow one. I also stole a hammer from his workshop, and slung it into my dive bag whilst he answered the phone, so we should be set.'

'Why are we going parasailing, surely the gold is of more importance?'

Richard throws his eyes to the heavens and mutters something indecipherable.

'I do despair, Jack, the parachute is so we can attach it to the flight case and inflate it with the spare cylinders to bring it to the surface.'

'Ahhh, I knew that,' I lie, extremely unconvincingly. Wendy then appears in a towel that is just on the short side of being decent.

'You boys talking shop then? Is there any more coffee, darling?'

'Yes and yes, it's on the side in the kitchen. Hop through the shower and we'll set off in twenty minutes.'

'Yeah right, Babe, see you in forty-five.' And with that she disappears through the flowing white linen. I marvel at the sight of her two white cheeks poking naughtily out of the bottom of the towel.

Victoria then appears through the shadows of the palm trees bearing arms full of fruit. She floats effortlessly up the steps to the deck and rolls the perfect, soft-skinned food out onto the table.

'Breakfast has arrived, boys!' She smiles, then plonks herself squarely in Richard's lap, planting a long and passionate kiss to his perfectly pampered lips. She turns to me and just radiates a beauty that I hadn't noticed before, a natural perfectness that cannot possibly be contrived or shaped with a surgeon's scalpel or Photoshop blend tool. Yes, Richard has truly struck gold with Victoria, yet seems to show only indifference towards her. I still can't work them out as a couple.

'Right, Jack, you give your better half the hurry up, and we'll be waiting down at the boat,' Richard commands, ousting Victoria from her perch on his lap and onto her feet. They leave without further comment and I head back inside to check progress.

Almost an hour later we leave for the jetty, a fifteen minute walk away, so I know Richard will be warming gently under the collar by now. When we arrive, he and Victoria are talking to a local who is moored next to the Rib, they're discussing the merits of European investment in this little patch of paradise, although Victoria, it must be said, looks somewhat bored and is pleased to see us.

'Right, Richard, any time you're ready, dear,' I mock, he swivels his head with narrowed eyes, giving a sarcastic smile. We board the adventure tour to wealth beyond our wildest dreams, and cast off in hope of a golden future.

After several tedious miles of playing follow the

magic arrow on the G.P.S. we hit the jackpot. I drop a line into the ocean and run through the procedure once more with everyone listening attentively.

'Right, we have sixteen cylinders. That means we have two each to use, and two each to spare, half with regulators. The way I see this working is as follows; we all sink to the bottom as quickly as possible, the girls will probably need to equalise their ears half way down, then all convene at the crash site, where I will have begun to unpack the parachute. This I will lay out as best I can, given the undercurrent. Then Richard and I will both tie the straps around the case as you, Victoria and Wendy, inflate the parachute with the spare cylinders. Once the first is under way, Richard and I will work towards getting a second case free, and move that to the front opening of the plane. As soon as the girls have inflated the parachute enough that it begins to rise to the surface, we all rise with it, remembering to stop at five metres, and then manhandle it into the boat. Any questions?' Nobody queries the plan, so we set to it.

Spadoosh! Once again, and we're finning our way back through our spectacular yet alien environment. The relentlessly active fish dart amongst us with predictable curiosity, but thin as our depth plummets. The four of us split after eight or so metres as the girls slow their descent, but the acclimatised Richard and I continue down into the depths relentlessly. We reach the ridge in what seems to be moments, scanning ahead for our wreck. After only a couple of minutes scouring, I see the remains of the aircraft below us and signal to Richard the way forward. The girls will easily see the bubbles from our exhaled breath rising to give them our location. Once again we penetrate the body and re-affirm our findings. The case we had moved the day before sits expectantly on the edge of the gaping hole in the fuselage, so I immediately set about discarding my spare tanks and unravel the parachute on the bed. Moments later Wendy and Victoria appear, whilst Richard has already set about fastening the straps to the heavy box. The girls begin to inflate the chute from the spare tanks, and it starts to take shape immediately as the final securing knots are tightened around the case. I can feel the buzz of endorphins spin happily around my circulatory path as I watch our dreams come true, slowly in front of my eyes.

The ropes and straps begin to grow in tension as the air displaces the water from the dome of the chute. It only strikes me now, the relief that the parachute is indeed the old traditional round dome style as opposed to a foil rectangular type which would have been completely useless in this operation, obviously a sign from the Gods that we are truly destined to have this illicit gold. The dome now rises from the bed, but is still only feebly inflated, so lacks the strength to lift the cargo yet. This, however, also raises an unforeseen problem. As the dome rises, the girls need to also rise above the bed in order to stay with the parachute. Wendy and Victoria both seem to be having trouble with the *two tanks each* scenario though, so as Richard appears to be sorted with the straps, I signal to him that I'm going to lend a hand with the inflation process. He responds with an 'O' for okay signal and I gracefully float up to the girls. From just a moment's observation it's obvious they are struggling with the dead weight of the extra cylinder. The B.C. gives their body the required buoyancy, but they have to use the fading strength in their arms to hold the second cylinder in front of them as it has no fixings to attach it to their B.C. After a quick moment's thought I signal for Wendy to drop back to the carcass of the plane in order to help Richard guide the case out once the chute has inflated sufficiently, then take the spare cylinder from her and fin my way over to Victoria.

I grab her spare cylinder also, and gesture for her to help me hold both of them together, making the task in hand somewhat easier, shared between us. I roll over onto my back, adopt a sitting position, and then allow both cylinders to rest horizontally in my lap whilst she guides the air from the open regulators into the parachute. This allows my B.C. to do most of the buoyancy work whilst I can monitor progress, I continually twist and turn with the movement of water and instability of the unusual weight distribution, but succeed in remaining still enough to carry out the task.

Slowly the inflation process completes its desired effect, and the box begins to move. At first just a scuttle, then slowly but surely it begins to glide. Wendy and Richard struggle to control it as the underwater currents play havoc with the chute. It then begins to rise quickly but the lines snag on a section of the aircraft, halting progress, jolting the chute to one side. Suddenly I am shocked as the body of a large grey shark barges into me from my blind side, it swirls and darts away, only to return a moment later with three friends. We all panic, Victoria drops the spare regulators and wisely makes for the surface whilst Richard and Wendy seem frozen to the spot.

A sharp tug on the lines then confirms that a shark has become entangled in the body of the parachute, as I stay static, with the regulators pumping more gas into the now overly buoyant chute. The struggle for power then spirals out of control as the shark tips the chute to one side, sending both of them darting diagonally, the lines entangle both Wendy and Richard, moving violently as the reef shark fights for freedom, pulling the lines like a crazed puppeteer and smashing Richard's face into the sharp edges of the mangled plane, killing him instantly. The lines then twist back, around to the rear of the plane's body as the finned beast fights for survival, Wendy also meets her fate with the tangled mass of ropes that then garrotte her with one snap of the shark's tail fin. I fumble for my ring and press the three sapphires as hard as I can, I must stop this monstrous mass execution immediately.

I shudder and shake as if a lightning bolt of ice is plunged through my very heart, then notice all around me has stopped, completely still once again. The shark entangled in the lines of the parachute looks angry and frustrated in its quest for freedom, its fierce open jaws ready to hack any man's limb that comes into range, its savage teeth ready to shred any who dare to encroach on the personal space of this submerged hunter. I float up in fascination of the captured creature, and inspect it in every detail, running my hands across its sandpaper like skin, and probe my fingers through the louvered gills that seem curiously soft to the touch. Its teeth are savage, and I try my arm inside its mouth for size, hoping it will stay in this frozen state whilst I do so.

I'm amazed as I suddenly realise how calm I am about everything; the savage shark, the death of both Richard and Wendy, and the whole scenario in which I now find myself. I bleed some air from my B.C. and sink down to inspect the carnage in the plane below. A plume of cloud-like blood has exploded from Richard's mangled face, the jagged edges of the aluminium skinned aircraft having lacerated it badly and smashed his skull. Wendy is not much better, the nylon cord that links the parachute to the flight case has wrapped itself around her throat, and snapped her neck cleanly with that one jerk of the shark's fin. I hold her hands and begin to well up inside, I can feel the emotion building and building as I fight the tears that begin to fill my slowly fogging mask.

Then, I notice another diver swimming towards me through the crystal clear blue, his regular breath sending plumes of exhaled bubbles to the surface in neat clusters. He is the only other living thing in this world of stillness around me, *'Saint Peter'* I think to myself, as he draws ever closer. His shape is curiously different though, gone is the white hair and older frame of Michael Caine, to be replaced with a muscular blond-haired man in his late thirties.

He arrives in front of me, then gives the *'okay'* signal, followed by a *'thumbs up'* to head for the surface.

Once back in the fresh air, I discard my regulator and bob in the water, amazed at how the entire ocean has frozen into complete stillness as far as the eye can see, with only my movements causing small ripples to punctuate the calm that surrounds me. I look to the Rib, where Saint Peter sits with his back to me, inspecting his kit. He had risen straight to the surface without needing the usual five metre safety stop to recalibrate, so was dry before I have even surfaced. I fin over to the side of the boat and he turns to greet me.

'Bugger me, Mister Bond I presume,' I exclaim. Daniel Craig then smiles as he lends me an arm to pull me up into the Rib.

I look at this fresh faced Bond in curious bewilderment.

'Get bored of the Michael Caine look then did we?' I question.

'As I told you, Jack, on the coach, I appear to you only as your subconscious sees fit. You alone have manifested this image of me, because I am really just a soul, invisible to the human eye. I come to visit now and then, as does Satan and God, but not as you might think. Whenever your conscience gives you a sudden jolt, that's me, just passing through to keep you on the right track. Satan however, manifests in the feeling of desire, of all things you know are wrong, yet you do them anyway. God on the other hand is more of a giver, so when you find yourself slowing your car to let people out of a junction, or offering your neighbour a hand to fix his lawnmower, that's him at work, doing the little stuff that makes you feel good. He does some pretty big stuff too, but I won't go into that now. There are, of course, hundreds more of us, Thor, Zeus, Buddha etcetera, all giving you the emotions you feel every second of every day. Bob Geldof was a great one of mine, but I think I went a bit far, turning a scruffy punk into a saint to feed the starving of Africa, but I was just showing you guys what's possible with a little belief. Mother Theresa was one of God's finest projects of course, but try as we might, we lost a couple along the way.

'That gold down there for example, that's currently costing you your fiancée's life, it was also paid for in blood many times before, and stolen from the most humble and loving people on your planet. Yes, Satan did an admirable job on Adolph Hitler, a mouthpiece for Hell with the gift of persuasion stronger than any I have ever seen. There are many examples of our positive projects, out there walking the earth every day, just helping the world to get along.

'So, tell me Jack, what do you hope to achieve by calling me here, what are we going to do about this mess down below that you lot have entangled yourselves in?'

'I was hoping that's what you'd tell me,' I feebly reply. Daniel shakes his slightly dipped head slowly, then looks me in the eye.

'There's nothing I can do directly, as I told you before, but I'm here to advise you, and help you along a little bit. So have a think, and come up with some questions that might be of use to you, I'm going for a swim, I'll be back in an hour.' And with that, he tips over backwards, spadoosh, and he's gone.

An hour is an extremely long time to be sat in a boat in the middle of nowhere on your own, with your watch arms frozen to eleven thirty-two. I run through every possible scenario I can think of, and finish with just one that feels viable. I need to cut the section of rope that kills Wendy as soon as time is reinstated, that way at least she will be saved. As Richard was pulled into the wreckage so violently, and probably just under thirty seconds before time stopped, I hold little hope for saving him. Richard, sadly, is history. I do also have further concerns though; I know that the amount of blood pumping from Richard's body will act like an alarm bell for all the sharks in a five-mile radius, bringing them here in search of lunch within minutes. We have to make ourselves safe, and haul his body up into the boat as quickly as possible in order for us to have any chance of escape whatsoever, all this done with an extremely pissed-off shark caught in our parachute and his three circulating buddies for an audience. I feel like a gladiator without a weapon. I lie on the floor of the Rib and close my eyes in the sun, drifting off as it warms my numbed brain and body.

I'm startled with the splashing sound of Daniel breaking the placid surface of the ocean. He bobs a moment to remove his mask, then throws a few lifeless fish into the boat.

'Here, I got you some dinner, it's easy when they're stationary,' he chuckles as he hauls himself into the boat. He pulls his B.C. off and thumps the bottle down onto the floor of the boat. 'So have you decided what you're going to do then?'

'Er... yeah, I guess so, but I can't figure a way to save Richard.'

'Well that, old boy, is just unavoidable. At least you can save Wendy again, she certainly owes you now, doesn't she,' he says with a smirk, 'okay, any questions before I disappear back upstairs?'

'Yeah, too right I have. I kept seeing ghosts of all the people I saved on the bus, dead and mutilated at the hospital in Morocco, can you explain that to me, or am I just going mad?'

'No, Jack, this may come as a surprise, but you all have a pre-destined path through this life, everything happens at precisely the right time and for just the right reason, without this there would be universal chaos. There are five hundred and ten million square kilometres on this earth alone, with six point seven billion people living in various countries around it – do you realise what havoc there would be if it were left up to you lot to sort out, hell it takes you fifteen minutes to make your minds up on what you're having for lunch if a menu has more than three options on it, let alone finding the love of your life in a maze of all those people in all those countries. Christ, it gives me a migraine just *considering* the mess you lot would make of it. No, the ghosts you have seen are echoes of the future lost. Let me explain; whenever you, or any past or future ring bearer decides to stop time, a ripple is sent out through the fabric of the universe. This ripple contains all the information for the future that has been changed, and the ghosts are the witnesses of that lost future.

'What you saw at the hospital was the sequence of events that *would* have taken place had the natural and intended course of history not been changed by your use of the ring, so the mangled bodies you saw, were those of the coach passengers that were indeed due to die that day. You effectively changed their destinies, and all that would interact with them from that day on. Shirley Bissett, for example in row three, was due to have her head smashed by a rock as she flew out of the windscreen down the cliff edge, so congratulations, you saved her life. However, in changing her destiny, Shirley's daughter Deborah, who was scheduled to fly out to identify the body, was no longer required to, so she missed the opportunity to meet her future husband who was also due to be on the same flight, in the seat next to her, travelling out to identify his brother who would have also perished in the crash. It leaves us with the unenviable task of trying to twist fate for them both to meet at a later date without too much damage to the timelines of the other people around them. Sometimes it proves impossible, and people die feeling they've not achieved their true potential for no reason other than the person they were destined to meet was diverted from their path by a change of events that could have possibly happened over a hundred years earlier. So be warned, Jack, as I told you before, you have in your hand the potential to change the world as you know it, forever. Treat it with respect, and consider every action you take with it for both its positive and its negative implications.

'You will see today, the ghosts of your future history. A clone of you, Wendy and Victoria will be born, as would one of Richard, if you are able to save him, but looking at it, I doubt it. Although you don't save Victoria's life, the result of your actions will alter her future dramatically, so a clone is born for her as well. The clones of your future history are only ever visible to you, the ring bearer, and they will show you the paths your lives, and the people you interact with, would have taken had you not had the opportunity to change them. Most people have a sensation of shuddering and extreme cold for a moment when they see their clone, this will reduce as time goes on, but can be quite strong to start with, as you know from the hospital.

'An interesting side effect to this, is a phenomenon humans feel regularly, a mild shuddering and cold sensation for no apparent reason, some people believe that another person has walked over their grave. This is almost right, it is, in fact, an echo from a previous destiny change that would have affected the direction of their lives. Right now, you have sent a shudder out to both your entire family, Wendy's family and all of your friends. Provided you save her, they won't be attending her funeral. So you have effectively changed all those destinies with just one command to the universe. It amazes me every time this happens as to the knock-on effect it all has and the mess we have to sort out as a result. I curse the creator of the ring every time it is used.'

I'm dumbfounded.

'Oh, and another thing I should probably mention,' Daniel continues, 'you've used your second ring privilege, so you only have one left before you need to pass it on. Remember though, if you give it to someone else to wear before the third one is used, you lose that last privilege, and the new bearer still only gets their three. Is there anything else I can help you with today, or is that it?'

'When am I going to die?' I ask with some trepidation.

'You are the ring bearer, the only human on this planet who is in charge of his own destiny. It's something I can't possibly answer. You've changed the predestined time of your death twice already, and yes, you were meant to have a chunk taken out of you by one of those sharks in a moment's time, just a hint. You've veered so far off your original timeline though, I've got no idea where you're heading. Most people use the ring to try and fix a failed chat-up line or embarrassing "caught at work shagging the secretary" type of scenario, but you've done the cheating death one quite well so far, so well done, mate.'

'So what now?'

'I think you know the drill, press the stones, and after you've grabbed your dive knife out of its scabbard and defended yourself against the shark that will appear to your right, whoops, wasn't meant to tell you that,' he smiles, 'swim furiously to cut the ropes that lead down to wrap themselves around Wendy's throat. The rest is up to you, but one thing I would point out, is that a fully inflated B.C. will bring a man to the surface rather quickly.'

'Thanks,' I reply, slightly puzzled, 'I owe you one.'

'You have no idea.'

Daniel then kits up with me, and we plunge backwards in unison. He disappears as soon as we enter the water, and I make my way back to where I was when the trauma ceased. Curiously I find an air pocket the same size and shape as my vacated body, exactly where I had depressed the stones. I return to the position that fits it perfectly, and draw a deep breath in preparation of the mayhem I am about to unleash.

One, two, three… I depress the three stones simultaneously, immediately the bubbles rise from my exhalation, and I grab the knife strapped to my leg, swinging instantly around to my right, striking a deep cut to the inbound dorsal finned predator. It scurries away to the bed, followed by the other two sharks who seem to like the taste of the blood that pours from its open gashed side. I immediately kick my fins with furious anger to head towards the ropes of the chute. I slash and cut at the chords violently, cutting all around me, allowing Wendy to rise up to the safety of the surface, and the Rib that rests upon it. I hope she and Victoria both have the presence of mind to take their stop once they're near the top and clear of the carnage, as I don't hold out much hope of finding a decompression chamber on the island. I immediately drain my B.C. of air, and plunge down deep to the bottom as fast as possible. Once I reach Richard, I inflate his vest and see him whoosh to the surface quickly, sending a plume of blood with him as he goes. This, is a Godsend. The last remaining shark is so intent on following the trail of his blood, still entangled in the cables of the parachute, that it completely ignores me, leaving me to rise at a reduced rate in order to preserve my blood levels a little. I pop out onto the surface after an agonisingly slow climb, and swim to the Rib immediately. I clamber in, and sit in awe of the number of dorsal fins that now abound. Victoria is whimpering, curled into the foetal position on the floor of the boat. Wendy sits, just staring vacantly at the horizon. They are both in such deep shock they've gone into shutdown. I spark the boat into life and guide it to where Richard's lifeless body bobs, occasionally jolted with the random bites the sharks are taking from what's left of his corpse. I dread Victoria's reaction once we see the state of him, and feel quite relieved when she merely stands in a complete daze, and sits next to Wendy, embracing each other, shivering with eyes closed. I place a couple of towels around them, and set about hauling Richard into the boat. After a couple of attempts, I manage to drag his torso over the side, and what's left of him lies in the boat, slowly filling it with blood. His face is just a mess of flesh, he has one arm missing from the elbow down, and one of his legs is completely gone. I return to the wheel and we head back to shore in complete silence.

*****

We dock at the jetty some time later, the girls are reacting mechanically to any input, and both remain silent. They step ashore and leave me to secure the boat. A moment later they have walked the length of the jetty and are sat together on the sandy beach. I follow them onto the sand, and tell them to stay put whilst I get some help. I jog for five minutes until I reach the poolside bar, where I see Robert, one of the managers.

'You've got to come and help us, we've been attacked by sharks, and one of us is dead.' I say almost calmly, I cannot believe the detachment I feel, even after witnessing the scene with such clarity. I guess I must also be in shock, but I'm yet to fully realise it.

'Oh Christ, is anyone else hurt?' he turns to the barman, 'Raymond! Raymond! Get some medics to the jetty immediately, we have an emergency.'

The other holidaymakers that drape in the recliners instantly drop their newspapers to observe the goings on, but I'm too confused to care. Then, a sudden rush of horror washes over me. I shudder and shake like never before as my body goes into a state of numbed detachment, my legs begin to weaken and I reach out to a table for support. My ghost-like clone figure then runs right past me, shouting and screaming to anybody that will listen. He's frantically trying to get help to the jetty to save his fiancée who has had a diving accident, he's so charged with adrenalin and denial that he refuses to believe that Wendy has already died in his world. I pity him instantly, and wish I could comfort my former self, and tell him things didn't work out that way, but quickly realise that it would just be futile. The feeling of horror melts slowly into one of relief; I have averted this tragic scenario that is playing out before me with my changing of our destinies, I tell myself it isn't real, yet feel strangely saddened to watch my true, yet former life path unfold so devastatingly before my very eyes.

'Sir, sir, are you alright? Maybe we should get you checked out by the medics as well, you look rather pale. Take a seat and I'll get one over here as soon as possible.' This is all I need to knock my brain back into reality. I recover my senses and sprint back to Wendy and Victoria on the beach. Small crowds have formed around both them and the Rib, with people offering help and advice. I check the girls first, who are both shivering and shuddering uncontrollably, someone has brought a blanket for them, but they are in such shock it has little effect. After a few words of comfort I head over to the Rib.

Again, I'm struck with the most violent of shudders, it almost takes me off my feet. When I manage to get to the boat I realise why. I'm shocked again as I see Richard's lifeless corpse remains face down in the boat, but Wendy's clone lies beside it, with the obvious open neck wound having spewed even more blood into the boat, whilst Victoria's uninjured yet bloodied clone just lies upon Richard's dead body sobbing and whimpering like a mortally wounded puppy. She sits up and looks around as if looking for an answer that doesn't exist, before slowly resting back down in denial of the nightmare her reality has dealt her. It's horrific, I just have to turn away, I'm incapable of thinking straight. I crave the morphine of the medic to just take this all away, and as my legs buckle under me, my consciousness fades. The only thing I register is my face smashing into the harsh wooden deck.

17. Shoes

The following day greets me with some uncertainty. I was released from the medical centre at ten o'clock. Victoria also was released, and has flown with Richard's remains back to the mainland by the helicopter that brought us here. Wendy was then released from the medical centre this afternoon after further tests, but is in no mood to talk to me. She blames my greed for the whole thing, and there's nothing I can do about that at the moment, as she won't even acknowledge my existence. She's gone to be immersed in treatments of varying kinds, so as to take her mind off it I suppose. The day has disappeared seemingly as soon as it had started. It's Wednesday, our wedding day, or should have been, I might clarify.

I sit watching the radiant orange sun slowly descend from the cloudless blanket of blue paradise. The waves breaking regularly on the golden sand are all that lie between our deck and the next island, I check the time on my beaten but trusty Nokia phone, ten past five.

'I could probably make it for a swift sharpener before sundown if I hurry' I whisper under my breath, squinting towards the corrugated iron and bamboo bar at the end of the jetty, around the far side of the otherwise desolate bay. Not wishing to bump into Wendy accidentally, I decide this locals' bar outside

the five star complex might also suit my dour mood a little better. After a moment's mental struggle, I rise from the recliner and pad my way into the bedroom.

Reaching into my large but well travelled brown leather bag, I retrieve a grey shoe box. This, however, is no ordinary shoe box. Clues to the quality of footwear contained therein are clear for even the simplest eye to see. These are the shoes I was to take Wendy to be my bride in, I had ordered them months ago in preparation for the big day. A green ribbon crosses the length and breath of the box, and then fastens centrally with a neat but un-fussy knot. Beneath this lies a gold leaf embossed coat of arms bearing the title of 'The St. James Footwear Company, by appointment to Her Majesty the Queen.'

I rub the tails of the ribbon between my coarse thumb and forefinger, drinking in the sheer quality, before a deft tug pulls the ribbon effortlessly undone. A mild whooshing sound ensues as I draw the lid upwards, causing a momentary vortex as the clean fresh air gasps in.

My eyes are greeted by a perfectly folded Chamois leather wrapping, fastened by the traditional red wax seal, also bearing the St. James coat of arms. After taking a moment to carefully break the wax along the edge of the perfectly stitched seams, I slowly fold back the soft leather to reveal the box's contents.

A bespoke pair of 'Tuscan brown' leather-soled loafers sit proudly in their cosy surroundings, I pluck one from the box and slide it onto a Ralph Lauren socked foot; it fits perfectly. The other loafer follows, then I stand to admire this little indulgence in the mirror. A cream coloured Hugo Boss short-sleeve shirt is then donned, worn outside dark brown Levi 501s that are held by a tired but perfectly serviceable Armani leather belt. The Rolex watch is next. Not a fussy affair, in fact quite the opposite. During the war, Rolex were commissioned to supply some of the, retrospectively inactive, Swiss servicemen with watches; my grandfather being one of them. The sun bleached timepiece wears its barely decipherable silver index marks on its watery grey face, with the once bold black hands now as faded as the memories of the Norman invasions. A pair of Ray Ban sunglasses sporting gold half-frames and iridium green lenses completes my dated but tasteful appearance. After a quick splash of Calvin, I leave the pavilion and set off along the isolated beach.

Wading through the deep sand, my first goal is the firmer, compressed and still cooler footing left by the weight of water at high tide several hours earlier. Upon reaching it, I shake off the excess golden powder from my shoes and press on towards the amber nectar at the other end of the isolated beach.

After what must have been ten minutes of walking, I look toward the bar. Strangely it seems further away, a trick of the eye due to this new point of perspective further around the irregularly shaped bay maybe? I continue unperturbed, until I come across a rather strange fish that must have washed up onto the sand earlier this afternoon.

I crouch to inspect it, the rouge faced sun glints off the dried scales giving their formerly silver colour a pinkish orange hue, almost like a red snapper's scaly skin, but this specimen is also streaked with sporadic wispy stripes of yellow and green, culminating in a rather large turquoise coloured fin towards its rear. The fish is quite a size, almost half a metre in length, with a ferocious looking mouth that sits wide open, as if it were frozen whilst taking a desperate last breath. The jagged teeth have taken on a translucent grey quality within its dark menacing mouth, and the eyes are now drawn back into the head with the onset of complete dehydration. It smells of death, so after a quick inspection I pull myself back to full height and think again of quenching my own oncoming dehydration. I continue along the beach, noting for the first time the speed of the incoming tide.

Off into the distance, probably half a mile away, I see a tall outcrop of rocks, tapering down as they advance towards the water. I estimate I will be safely around them by the time the sea seals off my path, but think a quickening of step should be adopted in order to ensure this, so my leisurely amble becomes a little more of a walk.

After only a couple of minutes at this invigorated pace, it becomes increasingly obvious to me that a little more speed is in order to safely clear the outcrop before the tide reaches it, so I lift the tempo to a swift march. The sun is lowering ever deeper towards the horizon, but the heat of the day still radiates from the trodden grains beneath. The renewed pace has my pores opening in sympathy with my rising temperature and my formerly fresh and crisp shirt now clings to my back with the dampness of sweat, as my arms slide to and fro in their now lubricated sockets. I wipe my brow, and raise my pace further, to a trot, as the tide seems to react with a renewed urge to close the decreasing gap sooner.

I curse as I see the first gentle surge of saline lick the lowest tip of the rocky outcrop. I continue at this now fraught pace, aiming to hop across the incoming tide with a simple bound once the obstruction is reached. As distance diminishes, so does my hope of reaching it dry footed. One particularly large swell engulfs my new loafers, as I dance precariously on tiptoe to avoid the inevitable dousing they now receive.

I'm beginning to anger, and wish I'd joined Wendy at the spa for a massage instead of my current choice of destination. The light tan I had so carefully chosen at The St. James Footwear Company now more closely resembles the tone of ox blood, albeit with a slightly less ruddy hue than my now flushing face.

I press on, resigned to the fact that my only wedding day indulgence is now as sodden and soiled as my relationship with Wendy; *'she'll calm down in a day or two,'* I think to myself, as I eye the shack that serves as a tropical bar with renewed determination, and reach the rocks swiftly. The now sporadically submerged stones prove a little trickier than I anticipated though, as a misplaced damp loafer loses purchase, and slides, staccato, from its holding and topples me onto the harsh rocks.

Once fallen, I register the blood from my now gouged palm, and inspect it for a moment before realizing there is also blood entering my left eye, from a forehead wound I had not even noticed. My sunglasses have also disappeared, carried away on the tide no doubt. In the absence of a mirror, I use the polished dial of my cherished watch to cast a reflection onto my face. A small cut of probably only an inch streaks diagonally from my eyebrow, *'nothing to fuss over,'* I think to myself, then rise, albeit a little light headed, to complete my journey.

The lowering sun now irritates my blinking eyes, its deep orange colour serves as a hindrance to my previously swift progress and I now find myself meandering left and right along the gently curved bay, unable to decipher shadows from form as the ingress of water pushes me further inland, towards the palm tree lined outskirts of the tropical forest.

'Hey, White boy, what you doin' round my part of the Island?' comes the distinctive voice of a local from behind me. I turn on my heel to be greeted by a large cutlass shaped blade inches from my nose. It is held by the outstretched arm of a slim, but no less menacing man in shabby clothing. His smile, whilst not in the slightest way comforting, depicts a story of exuberance and poverty as close akin to the inner cities on the mainland, no more than fifty miles away; the rotten stump of decaying enamel that once was a perfectly serviceable incisor on one side of his jaw, is now sat next to a bright gold replacement on the other. No sooner have I foolishly wondered where he will find the required funds to complete his set of C3-PO style stumps, do I feel the sharp intrusion of his blade at my gulping throat. Several more men then appear from the shadows to surround me. My tumbling stomach sinks past my testicles as the shock and horror of my fate now hits home with a sharp strike. I feel my face drain of colour, my brain shudders a last gasp of consciousness before closing down completely. My knees hit the sand as my torso follows, falling forwards, exchanging the vivid colours of life for the monochrome nightmares of fear and vulnerability.

*****

I wake some time later, it's dark now, and I have no idea how long I was unconscious. Whilst slowly coming to my senses, I methodically move one limb at a time, ensuring they are all still intact and functioning. A few bruises, but nothing broken, thank God.

I reach to my back pocket, empty. 'Bollocks!' I cuss, the thieves have taken my wallet. I then check my other pockets, also bereft of any funds. My watch I find also vacant, as are my shoes.

'My shoes!' I cry, 'The bastards have stolen my

shoes!' I pound the sand with clenched fists at the frustration and anger that now floods from my weakened body. Eventually I tire, and draw to a rest, staring out towards the dark horizon. It's only then, that the twinkling of light from the peninsula bar reclaims my attention. *'My drink,'* I mutter, as I rise to my feet and resume the quest for my nightcap.

I arrive at the strange yet welcoming structure some time later. I would estimate half an hour or so, but as I have no inkling as to either what time I had regained consciousness, or the current time due to my lack of timepiece, I will have to forgo this little detail. I rub the sand from my tired and sore toes, their new pink appearance a direct result of the friction the coarse grains have forced onto my usually pampered feet. I wince as the gash in my hand catches a toenail, breaking the fragile scab and refreshing the flow of blood to my palm.

I enter the sparsely populated bar, it contains mostly locals, a few groups of Hispanics and a ruddy faced but unshaven American, or so I presume, sitting at a table in the far corner. He appears to be in his late fifties, but the light is dim and my brain addled. The corrugated iron walls cover two sides to full height, the remaining two, only to waist height. These shorter walls are topped by a tightly woven bamboo counter top that bridges the customers on the plywood patio with the barman inside. The pitched roof is a similar affair of woven bamboo, and is in quite a state of disrepair. In fact the whole place looks as if the slightest hint of wind would have it razed to the floor, let alone a tropical storm that these islands are notorious for. I make my way uncomfortably to the bar and instinctively point to a bottle of Brahma, a local beer that is now with the marvels of modern society, available in most branches of Tescos.

I loft the chilled bottle to my parched mouth and luxuriate at the tingling sensation of the bubbles cascading down my throat, noting the oval shape of the vessel resting perfectly in my hand. Pure ecstasy.

I slam the empty bottle onto the countertop, and gesture for another, belching quietly as I do so. The large dark-skinned man behind the bar reaches back into the refrigerator, that I notice from the faded 'Walls' logos used to be an ice cream chiller, and retrieves a second bottle. He takes the opener that hangs from his key chain, tethered to his makeshift belt and pops the cap. Handing it to me, he gruffs, 'Six Reais.' I nod in acknowledgment, and take the beer.

'Six Reais,' he insists, this time a little louder. It then strikes me that I have no means of paying him.

'I've no money, mate, I've just been mugged,' I pathetically offer. The barman then frowns at me and repeats again; 'Six Reais, now!' He appears to be getting a little upset. He bangs his fist on the bar and then shouts something in Portuguese, throwing the bottle cap at me. Surprised, I take a step backwards, barging straight into another local who has come up behind me, and I'm absolutely panic-stricken for the second time today.

The white man in the corner shouts something to the barman, the local behind me backs off immediately and the atmosphere seems to settle into a tranquil normality. I make my way over to the darkened corner in order to thank the American.

'Whatever you said, I really appreciate it. I thought I was in for even more trouble there for a minute.'

'No problem,' the man returns in a strong Edinburgh accent, 'I told them your younger sister is picking you up in twenty minutes and gives the best blowjobs this side of Hollywood Boulevard for less than a fiver.'

My look must be of pure terror, I feel the dryness of my mouth, made apparent by the parched stiffness of my tongue telling me that my mouth had fallen open.

'Doon't worry, I'm only joshin' with ya. I told them you were with me and to stick it on ma tab. It's not often I get to see a face from home around these parts. Most holidaymakers stick to the resort, and by the looks of you, wisely so.'

'Yes,' I reply, 'you wouldn't believe the diabolical luck I've had since I stepped foot onto this godforsaken country.' I sense a twitch from the locals, and the eyes of my new found friend widen a little, 'but the hospitality of the people here have truly lifted my spirits no end,' I lie, sensing that instant reprisal is just a little too close for comfort. 'My fiancée Wendy and I booked this holiday to enjoy our wedding in paradise, but since we've arrived it's just been one disaster after another. We met a lovely couple in the hotel on the mainland, Richard and Victoria, who had booked the same package. They were due to marry the same day as us, so we became instant friends. Once we got talking it was truly amazing the number of similarities and co-incidences that have threaded all of our lives together over the last few years. Anyway, to cut two weddings and a funeral to a beer, there was a diving accident, and although I managed to save Wendy, I couldn't save Richard. This led to the cancellation of both our weddings, and a falling out between not only Wendy and I, but Victoria will have nothing to do with me either. In a state of depression, and after yet another row, Wendy disappeared off for a massage so I decided to foolishly set my sights on this place.'

The locals become animated again, I hadn't realised so many of them were eavesdropping our conversation. The combination of strong sun, a blow to the head, no water for a couple of hours and a swiftly downed beer has sent my senses just south of numb.

'Halfway here I encountered some bandits, who not only robbed me of my money and my wallet, but also the watch I had been given by my now deceased grandfather, the only thing he ever gave me I hasten to add. That I can accept, but they even stole my Church shoes, my Church shoes for Christ's sake! It takes months for them to craft them from the moulds they take of your feet, each one is hand-made to fit your body exactly, as God intended. The sheer precision and perfection that goes into a pair of shoes like that is unimaginable to the thieving scum that forced them from my feet. They won't even bloody fit the bastard, they're mine, mine I tell you and they've been stolen from the very feet that they were made to be worn on!' I realise I'm beginning to sound foolish, so quieten down for a moment.

'I'm sorry to hear that, young lad, but surely a man of your calibre is able to replace them ten fold?'

'Yeah right, they were nearly a thousand quid. You don't just find that dangling off every apple tree now do you, and if you did, it's the justification of it. No, those shoes were made for me to be wed in and now it's all gone to shit because of some thieving bandits that have nothing better to do than rob the people that support their economy by way of their tourist trade.'

'I thought you said the wedding was cancelled due to a bereavement.'

'Yes, but it's the principle of it, isn't it. They were my wedding shoes and that's the end of it. Anyway,' I sense a change of subject would be advisable, 'what's your game? Why are you here in this dive of a bar, what's the story behind the only other white face amongst us?'

'Well mine is a rather simple tale,' the Scotsman replies, 'about five years ago I was ferrying folks like yourself and Wendy here from the mainland in my little Cessna fixed wing, we'd fly around the coves and bays a while, as the lovers embraced and kissed on the rear seats. I thought of myself in those days as a high altitude tropical limo driver with wings. I had a girlfriend here too, but one day that all changed. The weather was fine, it always is mind, and there was hardly any cloud cover. Suddenly, completely out of the blue, came a bolt of lightning that struck the engine and fried the electrics in an instant. I struggled to control the wayward aircraft and fought it all the way to the ground, but my cause was hopeless from the instant we were struck. I survived but the honeymooners were dead upon impact. They had removed their seat belts apparently. Clunk click every trip, as they say.'

'Jeez, I'm sorry,' is all I can muster. 'Yeah, but my bloody shoes were a grand!' I add, almost by way of an apology. 'I loved those shoes, short though it was.'

'I think my ride has arrived,' he says. I turn to see the most perfect Brazilian angel walk into the bar wearing little more than a sarong and bikini. 'Let me settle our tab at the bar before I go,' spouts the Scotsman, 'Eddie's the name,' he says with an outstretched arm to shake, as I am yet to introduce myself to my host. He rocks to and fro in his chair, as he breaks free of the table. It's only then that I see he is in a wheelchair, his legs gone from the thigh down.

'Lost my legs in the crash,' he says, 'hope you find your shoes.'

18. Clones

Thursday dawns, I wake late, wrenching myself from the most horrific nightmare whilst bathed in a pool of my own sweat. Wendy has already gone out by the time I make my way into the kitchen to rustle up some food. As I walk back into the lounge the shudder returns, I lose grip of my plate and it smashes with my toast on the hardwood floor. The shudders reduce quickly, and are, as St. Peter predicted, lessening with their every occurrence. My clone is sleeping on the sofa, several beer bottles lie sprawled around him, mostly drained of alcohol. A Vodka bottle lies cradled in his arms, and the crusty stain of dried vomit surrounds his makeshift bed. The emotions of horror and pity burst into my body as my stomach drops at the harrowing scene in front of me. I feel ultimately helpless, like I am in some way indebted to help this fractured model of myself.

I go to clear up the bottles, but I'm shocked as my hand passes straight through the first one I reach for, another deep shudder shoots up my arm as the mirage remains unaltered. I sit on the sofa next to him and just observe for a moment. I wonder what I can possibly do to affect his world for the better, he seems untouchable, sad and so very alone. The strength of feelings build again inside me as the turbulence of emotion rises once more to the surface, I struggle to hold back the flood of tears, but surrender to the power that bursts from within me, struggling to escape. I dip my head to my lap and lose all control of my wayward emotions as I surrender to the onslaught of tears that cascade from my eyes. I am emotionally spent.

After probably an hour of helplessness, I manage to summon the energy to return to the kitchen in order to try again with the toast, only to realise that the last two pieces of bread were chucked into the bin with the broken plate only a moment ago, damn.

A shower helps, but I'm still in a daze, so decide to walk to the poolside bar to see if they have begun serving lunch yet. The barman takes my order of coffee and a toasted cheese sandwich, then I find a recliner in the shade that a large palm tree offers. As soon as my punch-drunk muscles feel the warmth of the soft green cushions, I slip into another dimension. I begin to dream once again, at first soothing thoughts of floating up, just above my own body, but these visions soon return to the horror of violent sharks, ripping Wendy to pieces whilst I look on in a numbed security, unable to affect the outcome, in an overpowering sense of reoccurring helplessness.

'Sir, your sandwich.'

I wake with a start, almost knocking the tray from the waiter's hand as he attempts to place it onto the low level table next to me.

'Thanks, pavilion seven.' I offer him the credit style card for him to swipe through his machine, then sign the electronically produced paper chit. I eat the food quickly and in silence, I hadn't realised the extent of my hunger until now, and feel somewhat relieved at its reduction.

Wendy appears a short while later, and sinks into the recliner next to me.

'Babe, I know all the horrific stuff that has happened isn't *all* your fault, but I just feel that if we hadn't been so greedy to claim all the gold ourselves we might have been able to get some help with it, and maybe not lost Richard. Victoria is absolutely devastated, I don't know what she'll do back on the mainland with no one for support, do you think we should head back early to help her out?'

'Yeah, I suppose she'd really appreciate a friendly face, best get packed. I'll inform the staff so that they can get the helicopter prepared and I'll see you back at the pavilion in a few minutes.' Wendy rises without even giving me a peck on the cheek, our relationship has screeched violently into plutonic mode, there's not even the slightest hint of intimacy, and I struggle to see a reversal in the near future.

Once back at the pavilion I again fall victim to the shuddering presence of my clone, this time sat on the sofa with Victoria's clone to comfort him as they weep together. I move to the bedroom and help in numb consciousness with the task in hand. The helicopter ride is spent in silence, and I reflect on the hope and optimism that we had last time we were aboard, less than a week ago.

Recife seems harsh and unwelcoming as we mix

with the lost souls to find a cab that will take us to the downtown police station where Victoria is being interviewed. I feel that life is empty, sour, and little within it can comfort me. Once at the station, we both give a brief statement as to the underwater events that led to Richard's demise, but thankfully the police have little interest in a rich tourist who died whilst on a luxury holiday. We had all agreed beforehand to be vague about the location it happened, and omit any details of the plane or its cargo. A week's interrogation whilst being a guest in a Brazilian cell is the last thing any of us need. We arrange the transportation of Richard's body and head to the airport as swiftly as possible. With a little luck and a well timed phone call we find ourselves sat on a plane home within ten hours of leaving Shambhala.

19. Reflections

'So we're all sorted then?' I ask Brendan over a pint in The Crown's beer garden.

'Seems to be, we have the contestants, a lovely girl called Jo and her boyfriend Sean. He works in a graphic design studio in Chelsea, so we can arrange for a new sandwich delivery girl to call into the office. She's called Teresa, an ex-model who, despite going to drama school, decided that displaying her rather generous norks in the tabloids was the quickest way to make some serious cash. She's had enough of the whole modelling game now though and is quite keen to get her face on the television. She came sniffing around the office whilst you were away getting un-married on a haunted desert island, or whatever you were doing last week.' Brendan sniggers at my misfortune, so I punch him squarely on the arm.

'This girl, Teresa – what are her stats, is she a looker?'

'She's absolutely perfect for tempting Sean I tell ya. 34D up top, five foot eight in a good set of heels, long bleach blonde perm and a waist thinner than your wallet. We've set the first encounter for tomorrow at eleven o'clock. The techies have been into Sean's design studio over the weekend and have it fully wired up. We've also got clearance from the council to set up a faux gas pipe repair outside Sean's office for the week, so we can leave a van there with all the mobile studio gear inside, close enough for a real good signal from the transmitter we've hidden on top of the air conditioning unit on the outside wall of the building. We really are all set to go, we just need your smooth commentary over the top and we can clear the mantelpiece in preparation for all those awards.'

'Has Hess been given the heads up on all of this, and what did you decide on scheduling with Sammy?' I enquire, then draw a long slug of chilled Budweiser into my mouth, holding it for a second to savour the bursting bubbles before washing it gently down my throat.

'Charles told Sammy to go all out and get us on the air immediately. He wants the mess of *Bully* eradicated from people's minds, and replaced with something a little more successful.'

'Successful!' I scoff, 'You can't get much more successful than a reaction provoking reality game show provoking a rather extreme reaction. I think the point here is; we're too bloody good at our jobs, people want a reaction and that's exactly what they get. In spades.'

'Yes, Jack, but complaints is what we actually have in spades, and talking of digging, let me remind you it'll be both of our graves you'll be digging with those spades of yours if it all goes tits up. Having the contestant pummelled till he bleeds all over the set isn't exactly Saturday tea time viewing, now is it?'

I snigger into my pint at the thought of Melvin, Malcolm or whatever his name was, flapping on the sofa like a chicken with a wolf in the coup.

'So, Brendan, what's been decided then?'

'We do the interview with Jo tomorrow afternoon in the studio, whilst Teresa makes initial contact with Sean, as I said, at his office. She's had a briefing from the usual sandwich girl, an atrocious minger with breath to clear a dungeon I might add, whilst Cathy from wardrobe has found her some rather revealing, tight busty tops, probably from Angelina Jolie's cast-offs drawer.'

'Sounds like it's all set to go then.' I drain the last of my pint, then see through the glass bottom a familiar figure approaching. Brendan stands to greet the chap. I, however, have a few questions…

'Jack, have you met the new effects guy, Hazy. He's just joined our merry band of rebels and is in with us on *Dangling the Apple.*'

'Yes, we met him here a couple of weeks ago.' I turn towards Hazy as he arrives at our table.

'Yeah, you're Jack Todd aren't you, the host of this wind-up show. My uncle, Jack Klein, who's head of special effects in Shepperton got me this gig after I lost my job working for Vertex, the motorcycle race team, last week. He knows I'm good with my hands, and love a practical joke, so he thought I'd be perfect for it.' I eye our new crew member suspiciously.

'Forgive me for asking, Hazy, but was it *you* who I saw on the bridge to Desborough Island in the early hours of the morning, the day we first met?'

Hazy laughs loudly, 'That was you was it, you

scared the absolute crap out of me. We had this whole prank going on and it had all started to go wrong. The next thing I know, we're bundling carpeted corpses into the Thames, it was so scary I can't even begin to tell you.'

'What!' exclaims Brendan, and I must admit, he'd certainly captured all of my attention as well. Then there's a surreal moment, as a mumbled rendition of Eric Idle's *'Always look on the bright side of life'* destroys the silence. The volume of which escalates rapidly as Hazy retrieves a rather mangled specimen of a phone from his pocket. He checks the display for the caller's I.D. and with a raise of an eyebrow he's off like a shot.

'What in Mary mother of God's name are you talking about now, Jack? Ghosts in Morocco, death and more ghosts in aeroplane wrecks at your failed wedding, to such a degree that Wendy will hardly even speak to you now, let alone marry you. To top it all, we've even got dead sodding bodies in the river now! I'm really starting to worry about you, Jack, seriously. Have you seen a doctor about this yet?'

'Brendan, Christ, we've known each other for years. Have I ever given you even the slightest reason to doubt me?' Brendan does a double take, but I continue before he can answer, 'I'm telling the truth damn it, death is all around me, and I'm the only one who can stop it. When are you going to believe in me? I really, really need you to.'

'No, what you really, really need to do, is pull

yourself together and give the nation a show to truly stimulate the mind, to draw on the bare emotions of humanity and deliver them in a neat controlled package to the brain-dead viewing public, two weeks Saturday, at six o'clock sharp.'

'Jeez, we'd better get a move on with all this then hadn't we?'

'Don't worry, Jack, it's all on hand, all you need to do is run through Jo's interview with me so we can plan the questions, then guide Teresa to act in a certain way at a certain time and we should be away. Oh, and turn up sober next Saturday.' I view Brendan with a frown, I have never appeared on live television drunk, tipsy maybe, but never drunk. I just hope it stays that way. Brendan drowns the dregs of his pint and we head towards the car park.

'I'm just nipping in for a slash, Brendan, I'll see you at the studios tomorrow.' The tubby Irishman waves without turning around, as he waddles his way in the bright sunshine back to his car.

I blink repeatedly in the dim light the interior offers, the usually off-white walls appear a speckled greeny yellow as my colour balance slowly returns to somewhere near normal. Looking to my left for the familiar Ladies and Gents signs, an overwhelmingly strong shudder fills my body again, unbalancing me suddenly and sending my hands groping to find the sticky edge of a wooden table for support. After a moment's pause, I continue. The creak of the toilet door turns the head of the lone customer sat at the bar as I step inside for a pee. I cringe at the strong acidic aroma of freshly splashed vomit, and at the sink crouches the only other occupant of the small stark room. As my eyes are still yet to return to normal, I notice nothing strange until he rises, then I stop, dumfounded as I am confronted by my own slightly translucent form, stood next to my real reflection staring back at me in the mirror.

'*My clone,*' I mutter, shaking my head in disbelief. He remains completely oblivious to my presence, and carries on at the sink, staring into the mirror and splashing water onto his face. I notice the Rolex watch sat on the sink next to him, stolen from my arm by the bandits on Shambhala, and bend down to inspect it. It's mine alright, but I fear I will never see the real one again. My eyes revert to the clone, he looks awful; the pale complexion heightened by the slight opaqueness of his shape, although the deep black circles under his red puffy eyes show the magnitude of pain he must be feeling. His hair, unkempt and greasy, remains at odds with both gravity and style as he douses it with water from his cupped hands. I'm shocked and sad, yet somewhat relieved at my apparent choice of destiny. I approach him with curious interest, getting a slight whiff of body odour as I near. He's in a bad way, the obvious signs of absolute breakdown are there, broken and dirty finger nails struggle with the buttons of his grubby shirt as he tries to remove it in order to wash some of the splashes of puke away. I feel like I should help, but remain frustratingly absent in his world of pain.

'Can I help you with that?' I enquire, as I reach forward to assist. My question ignored as my hands glide through his, as if passing into the illusion of a hologram. The shudder returns, this time stronger, sending me sideways and barging into the next sink along. I slip on the wet floor tiles and fall to my knees, bashing them harshly on the unforgiving floor. Bang! The door opens swiftly, causing a momentary vortex as the dust swirls around the edges of the curved bottom walls where they seamlessly meet the floor.

'Are you okay there, Jack?' booms Dave the landlord, as he enters the room, unzipping his fly as he walks.

'Yeah, just slipped on the wet floor,' I lie, 'I'll be out in a sec.' I rise slowly as Dave whistles an indecipherable tune whilst splashing away in the urinal. I manage to stand, and make my way over to the next porcelain piss hole on the wall.

'I hear you've got a new show coming out next week.'

'Yeah, how do you know about that?'

'Hazy, he was in the bar earlier and said he's got a slot on the special effects and set building side of it, says he'll be there to make you look good.'

'I don't need any help in that department.' I boast, 'Brendan on the other hand...' Dave smirks, shakes and zips, then wanders over to the sink, straight through the clone, who continues to rinse his soiled shirt, and washes his hands with no detrimental effect whatsoever.

'What?' enquires Dave, as I realise I'm staring.

'Er… nothing, just daydreaming.' I shake my head to try and gain a little clarity, but the image of Dave washing his hands in the same space as my clone dousing his shirt is just a little too bizarre for me to fully take in. I follow Dave with a shake, a zip and a wash, but chose the next sink along to avoid any more uncontrolled shuddering sensations. I look over to the clone, and as his scrubbing becomes increasingly invigorated, tears begin to roll down his saddened cheeks. His frustration and pain are getting the better of him and his whole body begins to shake with increasing magnitude. After a few short moments, he releases a hollow moan and slams his shirt into the sink before pounding his fist into the mirror, cracking the glass that streaks a few fine lines of descending blood from his gashed hand. He staggers backwards into the wall, collapsing to the floor, and then slumps forward whilst sobbing uncontrollably. I stare in shock, momentarily rooted to the spot. It's not until the door creaks open again with another punter that my trance breaks, and I rush outside for some much needed air.

20. First bite of the apple

I sit glued to the screen in the director's suite. Teresa has entered Sean's design studio and is making quite a show of her wares, in more ways than one. Several of the other designers can be seen turning their heads in disbelief that the usual rhinoceros of a sandwich girl has been transformed into the most desirable female on the face of the earth. Sean however remains engrossed, clicking away no doubt at the next advert to shape the products we find instantly irresistible by the flick of a Photoshop brush, or swish of a rasterized vector mask. All gobbledygook tosh to all but the graphically well groomed I suppose.

Teresa manages to more than double the sales of her predecessor (what a surprise) and then makes a beeline for the preoccupied target.

'Anything you fancy nibbling on, young man?' enquires Teresa as she bends forward over Sean's desk.

'Nah, yer alright,' comes the disinterested response as his eyes never leave the screen.

'Bollocks!' I cuss, as we seem to have fallen at the first hurdle. Brendan then enters the dimly lit room to join me.

'How are we doing, Jack, got anything juicy yet?' I gesture towards the screen at out target's complete lack of interest with a shrug.

'Fuck,' is all Brendan can offer, until something

strange happens. All the other employees begin to tease Sean about his inobservance, the perfect babe that has just walked out of his life because he was too busy chasing deadlines. He rushes to the window in order to catch a glimpse of what he had missed, and tuts as he sees her hourglass figure walking into the distance.

'I think all may not yet be lost, Jack.'

'Hmm, I think you're right, but I'll have to try and predict his reactions for tomorrow, as I'm due to interview Jo in a couple of hour's time. Let's get Teresa in here and see what we can set him up for.'

'Good plan, Jack, I'll get the boys to bring her up as soon as she's back.'

* * * * *

Two weeks Saturday, has arrived, we have the first three shows lined up, with interviews done, filming filmed and all that's left to do is the live performances. I'm feeling quietly confident with the reactions we've had so far from both the contestants and the targets, it's all going smoothly. The familiar voice of Brendan invades the now quiet studio with his usual;

'And on in five, four, three…' then silence as he mimes the last two digits.

'Good evening, ladies and gentlemen,' I burst onto centre stage as usual, albeit this time with a fresh set and fresh set of challenges. 'Let me introduce the beautiful Sally, who will be my assistant for this, the brand new series of *Dangling the Apple*,' Sally takes her bow, 'and welcome you all to the latest, cutting-edge style of show, that's beamed to you lucky viewers live every Saturday evening, at six o'clock sharp.' A roar of applause raises the roof as the dweeb wanders to and fro in front of the studio audience with his 'CLAP NOW' placard planted firmly on his shoulder. Brendan is smiling for once, and I hush the audience in preparation for our first guest.

'Well, ladies and gentlemen, it is truly a pleasure to be back on your screens after our short break. You will be glad to know, that we used the time wisely to formulate the ultimate game show, that will within moments have you drawn to the very edge of your seats in nervous anticipation of the next move, the next answer, and ultimately, the next big winner. This, however, is a game show with a difference. There is only one contestant, only one winner, and ultimately only one loser. Sally, please could you bring on Jo, our first contestant for *Dangling the Apple*.'

The applause explode again, and a rather confident but heavy set woman enters the spotlight, her face an unfortunate blend of masculine features masked by long lifeless brown hair. I instantly think I'd better refer her to one of the makeover shows once I've finished with her.

'So, Jo, welcome to *Dangling the Apple*, you are the first ever contestant on this brand new style of show, how do you feel about that?'

'Quite good I suppose,' she replies in a monotone drawl.

'And tell us a little about yourself, Jo.'

'I was born in Cornwall, but moved to Essex when I was six. I'm unemployed, but do a bit of office cleaning for cash, you know, in the evenings.'

'Right,' I interject before she incriminates herself any further, or begins to go off on a tangent about her brother Desmond's oddly shaped carrot collection. 'Cutting straight to the game then, let me explain the rules to you once again for the benefit of the viewing public. You responded to an advertisement we placed in the newspapers for a wife or girlfriend who believed they knew their partner inside out. We then interviewed you two weeks ago in our studios to get some background information as to how you thought your relationship was going. We then, unbeknownst to you, had our camera crews follow Sean, your boyfriend, around for two weeks. This we also recorded and will play back to you in a moment, accompanied by a series of questions relating to his behaviour. At specific moments throughout the short film we've compiled of him, we will freeze the picture and ask for your opinion as to what decision or action he will make. Each question will be accompanied by four answers that will appear on the frozen screen, one correct, three incorrect. For each correct answer you will receive points, the more adventurous the question, the higher the points and, as we all know, ladies and gentlemen;' I turn to the audience with raised hands and we all shout in unison; 'Points make prizes!'

'Are we all clear on that before we continue, Jo?'

'Yes, Jack, ooh I'm really excited.' *'Hmm, thrilled*

when you see what your fella's been up to, I'm sure,' I muse to myself. 'Sally, could you lower the screen please.'

Sally then reaches for a branch of one of the theatrical trees that line the new set, and pulls it down like a lever. Another wave of applause erupts as the lights in the studio dim and a large green three dimensional model of an apple, three metres across, is then lowered from the ceiling. A flash and a bang from the overhead pyrotechnics sends fluttering thousands of small silver leaves, floating to the floor as the spotlight tracks the apple's downward progress. Once at eye level, the apple rotates slowly around to reveal a screen that is punched squarely within it, upon which Jo is going to have quite a surprise I think. The lights begin to brighten again, and Jo looks solemn and unmoved by Hazy's exuberant display.

'Okay, ladies and gentlemen, could I ask for quiet please, as we are about to play… *Dangling the Apple!'* A roar of cheers goes up again as the band play their intro, then quiet falls suddenly with the wave of another off screen placard.

'Right, Jo, you may recognise this scene as being shot in Sean's design studio; we placed cameras there last week, and recorded this snippet of film for you. Sally, will you roll the first clip for us please.' The logo on the screen disappears and the scene from the first days filming springs to life. The overhead mounted camera switches from Sean to Teresa as she enters the room, we see her sell a few sandwiches to other people within the office, then set her sights for Sean. When she arrives at his desk, she leans forward to give him a bit of an eyeful, then the film clip freezes.

'Okay, Jo, your first question starts now, as you know your boyfriend so intimately, we wondered what you might think his next actions might be. Did he; A. Look briefly at the choice of sandwiches and decide not to bother,' the first answer appears on the screen over a slightly bleached-out still shot of Sean and Teresa, 'or did he, B. Dismiss her altogether, saying he was too busy to look,' again, the answer appears on the screen, 'answer C. Did he grab the first sandwich that came to hand and pay for it, refusing the change, or did he D. Stare longingly into her eyes and smile seductively before asking her name?'

'Answer B. Definitely, he's always too busy to eat, even at home.'

'Okay, are you sure that's your final answer?'

'Yes, Jack, I'm sure, final answer.'

'Good, but before we go any further, we have some footage of our initial interview with you two weeks ago, done in our studio. Sally could you play the footage please.'

The screen springs back to life, as the scene switches to a drably decorated interview room. Central in the picture is Jo, dressed slightly more casually, and we hear my voice in the background, asking: 'So Jo, is your boyfriend a fussy eater, or is he one of those *eat anything* kind of guys.'

'God no, he won't sit still and eat for five minutes, you could starve a mouse on what he eats in a day, always too busy he says.'

The screen reverts to the previous image with the answers punctuating the screen.

'Well, Jo, let's see if you're right, and I might add, that this question is worth five points.' I turn and raise an eyebrow to exaggerate the point. 'Sally, would you show us the correct answer please.' Ping! The correct answer changes to bright yellow on the screen as the incorrect ones fade away. The film resumes to show Sean completely ignoring Teresa, and five points are shown on the digital scoreboard above the screen.

'Congratulations, Jo, you've won five points, and we all know what points make…'

'Prizes!' comes the roar from the prompted audience. I feel like I'm in a sodding pantomime. Jo settles in her seat a little deeper, obviously more comfortable with getting the first correct answer under her belt.

'Right, well done again, you now have to repeat the process with the second clip.' The screen resumes animation as it shows the following day's activity. This time, Teresa is seen to perform her sandwich round duties throughout the entire design studio, but completely ignores Sean and bypasses him. The film is then stopped as she approaches the exit.

'Right, Jo, we have now your next set of answers to the following, and glowingly predictable question of what happened next. Remember, this will be cross referenced for congruency with your initial interview. Answer A. Sean continues to ignore her and carries on with his work. B. He shouts across the office that he has been left out, and would like to purchase some food. C. He rises from his desk and rushes over to the exit in order to buy a sandwich. Or D. He also rushes over to the exit, but this time in order to ask her out to lunch. Jo, the clock is ticking, you have thirty seconds to make up your mind, and may I remind you that this question carries a healthy ten points, double that of the last question. So what is it going to be, Jo?'

'I don't need thirty seconds to confirm he never eats now do I? A, Jack, my answer's A.'

'Final answer?'

'Yeah, course it bleedin' is.'

'Okay, Sally, please roll the film of the previously recorded interview.' Again my dulcet tones grace the speakers as the scene reverts to the dim studio; 'So, Jo, would your boyfriend ever chase after food, given a slightly missed opportunity, say to get a sandwich for lunch, something like that?'

'No, ain't you listenin', he never eats, he'd be as likely to fly a bleedin' jumbo jet to China than chase a bloody sandwich.'

I look to Jo and enquire; 'A, are you sure?'

'Sure.'

'Okay, Sally, let's resume the footage.' The screen flicks back to the design studio, Sean is then seen to jump up from his desk and make a hasty march towards Teresa at the exit. He reaches her before she leaves and buys a chicken, bacon and avocado baguette.

'What! 'E never eats a thing, let alone sodding avafu-Beeeeep-incado.'

'Sorry, Jo, as you can see,' I wave my hand to the now yellow answer upon the screen, 'the correct answer is, in fact, C.' I smile as the hornet's nest between her ears begins to stir. 'And may I remind you that this *is* live television, and although the censors love to have their fingers hovering above the beep button, we would like it if you could refrain from swearing please.'

'Sorry.'

'So, Jo, we move on to clip number three. Our location has changed somewhat to the local convenience store your boyfriend Sean stops in at occasionally on his way home from work. Sally…'

The film shows the interior of a typical twenty-hour-a-day convenience store. The bright fluorescent lights play havoc with the cameras, but a good clean shot is achievable with the marvels of modern digital technology. Sean enters alone, and after perusing the top shelf entertainment, he focuses on the ready meal section, purchasing a chicken madras for one and a solo portion of pilau rice. He then heads for the alcohol chiller. At this point the film grinds again to a faded halt.

'Okay, Jo, in this midway section of the show we can give you a swift *yes or no* twenty point bonus. Are you willing to take it?'

'What's the down side?'

'There isn't one, you answer correctly and you get the bonus, you answer incorrectly and you don't. It's a fifty-fifty chance, with no loss, are we going for it?' I ask in a somewhat condescending voice.

'Yeah, s'pose so, what's the question then?'

'Does Sean, or does Sean not buy a bottle of Champagne?'

'Pah!' Jo scoffs, 'he wouldn't even buy Champagne for his Uncle George's funeral, who he hates with a passion, let alone a random Tuesday or whatever in May.'

'So your answer is no then?'

'Too bloody right, give me those points.' The film then resumes to the recorded footage of the interview room. I question; 'So would Sean have any tipples other than the beer you have mentioned, would he ever buy wine or Champagne for example?'

'Never, he says it's for stupid toffs who don't know their twats from their toenails.'

'So he would never come home with a special bottle, even for a celebration?'

'No, a bottle of Newquay brown is his idea of a celebration, other than that it's pints all the way.' The film freezes again.

'So, Jo, your answer is no, he would not in this instance buy a bottle of Champagne, I presume from your categorical tone this is your final answer.'

'Final answer, now give me them points.'

'Not just yet, Jo.' I turn to the camera, 'And now

we are going to have a short break, we'll be right back after these important messages.'

The studio lights fade slightly as our broadcast is paused to the nation, allowing them in to be brainwashed into buying a brighter, bolder washing powder or funkier flavoured fruit chew sticks for Fido.

Moments later the music cranks up again as Brendan directs the crew for the continuation of our fabulous new game show.

'Hello and welcome back to *Dangling the Apple*!' The predicted explosion of feigned enthusiasm fills the air for a moment, before silence again falls. 'For those who have just joined us, where on earth have you been? This is the latest in cutting-edge television, that mixes human behaviour with a little familiarity, then blends it with a little spice of a life unknown, until now! Sally, would you roll the rest of the clip please.'

The shot resumes to show Sean approaching the chiller cabinet, he checks the sell by date on the bottom of a four pack of Fosters before adding them to the basket. Then, he seems surprised to see Teresa appear to his right, standing in the queue for the checkouts. He instantly ditches the basket containing his microwave meal and beer, then heads towards her. They speak for a moment, but the microphone is out of range until they reach the check-outs together. Whilst Teresa has her basket of salad and fresh tuna steaks blipped across the scanner, Sean is standing at the check-out next to her and can be clearly heard ordering the most expensive bottle of Champagne in the store. This provokes a response from Teresa, to which he answers;

'It's a girlfriend's birthday, so I can't very well meet her for a drink without a little token of celebration, can I?'

Teresa flutters her eyelashes and gives a cheeky smile. Sean reciprocates with a smile of his own, and asks Teresa her name.

'Teresa, I didn't think you'd noticed me in the office, you're a hard one to read.'

'Are you good at reading people then?' Sean replies with another flirtatious smile, his eyes locked into hers.

'Forty-six pounds please sir,' the slim Pakistani man behind the counter insists, 'We have queue behind sir, so forty-six pounds please.'

'Yes, sorry.' Sean breaks his trance, fumbles with his wallet and hands the guy a fifty as Teresa begins to walk away.

'Keep the change,' he turns towards the exit and calls; 'Teresa!'

The film grinds to a halt again. 'Sorry, Jo, wrong again, although you have been consistent with your interview answers, so we'll give you three points for that. Ping! The scoreboard displays a digital number eight. Jo is sat with her mouth open, obviously trying to work it all out. Before the penny drops all the way to the floor I ask Sally for the next clip.

'Okay. Here, Jo, we have two hidden cameras, one placed outside the design studio front door, showing the street ahead, and one from the usual angle, where we see Sean looking rather agitated at his desk.'

Teresa is then seen to approach the door and walks inside. The camera switches to the familiar interior scene, showing Sean glance furtively in the direction of the incoming blonde, who makes a sale to each and every member of staff as she makes her way slowly towards him.

'How was the Champagne?' she asks once stood at his desk, with a broad smile stretching across her lips.

'Very well received actually, so much so I thought of buying another one.' The screen screeches yet again to a faded halt.

'So, Jo, two bottles of Champers in a week. Not quite the man you thought you knew, now is he?'

'Too bleedin' right. Come on, what's the question, Jack, I want to see what he's been up to.' The dangling fruit is now obviously working on both sides of the camera.

'Okay, Jo, just to recap on what we have seen, Teresa has entered the office on her sandwich round and now seems intent upon offering all her attention to Sean, who has admitted to purchasing a second bottle of Champagne, but for what ends we are yet to discover. So, for ten points, can you tell us if he; A. says that he'll keep it for a special occasion. B. asks her to share the bottle after a walk along the river. C. tells her he's bought it for you, his girlfriend, or D. asks young Teresa out to lunch.' She looks aghast at the prospect of her former dearest taking another woman to lunch, but after a moment to regain her composure, she answers:

'Up until now, I would have laughed out loud at any of those answers, but given the little bast-*Beeeeep* has been up to no good, I'll go for answer B, he asks her for a walk along the river, Champagne in hand, although he's usually too busy to even get his own dinner from the kitchen, let alone wander down the bleedin' river.'

'Okay, so your answer is B. Sally, could you show us the interview footage for this question please.' The screen bursts to life once again, and we revert to the rather miserable looking Jo sat back in the dimly lit studio of two weeks ago.

'So, Jo, tell me,' I ask, 'would Sean ever take it upon himself to go out for a romantic walk, along the river maybe, with a bottle of something special for a small celebration possibly?'

'You're joking, Jack, he comes home from work knackered, and plonks himself straight in front of the football, demanding his dinner. Even my birthday this year was spent in the pub on his way home from the office, so cosy walks in the countryside are about as likely as Bill Gates going skint.'

The screen then fades, and back comes the image of Sean and Teresa with the answers hovering in thin air on top of them.

'So, you opted for answer B, a complete contrast to your earlier judgment of his character. So, do you want to change, or is answer B where you feel most comfortable?'

'Yes, Jack, answer B. I'll bet he takes that tart for a bloody snog down the river, she looks like a marriage wrecking slut.'

'Yes, quite. Sally, the correct answer please.' The three incorrect answers then fade away, leaving the predicted answer B glowing yellow on the screen.

'Answer B, Jo, is the correct answer. As you have deviated from your original answer we can also not only give you the ten points for the correct answer, but a bonus two points for initiative, bringing your total to twenty points.'

A burst of applause then ensues as Brendan continues to give me the thumbs up off screen, then indicates we are pushed for time by pointing at his watch.

'Sally, could you resume the clip please, so as we can all see the outcome.'

The yellow text then also fades as the action continues inside the office. Sean leans forward, and whispers to Teresa that he can leave work at four o'clock, and thought she might enjoy a glass of Champers on the nearby river bank. She confirms with an exaggerated lick of the lips, and their date is set. Jo, back in the studio is starting to boil. Her lank greasy hair seems even more lethargic than when she arrived, and her face is flushed to a tone of crimson that would seem more appropriate for a whore house's curtains.

'So when did this slut begin to wreck our relationship then, Jack?'

'The footage, if that's what you are asking, Jo, was

shot last week. But I must point out, that Teresa is merely an actress that is to remain neutral in all situations, and will have no further contact with Sean after this show. She is merely playing a role to fulfil a study of his behaviour. After all, it is indeed Sean who appears to be making the moves, wouldn't you agree?'

'I don't know about that, she's still a cow.'

'Sally, could we roll the next and final clip please.' I raise an eyebrow to the formerly jolly Brendan, but he gives me the okay signal so I breathe a sigh of relief. The screen reanimates for almost the last time and floods with an image of the riverbank, although it's not Chelsea, nowhere near in fact. The lush green lawns that line the flowing water are far more suburban, Richmond possibly or even further afield. The scene opens with Sean and Teresa walking together, close, but not intimate. Sean indeed holds a Gold topped bottle in one hand and a pair of flutes in the other. They appear to be laughing and joking, although the volume on the microphone that Teresa has concealed is muted. They sit on the grass and watch as the spring sunshine illuminates the river goers in a cloak of bright light. The volume of the microphone is then brought up to a more clearly audible level. Sean appears to be quite inquisitive as to Teresa's relationship status, and continues to press for information. Then, once the currently abusive boyfriend is flushed from the trees, so to speak, we hear a rapidly escalating personal sales pitch from Sean, as to how his current situation with Jo is going nowhere, and how he really is on the verge of leaving her. The clip then freezes at the crucial moment in anticipation of the now familiar four answer format to the question I'm about to pose.

'So, Jo, last question. This is worth an astounding twenty-five points, and as I'm sure you have grasped, involves a little courage on your behalf. But we all know what points make...' The crowd erupts with a rendition of the word 'PRIZES!' and then falls quiet again.

'So, Jo, the question is, and I know this'll be a hard one, does Sean A. tell her that; in him she will always find a friend. B. offer to have the offending boyfriend's legs broken. C. talk dismissively about all girls wanting a bastard of a boyfriend, then all they do is whinge about it afterwards, or D. offer to leave his current situation in order to save her from this toe rag of a man, then live with her happily ever after.'

'Oh that's easy, Jack, it's B. again. He knows loads of dodgy people who certainly aren't afraid of swinging a sledgehammer at a pair of shins.'

I cringe at the thug I've obviously underestimated who is waiting in the wings for a confrontation of no doubt mammoth proportions.

'And, once more, can we have the recorded interview please, Sally.'

The screen fills with the darkened interview room one final time, as my voice asks the leading question, 'So, Jo, would Sean ever be unfaithful to you, or possibly leave you for another woman, do you think?'

'Oh you can't be serious, we're like peas in a pod us two, Hell on Earth wouldn't be able to split us two apart.'

'Okay, Jo, B, final answer for twenty-five points?'

'Final answer,' she says determinedly.

'Sally.' I nod in her direction, cringing as to what is about to be released to the viewing public. The screen then fades the incorrect answers away to leave the one that poor Jo least expects; answer D. Her shoulders visibly drop as she bows her head in shame, I sense she's about to cry, so take the initiative and stand, microphone in hand and introduce to the crowd, the absolute rat of a boyfriend called Sean. The audience are prompted into a frenzied whirlwind of applause as a whole clan of placard dweebs meander in front of the seats, encouraging whistles and cheers from all present. Sean strides onto the set like he owns the place, for a moment I'm fearful of a repeat of the bloodbath from the final *Bully Boys* episode, but this time with *my* face on the receiving end of the fist, but thankfully he continues straight past me, then hugs and kisses Jo as he takes his place next to her on the sofa. She's all of a sudden become a nervous wreck, cowering in his presence. He leans in and whispers something into her ear. This instantly provokes an uplifting response from her as she draws herself up straight and proud, beaming next to him on the sofa.

'What on earth could he have said?' I wonder, but the answer comes swiftly as the microphone is thrust into her face.

'So, Jo, what do you have to tell the viewing public about this most enlightening of experiences?'

'Oh, he's so clever my Sean, he says he sussed the cameras almost immediately,' *'what a load of Bollocks!'* I cuss under my breath, 'and then played along to make good television, didn't you, Babe?'

She smiles inanely at her fella as I inwardly cringe at the lies this lowlife has just created to get himself off the hook. With a moment's reflection though, his lies have also let me off the hook of an impending broken nose, so I don't feel quite so hard done by. Brendan is positively beaming with pride for a show well executed, and so I close the event with a short speech on the immorality of infidelity. The band strikes up and the credits roll, as we all celebrate the success of our bright new future on prime time television.

As soon as I get the signal, I leave the stage hastily.

'Jesus, Brendan, I'm glad that's over. Let me treat you to a pint.'

21. Petworth

We sit in designer aluminium armchairs outside the bar named simply *'The Bar'* in Esher High Street. The pavement awash with evening socialites drifting from one alcoholic establishment to the next, their ages stretching from late twenties to mid forties, yet all seeking out the same thing; the next candidate on their hit list of eligible partners. The girls are trimmed, plucked, botoxed and waxed into a state of near Barbie doll perfection, wrapped neatly in Karen Millen's finest, whilst the boys wear a blend of neatly pressed Armani and Hugo Boss uniforms over a dash of Kenzo, bleach blond spikes and a pair of mirror polished Oliver Sweeney's joining them to the pavement. The conversational tempo is strong, a good week so it seems, and animated gestures from the confident men enthral the attentive nature of those less dominant, the girls laugh and titter, the boys boom and josh. A lively hubbub of the universe indeed.

'So Brendan,' I ask, feeling a little conspicuous of our drab attire, especially his, 'did it really go down as well as I think it did?'

'We absolutely knocked them for six, Jack, believe me. Charles Hess is going to have our picture on his wall under a bleedin' spotlight before the end of the year, you mark my words.'

'Now *that* I would love to see, here's to success never ending.' We raise our glasses and chink them together before both taking a long and well deserved gulp. I replace my pint on the table and, looking up, see Hazy approaching our table.

'It was this very spot, Brendan, that I was sat in last autumn when that that guy got run over who gave me the ring, moments before he died you know.'

'Yes, Jack, but don't be going on at me with any more of that hocus pocus shit about ghosts. I've heard enough of all that thank you very much.'

'Hocus pocus ghosts,' interrupts Hazy as he arrives at the table, 'this sounds like an interesting conversation, mind if I join you?'

We both raise our eyebrows non-committaly, so he draws up a chair.

'So go on, what are you two talking about, sounds fun.'

'Jack here has lost his marbles,' the Irishman starts, 'He believes he can see dead people wandering the earth, and has the ability to change history or something. Why don't you explain, Jack, see if Hazy has any ideas as to which psycho ward we need to have you committed to.'

'Ha bloody ha, Brendan.' I turn to Hazy in order to give a slightly more credible explanation.

'Well it all began last autumn, I was sat here having a swift pint before the show when...' and so it went on, for half an hour in fact.

'You know what,' Hazy returns, 'you should go and see my friend Jerry, he works as an estate manager down in Petworth, Sussex. I'm sure he knows all sorts of stuff about this kind of thing, an' he could probably point you in the right direction if you want to find out a bit more about it, let me give him a call, see if we can't get you two together for an afternoon.' Hazy then punches a few keys on his mobile phone. 'Bollocks, answerphone, I'll leave him your number; Hi Jerry, it's Hazy, can you give a mate of mine called Jack a bell, his number is 07836 278376, I think you'll have a lot to talk about, he's as nuts as you. Laters.'

Hazy terminates the call and returns his battered phone to his jeans pocket. 'Yeah,' he continues, 'Jerry used to have a real deep interest in all things supernatural, he's travelled all over the world talking to people about this shit, he believes in parallel universes and the hidden un-dead that walk amongst us, influencing our lives. I think it's all a load of old tosh personally, but each to their own I suppose.'

The shadows lengthen across the road as evening becomes night. At ten o'clock I decide to head home, and clamber in behind the wheel of my trusty B.M.W. after more than a couple too many.

*****

I wake to the *'bleep bleep...bleep bleep'* of an incoming text message; it's ten past five in the morning. I stagger to the bathroom for a leak as I open the message, it reads: *'Jerry here, was told to make contact, call me on this number.'*

'Maybe in a couple of hours, mate,' I say out loud,

causing Wendy to stir. I return to bed and snuggle up to my beautiful, if still slightly fractious, fiancée, or is that ex fiancée, come reverted girlfriend? Who knows, in fact why *do* relationships have to have such specific terminology?

'Go away, I'm sleeping.'

'Never stopped you before we were attacked by bloody sharks,' I say just a little louder than intended, causing a snatching of the duvet and an invisible yet impenetrable barrier to descend between us. I take this cue to leave the bedroom and head downstairs for a cuppa.

'Hi, Jerry, you don't know me, but I was given your number by Hazy at the studios. The name's Todd, Jack Todd. He says you might be able to help me make sense of a few things that have been going on in my life recently, real strange stuff, he said you'd understand.'

'Jack Todd eh? The chap off the telly last night then.'

'Er… yeah, what did you think?' I regret this question the moment it has registered in my brain as having passed my stupid lips.

'Not bad, but you need to attract something with a little more intelligence than a Marmoset's faeces if you want to retain something approaching a reasonable audience base. Novelty is like a fad, young man, it is extremely powerful, yet grows tiresome with a speed to astound even the most pessimistic amongst us.'

'Thanks, Jerry, I'll keep that in mind. Anyhow, the reason for calling is that I keep seeing ghosts of the past, not just any old past mind, my own, and that of the people around me whose destinies I have changed. I was given…'

'A ring,' Jerry interrupts.

'Yeah, how did you know?'

'You'd better come and see me immediately. I'm on the Travers estate just outside Petworth, come as soon as you can.' Blip.

And with that he was gone. After ten minutes in my office, glued to *Google*, I find the estate, print a map with directions and then download and print a further twenty-three pages on the entire chronological history of the place, care of a misplaced jab of the keyboard.

The traffic is predictably light at ten to seven on a Sunday morning, so with the roof down and the wind in my hair I find myself heading south past Guildford and onto the A283 towards Sussex in no time at all. I make Petworth in a pleasing thirty-five minutes, ignoring all speed limits as I go. The Travers estate, named Brackendene Manor, resides in a valley just south of the picturesque market town. I count a quarter mile past the golf club as instructed by Jerry, then enter the foreboding gates with a little more trepidation than I had expected, passing a decrepit and burnt-out lodge house that sits to my left, before arriving at the stables to the far right-hand side of the main house. The yard is full of life, horses brought to and fro, saddles thrown upon them in anticipation of an imminent hack, some taken to the school for juniors to learn and others being fed behind their half height doors of incarceration. The hive of activity is dizzying to a city day-tripper such as me, who simply seeks a slither of knowledge from he who may know the route my life is about to take.

I pull into a parking slot outside the closed gates of the yard and walk in. I spot a man, who from his appearance I guess to be Jerry, imparting orders to a young stable hand at the far end of the newly built, yet classically styled stable block that's home to the twelve horses it houses. Once finished, Jerry checks his watch, and then disappears through a doorway. I follow him, down a short corridor and watch as he enters an office. I reach the doorway and peer in to see him sat behind a large but rather untidy desk.

'Hi, may I come in?'

'You must be Jack, yes, come in and take a seat.' I enter the room fully, and sit on an old leather armchair that sighs as I recline into its backrest. Jerry sorts some papers on his desk and then begins to write a series of paragraphs in his large open desk diary with a broad tipped fountain pen. He's mid fifties, with longish grey but thinning wispy hair to suit his tall, thin and wispy build. Dressed in a muted brown and grey check shirt with dark brown jeans, held by a well worn but obviously high quality leather belt, his rugged yet neat appearance is exactly as I had expected. His handwriting is large, bold and flows from his wrist with almost musical pace, covering the top half of the page in only a few moments. He stops writing, places a ruler across the paper, and divides the page in two with a dash of his pen, he then begins to sketch what looks like some kind of three dimensional mechanical contraption involving cogs and wheels linked by chains and belts. Without looking up, he comments:

'So you are the current ring bearer, interesting choice I must say.'

'What do you mean?'

'I think you know what I mean, if you are seeing ghosts, or clones as they are called, of your altered destiny then you are truly a lucky man.'

'Lucky, I'd certainly agree with that, my clone is having a hell of a time. We were due to be married, not the clone mind, me and Wendy, my fiancée, or ex fiancée, to be precise, and it all began to go horribly wrong.'

'Let me stop you there, young man, you're not really making sense. I'm working on a pulley system for the girl's tree house that I need to make some progress on. I've just had an idea that I wish to try out, so please, do follow me to the workshop so as we can continue this conversation without my work schedule falling behind.' He stands, tearing the page from his diary and walks silently from the office.

Once back out in the sunshine, Jerry stoops to collect up a red tennis sized ball, then throws it with a powerful stroke to the overlooking field.

'Go on Foggy, fetch!' cries Jerry. A grey

Weimaraner scrabbles swiftly to his feet and tears across the yard in pursuit of the red bouncing sphere.

'They used to be called the grey ghosts, Weimaraners that is. Apt name given our topic of conversation today don't you think?'

I smile at the rhetorical question and continue to follow Jerry out of the yard and down a pathway towards another wooden building. This one seems far older, and somewhat weather beaten with its bleached shiplap walls and shingle roof. We enter the building that stands probably six hundred square feet in footprint and two stories high, although hollow inside, save for a small partitioned kitchen area of predictably rustic style. A wood burner sits to one side, but with the rising temperature of early summer it remains unlit. A dizzying myriad of both woodworking and mechanical tools hang from the wall mounted pegboards that sit above the fitted wooden workbenches gracing three of the four walls; their worktops worn with many years of industrious labour, soaked over the ages in the sweat of those workmen keen to please the lord of the manor, and the impeccable maintenance of his estate. In the centre of the room is a smaller wooden building, I eye it with curiosity, wondering the purpose of a building within a building, before realising that it is in fact the tree house Jerry spoke of. Jerry pins the sketch from his office onto the notice board above a bench upon which a selection of wheels and cogs lie. He draws up a stool and gestures for me to do likewise; I do, and then watch as he begins to piece together the pulley system he had been previously working on.

'Can't seem to get the leverage ratio right,' he says out loud, though not to me directly. He refers to his sketch, and then re-arranges the order of the cogs on their metal backing plate, then measures the lengths between them, presumably in order to find new belts to suit.

'So tell me, Jack, what is it you wish to know?'

Once the measurements are complete he scribbles the figures onto a piece of scrap paper, then stands, gesturing for me to follow.

'I want somebody to make sense of what's happening, and how it all works.'

'The ring you mean, you wish to uncover the secret of the ring's power?'

'Yeah, I suppose so. I just need to know what I can and can't do with this stopping time thing, and how it affects everything else around me. Where it came from and what do I have to do with it once I have used my three privileges.'

'Wow, inquisitive little bunny aren't you. Well let me see how I can help.' Jerry stands and makes his way over to a wardrobe on the far wall. 'So far as I know, there is only one ring, the one you are wearing. It has been passed down through generations and generations. The true age of the ring has never been ascertained, although it is thought to be more than a thousand years old. People have speculated about its origin, but none can agree. The truth is, I don't think anybody really knows. Sorry, could you just hold that a moment please.' Jerry hands me a loop of rubber toothed belt, retrieved from the old wardrobe that houses an array of them in varying lengths, which he then proceeds to measure with an old wooden yard stick. 'Perfect, young man, could you put it on the bench with the pulleys and come back to help me with another one. Where were we, oh yes, the speculation. Well apparently it was made from the melted nails of Jesus' cross according to one source, it also comes from outer space, and is used as a tracking device by aliens if you subscribe to others ideas. It's also all gobbledygook if you take the more universal opinion; but you, Jack, probably know different, don't you.' Jerry refers to his scrawled notes once again, then hands me another belt to measure. 'Perfect, right, back to the cogs.' He shuts the wardrobe and we take our places at the bench once more.

'May I see it?' he enquires.

I remove the ring from my finger and place it in Jerry's palm. He regards it with the curiosity of a child, turning it repeatedly, smelling it and testing it for hardness with a blade.

'It's the real thing alright, so far as I can tell. Amazing how hard the metal is, not one scratch in all these years, look even where I pressed my blade into it, no mark whatsoever, unbelievable.'

'So what else can you tell me about it, am I able to influence the people whose lives I have changed? Or do they just drift along their new life path oblivious?'

'I don't know is the honest answer. Although I have followed as much of the ring's history as I can, there is very little reported by the actual bearers of the ring, it all seems to be second-hand information spread by their friends and family who mostly claim that the bearer has gone mad. This information is notoriously inaccurate, and sometimes even quite venomous. The bearers throughout history have had a range of fates from being burned at the stake to hailed as a God, depending upon which century you look at. Allow me to give you a little history lesson from the area of the ring's ancestry I have been most closely following:

'As you may have noticed upon your arrival, there sits a lodge house to the left of the estate's entrance. This is my home, and although unfortunately gutted by a recent fire, it is a building of great historical interest. It was the home of Sir William Pitt the younger, prime minister to George the Third during the time of his reign. George the Third inherited the crown from his grandfather George the second after the unexpected death of his father Fredrick, Prince of Wales. Young George made many foolish decisions during his youth that he bitterly regretted. He fell deeply in love with Lady Sarah Lennox, daughter of the Duke of Richmond, and wished to take her for his wife. An influential Lord Bute, however, advised against the match and George abandoned his thoughts of marriage.

'As the young George approached his eighteenth birthday, his grandfather the King offered him a grand establishment at St. James's Palace, but George refused the offer, again on the advice of Lord Bute. These were two decisions that were to shape his future more than he could ever imagine. The king also proposed he take the hand of Princess Sophia Caroline of Brunswick-Wolfenbüttel in marriage, again he refused to accept his grandfather's advice, as he remained heartbroken by the subsequent loss of affection from Lady Sarah. This, as history proves, was a mistake so crippling for him that it eventually cost him his sanity.

'The king saw the angst and pain in young George's eyes for the loss of his former love, Lady Sarah, and offered him a ring as a token of compensation. A ring that would allow him to never again feel the pain of regret, it was a ring to change the path of his destiny and revert any future unwise decisions with the mere pressing of its three stones. That ring is the one you now wear upon your finger, so treat it with respect, young man. The story as I'm sure you know has far from a happy ending. George the Second died, passing the crown to the now married George the Third. A troubled man then stood at the helm of a troubled country, that quickly saw the development of civil war in the Americas, the French revolution and the Napoleonic wars, leading to the decline of world power that the English had held strongly for so many years. He became confused with the myriad of decisions and possible outcomes that this powerful ring could offer, his mind raced out of control and sent him mad. He found it impossible to decide when and where to use the ring, agonising over decisions for months with his close confidants. The answer came swiftly though during an attack by Margaret Nicholson in 1786, who stabbed him in the chest with a carving knife. Facing certain death, the monarch had the presence of mind to depress the three stones and avert his imminent death. He is then reputed to have replaced his attacker's carving knife for a fruit knife from the kitchens of the palace. This explains the apparently bemused face of the attacker and the background to one of his most famous quotes:

"This is a fruit knife, madam; it couldn't cut a cabbage, much less a king."

'This gave birth to the clones. He watched as his clone body lay in state, the hurt and helplessness of watching the clones of his queen and fifteen children mourn his death. More importantly though, a clone was born of his detested eldest son, who took to the throne in his now altered universe. Every day the king would see his clone son make decisions against his will, and he wept as this evil clone banished his mother, the king's beloved wife, to the tower to rot the rest of her life away. This was the beginning of the madness King George was famed for, these images of a life averted drove him insane. Instead of rejoicing at the new destiny he had created for himself, he spent his entire life trying to ensure his son never ruled England. Ironically this preoccupation caused such stress for the king that he was declared unfit to rule and he himself was banished to Kew for intense therapy by his newly appointed doctor, Francis Willis.

'This Doctor, as the history of the ring has shown over and over again, was the ring's guardian. A figure sent to make sense of the awesome power the ring holds, and bring it back into perspective for the ring bearer. King George would have truly lost all control had it not been for Willis. His outbursts were all too understandable to Willis, the only spectator with the knowledge of the ring, yet all around him thought him simply mad. Willis became both the king's mentor and friend, a calming influence in the sea of peril that surrounded the monarchy from the escalating rebellions of both America and France. A further attempt on George the Third's life took place whilst he stood to attention during the National Anthem in the royal box of the Drury Lane Theatre on the 15th of May 1800. A certain James Hadfield stood in front of the orchestra pit and fired a pistol at the heart of the king, killing him almost instantly, I say almost instantly because he had the presence of mind to call the power of the ring into action, halting time as the bullet smashed through his ribs on its deadly journey. Seconds before death, King George was able to cease the sequence of events and plot the exact path the bullet had taken, allowing himself the time, once rewound, to dodge the incoming projectile with deft precision.

'King George had the pleasure of Dr. Willis for his guardian, I fear you may not be so lucky.' Jerry glances down at his classically styled but faded gold faced watch, 'It's time for morning break, we will take tea by the marquee I have been reliably informed by the imposing Mrs. Jaques, head of kitchens here, as Mr. Travers is in London today. Whilst the cat's away, as they say.'

Jerry downs tools and we return once again into the mid-morning sunshine, up a short hill and past the front of this most imposing house we walk, with Jerry holding a surprisingly swift pace.

'Come along, Mr. Arnold, tea waits for no man,' Jerry hollers to an older man tending the flowerbed encircling a central fountain that serves as a roundabout for the immense driveway. The white-haired man nods in acknowledgment and we continue around to the far side of the house, where upon a perfectly manicured lawn sits an enormous white marquee.

'Big party last night, hundreds of bloody toffs all over the place, went on till four in the morning, what I would have done for a large incendiary device,' Jerry muses as we approach the enormous tent. Once through the flap that serves as a back entrance, we progress through the maze of naked tables and chairs, all being methodically broken down and stacked neatly into the back of a large lorry.

Once we reach the grand entrance, I see columns brimming with floral bursts line the way as we find ourselves in a short fabric corridor that leads out once again onto the main lawn, punctuated by an almost

Olympic sized swimming pool. A twelve foot wide strip of slate paviours line the pool, and a selection of tables and chairs are also spread throughout the surrounding area, with the number of seats there appears to be I'd estimate around three hundred guests were enjoying Mr. Travers' hospitality last night. A stage sits at one end of the pool, at a right angle to the marquee, and wears a backdrop of New York's skyline with the text 'The Franco Sinatra Band' picked out in metallic gold. All of a sudden, I sense something odd about the immediate area, something I find hard to quite put my finger on. I look beyond the stage, and to the left of it there is a rather large hole in the hedge, showing the road beyond the estate. With the length of the meandering drive I would never have imagined the outside road to be so close. The corner of the marquee corresponding to the hole also looks somewhat makeshift upon closer inspection, and to my dismay, I then notice the skidmarks from a wayward car that slew along the lawn, through the corner of the marquee and continue right up to the slate paviours, beyond which is the edge of the pool with what appears to be a blue car sitting at the bottom of it.

'My God, Jerry, what on earth happened here last night?'

Jerry turns and smiles, 'A couple of lads lost control of their car and punched through the fence, followed as you can see, by the marquee, narrowly missing a table full of people, only to finish up landing in the middle of the swimming pool. Mr. Travers was so amused he let the two little reprobates stay for the party as honorary gatecrashers. It's up to me of course to get the bloody thing out now.'

Mrs. Jaques has set her tea service up at a table to the side of the stage, and there is a gathering of probably twenty staff, all enjoying the sunshine around the pool whilst nibbling on sandwich triangles and miniature éclairs. I sense that if Mr. Travers were to return earlier than expected, activity resembling a scurrying of rats would ensue. I sit at a table with my host for the day and ask;

'So, Jerry, what more can you tell me about what is going on in my life?'

'Not a great deal I'm afraid, I have only studied the history of the ring for the specific period that relates to my house, and the involvement of William Pitt. It's quite co-incidental that George the Third was one of the most famous ring bearers really, I've not got a vast amount more information to pass on, other than details of the Guardian that is.'

'The Guardian, who's the Guardian then? For me that is.'

'The Guardian of the Ring, as history seems to have shown, is usually a complete pain in the neck; arrogant, obnoxious and self-righteous. Willis was King George's, and as I said, I have a good idea who yours might be. There is a professor who goes by the name of Dr. Richard Bandlaman. He lives in a large chateau overlooking the sea that boasts gothic architecture to strike fear into even the boldest of men. It can be found on the northern coast of France, just outside the walled city of St. Malo. It's also near the famous monastery of Le Mont St. Michelle, so you could always stop in there on your way back to recover.'

'Recover?'

'Yes, although I have never met with the great Dr. Bandlaman, his reputation certainly precedes him. He has searched the globe for even the merest snippet of information or proof of the ring's existence. Originally from the west coast of America, he travelled over here in the mid seventies, the long way around. Starting with just a beaten-up V.W. camper, he drove south, taking in as much of South America as he could, learning from the tribes that border the Amazon, the descendants of the Incas and any who had something to say that contrasted with traditional Western culture. From there he crossed by sea to Japan, and travelled by road through China, Mongolia, Russia, India, then down through Saudi, Egypt and the Sudan. Eventually he reached the Congo, where he lived for three years gathering and studying all the information his travels had given him. From there he went north again, through Romania and Belarus, continuing up to the Nordic lands, each time seeking out the gurus, the teachers and the shaman to learn from all who would teach. He then sailed from Norway to Scotland, travelled through our green and pleasant land, eventually crossing the Channel when he reached

Portsmouth. Finally, after a month in Paris, he decided to settle in Normandy, where the ring was supposed to have last been seen, several years ago. This remarkable journey took him nine years, he absorbed more knowledge than any man could ever do by merely reading text books and is reputed to have learned the language of each and every country he visited. Some say he is a wizard and a sorcerer, others a fake and a sham. I fear this just represents the opinions of those who have not yet met him. Bandlaman is the only person alive who can help you make sense of the ring, you must go to him as soon as you can, but be warned, he speaks with a tangled tongue in more ways than one. As you listen to a seemingly innocuous story, he will be working on your subconscious mind, through hypnosis and metaphorical speech. Don't try to make sense of what you hear, it should all become clear in the days following your visit. Listen with your heart, open your eyes and close your logical mind, he is a genius and a guide; just don't try to follow him.'

'So I have to go to St. Malo?'

'Yes, leave as quickly as you can, he lives at the end of the coastal road named "Rue de la Guimorais". You'll easily identify his residence, believe me.' Jerry gives a knowing smile. I, however, feel somewhat uneasy. After thanking Jerry and Mrs. Jaques for their hospitality I head back to the car, unsure of what I have really learnt.

*****

'I'm home, Babe.'

No reply, but I can hear muffled voices so walk towards the conservatory in order to investigate, feeling a mild shudder shoot through me as I do so. Wendy is nowhere to be seen, but my clone has tidied up his mess and is sitting on the sofa with Victoria's clone, they appear to be getting on rather well. Gone, it seems, is the moping morose shell of a man that he was, to be replaced with a more level-headed, and frankly tidier version of my alter self, so I sit in to eavesdrop.

'Well, Victoria, you certainly seem to be coping incredibly well with it all, I've been an absolute mess. My new show was meant to go out last week but I haven't even been into the studios since we got back. It's just been awful. My boss Charles Hess has left a couple of messages, but I can't even summon the courage to call him back. I just feel so utterly lost without Wendy.'

Victoria pulls him toward her in a compassionate embrace, her arms winding around him as they both begin to break down. I feel a strange sense of warmth at his newly developed relationship, and begin to wonder how I can regain some of the missing warmth that *my* life so desperately needs. Ironically, I muse, the clone is indeed becoming better off than me, even after I've moved Heaven, Earth and a few sharks to shape it this way.

After a swift look around the house, no clues to Wendy's whereabouts are apparent, so I grab my keys and head out the door in search of Mr. Hobbs, my favourite travel agent.

22. Reversal

With my ferry ticket booked for three weeks' time, I should be able to sneak off without it interrupting the programme schedule too much. Brendan is arranging all the studio recordings for the next four shows to be filmed in one hit over a couple of days next week, the outside broadcast unit is working overtime to gather all the incriminating footage and I'm warming up my vocal chords ready for a performance to thrill the nation into a state of near nirvana.

I sit in the otherwise empty canteen, enjoying a rather odd tasting cup of tea, poured from the ancient urn that was no doubt in service before the late Queen Mum. The click, click, click of high heels on the hard tiled floor breaks the silence as in walks Teresa, dressed somewhat smartly in a dark knee-length skirt, but with a hint of naughtiness by way of a half unbuttoned semi-translucent white blouse showing an intricately laced cream coloured bra. I'm quite surprised to see her back in the studios after her brief appearance on my show, but gladly take the opportunity to relieve the boredom of waiting for Brendan to arrive by gesturing for her to join me. She places her mug of tea and KitKat on the table whilst radiating a simple beauty which I'd failed to fully appreciate before.

'So what brings you back to this dismal place?'

'I had an interview with one of the guys from

Eastenders, he reckons he can get me a slot on the show, said I was just what they were looking for.'

'Cool, so you thought you would celebrate with a cup of shite tea from the worst cafeteria this side of Beirut.' Teresa laughs at my sarcasm, then replies;

'Well *lunch* wasn't part of the "B" list hospitality at the interview, so I guess a bar of choccy will have to do. How's things with you?'

'Yeah, not bad I suppose. The show has taken off, and we are on the second set of recordings. I'm off to France in a couple of weeks to sort a few things out, so on balance, quite good I suppose.'

'How was your wedding by the way?'

'Hmm, by the way would be about right. We had a couple of issues whilst in Brazil and called it off. Wendy has morphed into a zombie whilst I'm around, she refuses to talk to me or even acknowledge my existence most of the time, so marriage is so far off the agenda it's got a Norwegian postcode.'

'Oh my God, I'm so sorry to hear that.' She places her hand onto mine; it's warm from clasping the mug of tea, and lights a dormant emotion in the pit of my stomach. 'What do you think will happen?'

'No idea. Listen, I'm starving, Brendan's over an hour late, and I certainly don't fancy any of the deep fried rodents that appear to be sat cremated on the food counter, so why don't I text him that we've gone to The Crown for something to eat?'

'Good plan, Batman, let's get out of here, I could kill a glass of wine.'

Teresa stands, leaving her PG tips on the table and heads for the door. I follow in hot pursuit and find myself in the passenger seat of her sporty little red MR2 Roadster moments later.

*****

'Pint of Becks and a dry white please, Dave, what's on the specials for today then?'

'Kitchen's closed, Jack, chef had such a bad hangover this morning he vomited in the soup whilst warming it on the stove.'

I cringe at the vile image of what now floats in the pan, left bubbling on the hob. I doubt I'll ever eat here again, so return to the outside table by the river that we've chosen and rest our drinks upon it. Teresa is perusing the menu, her eyes flit from ham and chips to Cesar Salad as her conscience does battle with her desire.

'I wouldn't get too excited, they're not serving food due to a staff problem.' I gaze into her deep blue eyes, and realise just a moment too late that I too am having a battle of conscience versus desire.

'Hmm, okay, let's down these and get a couple of sandwiches from the deli in Queens Road, then eat them in the park?'

'Sounds good,' I reply, 'let's see what kind of a gal you are; down in one!' I raise my pint to my lips and draw a long series of gulps to drain my glass, noticing that Teresa is doing likewise. Moments later she slams her empty glass on the wooden table and lets out an almost silent belch.

'Beatya!' she exclaims as I drop my glass to the table with an inch or so of foam left in the bottom. We both grin inanely, and then laugh at our childish behaviour. Back in her car, I feel a little light-headed, no doubt due to the speed of our imbibed alcohol. We head to the deli, then walk to the park, recycled brown lunch bags in hand, bumping occasionally into each other as we go. I wonder if it's purely accidental on either of our behalves, we seem to be getting on just a little too perfectly.

The grass rises into a large mound in the centre of Weybridge Park, and we sit munching away at our crisply fresh baguettes. Teresa produces a small bottle of Vodka from her bag and tips some straight into my can of Coke, likewise with her can of Fanta.

'Just a little perky,' she says almost innocently. I don't complain and down half of it in one, only for her to refill it almost immediately. This time though the drink is far stronger as the cola is somewhat reduced. I'm really starting to feel a bit sozzled, so give up my battle with the unending crusty bread, leaving the remnants to one side for the birds to peck on whilst I lie down next to the bird sat beside me. Teresa does likewise, and we drink in the warm rays of sun together. A few moments pass before she breaks the silence.

'So what do you think will happen, with you and Wendy?'

'I have no idea, she seems so distant and uninterested, I wouldn't be surprised if she told me she'd started an affair to be honest, things really do feel that bad at the moment.'

'An affair, how do you think that would happen? After all, you seem so perfect.'

I smile, it's a long time since I've had a compliment, let alone been accused of perfection. 'You aren't so bad yourself,' I hear my mouth saying, without permission from my brain. I roll onto my side to face her. She looks at me with those fabulous eyes and I find myself leaning forward to meet her lips with mine as my arm closes around her shoulder and the rest of the world fades into soft focus. We kiss and embrace passionately, tongues entwined, but only for a few moments. Shocked, I stand and brush some imaginary grass from my trousers whilst apologising, then state that we should head back. I offer her my hand to help her rise and we walk back to the car in silence. The return journey is filled with polite but stilted conversation about nothing in particular, like that of incompatible strangers in a confined space. Quite the opposite, I think to myself, of our outward journey that filled the car's small interior with vibrant humour and animated conversation. A line had well and truly been crossed and we both knew it. If she goes to the tabloids with this Hess will kill me, just after Wendy has barbecued my bollocks with a dash of Oregano and Rosemary. I feel crap, again.

We reach the end of my road fifteen minutes later.

Teresa makes it perfectly obvious with her body language that even a peck on the cheek would be a violation of territory serious enough to involve the United Nations, so I thank her politely for the afternoon and head home.

*****

Sod's law, that's all I can put it down to. As soon as my key is slid into the polished brass lock of Todd Towers, my phone bursts into life with its rather dire ring-tone that I'm yet to learn how to change.

'Jack, it's Charles Hess. I need you to go to the studios immediately and iron out a few things with Hazy, he's unsure about the revised layout you wanted for the stage. Also, I'd like you to meet me tomorrow at my London office, it's in Covent Garden and Sammy can give you the address, I have a few things we need to go over together. Nine thirty sharp, okay?'

'Yes fine, Mister Hess, I'll see you then.' Click, he's gone. I turn around to be confronted with a clear driveway; Teresa had dropped me at the end of the road, and we both seem to have forgotten about my car that's still parked at the studios. 'Sod it,' I cuss as I call the knights in rusty Nissans to whisk me back to Shepperton as soon as possible.

Once there I head straight to the set, only stopping briefly to collect another cup of rank coffee from the cafeteria to sober me up a little on the way.

Hazy abseils from the rafters of the tall studio twelve building as I arrive; screwdriver in teeth and a mass of electrical wires under his left arm.

'Hey, Jack, I've changed the angle of the spotlights, but need you to tell me the exact height you want them pointing to.' Hazy un-clips his harness and walks to where the dust sheet protected sofas lie. He stands behind the contestant's side and hovers his arm at about their head height; 'About here wouldn't you say?'

'No,' I respond, 'a little lower. The contestants have all been complaining about the glare in their eyes, so I think we need to bring the lighting more in line with where they are sitting, and shine it down on them whilst lighting their torso from the sides. This should kill the shadows I would think, and stop them moaning at the same time.'

Hazy thinks a while, and nods in agreement. We discuss further the minor tweaks that need his attention and we finish on quite a positive note. It's only then that I notice a camera has its green light showing; it's filming us.

'What's that camera running for?' I ask.

'Checking colour balance for the skin tone with this new lighting, we'll be done in a minute, why?'

'Nothing, just wondering,' I dismiss, then head out into the sunshine once again. A mild shudder fills my body as I see my clone and Victoria drive past in my car, or should I clarify, a *ghost* of my car. It parks in the same space my real car occupies and they get out, walking towards the set that I'm stood outside. They walk straight past me and through the door, followed by a clone of Hazy who appears from just around the corner. I'm intrigued, so mooch back into studio seven to see what they're up to.

Incredibly only a few seconds have passed, yet the entire set has changed to one titled *Trampoline*. It shows cartoon images of stereotypical tramps all performing everyday tasks, in business meetings, plumbing, entertaining and every other job conceivable. It's almost set like a circus, with the bright colours and a really strong theatrical feel to it. I wonder what the hell is going on.

'Jack… Jack… JACK!' I'm startled by Hazy stood beside me (the real one). 'What are you doing? I thought you had gone.'

I shake my head, then look around me as the set has returned to its usual image of *Dangling the Apple*.

'Sorry, Hazy, daydreaming I guess. I think I'd better go and have a lie down.'

I return once again outside and head towards my car, then home for a nice quiet nap, unsure now more than ever of what on earth is happening to me.

*****

I decide the train is the best way to travel into London, underestimating of course both the number of commuters at eight in the morning, and the mortgage I will now need to apply for after purchasing a peak return to London Waterloo.

Hot, sweaty and skint, I emerge from the grand station. It's only about an inch and a half on the A to Z to Hess' office so should only take a jiffy or two. It's still early so I decide to walk the distance from Waterloo in favour of the further expense and hassle of a cab journey. *'The fresh air will do me good,'* I say to myself, through a slightly congested nose. I seem to be getting a bit of a cold. Trucks, taxis and cars come and go as I make my way along the embankment, past the wealth of splendour that the Savoy Hotel holds behind its clear but substantial doors. Memories of great banquets within, at my grandfather's table flood my otherwise vacant mind.

I take a left, continuing along Savoy place, then head north up Carting Lane, past the kitchens of this great hotel, where my friends and family had worked for many years, then on to the Strand.

I stand patiently with the few eager tourists, waiting to cross the road once the green flashing man deems it appropriate. A striking black Rolls Royce Phantom pulls up at the lights as they change to red, *Hess*, I think, and tap on the dark tinted window. The window remains closed, but a rather burly man in a suit opens the driver's door and leans out to glare at me. He's not Mr. Hess' chauffeur, and this is not Mr. Hess' car. Oops!

Once safely across the Strand, I walk along South Street, towards my destination. I glance at my watch; eight thirty-six. He probably hasn't arrived yet.

I cross the dormant piazza, and find at the far end the famous Drury Lane, home to the theatrical arts of our fine city. To my right I spot a corner shop, and enter for some much needed bravado, by way of a packet of chewing gum.

No matter how small or insecure we feel, chewing gum always offers a kind of *'look at me, I'm cool, and I've got fresh breath to prove it'* kind of confidence that we all sometimes crave. I pop two pieces of sugar coated magic into my mouth and chew.

The sky is broken cloud and sporadic blues, it looks a little uncertain, as does my relationship with Wendy, but best put that to the back of my mind and clear my head for the upcoming meeting with the Boss man.

Hess seems rather upbeat with the show and we discuss some further enhancements and tweaks. A national advertising campaign is suggested, and I'm given a new promotions manager called Edward. Edward is to cover the country in posters, leaflets and fliers, there won't be a glossy magazine or bus shelter without my face on it by the end of the month if he gets his way, so I like Edward; he's going to turn me from a celebrity into a superstar.

I return to the reception area, and cross the marble floor towards the sunshine with a rather large spring in my step, but then somewhat taken aback as I'm confronted by my clone on the other side of the glass door that leads out into the street. He walks right past, within inches of me and heads to the elevators. I'm surprised to notice that I had almost no shuddering sensation at all. In fact, I feel positively great. I could get used to feeling like this!

Out of the building and into the piazza, I stop for a

cup of coffee accompanied by a brie and grape croissant at an extortionately priced tourist trap. I care little about the price and just soak up the ambience. Pigeons come and go, as do street entertainers and shoppers alike, all encapsulated in their own reality tunnels, barely noticing the world around them. A second coffee slips down as easily as the first, and I decide to browse around the shops a while and maybe treat myself to something indulgent.

After half an hour of uninspired shopping I return empty handed to the banks of the Thames, taking my time to walk back to the footbridge that carries me south of the river and back to Waterloo. I walk with the crowds of tourists and businessmen along the pavement, and once over the bridge stop just outside the Royal Festival Hall. I'm quite surprised to see my clone sat there cross-legged on the floor talking to a tramp, or the clone of a tramp that is occupying the same space as the real tramp's body, although the clone is far more lively than his human counterpart. I move to the Mexican bar nearby, and take a seat at an outside table to observe the pair of clone's activities. I'm out of earshot, but can see them talking and laughing with animated gestures; they appear to be getting on like an inferno in a firework factory. After a while, the two of them stand, leaving the real tramp behind, who physically shivers as the ghostly figure leaves his body. They head off towards Waterloo together, so I follow from a distance to try and make sense of what they're up to.

After disappearing downstairs to the wash rooms for twenty minutes, the pair of them re-surface to scan the departures board, waiting for a return train to Weybridge. My clone buys some food from the Café Paris, and I suspect that's the most the tramp has had spent on him for longer than he can remember.

The directory flips the horizontal name slats around to show our departing train will leave from platform eight in ten minutes' time, so the three of us head towards the waiting carriages.

*****

I take a taxi from Weybridge station, leaving the clones to find their own way home, and once over the threshold, I make myself a nice mug of tea, then settle into the conservatory sofa for a quick snooze.

I awake, startled as the clones crash their way into the hallway, they're drunk and it's started to get dark. The clone Victoria has joined them and is singing Abba's 'Waterloo' at full volume in the hallway, presumably in celebration of the tramp and my clone's meeting place. I'm thrown completely, and as the party moves to the kitchen, I head upstairs in search of Wendy; only to be welcomed by an empty and unmade bed. The singing gets louder as my clone and the tramp join forces for the chorus and it all just gets a bit too much. I head out of the front door and plot a course for The Crown. By the time I reach my car I'm startled by the ghostly figures of Hazy and Tess walking down my driveway.

'They're in the kitchen, feel free to nick all my sodding booze,' I say, but the clones can't hear me as they walk past in their own dimension.

*****

'Pint of Becks please, Dave.'

I slide the amber glass from the bar and head for the corner. I'm not really in a sociable mood, despite my praise earlier today, so sit at a small round table with my back to the wall, sipping gently at the welcoming fluid that regenerates a glimmer of my previously positive feelings. After a moment I notice a familiar shape on the other side of the room, Brendan is sat with his back to me, partially obscuring Hazy, with whom he chats on the opposite side of the table. I try to make out their conversation from afar, but it's no good. I collect up my half drunk glass and take my half drunk body towards them.

'Jack! Great to see you, mate,' welcomes a somewhat over enthusiastic Hazy, Brendan then stands and shuffles around a bit to allow me enough room to join them at their table.

'So what brings you two out on a school night then?'

'Oh nothing really, we were just running through some techie stuff for the show and thought it best done over a pint, how about you?'

'If I told you, you'd think I'd completely lost it, so best leave it at that shall we?' Brendan raises an eyebrow, whilst Hazy questions;

'So how was your meeting with Charles today?'

'Brilliant really, he's happy with the first four shows and has employed a P.R. chap to make me *really* famous. We ran through the outlines for the next eight weeks and he seems over the moon.'

'And, Jerry, how did you get on down in Petworth?' Hazy continues.

I laugh, recalling my brief stay at the country manor and tell the pair of them all about King George, the car in the swimming pool and the mechanical lift for the tree house, which Hazy takes a particular interest in.

'So I'm off to St. Malo after the seventh show in this series, leaving you to sort everything during the week for the eighth, I should be back by the Wednesday evening in time to take up the reins once again.'

The conversation drifts from one vacant subject to another, as we all struggle to find the required enthusiasm to return to our homes. I eventually drag myself to the car at half past ten, mute the stereo once inside, and drive home in silence. Wendy is predictably asleep, and I see my clone sprawled out partly next to and partly through her. I'm further disturbed by the fact that Victoria's clone is in bed next to him, also half through the real Wendy. It's a rather disturbing vision, but I try to ignore it. I brush my teeth with numb repetition, then gargle and flush my plaque down the plughole. Returning to the bedroom, I pull off my Calvins and pull back the sheets to fall into a much needed relaxing sleep.

'Jesus Christ almighty!' I leap from the bed as soon as my body hits the mattress, it's like an electrical shock has burst into my nervous system. I shiver and shudder on the floor a moment, before Wendy rouses to see what all the noise is all about.

'What the hell is going on, Jack, you've woken me up.'

'The clone, it's in the bed with you and I can't get in,' I say confusedly, 'We can't occupy the same space, I've told you that before, what shou...'

'Oh shut up with all that fucking ghost stuff, you're driving me mad with it. Pull yourself together or go and sleep in the spare room, I don't care which, just leave me in peace.'

I gather up my clothes and retreat to the room at the back of the house in a daze. This is *not* good.

23. Rotten apples

It's Saturday, late afternoon, and as three weeks have passed, I'm off to St. Malo in the morning; alone. Wendy and I have been especially distant this week, I've taken to sleeping in the spare room full-time now, and moved most of my stuff into the wardrobes. My life is still surrounded by clones, but I tend not to notice them most of the time. Except, that is, when I want to sit in my armchair to watch telly whilst '*he*' is sitting in it, or log onto my computer whilst '*he*' is happily plugging away at the keyboard. On the whole we seem to be existing together quite well, unlike myself and Wendy. I stop at the bar in Esher for a relaxing pint on my way to the studios and *people watch* for thirty odd minutes. I love sitting out on the pavement as the world goes by, everyone busier than me. I like it that way.

My life has changed so much since I last sat here alone, I reflect; the long-haired ring bearer gave me the power to enhance or destroy my life with one easy swish of the hand, and I seem to be doing a pretty good job of ballsing it all up at the moment, at least the show's a success though. I glance to my watch and see it's indeed nearly show time, so drown the dregs of my pint and head back to the Beemer.

*****

'You're late, Jack, get your bloody face through make-up and be back here in thirty minutes on the dot, I despair at you, Jack, I really do.' Yes, that was Brendan tearing his hair out as usual. I head towards make-up, stopping to talk to Sally briefly on the way.

I sit in the chair, smock around my pampered neck, waiting for Julie the make-up artist.

'Hello, Mr. Todd, just the usual I suppose.'

Julie, bless her, is the most boring person on the planet. A gothic black appearance covers skin so pale I could almost mistake her for a clone. She has strands of bright burgundy red hair punctuating the mop of unwashed limp black locks that cascade lifelessly over her shoulders, her infinitely boring and monotone voice isn't helped by the amount of silverware that punctures her nose, and she lisssspss heavily due to a rather large piece of metal she wears through her tongue.

'No, Julie, didn't anyone tell you, we're doing a horror night tonight, so loads of blood, gouges and hanging flesh please, and don't skimp on the scars either.'

'No... Mr. Todd, surely you're having me on,' she drones, unable to note the sarcasm rich tones of my voice.

'Yes you're quite right, Julie, that's for the guest. Just the normal brush and tart up job please.'

'The guest? She's already been in, Jack, quite a looker I must say, not like the usual dogs you've had the last couple of weeks.'

'Yes, quite.' I sit in reflective silence as Julie does her thing, wondering what on earth she is on about. From memory, the girl for tonight is certainly nothing special, a bit rough around the edges actually. Julie must obviously have somewhat lower standards than mine, her boyfriend likewise. I close my eyes and meditate as the brushes blend the blemishes from my almost perfect face.

'All done, Mr. Todd, see you next week.' I remove the smock, astonished that thirty minutes had passed in the blink of an eye, and leave it in the chair I vacate, then head back towards the studio with only moments to go before the cameras go live. The intro is playing as I enter, and I walk straight out on stage without missing a beat. Brendan must be tearing what's left of his hair out somewhere, but I can't see him so carry on regardless, right to centre stage.

'Good evening, ladies and gentlemen, and welcome to yet another display of the unfathomable talent this country holds, hidden behind the closed doors of offices and houses alike, where the next unwitting star of *Dangling the Apple* may well be you.' I point my finger whilst giving a cheesy wink at the camera that zooms in for a close-up. 'Let me just remind you, the viewing public, that all the tempting girls we use, to entice the unwitting stars of our show, are professional actresses and have no further communication with the targets after the show. This is not a game of moral standards, but one of human nature, the choices made by the free will of the contestants and the behaviour of their spouses is purely an experiment in extreme conditions of temptation.'

I smile my best smarmy game show host smile at camera three and see Brendan re-appear to the side of it, no doubt somewhat relieved. He shakes a fist at me with a frown, but I know he's only joshing. I fire off the usual pre-prepared jokes and one liners to an enthusiastic studio audience and then begin the game.

'So, Sally, could we please have the lovely contestant for this week's thrilling instalment of *Dangling the Apple!* The crowd explode into a frenzy of cheers once more, which I of course lap up with another smarmy grin akin to that of an election winning politician. The grin drops, however, as soon as I see Wendy march from the wings, and onto the stage, meeting me in the centre. My stomach goes into freefall as the colour drains from my wax covered face.

'Er…Wendy, what are you doing here, where's the contestant?'

'I am the contestant apparently, Jack, so come on, let's find out *why*, shall we.'

Oh shit, I helplessly glare at the spotlights bearing down on me, I will never run a rabbit over again, promise.

Ever the professional, I try to carry on as normal, glancing to Brendan who looks even more shocked than I am. He exaggeratedly shrugs his shoulders with a ridiculous expression on his face as I guide Wendy to the sofa, my mind is sludge, churning at twice the speed of my stomach. I've never been nervous on stage, ever, up until now that is. I wonder if anyone has noticed my hands starting to shake. I stare straight into the camera and open my mouth, with no idea what the hell will come out.

'So, ladies and gentlemen, as it's not my birthday or any other marked anniversary, I wonder why on earth my girlfriend, the beautiful Wendy,' I gesture to the frowning female that sits scowling at me, 'has come to visit little old *me* at work.'

This raises a laugh. So, ever the entertainer, I respond with another cheesy grin. My brain is racing at a million miles per hour, yet bereft of clarity or ideas. I decide in desperation to stick to the script, and follow the autocue that prompts my commentary.

'So, Wendy, we've been together for almost eight years now, wow is it that long.'

'Stick to the script, Jack, I want this debacle over with as soon as possible, I just need to know what you've been up to.'

'Er... yes, sorry dear. So... Wendy, eight years, a long time.'

'Too bloody long, get on with it will you, this is embarrassing.'

'Sorry, so... Do you think in those eight years you've really got to know me, to trust me, completely?'

'I'd always trusted you, you might be mentally unstable but trust was never an issue. Until I got asked to come on your bloody show, obviously.'

'Right.' I stop to gather my thoughts, but they appear to be running away, waving a white flag. 'Okay, Wendy, I presume you know how this part of the show works, we will run some previously recorded footage and I will ask you a question. Four answers appear on the screen, one of which is true, three of which are false. You need to pick the correct answer to receive five points, and we all know what points make,' I turn to the audience and whoosh my hands in the air…

'Prizes!' comes the predictable response, and welcome break in the awkward atmosphere.

'Right. And now, ladies and gentlemen, let's play; *Dangling the Apple!* The audience cheer again as the large plastic apple drops theatrically from the ceiling once Sally has feigned its operation with a downward tug of the fibreglass branch.

'Sally, dare I ask for the first roll of footage please?' I cringe as the screen bursts into life, showing me sat on my own in the canteen of Shepperton Studios, innocent enough, but I know what's coming, and it isn't anything to be proud of. The familiar tap, tap, tap of Teresa's high heels invade the studio at ten times the usual volume. I'm done for, somebody give me a gun, I need to end this right now.

The screen freezes with Teresa leaving the servery aisle, looking for somewhere to sit.

'So, Wendy,' I ask, again reading the autocue, 'do I, A. ignore her completely, B. offer for her to join me, C. make a lewd comment at the mountain of flesh showing from the number of undone buttons on her rather revealing blouse or D. insist she sits at another table as I have clients coming in a moment?'

I look to Wendy with wounded puppy dog eyes, but it doesn't work.

'I would normally say A. you ignore her, but given your current random behaviour I'll go with B. you ask her to join you.'

'We have some previously recorded footage from an interview that apparently,' I read the autocue, 'a member of our staff took with you earlier this week. Sally, would you roll the film please.' I shake my head as the screen bursts into life and the now familiar dimly lit studio environment shows Wendy sat on a chair, legs crossed, being interviewed. I recognise the voice of the interviewer, but cannot place it.

'So, Wendy, if Jack were to be left to his own devices, in a bar or a café for instance, would he initiate contact with a member of the opposite sex, have them sit with him and such like?'

'No, not at all. He's quite quiet off camera, so I wouldn't expect him to be talking to random strangers at will.'

The screen then freezes and it's my turn to speak again.

'So, Wendy, you've chosen answer B. I invite Teresa to come and sit with me. Final answer?'

'Yes, Jack, get on with it.'

'Sally, would you show us the correct answer, and can we have the rest of the clip please.' I close my eyes in shame as the incorrect answers fade, leaving answer B glowing for all to see. The footage then resumes and the studio fills with my smart-arse comments that bring the planted beauty over to my table. How on earth could I have been so stupid?

'Congratulations, Wendy, you answer is correct, I do indeed ask Teresa to join me at my table. And for that correct answer you receive a healthy five points, and we all know what points make!'

'Prizes!' comes the thundering roar from the audience. The footage resumes once again, after a few minutes it pauses just before the point where I tell her Brendan's an hour late. It suddenly strikes me that he's in on it and must have helped set me up, bastard. I break my thought at the sound of silence, everyone is looking at me.

'Sorry, I was miles away. So, Wendy, the film has paused at a pivotal moment.' I glance to the autocue to see the inevitable question appear.

'Okay so, for ten points, can you tell me what happens next, do I, A. ask her to leave as her breath is putting me off my tea, B. ask her to get me a sandwich from the counter, C. stare deeply into her eyes incapable of speech, or D. ask her to lunch at a local pub. And remember, Wendy, there are ten points at stake for this question, so choose wisely.'

'Jack, I couldn't give a toss about the points, and it's our relationship that's at stake here, not some bloody prizes.' I'm struggling and she knows it, I fear that if I slip out of 'game show host' mode I'll just become a jabbering wreck, so continue regardless.

'So, Wendy, do you have an answer for us? I don't want to rush you, so please feel free to take your time.' She heaves a deep sigh, then continues with the façade.

'A. is unlikely, B. a possibility, although you always moan about the miserable canteen. C. is ridiculous, you're never short of something to say and D. is, I suppose, the most fitting for this show, so D. you take the tart to lunch.'

'Are you sure?'

'Yes, Jack, I'm sure.' She rolls her eyes to the heavens.

'Great, could we roll the interview footage then, to see if it's congruent with your current answer, Sally.' The screen does as predicted and shows Wendy once again being interviewed. Suddenly I twig the voice of the interviewer, it's Hazy! I cannot believe the special effects guy has set me up like this. I'll kill him, beat him to death with one of Brendan's limbs that I'm going to cut off with a blunt carving knife. Wendy answers the interviewer's question that, given the opportunity it would be extremely unlikely for me to invite a random woman out to lunch. I cringe as I ask Sally to do the inevitable:

'Sally, could we have the correct answer please.' The screen pings as the three incorrect answers once again fade into the stratosphere.

'Congratulations, Wendy, answer D. is correct, I did ask Teresa out to lunch last week.' I cannot believe I'm doing this on live prime time national television. 'And as you once again broke with the pre-recorded interview answer, I can offer you a three point bonus, taking your score to a maximum eighteen points!' The crowd go ballistic, as instructed by the placards being waved at them. I know what's coming next and hate myself for it. The autocue reels off the next question and I cringe a little more.

'Okay, Wendy, we have the scenario that I'm now taking Teresa to lunch, for a ten point bonus, could you please tell me whether I get into her car with her or do I take my own?'

'No idea, Jack, you tell me.'

'It's worth ten points...' I raise my eyebrows.

'Oh shut up about the bloody points, did you or didn't you?' Cornered, I did what any frightened animal would – I stare into the camera, and with as near to a smile as I can muster, utter the words:

'We'll be right back after these important messages from our sponsors.' I point my finger at the camera and hold a wink until the light on top of it fades, signalling we are off air. I stand, shouting 'Brendan, Brendan where the fuck are you, you coward. Come here and get punched you absolute tosser.'

Brendan is nowhere to be seen, I glance around for Hazy but likewise, he has thought fit to hide. I turn around to see Wendy still sat on the sofa, she appears to have a tear rolling down her cheek. I sit next to her to comfort her.

'Get off me, you pig! Where's this leading, Jack, what have you done to me?'

'I, I, nothing, I haven't done anything to you. I promise.'

'Who was that slut then, and what the hell were you doing with her?'

'It was Teresa from the first show, remember I told you all about her.'

'You didn't tell me you were taking her to bloody lunch. Have you slept with her, I need to know before we go any further with this.'

I wonder how far indeed we are going with this. I hope for the best and optimistically presume the footage ends at the pub.

'No dear you've nothing to worry about, it was just...'

'And on in five, four, three,' with the last two digits mimed, Brendan disappears out of sight again. The band strikes up and I welcome the viewing public back with open arms, to the most watched show on television. It will no doubt be the most talked about too in about twenty minutes' time, but best not think about that and just get on with it, eh.

'So, hope you all enjoyed the break, we *certainly* did here, and I'd like to welcome back to the second half of this week's *Dangling the Apple!'* Applause shower once again as I drink up what could well be my last fifteen minutes of fame, ever.

'So, Wendy, with a swift breather and a few minutes to think about it, do you have an answer for us that could net you a whopping ten points, and we all know what points make…'

'Prizes!' comes the predictably crass response.

'I really don't know, Jack, nor do I care. You took your own?'

Ping! The correct answer flashes across the screen with some footage of the pair of us in her red convertible zooming out of the studio's gates, it seems to look far worse than it was, or am I just kidding myself. Wendy glares at me with a venom I've never seen in her before, suddenly I'm scared of her. The footage then skips to the pub, shot from the outside. It shows the pair of us arrive, then Teresa walks to the garden to ensure we sit at the table near where the camera is set up whilst I disappear inside to get the drinks. Again the film slows to a halt and the question pops onto the autocue screen.

'So, Wendy, the question is, as predicted, what happens next. Sally, the options please. Answer A. then pops onto the screen; 'I decide it's all a bad idea, make my excuses and call a taxi home. B. I return with two cokes and chat politely for twenty minutes whilst our food is prepared. C. return with a pint and some wine in order to get her tipsy, or D. return empty handed and suggest we move to somewhere a little more intimate.'

Wendy sits shaking her head, she's finding it hard to comprehend what's going on. I flash her a little smile of encouragement, but it's wasted as she just closes her eyes and answers with a heavy outward breath; 'C. Jack, I presume it will be C. God knows I'll kill you if it's D.'

The screen reverts to the previously recorded interview where Hazy asks Wendy if she thinks I would take another girl out to lunch, get her tipsy whilst having a few beers myself. The answer is a categorical 'no' from Wendy, as she states clearly that she's never known me to drink during the day, not even whilst on holiday. This is, of course a total contradiction to the answer on the screen that she has chosen, so I ask her to confirm the choice once more.

'Yes, Jack, I'm beginning to learn quite a lot about your secretive behaviour, so yes, you do get the slut tipsy, and also yourself no doubt.'

'Ahh, I take it that's your final answer then.' Wendy closes her eyes in contempt. 'Sally, could you reveal for us the correct answer please.' The correct answer C. then remains on the screen, as the footage resumes to show not only my returning with two drinks, but acting like a complete child by challenging her to down it in one. I'd forgotten about that bit, oops! I know from the show's format that there is only one question remaining, I pray they haven't followed us to the park and cringe as I ask Sally to resume the footage. It's like playing Russian roulette up here, and I think I'm the one that's going to get shot.

The film skips to the park, the pair of us lying on the mound, laughing and joking whilst drinking Teresa's Vodka. My heart ceases to beat and I can feel a wave of nausea wash over me as I fear what's about to be revealed. The film clip freezes as we both lie back in the sunshine. I have an irresistible urge to run, but I know it will do me no good, I've just got to stand here and take it like a man, a very frightened man.

'So, Wendy, I really don't want to ask you this,' I mumble pathetically, 'but what do you think happened next?' I cower at the thought of what's coming, expecting the worst.

'Sally, dare I ask you for the options?' Sally smiles, no doubt enjoying my absolute dread at the next few minutes of my sad and sorry life. Ping! Answer A. appears; they both relax in the sunshine and fall asleep together. Ping! B. Jack falls asleep, and Teresa disappears back to the car, leaving him there to snooze, *so far so good* I think to myself. Ping! C. Jack falls asleep with his mouth open, and then Teresa pours the bottle of neat Vodka down his throat, causing him to choke. Ping! D. I cringe at the outcome of this, but it comes anyway... Jack sits up, startled, and bursts into conversation at this wonderful idea he's just had.

Eh? I scratch my head, bemused at the answers. Maybe I am going mad after all. Ping! Bonus answer E. Jack leans across and kisses Teresa passionately. 'AAAGGGHHH!!' The voices inside my head scream as I try to keep some decorum. I fight the internal war that's waging and politely turn to ask;

'So, Wendy, interesting one this, what is it to be?'

'I don't know, Jack, give me a hand will you, did you snog that slut in the park in front of everyone, did you? Come on, Jack, you can tell me, after all I *am* your girlfriend and this *is* live television. Okay, scrap that, call me stupid, but I'm going for answer A. you both fell asleep. And yea Gods I warn you it had better not be answer fu..Beeeeep..ing E.'

'Sally, scrap the final studio footage, let's just get this over with. Roll the rest of the clip,' I almost whisper, resigned to the imminent humiliation. The screen flicks back to life as we see the pair of us roll around on the top of the mound, fully entwined as our mouths are pressed together in a passionate kiss.

'Answer E. you absolute tosser! You snogged her, you unfaithful pig! I hate you. Hate you, you vile piece of shit, you hear me? I never want to see you again!'

Wendy launches off the sofa at me and flies into my face, beating me with clenched fists and biting my arm that I lash out with in self-defence. A random elbow catches Wendy's nose and the blood bursts from it as the stage becomes mobbed with people trying to separate us. Once she is pulled clear of me and held at a safe distance, I see Hazy nearby, so then launch at him with a frenzy of fists, pummelling any future hope I had of working in this industry ever again as we hit the floor in a mass of writhing limbs.

*****

I don't really need to tell you what Charles Hess said, now do I?

24. St. Malo

The drive from Cherbourg is pleasant, although the French seem to take Sunday as the day of rest a little more literally than the British, moving at an even more sedate pace than usual. I take a diversion through the town of Bayeux, but fail to see any signs for an outstanding piece of ancient needlework, so carry on through towards my destination without stopping.

I arrive at the awesome walled city of St. Malo some time around dusk and decide to head straight for the 'Hotel le Jersey', located apparently on 'Chaussée du Sillon', a road that heads out of the city and to the east, along the picturesque beach. Convenient for the wealth of restaurants the locality has to offer and apparently within easy striking distance to the home of the great Dr. Bandlaman, although I'm yet to find out exactly where he resides, maybe some locals can tell me. I pull into the small car park and feel a sense of concern as to the size of the building. The tiny hotel is wedged between two larger hotels, and appears a little dilapidated. After checking in, I drag my bag up the eternally winding narrow staircase, laid to a nauseating purple and black Paisley carpet, until I reach the fifth floor, where I find room number 15. I throw the flimsy hollow cardboard door open to find a disappointing room the size of my broom cupboard at home. I had booked a double room with an en-suite, and to be fair, it did house a double bed, just, and a cupboard in the corner with a shower, so I guess they stuck to their side of the bargain, it just isn't quite what I had expected to find after a short trip in a civilised country. Bangkok maybe, Brittany maybe not.

I throw my light holdall onto the bed, it creaks as I do so firing a worry throughout my cerebrum as to its ability to support my weight for the next couple of nights. The window is ajar, and a light breeze flutters around the confined space. I walk to the window and melt somewhat at the view. The room may be inadequate, but the scenery's just fine. I poke my head out of the opening and drink in the fresh salty taste. A slight chill fills the air, so I close the window and don a light sports jacket over my plain Ralph Lauren polo shirt before heading down to reception for directions to the best restaurant within walking distance. This, of course was a mistake. Pascal, as his name tag informs me, gestures to the manky excuse for a restaurant on the other side of the entrance hall. I almost say; *'no, I said decent restaurant,'* but manage to hold my tongue.

'I'll just go for a walk first, thank you, Pascal, I'll be back later.'

'Non, ma name is Raymond, zis badge is ma brothers, he works ere in the moorning.' Bemused, I ask; 'So why are you wearing his name tag?'

'Because e iz wearing mine of course. We got all mixed you know.'

'Er... right. See you later then.' I turn and escape as quickly as possible. Once outside, I notice the wind has picked up, sending a chill right through me and my flimsy attire. I walk along the promenade towards the darkly imposing gothic walls of the city.

Before I reach St. Malo, I come across a rather stylish looking restaurant. Mostly glass walls form a light and modern looking building with busy staff running to and fro, carrying plates heaped with culinary delights. Perfect.

I'm shown to a small table near the edge of the restaurant closest to the beach, and sit facing the sand, ignoring the frenzy of activity behind me reflected in the plate glass windows. It's dark now, and I look forward to some much needed nourishment. A man sits to my left, also alone, or so I think until his small white dog makes himself known with a yelp after a misplaced foot compresses his tail into the tiled floor. A comforting stroke from the owner has the canine happy again and I offer a smile in their direction. The man returns the gesture, then in a surprisingly English accent asks;

'How you doin' there boy, been in town long?' I regard his thin, slightly scruffy appearance and guess at early sixties from the white hair and beard. His plain shirt sports rolled sleeves and is drab olive in colour. He smokes a thin pipe with a small round bowl, like those of a traditional seaman, and has a ruddy hue to his hollow cheeks.

'No, just arrived. Drove down this afternoon for a

meeting with someone who lives near here, an American. I don't have the exact address though, just the road name.'

The white-haired man raises an eyebrow, then with a smile answers:

'I'm sure if you've travelled this far, a small detail like a house name won't hold you back. When are you due to meet him?'

'I don't have an appointment, as such. I'll start looking for his house in the morning, probably after a run on this fabulous beach.' I gesture outside, as if it needs pointing out. A basket of bread arrives, and I chat on and off with the amusing man for the duration of my undercooked steak, *frites* meal. He sits and smokes, picking occasionally at some bread and sardine paste, but other than that he just drinks his coffee.

'Good luck with tomorrow, young lad, hope you find what you've come looking for.'

I thank the man for his conversation and scoop half of my change from the silver plated tip tray as I stand to leave. Walking back along the seafront I feel a real sense of power, of achievement, then I remember the piss poor hotel room I'm yet to try and sleep in.

*****

Monday dawns, predictably, at dawn. I know this because my broom cupboard of a hotel room has no curtains at the window, so the blaring sunrise illuminates my room like a Belisha beacon. I head down to breakfast at six o'clock only to be informed I have another hour to wait before the kitchen opens. I try explaining to Pascal, sorry *Raymond*, that I don't need the kitchen to be open in order to eat a bowl of cornflakes, but he's just not having it. I guess he's upset at my boycotting their dump of a restaurant last night. Ho-hum, a breath of fresh air will do me good I suppose. I wander out into the early morning streets and savour the relative tranquillity this time of the morning brings. On a whim, I decide to grab a couple of croissants and a take-away latte from a local *boulangerie* and enjoy breakfast on the sand, sod Raymond and his dire restaurant. A wave of lethargy sweeps my body after eating and I decide to forgo the run along the beach for a swift stroll followed by the initiation of my quest for Dr. Bandlaman.

I hop into the Beemer and thumb the roof switch. It judders down and back behind me allowing the glorious rays of sunshine to fill the open car. I select first and roll out of the tight car park, turning left towards my destiny. The road sits slightly inland, with only one row of houses obscuring my view of the sea. These beautifully designed and crafted stone creations thin out somewhat as the road heads north-east towards Rotheneuf. I admire the style and work that has gone into these fabulous homes, and feel it such a shame that our English coastline is littered with such uninspired creations that reek of sad samey sixties cubism. As the plots of land grow in size the further from the city I drive, as do the houses in equal proportion. By the time I reach La Guimorais, a northern peninsula, the properties have grown to a quite breathtaking size. I pull onto Rue de la Guimorais, initially a normal road that then narrows to a single track. This track becomes a dirt road after half a mile or so, that leads me out to a rather barren spot of land, surrounded by cliffs on all sides, with the exception of the thin road that feeds it.

I find 'Chateau de Bandlaman', and enter the imposing gates. The long gravel drive scrunches under the weight of the Beemer's well worn tyres, and when I eventually reach the house, I park it out of the way. Once stood beside my car I can fully appreciate the absolute majesty of this castle, for that's what it is, a castle. As the saying goes, if every man's house is his castle, they should come take a look at this place, this is not your everyday residence. Four round turrets reach thirty metres into the sky, with perfectly tiled wizard's hats atop each to protect them from the elements, all of which sport flags; one is simply a jumble of initials surrounded by a ring depicting the flags of the world, one the French national 'Le drapeau tricolour,' one the stars and stripes, and the last plain black, except the words 'Never surrender' in bold red text. I guess this guy has a sense of humour.

I stroll up to the front door, confident that I've

found the right house and knock with the large ornate brass eagle's foot clenching a ball door knocker. I stand back and wait a moment for an answer. Nothing, so I knock once more, this time though I notice a small plaque next to the door that informs me the door is open, and would I please step inside. This I do, arriving in a small atrium with nothing but another door, this time painted red. The plaque to the side reads; 'Please notice the surveillance camera above you.' I look up to see a glass half-dome fixed to the wall that I presume houses the camera. A plaque to the side states; 'All salesmen or religious representatives please wait here, I know you are waiting and will be with you shortly. All others please come through the door.' I turn the handle and push the heavy wooden door, then step inside, finding yet another atrium and yet another front door. I feel like I'm Alice in Wonderland. This time the door is dark green. Instinctively I grab the heavy brass door handle to open it, but it appears locked. Again a plaque to the side states; 'All salesmen or religious representatives please leave, you obviously are incapable of following instructions. All others please use the door around the back of the building. Thank you.'

Bemused I return outside and walk around to the side of the building where a large grand set of double doors appear, housed in an ornate frame and covered by an immaculate glass pitched roof porch. Again I approach the door, this time somewhat hesitantly, and try the handle. It turns easily in my hand so I push the door, nothing. I then think to pull it towards me and it glides open easily, only to reveal a brick wall behind it bearing a plaque that reads: 'This is not the back, pay attention.' I chuckle lightly, half from amusement, half from embarrassment and continue around to the back of the building.

A large and perfectly flat lawn lies to the rear of the castle, punctuated with croquet hoops and four men dressed in black Karate suits practising some martial arts moves. I sit at a bench and watch as the dark figures 'huh!, hiiiyahh,' and generally grunt their way through their training session. The sun warms my body and my eyes find themselves heavy, the fitful and inadequate sleep from last night taking its toll so early in the day. Slowly I drift off into a pleasurable oblivion.

I rouse some time later to the sound of silence. The lawn is naked, as the ninjas seem to have retired so I gather my thoughts and stand a little too quickly for my addled brain. Once balance is restored, I walk a little further along the building to find a large set of glass doors, beyond which appears to be an entrance hall. I open the door and walk inside. The air is much cooler than the outside temperature, and the high ceiling gives an air of peace and tranquillity. The décor is sparse yet modern; a mix of mostly whites, set off with occasional greens, creams and greys. A large circular table sits central to the room, mahogany I guess and upon it a burst of floral colour in a large silver vase. Above this an enormous chandelier hangs, although it's modern in design, not all dangly glass and fake candles.

'Welcome.'

I'm startled momentarily, a large man in his late fifties stands before me. Heavy set with long grey and black hair tied in a pony tail. He wears jeans and a black shirt, several rings adorn his fingers and a silver chain hangs from his neck, upon which rests a sizeable gemstone. His aura commands attention, even though he has only spoken one word. A modest smile grows across the lower part of his face, and he gestures for me to approach.

'Come on in, we've stuff to discuss.'

As I approach, he holds out his hand. I draw mine out to shake his, but in doing so he interrupts the motion by grabbing my wrist with his left hand, swinging my open palm up towards my face.

'Notice the swirling patterns of skin on your hand, and the changing focus of your eyes as they close down deeper into a state of complete and utter relaxation.' My eyes fall closed as Bandlaman continues his hypnotic induction, 'and notice how the warmth of the room helps you fall easily to where you know you need to go and find the resources you can use to go down deeper inside, that's right, all the way.' Bandlaman moves my hand from my face, keeping it at the same height as he continues to talk in his deep throaty voice. I co-operate automatically as he continues; 'and I want your hand to drop down from this place, only at a rate and speed that's appropriate for you to go deeper into a state that you find out all you need to know that I know you are beginning to know the direction this relaxing feeling is taking you.'

Okay, this I must admit, is a little weird. I can hear his voice, and have the free will to stop what is happening, yet remain obedient to his commands, and indeed, the lower my hand falls, the deeper I feel the relaxation growing throughout my whole body, it's almost addictive after only a couple of words in less than a minute.

'Now what I want you to do, is with the unconscious part of your mind, let me know when it's ready to communicate by moving the index finger on your right hand.' I lift the finger slightly to signal, yet am chastised immediately by my host.

'Not that mind! The *other* mind.'

I hear him take a few paces away, then miraculously I feel a deeper wave of relaxation flood through me. I remain standing, but it's as if my outer body has been sprayed with concrete, allowing the inner sub skin body to totally relax without the muscle tension to keep me upright. It's a very bizarre feeling. Suddenly I feel my index finger twitch, all on its own, kind of like a nervous jitter.

'I'd like to thank your unconscious for communicating with me, and let it know that I would like this to become a "yes" signal for me to access at any time during your stay here, if it is agreeable with this could I have a further yes signal to confirm.'

Again my finger twitches completely on its own, sending a mild electrical pulse down my arm as it does so.

'Right, as you become slightly more aware of your surroundings, the coolness of the room and the sounds within it, I'd like you to be fully awake as I count backward from five, four, bright and awake, three, two, feeling alert, two, one and welcome back to Richard's planet.' He lets out a deep hearty chuckle, then takes my slightly numb hand and shakes it this time.

'Hi, I'm Dr. Bandlaman, you can call me Richard, but I guess you know that as you've travelled all the way here. How can I help you?'

'Hi, Richard, my name's Jack Todd. I was told you'd be able to help me with a few things I'm trying to work out.'

'Don't tell me, you're the ring bearer and you need to know how to revert your life path to where it would have been had you not messed with it because you've fucked everything up. Am I right or what?'

'Jesus, that's incredible. Are you, you know, telepathic or something?'

'No, I saw the ring whilst you were asleep outside, and I know that you guys *always* fuck it up.' He chuckles again, 'Tea?'

'Yeah, that would be great.'

'Earl Grey?'

'Yeah, great.' Bandlaman turns and gestures for me to follow. We walk through the rooms of this awesomely impressive residence, upon the walls of which hang original oil colours, works of oriental tapestry, scrolls and photographs of the man himself in all corners of the world. I wonder if there is any facet of life Bandlaman *hasn't* yet experienced. We pause outside a large bare wooden door that sports a heavy iron handle. The picture immediately next to the door is an original painting, acrylic I deduce, by the starkness of colour and opacity it's painted in, of Bandlaman talking with the burgundy and gold robed Dalai Lama over a low level table, laid out with a simple china tea service. I presume the picture depicts the Dalai Lama's home of Tibet, the background showing a white-capped mountain range from the window of the room in which they are sat.

'Cranky old guy that one, took a while to chill *him* out.' I smile at Bandlaman's irony, but all he returns is a raised eyebrow. The door sweeps open to reveal an immensely stocked library, a world of culture and knowledge whisper and chant information from the dark hardwood shelves to fill the room with such a wealth of words it's almost dizzying. I slowly enter in a state of awe.

Although a large floor-to-ceiling window punctuates the opposite wall, the room seems strangely dark.

'Sit here for a spell,' he gestures to a chair near the centre of the room, 'and as you sink down into the comfort of the chair, you might notice how much deeper you can relax. Absorb the knowledge that surrounds you, I'm going to make us some refreshments.' I do as instructed and recline into the burgundy buttoned velvet armchair. I close my eyes for a moment as the door does likewise, then sit surrounded by the thoughts of the greatest writers the world has ever known.

Rousing once again, some time later, I'm unaware of the length of time I've been asleep. I stare at the ceiling that is painted in a deep dark blue, with all the constellations of our galaxy mapped out in gold leaf, along with numbers and figures, lines both solid and dashed, straight and curved. All the signs of the zodiac are also marked along with collections of planets and stars that bear familiar names of both ancient gods and mythical heroes. Rising from my chair, I make my way to a large desk that sports an old dusty leather bound volume; *Transderivational searches and the analysis of automatic responses, part three*, by Dr. Fredrick Von-Felps. I flick idly through the thin yellowed pages, grasping little of the message Dr. Von-Felps is trying to convey, then turn my attention to finding something a little easier to digest. The shelves are filled with mostly non-fiction books on everything from physics and quantum mechanics to language, hypnosis and biology. There's an occult section with tales of bogey men throughout the ages, sacrificial worship guides and general wizardry next to the area reserved for magic, most of which appears to be in French, but I pull a book from the shelf to nose anyhow. A few simple tricks are outlined pictorially, and I try a few for size. My fumbling digits, however, find the necessary co-ordination somewhat lacking, and after dropping the coin I was attempting to make disappear seven or eight times I return the book to the shelf and search for something a little less taxing. I scour the shelves further and settle on the biography of one Henry Jackson, a soldier embroiled in the First World War who appears to have found a ring with mythical powers to change the world. I turn to a page headed 12th July 1918. It depicts life at the harshest moments imaginable, the front line troops that surround him are wounded and ill with what they call Mountain fever, some have lost the use of their legs due to it, but Henry is saved the discomfort of illness, only to be ordered *over the top* to a further trench. A letter to his wife is transcribed on the opposite page, so I read it with fascination:

Dear Margaret,

How I miss your face, your scent and your smile. I trust all is well back home, and you continue to nurse mother. I know you will always do a sterling job and feel it only a question of time before she can return to full health. Give her my love.

On the subject of health, I had a scare this week, don't want to frighten you Poppet, but I feel I should share this with you. We have had some trying jobs lately, in front line, on advance manoeuvres with what they call sacrifice posts. Out all night about a thousand yards in front of our own wire and we have to stick it and only retire in case of a big bombardment, any minor raids we have to stay put at all costs. A ruddy scare at times I can assure you. It was during one of these ops that a damned Jerry went and plugged a bullet straight through my chest, my ribs exploded as the offending piece raced through me and into my lung. Don't fret dear, I'm fine though. That ring I was given by the dying man in The Battle of the Somme, almost two years ago, was my absolute saviour. I did as he had told me, and remarkably it worked! I certainly wouldn't be writing this letter if it hadn't my darling, as you can imagine. It was incredible, and I hope you don't think ill of me, or shell shocked or mad, but I managed to cease time for just a moment, to avoid the deadly projectile. I have only this single sheet of paper, and space is evaporated so must close this letter now, but assured I will return once again to my darling beautiful wife that you are.

God bless, love always, Henry.

Moved by these words, I hold the book in my hands, assured of my own sanity in a simple page. I have been right all along, my fragile mental state has not caused delusion at all, Wendy must read this, I will take this book and use it to prove the power of the ring and win back her heart. Mind you, it may take a little more work than that, given my final *Dangling* performance with Teresa. I sit back into the armchair once again and begin to read the further writings of Private Henry Jackson to the hypnotic tick, tock of the grandfather clock in the hallway.

Again I rouse from sleep, this time with a start as I hear a door slam in the wind. Glancing to my watch I see it's almost three in the afternoon, this is confirmed by the hollow feeling in my stomach that growls as a gentle reminder.

'Ahh, you're back with us,' Bandlaman exclaims as he returns to the room, carrying an oval silver tray upon which sits a tea service and a selection of crustless sandwiches, cut neatly into quarters.

'Where on earth have you been, it seems ages.'

'I had to go to the store to get some tea, it's about an hour and a half's walk each way, and I stopped by a friend's house on the way back. Why, did you run out of books to read?'

'No, I reply somewhat confused, what's in the sandwiches?'

'Oh did you want one as well, sorry.'

'I, er…'

'Just kidding, they're cheese salad, that okay?'

'Yes, fine, thank you.'

Bandlaman rests the tray on a low level table in front of me and pours the drinks.

'So,' he begins, 'how much of this stuff do you already know?'

I burst into an account of all my discoveries over the last year, and the wise man just listens, occasionally sipping from his saucered cup.

'So you seem to be quite a way down, the path of knowledge, and that can be helpful. Although presuppositions are drawn, that's things you pre-suppose by the way, that are not entirely correct me if I'm wrong, but what do you think you thought you knew about the things you weren't so sure that you were clear about now you have come to, listen to my advice?'

'What?'

'Okay, let's see. The knowledge you seek is that of the future, but with all things historical, in order to see the future, we need to look at our past. I have studied the history of the ring like no other, centuries have passed through my hands at the tips of my fingers that touch the pages of the books that I have held, or by the ear that I listen to the mindset and knowledge of the wisest men on the planet. I have learned more in the last two thousand years than you could amass in ten thousand people's lifetimes, so listen dear friend, for what I am about to tell you holds as true today as it did two thousand years ago, at the birth of the ring.

'The great Norse God Odin was the creator, he was born of giants named Borr and Bestla. He helped in shaping the earth from the slain body of Ymir, and created humankind from an Ash and an Elm tree. Odin is depicted as a strong and tall middle-aged man, with a long beard and only one piercing blue eye. His other he sacrificed to the three goddesses of destiny, but we'll get to that in a moment. He often walked in the mortal world observing the ways of men; he would always appear in a blue cloak and a wide brimmed hat, which was pulled down over his face to hide his single eye and therefore his true identity.

'Odin was all knowing and all seeing, and depicted as a leader of the wild hunt. He roamed the countryside with his pack of hounds searching for the souls of men upon his horse Sleipnir, which had eight legs and could ride faster than any mortal horse. It is said, that Odin forfeit one eye in order to free the human world he had created from death and regret. He commissioned a ring to be made by the Greek blacksmith God Hephaestus – after his ejection from Mount Olympus – who had also crafted much of the other magnificent equipment of the gods, being Hermes's winged helmet and sandals, the Aegis breastplate, Aphrodite's famed girdle, Agamemnon's staff of office, and Achilles' failed armour.

'A deal was then struck with the three Norns; the goddesses of destiny. These were named: Urd, meaning fate, Skuld, meaning future and Verdani, meaning present. The three blue gemstones that are set into the ring represent the wisdom of the three goddesses, which can be called upon three times during one's ownership of the ring. These three gemstones were exchanged with Odin for one of his eyes.

'The summoning of the Norns is done, as you know, by the pressing of all three stones together, thereby stopping worldly time to allow a decision to be retracted and thought about, before the reinstatement of the space-time continuum we know on earth as life. The three Norns however, are not allowed to influence you in any way, so an advisor was sought to assist humans in this confusing process, hence Saint Peter appearing to all who call the power of the ring into being. Saint Peter is also known as Shimon, or in Hebrew *"Keipha"* which means stone, so calling the power of the stones means you are calling the power of Saint Peter, follow?'

'Phew! Yeah, I think so. What relevance does the "Daz, Aparip, Aka" text have, that's engraved into the ring.'

'That, Jack, is not engraved. It was forged by Hephaestus to appease the great god Kalki, the tenth avatar of Vishnu, the god of eternity. It's written in Sanskrit, and the literal translation is: *"To change one's destiny."* Therefore, presumably postponing a meeting with Kalki, and the eternity he represents.

'The ring brings with it many examples of the perfect way the universe works, the book you were reading for example, written by a virtually unknown soldier named Henry Jackson shortly after the First World War. As you know, it's about a ring he inherited from another soldier, Thomas Kettle, that lay dying in the hell of a live battlefield during the Battle of the Somme on the 9th of September 1916. This may seem an unremarkable feat in itself, but a monument to Thomas Kettle was erected in St. Stephens' Green in Dublin, Ireland, also in itself a fairly unremarkable feat, until you notice a circular pool opposite, lined by a ring of neat stones, and with a bronze statue placed in the centre. The statue was given to the Irish by the Germans, who ironically killed Thomas Kettle, and it's called the *"Three Fates"* and yes, as you have probably guessed, it depicts our friends, the three Norns that helped in the creation of the ring.

'Also, within the same park in the centre of Dublin we find the great writer and poet James Joyce, also a ring bearer many years ago, so you're in good company, young man. The writer Joyce makes numerous references throughout his work as to the power of destiny and alteration of it, indeed he even created an alter ego by the name of *"Daedalus"* who is in Greek mythology termed as a *cunning worker with many images that appear to move about independently*. Obviously a reference to the clones you are now seeing.

'In mythology, Daedalus has two sons, Icarus and Lapyx. Both of these are speculated to be clones of Daedalus. Icarus was released by his father, Daedalus, on feathered wings, but as the heat of the sun melted the wax with which they were held, he plummeted back down to earth and was killed instantly. This is a metaphor for the killing of a clone, removing a path of fate. The other and more interesting son, or clone, depending on what you believe, Lapyx, was a healer. One to cleanse the body and soul of all whom he met. There is a famous portrait of him in the Museo Archeologico Nazionale in Naples that was originally found in Pompeii around 79AD. It depicts him removing an arrow from, and therefore saving, Aeneas, a Trojan hero. This again seems pretty innocuous until you realise that Aeneas is the son of Aphrodite, former wife of Hephaestus, the blacksmith, you will remember, who was tasked to make the ring of destiny by Odin.

'This also follows on to the work of Joyce. The character portrayed in this work is called *"Odysseus"* or *"Ulysses"* as he was known in Roman myths. Indeed he makes reference in this volume to the Cyclops, dedicating a whole chapter to him, the Cyclops of course being Odin. My favourite Joyce quote from Ulysses is this:

"A man of genius makes no mistakes. His errors are volitional and are the portals of discovery."'

'Woa, woa, woa. Let me get a handle on this, you're going a bit too fast here. The ring was made by Hephaestus, the blacksmith who was married to Aphrodite.'

'Correct.'

'Aphrodite had a son called Aeneas who was saved by Lapyx, who was a clone of Daedalus – Joyce's alter ego.'

'Correct.'

'Lapyx and Icarus were both clones of Daedalus, who as we all know was in fact an earlier incarnation of James Joyce.'

'Kind of, go on.'

'And James Joyce's statue sits in a park with a

bronze of The Three Fates, being the three goddesses of destiny who also helped make the ring.'

'You're getting this, keep going.'

'The bronze of The Three Fates sits opposite a statue of Thomas Kettle who was also a ring bearer and gave the ring to Henry Jackson whose autobiography I was reading when you came in.'

'Got it! Now the plot thickens when we study Joyce's work titled *Ulysses* further, but I won't go into that now. As you mentioned earlier, you know many things already as to the source of wisdom and knowledge that the ring holds you to your decisions previously thought to be where you think you thought you wanted to go, but didn't due to the consequences it unfolds for you to realise it wasn't where you were destined to be anyhow. My favourite quote from the period when King George the Third was in possession of the ring was by Sir William Pitt in 1770 whilst addressing the House of Lords in your English Parliament, he stated;

"There is something behind the throne greater than the king himself."

'Most realise this is a reference to the great Doctor Willis, but few realise just how powerful Willis was in returning sanity to the addled mind of the monarch. The ring has found itself onto many leaders' hands, causing radical changes in destiny and behaviour, a more recent and frankly obvious example is that of Ronald Reagan. How on earth he got away with using the ring so obviously without arousing great suspicion is completely beyond me, let me elaborate a little. Ronald Reagan was no big shot, he inherited the ring from a man who was too scared to use its powers even once. Arnold Wainwright used to own the small corner shop that Reagan visited every week as a teenager for his edition of *Variety* magazine. When Wainwright decided to retire off to the lake at sixty-three years old, he gave Reagan the ring as a good luck charm for the acting career the young man so desperately wanted. In 1937 he got his big break and walked not only onto the silver screen, but into the annals of time. Reagan was at last following his dream, you can follow yours as well, if you just pay attention, I always look to the fifth to take my cues as to where you need to go. Keep schtum and follow the leaders. Don't you just love it when they catch a leader in the headlights and he pleads the fifth? Anyhow, where was I leading you, oh yes, the ring. Reagan then burst into the "B list" movie scene racking up dozens of films, he was living the dream, and almost gave the ring to a girlfriend, thinking life so perfect he'd never have a need for it. But a tiff on the night in question saved his life, twice, although he didn't know it at the time.

'In 1954 whilst filming *Cattle queen of Montana* Reagan plays a hired hand to help rid a ranch of horse thieves, and it's on this set that he accidentally falls from a covered wagon as it races across the plane, plunging down between the horses who trample his legs, smashing them to pieces. He keeps, however, the presence of mind to use the ring and cease time, rewinding it the vital thirty seconds required to ensure a better foothold and prevent him slipping from the moving wagon. As the great comedian destiny is, you can find the poster of this movie clearly displayed in several scenes of the later eighties' film *Back to the future* as Marty McFly tries to reverse the path of altered history by using his persuasive powers on his father George.

'The script for *Back to the Future* was originally written by another former ring bearer Robert Zemeckis, also famed for writing the Harrison Ford movie *What lies beneath,* ironically about a housewife that is haunted by the appearance of ghosts in her own image. Are you seeing a theme here? Anyhow, I digress. Back to Reagan, during the filming of the 1963 classic Hemmingway adaptation *The Killers.* Reagan plays opposite Angie Dickinson. Off set he makes a wisecrack about the alleged affair that she was having with John F. Kennedy, only for a lad to run in moments later with the shocking news of the assassination in Dallas, Texas. Stunned at the insensitivity of his previously innocent comment, Reagan summons the halting of time, to rewind it thirty seconds, and literally eat his own words, intending to replace the irresponsible comment with praise for the great president, but once time is ceased Reagan has an epiphany. He decides to use this advantage of free movement in a stationary world, and formulates what would seem like a wild and crazy plan to turn his career from being a "B list" actor into the most powerful man on the planet, just with a simple change to the beliefs of his own destiny. Immediately he plotted a determined course for the White House. Whilst time stood still, Reagan realised that in the wake of Kennedy's death, anything was possible. He arrived in Washington several days later, transport was difficult due to the world being frozen of course, and marched into the White House in order to get a real feel for the Oval Office, upon which he had firmly set his sights. Once there, he made numerous notes as to the layout and structure, took photographs, copied down telephone numbers of all the people he thought may be influential in helping him rise to the top of the pile and left subtle messages and hints everywhere so as people would be more familiar with his name in the context of the White House, rather than the actor he then was. He even put memos on the computer system to randomly bring up his name on certain days in the future in the offices of key government figures. He walked through the halls, slept in the president's bed and acted as if he were truly president. This week-long role play, although seemingly silly, was what convinced his sub-conscious that it was achievable. Bam! Eighteen years later he's gracing all of our screens again, but this time there's not a cowboy in sight. He's waving on the front lawn after his election victory. Never underestimate the power of suggestion when your unconscious now knows the continued path that's most appropriate for you to follow my words and you'll find the treasure at the end of your nose where to go. Where was I, oh yeah, on the front lawn. Sorry I just kinda slip off occasionally. Dallas, now there's another co-incidence that links these two presidents. John F. Kennedy was shot and killed whilst riding in a motorcade on Elm Street, Dallas, Texas. Ronald Reagan was shot in an assassination attempt by a man called John Hinckley, who purchased his gun from Rocky's Pawn Shop on, you guessed it, Elm Street, Dallas, Texas.

'The attempted assassination of Ronald Reagan, once in office, was the third and final use he had for the powers of the ring. Yea Gods I don't know how the press ever missed this one. Let me tell you a little of what went on that day, March 30th 1981. Here's the outline; Reagan was making a speech in the Washington Hilton, the distance from the door to his armoured limo was about thirty yards, tops, and a group of photographers lined his route. Within those photographers was the assassin called John Hinckley. He fired off, at almost point blank range, six rounds from his revolver, whose bullets were all tipped with a chemical called Lead-azide, which is so volatile it will explode even if dropped six inches to the floor, let alone fired from a gun. How then was it ever explained that Reagan not only survived the shooting, he also was only hit after a bullet ricocheted off of the limo and penetrated his lung just under his armpit, breaking his rib. You will recall that this is the exact same injury sustained by the World War One soldier Henry Jackson you were reading about. The doctor who removed the bullet from Reagan even commented that it still had the paint on it from the car it had hit first. So a gunman manages to miss a human target a few feet away, six times in a row. *Please!*

'What happened in reality though, was a simple case of preparation. Once Reagan had been hit by the first bullet from Hinckley's gun in real time, he again summoned Saint Peter and the three fates to freeze his current situation and allow him the time to think of a solution. It was a dull overcast day, but the sun made an appearance when the group exited the building. This gave Reagan a clue as to how he could deal with the situation, and ingeniously he decided to blind the attacker with the reflection of his watch. The only problem being that he was wearing a quite small formal watch, a larger faced, more casual one sat back at the White House, a gift from his wife. It was one he usually just wore around the house, not to any public occasions due to its informal appearance. Today, however it would be perfect to blind Hinckley with its reflection of the sun for long enough to jump into the armoured limo's safety, dodging the bullet that had in this previous reality already hit him, as he would have thirty seconds "back time" to play with before it was fired, once the continuation of time was re-instated. The other interesting thing Reagan did, was head to the library whilst the world stood still, and looked up what coating the bullets were wearing, and a pacifying liquid mix of ammonium acetate and sodium dichromate was then sourced to reverse the explosive properties of the Lead-azide. Once the neutralisation of the bullets and the exchange of watches was complete, Reagan again re-started time. The rest, as they say, is history. It's interesting to note that he even covers his tracks in a later interview by making humorous comment to the watch his wife Nancy gave him, and apologising as he apparently forgot to duck the last bullet. Watch the footage, with the knowledge you now have, it all makes perfect sense. You can clearly see Reagan wave with his right hand, then lower it and raise his left to cause the reflection that blinds Hinckley. He wore his watch face side down to ensure this was possible, and times it perfectly. He's even smiling as he does this. Who ever said he was a duff actor?'

'Jeez, I never realised so many people were involved in all this, how many know about it now?'

'I've no idea, son, what is of consequence to you though is the information I can give you, what more do you need to know? You obviously came here for a reason.'

'Well, yeah. My life has turned around since the second time I used the ring. I saved Wendy, my fiancée's life, yet she can't see it, she just thinks I'm going mad. My clone had an initially bad time once the clone Wendy was killed, but he seems to have his life back in order and is making more of a success of it than I seem to be. How can I revert back to my unchanged self, to live the life I should be living?'

'Now steady on there, Jack, the life you should be living, you told me, ended over a Moroccan cliff aboard a sightseeing coach. If that's what you want I'll throw you off the damned cliffs outside right now. You have to be more precise about the future you want or you end up in the kind of mess you're currently trying to get out of.'

'I mean that I want to change places with my current clone, he seems to have everything going his way now whilst I'm just falling further down.'

'Okay, you have the tools you need to do all of this, after all your clone is managing it and he *is* just essentially you. All you need to do is replicate what he is doing. You can follow him around and see how he does it, then just copy.'

'I don't think it's really that simple, I've lost my job, and after the debacle on national television two shows in a row, I'll never work in the industry again. Wendy just thinks I've lost my mind, as do most of the people I know. The only person who might understand is Victoria, and last time I saw her she accused me of killing her fiancée because of my greed, so I don't even think she'll give me the time of day.'

'Okay I only see one solution. I'll tell you later.'

'What! tell me now!'

'I can't.'

'Why on earth not?'

'It's time for my massage.'

Frustrated, I exhale deeply, and realise how tense I had become whilst talking with Bandlaman about my immediate problems.

'I'll arrange for the lovely Cassie to come and give you a once over after she's finished with me. I'll be a couple of hours, so make yourself useful and relax. There's a hot tub in your room, a sauna by the swimming pool in the courtyard and a solarium just down the hall from that. John mentioned that you enjoy running, so if that helps you relax then you're welcome to use the castle's grounds.'

'John?' I question, 'who the hell is John, and how does he know I like running?'

'He'll show you around, I believe you've already met.' The thin man from last night's restaurant appears around the ajar door and nods his head with a smile. 'We're dining at eight in the great dining room.' Bandlaman continues, 'I've told housekeeping you'd be staying, so everything is arranged. Tell John where your hotel is and he'll go get your stuff and check you out.'

Bemused, I find myself agreeing to the hospitality of this complete stranger. John leads me through dark windowless bare stone corridors to an elegant room with a four poster bed in the middle of the back wall. Deep burgundy gold and blue fabric adorn the room in the form of sofas, curtains and throws. A tapestry hangs from one wall nearly three metres square, depicting a castle with a gallant knight approaching. I look to the small window, and look out over the cliffs and sea below, exaggerating the altitude of my room. I turn to ask John a question, but he's slipped silently away. Spread on the bed is a robe, a pair of new swimming shorts, one size too small, but they'll do, and a towel. I change quickly, cringing that the shorts are just a little on the tight side, but serve their purpose, then leave the room in search of the pool.

Winding through the maze of corridors and dead ends, I feel like I'm Harry Potter or something, expecting a wizard or toad around every corner. The paintings on the walls give me the creeps, I even imagine the eyes following me as I pass them by. After ten minutes of vacant searching, I find the right combination of stairs corridor and doorway to land me out into the courtyard where the swimming pool lies. I drop my robe and towel onto a wooden lounger and take to the pleasingly warm water. A dozen or so lengths later and I retire from the pool to relax on the lounger a while. After thirty minutes, a session in the solarium seems appropriate, so I head down the corridor in search of my next luxury. Once tanned, I return to the courtyard to find that tea has been served, accompanied by some fresh cream scones. These I enjoy, then slide once again into the pool for a further five lengths before a stint in the sauna. This is again followed by a bob in the pool to cool down, and the rest of the second hour is then spent back on the lounger, in the glorious sunshine.

'Cassie is ready for you in the gymnasium, if you'd like to follow me.' John is stood at my feet, but with the sun behind his head I'm unable to fully make out his face. I sit up a little too quickly and need a moment to reset my brain to vertical mode before standing. I follow the thin, slightly stooped character back into the gloom of the castle, and continue down seemingly unending corridors. The door to the gymnasium lies open at the end of one such hallway, and entering gives me quite a surprise. The room is full of all kinds of modern machinery from treadmills to weights machines and computer controlled cardio cross trainers. An enormous picture window looks out over the sea, offering a spectacular view as the sun's rays glint on the animated surface. I presume we are facing the same direction as my room above. Cassie greets me with a smile, then enquires if any particular part of my anatomy needs attention.

'My brain.' Isn't the answer she's looking for however, so we decide on a general once over with extra attention on the neck and shoulders in order to ease the tension of my recently stressful life. Her hands glide their lightly lubricated way over my lower, mid and upper back, stretching out the muscles in my legs, arms and neck as she goes. The conversation light, polite and interesting.

'So you think there's a real chance you'll be picked for the England women's cycling team for the Olympics then?'

'Well yes, I've done well in all the preliminary tests, and my race results are encouraging this year, so I'm talking with David King who has the final say next Tuesday, it all looks pretty good though. How about you, aren't you something to do with the telly, didn't I seen you hosting a show on Saturday night?'

'Oh God, don't. It was such a mess, I don't know what to do. My girlfriend Wendy won't even speak to me after that, and I lost my job the next day because of it.'

'I'm not entirely surprised on both counts, you were shown to be an untrustworthy unfaithful rotter on national television, in fact we even saw it here in France, so make that *international* television.'

'Are you trying to make me feel better?'

'Your back or your brain?'

'Either.'

'Yes and no.'

'Thanks.' I then go on to explain, without the additional information of the ring, clones and Norse Gods, how I feel I would be better off with Victoria instead of Wendy, hosting a different show and basically living a different life.

'So why don't you just show up on Victoria's doorstep and tell you her how you feel. Surely that's the best way forward, you'll at least know where you stand.'

'That's a very practical approach, I must say. Don't quite know how it would work though, as she thinks I'm responsible for her fiancé's death.'

'You never know, fate's a rather strange beast, sometimes it befriends you when you least expect it. She might be pining for you to make a move without even knowing it herself, what've you got to lose? You appear to be pretty screwed as it is, what's the harm in just *one* more person not talking to you, when you jeopardise your whole life's future happiness by *not* talking to her?'

This takes a while to sink in fully. I wonder at the wisdom of this girl fifteen years my junior and quietly ponder my options. The silence is cathartic, and finishes the session perfectly.

'You may ache a little tomorrow, but just be aware that it's totally normal.'

'My brain or my back?'

'Both if you've spent the day with Doctor Bandlaman and then me.'

I smile at her wit, then rise slowly back to a sitting position.

'Right, do some stretches in the morning, I'll no doubt see you tomorrow at some point, Richard usually keeps me busy three or four days a week. Enjoy dinner, I believe it's roast boar.' I raise my eyebrows at the thought of something new to stimulate my taste buds and head back into the gloomy corridor.

*****

Dinner is an extremely pleasant experience. The wine perfect, the food exceptional and the company stimulating. We sit opposite each other in the middle of a table large enough to seat twenty people comfortably. Bandlaman holds the conversation almost exclusively, asking questions that require only simple answers. I get the feeling he's testing me, trying to fish out information by creating scenarios I respond to non-verbally. He's a smart guy.

'So what I believe you need to do, is eliminate the clone from your life, that way you won't be constantly looking to him for where you think your life might be going in the opposite direction that it should know where to go towards. That way you get to live on your own terms in your own direction. You should always move toward pleasure, not simply away from pain. What you see around you now just reminds you of the pain you are moving away from, not the pleasure you should be seeking now the tools to dig up your true future relies on it. Move house, another town, new job, new friends, shed the image of where you think you ought to be yet cannot go.'

'But I can't, I don't want to move my life around just to appease the clone as it shows me how good it really should be, I want it to *really* be that good.'

'Excellent! If you'd agreed with me I'd have kicked your butt off the battlements of this castle. Right, let's get to work.'

'What do you mean, work?'

'You have to devise a plan.'

'A plan, what for?'

'To kill the clone of course.'

'Kill, *kill* the clone, I can't do that!' Bandlaman looks at the floor and shrugs, 'Okay then, I guess you'll have to just move away, out of the area and out of his life.'

'No, I can't do that either, surely there's another way.'

'What did I tell you when we first met? That we have to learn from history, look at the past to predict the future. Have you listened to anything I've told you, or just sat there for the ride?'

'Of course I've been listening, but I don't get where you're going with this, why do I have to kill the clone?'

'Look at the past, King George the Third was sent into a state of madness and despair when constantly reminded of the consequences of his actions, the clones he saw haunted him as clearly as they would a paranoid schizophrenic. Is that how you want your life to pan out? Locked away and sedated until they take you quietly to your grave. Or would you rather take the role model of Ronald Regan, who gripped the forces of destiny to re-think and re-shape his whole life, laughing no doubt from his armchair in the White House at the occasional clone image that may wander onto his TV set late at night when a *made for television* "B" movie staring his clone, who never made the big time, would flicker onto the screen. No, he made his choices and made them well. You, however, didn't. The path of your altered life has taken you somewhere you'd rather not go, and your clone is reaping the rewards. Naturally you feel angered, jealous and hard done by, but that in itself is just not good enough, you need to rise above the challenge and either beat the clone, or I fear, he may just beat you.'

'So how do I do that?'

'Well, as I see it, you have only two choices, well three if you count running away, but that would disappoint me, and you wouldn't want to disappoint me, believe me. Your first option is to out-do the clone, become more successful, happy and confident than he is, therefore not care a damn what happens in his life. The only reason he has such a hold on your psychology at the moment is because he is beating you. He has the job, the girl, the future. You probably didn't much care about him when he was moping around the house in a state of depression after the clone of Wendy's death, but since falling out of favour with the real Wendy and destroying your job prospects, you're probably feeling somewhat regretful at the current sequence of events, am I right?'

'Yeah, you could say.'

'Right, so if you are going to become better than the clone, you'd better make sure it's a foolproof system, you get the girl, you get the job, and you get the smile all across your wiseass face, and mean it! Or else, if he ever starts to reel back his power, become more successful, happier and simply have more fun than you, you could end up in another downward spiral, so personally, I prefer plan B. Kill him, then he can never come back.'

'But I've never killed anyone before, and also, I can't kill him. Every time I try to touch him, my hands go straight through him, sending a shiver right down my spine.'

Bandlaman smiles, 'You can't touch him, but it doesn't mean that he cannot be touched. If he were, for example, to get into a car, and you glued up all the locks in the car so the catches didn't work, he wouldn't be able to get out. The only parameter that this has, is it cannot have been affected by him in any way, so if he were to move the car six inches forward, then the car he is driving crosses over to his dimension and becomes a clone car, that's a clone car, not a clown car.' Bandlaman smiles, 'So, if you try to glue the locks up on the car once it's moved six inches and therefore into the other dimension, your hands will just pass straight through it. Do you get it?'

'Yeah, I think so. Basically, I cannot touch him, but provided something remains the same in both of our dimensions, I can influence it to interfere with his world, and possibly kill him.'

'You got it, see, it wasn't that hard, was it?' I raise my glass and then continue to discuss the possibilities with my strange, but helpful host.

The following day I rise a little later than expected, having dreamed more vividly than ever before, and after a light brunch I head back towards my homebound ferry.

25. Trampoline

I drag my sports bag over the threshold of my hollow house, kicking a pile of bills from the mat as I do so. My body loose but sore after the deep massage of both my body and brain, followed by a particularly bad crossing. I head to the lounge where I frump down into the sofa for a moment's rest.

A minute or two passes, and the God of coffee must be obeyed, so I open my eyes in preparation to heave myself from the engulfing cushions to head to the kitchen. It's then that I notice a few things missing. Nothing serious like furniture, but pictures, ornaments and just 'stuff'. I wonder if we've been burgled in my absence, but the large black slab of a plasma still engulfs sixty inches of wall space, and the patio windows are still windproof, so I draw the conclusion that maybe Wendy's just had a bit of a tidy up. I mooch into the kitchen and flick the kettle on, it rattles and gurgles its way to boiling point as I stare vacantly from the large window. It's getting dark and slightly overcast, might rain. The kettle clicks off, and a waft of steam passes me by. I'm not quite *with* it today. Holding my hot cup of black stuff, I sit at the kitchen table to see what depressing news the newspaper holds, only to notice an envelope with my name upon it. It's Wendy's handwriting, and I instantly fear it may hold something far more depressing than the headlines.

I peel the envelope open, and draw a deep lung full of courage before opening the letter, it's short and to the point.

Jack, (charming, not even Dear Jack.) *over the past year I have been increasingly concerned about your mental health, and although I have voiced my opinion many times, you still refuse to see a psychiatrist. The humiliation I suffered on your show was mortifying, and just one step too far. You've pushed me over the edge. I fear for my own sanity if we are together a moment longer, so I have to leave. You need help Jack, I suggest you get some. I've changed my mobile number and email address, so do not contact me again, Wendy.* (No love, kisses or anything!)

I go to the lounge and top my coffee up with neat Scotch.

*****

Saturday dawns, I rise with a bleary head. Whilst painfully scraping a week's growth from my face with a blunt razor, I wonder where Wednesday, Thursday and Friday had disappeared to. I have no recollection whatsoever of what has happened for the last few days, other than a great sense of hollowness. I'm sober for the first time since I found the letter, and boy does my head like to remind me of it. I think to find some more alcohol, then recall what Bandlaman said to me about controlling my destiny or letting it control me. I decide to take control, and some bloody strong pain killers. I head back into the spare room and dress. I can hear laughing and frolicking as the clone is having passionate sex with Victoria in my bed, which sends a pang of jealousy straight through my heart. It's time to track down the real Victoria and grasp the destiny I should be living with both hands. First though, I need food.

The fridge swings open with a creak, *'still haven't done that'* flashes through my brain, so I head straight to the garage for some WD-40. A squirt and a swivel later, the fridge door glides open silently. *'Why did it take me six months to do that?'* I wonder. I browse the contents of the fridge, only to find delivery pizza boxes, delivery curry cartons and delivery Chinese dishes sprawled in a mess over the interior. The milk in the door pocket was more closely related to stilton than semi-skimmed, so I gather it all up and chuck the lot out. A blurred ghostly vision then appears of an abundance of fresh food in the now vacant fridge. *'Victoria's influence,'* I think as I close the door and head for the car.

Café One sits on the corner of Weybridge High Street and Baker Street, a great place to sit and watch the world go by. It's also a great place to gather information and overhear the local gossip. I ask around if anybody knows of a girl named Victoria, accompanied by my feeble attempt at a description and the fact that her fiancé was attacked by sharks recently. Blank looks and shrugs is all I seem to illicit though, and I'm beginning to doubt myself again. Maybe Wendy's right, am I going mad? I stop asking questions and take a seat outside after ordering a much needed Full English.

'You might want to take a look at the registry office, they have a list of all the births and deaths there, at least then you'd be able to ascertain his surname and possibly get an address,' a helpful old man comments as he leans towards me from a neighbouring table. 'Of course, thank you. I hadn't thought of that.'

The old guy then takes it upon himself to talk at me for the next thirty minutes whilst I drink my tea and munch through my fried farmyard, telling me of poor mister Gladstone the butcher, who survived the war, only to return and bleed to death after having his testicles bitten off by the Bull Mastiff he kept in the yard behind his shop. Just what I wanted to hear whilst eating sausage I'm sure!

Weybridge registry office is found on the main drag between the town and Walton upon Thames, a Tudor looking building with great presence. I enter the side door as directed and wait at the counter.

'Good morning, sir,' the skinny young clerk appears from a doorway to my right, 'I'm Melvin, and how can I help you today?' Wide-eyed and shocked, I'm speechless as I recognise the dweeb from *Bully Boys* who was pummelled in front of the live audience.

'Er… er… Victoria, no, Richard, I need to find someone called Richard.' The man looks at me curiously, then as a 'Ping!' of recognition enters his brain, he says;

'You're Jack Todd, you humiliated me in front of everyone in the country. My life is ruined, people laugh at me in the street and all the kids jeer and jostle me. My life's been hell since *you* messed it up on telly.'

I turn and leave as fast as humanly possible, I can't believe what's happening. Even real people are haunting me now, what the hell am I to do? I head back to the safety of my car and lock myself in.

*****

Once safely back at home, I sit and think. I scour my brain to remember any snippet of information that might lead me to the front door of the woman I am destined to spend the rest of my life with, but none is apparent. I decide to call Brendan and see what he has to say for himself. No answer, so I head into the kitchen for a brew. Once again I find myself staring out of the window of my neo-Georgian chunk of Surrey paradise into the lead filled sky that clouds both my eyes and my mind. A rush of steam and a click signals that it's time to find a mug, smaller than the one that's staring out of the window.

Again I sit at the heavy-set wooden table and leaf through the bad news that fills the paper. I discard it as nothing remotely uplifting leaps out at me and throw it towards the recycling bin, missing it of course, and sending a flurry of loose black and white leaves fluttering to the ground. Cursing I slide from the chair and begin to scoop them from the floor, scrunching them together with frustrated anger. I flip the lid of the bin, and see inside the ghostly images of a couple of letters. I try to pick them up, but my hand passes straight through them, sending a shudder down my spine. Once recovered, I tilt my head to read the clone's letter, it's from Hess Media Limited.

Dear Jack,

Due to the phenomenal success of the pilot for 'Trampoline,' I am pleased to offer you the following contract, subject of course to the amendments outlined in my letter dated third of July.

For initiation and marketing video shoots comprising of three days filming, the sum of £7,500.00 per day plus expenses.

Initial series of twelve thirty-minute shows, scheduled for prime time airing, for a season commencing Saturday second of August, the sum of £420,000.00. Payable in four instalments over the period to twenty fifth October.

All terms and conditions of contract remain the same as our existing agreement, and I thank you for this opportunity to extend our working relationship, and look forward to a successful season. Please find enclosed a cheque for £45,000.00 as the initial payment. All further payments will be via the usual system of credit transfer.

Regards, Charles Hess.

I glance to my watch to confirm the date, forgetting that Brazilian scumbag had stolen it, invoking a curse. I then check the date on the newspaper, August second, the new show starts tonight! I go to stuff the rest of the newspaper into the bin, then notice a letter beneath that of Charles Hess', it's a credit card statement for a Miss Victoria Freyvia, of Amberley Cottage, York Road Weybridge. Perfect, I'll pay her a visit on my way to the studios this afternoon. Out of the front door, and into the Bee Emm, thumbing the roof switch as I consult my Surrey Street Atlas in order to plot the best path to chez Victoria. The metal framework judders as it takes the cloth lid back over my head, making a slightly odd sound as it goes. *'Must get that checked out properly,'* I think as the motor seems to be straining a little with the last few inches. I sling the car into first, lift the clutch and head out towards my well deserved destiny.

I find York Road easily enough and spot Amberley Cottage opposite the pay and display car park a third of the way down. I pull into a parking slot perfectly placed for surveillance, and sit and wait. I hadn't planned what to do at this point, I just feel that I need to talk to her, persuade her that I'm her perfect and destined partner. Confrontation, that's the best plan, wear my heart squarely on my sleeve and tell her exactly how it is. No beating about the bush.

I hop out of the Beemer and stride purposefully across the road. A car's horn blasts as it swerves violently past me at high speed, sending me reeling as

I'm almost hit. I must think to look next time, as I've only got one chance left. Once on the safety of the pavement, I bend to swing the low gate open that heads the short but heavily weathered herringbone brick path to her house. Halfway down, I jump as the spring loaded gate clatters back into its frame behind me, I'm a nervous wreck. Standing under the tiled canopy I draw two deep breaths, and with eyes closed firmly grasp the tarnished door knocker. One final inhalation before I swing the weighty brass ring back and plunge it twice onto the door.

Silence, she's not in, I know it, or she saw me from the window and is avoiding me, what should I do? Retreat, knock again, run like a coward? My brain begins to race and I decide it's time to leave. I turn and face the closed gate, noticing it's in need of a lick of paint. At that moment, a clunk and glide has the door behind me opens. I turn to see Victoria, framed perfectly in the open doorway, her perfect hair lit by the sunlight flooding in from the classically styled open patio doors in the next room. I'm bereft of words, her face has stolen all sense of self and disabled my brain with its beauty.

'Hi, Jack, what are you doing here?'

'I… I need to talk to you, it's about *us*.'

'What do you mean, *us*, there *is* no *us*.' She looks quizzical, so I clarify;

'Oh but there is, the clones that were born when Richard died have shown me that we were truly meant for each other, we must give it a go for our own sakes, we're perfect for each other, I've seen it.'

'What on earth are you talking about? I thought you and Wendy were perfect for each other, that was until you were unfaithful on national television last week. Is that what this is all about? Am I the next in line to be humiliated? Haven't you done enough to me with your greed Jack, that you think you can come and finish off my life completely, I'm hollow and broken without Richard, and I… I…'

This isn't going to plan, in fact I've made a complete botch of my intentions and she now thinks me a fool, or mad, or both. This is my destiny, here on the doorstep in front of me and I've destroyed it with one conversation. This is my only chance to win the true girl of my dreams and I'm killing the moment as surely as the sharks that killed Richard. There's nowhere to hide, I cannot persuade her after what I have foolishly blurted out. With only one thing for it, I grab the ring and press the stones for the final time.

The familiar feeling of tranquillity is instantly upon us. A wasp captured motionless in mid air between us that I hadn't even noticed before time stood still. I stare longingly into the perfect blue eyes that adorn the face of my beloved. I step closer, and a shot fires through my heart like an incendiary device as I notice the welling up of a tear in the corner of her left eye. Mine also, at the sight of this, well up in sympathy of the hurt I have caused her again. I can put it right, change things back to where they should have been, I'm sure of it. A tear rolls down one of my cheeks, then the other. Before long I have broken down on the floor at the turmoil I have created with my own doing. I shudder, shiver and cry for quite some time, then become aware of a presence beside me. I look up to see the actor Will Smith looking down at me, shaking his head.

'What the hell you doin' down there boy? Getcha self up, dust yo'self down and quit that yakkin, we got a job to do.'

I sit up, bemused at this character I've summoned, wondering why he's here. 'Saint Peter?' I question.

'That's me, I've come to *hitch* you up with this little lady.'

'Ahh, from the movie, now I get it.' Smith then goes over to Victoria and eyes her up, top to toe whilst walking all the way around her, then lifts her delicate summer dress from behind whilst bending down,

'Stop that! Leave her alone,' I implore, 'Remember you're meant to be a bloody saint.'

'Oops, nearly forgot. You been scrabbling around on your ass like that you never gonna get anywhere with this girl anyhow, and mighty fine she is too if you don't mind me saying. What you gonna do now, you only have thirty seconds back time to make this right, so you best make a plan. As the saying goes; *he who fails to plan, plans to fail.* I'd take a note of that one if I was you, you seem to be ignoring it a little too much lately. What the hell was all that stuff in the park anyhow, *damn* you make my job so hard sometimes.'

'So how can I change this, what can I say?'

'*Say*, pah! You already said *way* too much. What we need to do is get your sorry ass out of here before she sees you. You only have three seconds once time re-starts to disappear, the door opens after that and you'll most likely screw it up again if you're stood there looking like a screwball.'

'Screwball, what the hell do you mean?'

'Man, look at you, K. Mart have a sale this weekend?' I look to my attire, a little tired but nothing too shabby. I shrug. Smith shakes his head again.

'Okay, let's get you suited and booted and see how you scrub up. Where's the nearest trendy clothes store round here, and I do *not* mean supermarket, we're talking Kenzo, Hugo Boss, Armani, you know the drill, don't be going cheap on me, Jack.'

'Sure, Will, there's a shop in the High Street called Establishment, they carry all the decent brands, so let's start there.'

'Cool, we'll walk.'

'Walk, but it must be two miles!'

'You in a hurry to fuck it up again, or you gonna trust me? Hell, I'm in no end of trouble with the boss for helping save you with that shark thing, I'll tell you, so don't be giving me no attitude or I'll just ping!' Smith clicks his fingers and looks at me.

'Okay, let's walk. I can't wait to hear what *you've* got to say,' I mumble unenthusiastically. I notice within yards the way he carries himself.

'What's that? The Saint Peter strut,' I jibe.

'No man, it's called confidence. Right now I'm gonna give you your first lesson in charming some twinkles into these fabulous ladies' eyes. You cool with that?'

'Er… yeah, I guess so.'

'So anyway, lesson one, posture my friend, and no, he wasn't a Greek philosopher, it's the way…'

'Yes, yes I know, what about it?'

'The golden thread, my friend, the golden thread. See you walk as if you have lead in your shoes, a weight on your shoulders and you're looking for a nickel on the sidewalk, what kind of a message do you think you is sending out to the babes you meet? I'll tell you, DON'T BOTHER! Man, you look like a retard on day release.' I'm affronted by this comment and snap back immediately.

'I happen to be an extremely successful presenter who has the nation's hearts and minds captivated by my charisma, week in, week out.'

'*Were*?'

'What?'

'You *were* extremely successful, your ass ain't worth shit now, boy, remember, I see everything up there.' I exhale heavily, stooping further forward. I get his point though.

'Right, Jack, were just gonna stop right here, you ain't goin' nowhere stooped like an old man, sharpen it up a little will you.' Smith presses his hand into the small of my back, then sets my shoulders square and tilts my chin up. 'That's better, be proud, fuck, you own this town, right?'

'Right,' I say, just not quite enthusiastically enough to be convincing.

'Man, shall we just start over?'

'No, no. I'm getting this.'

'Right, imagine a steel bar running across the base of your spine, horizontally from hip to hip.'

'Okay.'

'Now attached to the inside of your belly button is a golden thread that goes down to a loop on this steel bar just above your ass, then up through your body and out of the top of your head.'

'Yeah.'

'Now what happens if you misbehave and I yank that sonofabitch chord?'

'I stand to attention.'

'That's right. Now attention is what you ought to be payin' the whole time you's out in public. No way you gonna know who you gonna meet, capische?'

'Yeah, I think so.'

'So you best keep this golden thread with a little tension in it, to keep your head up and your ass and belly in line. Hell man, you be saving a world of trouble later in life anyhow with slipped discs an all, you're surgeon gonna starve when Mr. Smith finished wit' your ass.'

I try the posture, and it feels a little strange to start with, but the more vividly I imagine the thread the easier it gets.

'Next is them eyes, you always looking down at the floor, what you expect to find? Look up, it stimulates the brain you know. You guys down on earth all use your eyes to access different parts of your brain, anyone tries to remember something, where do they look, *up*, usually accompanied with the noise Urrrrr, but even I haven't worked that one out yet. They make a picture of a memory in the sky and that accesses the memory part of their brain, the same thing with imagination, see a group of school kids writing a creative story in a classroom and they all stare at the sky for inspiration, it's how you guys are wired. So if you want to be stimulating to talk to, stop looking at the floor! Right, are we nearly there yet?'

'What kind of a question is that, how old are you?'

'Just checking you were paying attention, 2009 years old if you must know, didn't anyone tell you it's rude to ask?' We walk down Baker Street, past the Grotto pub and on towards the outfitters.

The tall white framed glass doors welcome us into a wealth of style and sophistication, the racks of designer clothes line the walls, each piece clamouring for our attention. Will heads straight for the Hugo Boss section.

'Okay dude, we have here a light cloth, tailored into a perfect summertime piece for attracting the ladies like bees to a sticky ribs barbecue, a deep peat coloured blazer that will set off the black Armani jeans we gonna fit your ass into in just a moment's time. See how it fits.' Will throws the jacket, still on its hanger at me to try. I don the piece, and feel quite at home in it.

'Nah, too loose, gimme it back.'

'But I quite like it actually.'

'Gimme it back, you don't wanna make me come get it now do you?'

'No, quite.' I toss the article back; he catches it in one hand without even looking, then slots it back in the rack.

'Yo, try this.' He tosses another jacket, this time dark grey with an extremely subtle black dogtooth pattern. I roll it over my shoulders and pose.

'Hmm, maybe. There must be something better, oh wait, try this.'

Another airborne jacket comes my way before I've even removed the last one, almost having me drop it to the floor, but I catch it just in time. I swing the cream leather jacket around my shoulders and wait with raised eyebrows for approval.

'Black, yes, white, no. Get a tan, and gimmie it back in the meanwhile.'

I disrobe once again, musing that I've never put so much effort into appearance before.

'Here, try this.' Another leather projectile flies my way, this time calf skin, mid brown and classic three button blazer design.

'Perfect. Jeans?'

We repeat the process with slim fit, boot cut, comfort, button, zip, black and every shade of blue until a pair of indigo Banks button fly straight with light boot tapers is chosen, 34-34 if you must know. A pair of mid brown slip-ons follow; highly polished with gold stitching from the Sweeney stable, and a pair of Pier Cardin socks finish my feet. Now the all important shirt, racks and racks of the bloody things, Will has me in a frenzy trying on all manner of cotton and silk until we decide on three of his favourites; a plain white short-sleeve that I wear, then two long sleeve offerings, one light cream with burgundy embroidery to one side, and across the back of the neck, the other charcoal silk, he couldn't resist the touch, nor will Victoria he assures me. My bag is then stuffed with another pair of jeans, same cut but black, and a pair of matt Boss lace-ups to match the silk shirt.

'Jeez boy, you done twelve hundred pounds. Best ring it up and swipe that card o' yours.'

I look at him quizzically.

'These guys gotta eat, and you just done their store, so best pay up, amigo.'

'But I thought... er...'

'You want the babe right?'

'Yeah, okay. I get where you are coming from.'

'Cool, chip that pin and we outta here'

£1,248.32 later and we're on our way back. The return journey seems harder work, it's mostly uphill for a start, then there's the bags, the depleted muscles from the journey there, the...

'Will you quit that whining, I can hear yo thoughts and it's givin' me a headache.'

318

'You can hear my thoughts, are you serious?' Will raises an eyebrow, 'Shit, better be careful.'

'It's too done late for that, boy, I can tell you,' Will retorts with a smile, then shakes his head yet again.

'So, you got the threads, you got the posture, all you need now is the jive, and I don't mean no wiggle ass dancin' neither. You open your mouth and lord knows what shit you spout all over the place, you gotta keep a check on that tongue of yours, boy.

'Okay, when a girl says she's not lookin', that's exactly what she's doin', though not in your direction. What you gotta do is swivel them eyes of hers around so there ain't no other direction worth lookin' in, you follow?'

'I think so, grab their attention.'

'Grab it, man, you gotta yank their minds so fast in your direction a freight train at full speed seems slow by comparison, but don't be getting' confused, I don't mean brash and obnoxious, just controlled with power, poise and purpose. Show the lady you're independent and fun, yet popular and well liked, especially by other good looking girls, that usually triggers the little switch in their grey stuff that says "hmm, best not let *her* get to him first" and then they all start fighting over you, subtly though, all snide remarks and sideways glances, it's great, believe me. I'm a professional.'

'So let me get this right, in order to win Victoria's heart I have to flirt with other girls?'

'You got it, but only subtle mind, and tell her

they're flirting with you. What you need to do is create a carrot and a stick kind of scenario.'

'Oh *PLEASE!* Don't lecture me on *dangling a carrot*, shit could I tell you a story about that!'

'Best save it for another day, we almost back at Victoria's place.'

'Okay, so what do you suggest I do?'

'In the short term? Get your ass over that hedge into the neighbour's front garden and hide before she opens the door, confrontation is not the way to handle this right now. Just remember the old phrase; slowly, slowly catchy monkey. In the long term, you gotta have a plan, a strategy. Take her out, wine and dine her, but stay cool. She'll know when the time is right, and when it comes, she'll hold your glance for that second too long, squeeze your hand for that moment you didn't expect, and you'll catch her in the reflection of a window watching you for no real reason. That's when you've won the girl of your dreams, short sharp seduction works most of the time, but that's usually where it ends up, short and with sharp tongues at the end. Pace yourself, learn the art of conversation with complete strangers, how to cook, how to sell yourself in the best light. Hell; magic, languages, philosophy, art and all sorts of things to stimulate the mind. But above all, never surrender.'

'That sounds familiar; it was on a flag above a castle…'

'Ahh, Richard, one of my best students. You met I recall, such a colourful character, with a wealth of knowledge to humble an encyclopaedia. A legend, one of the best ring guardians we have ever had. I love Bandlaman and all his quirks, boy does he have his quirks. Right, here we are, throw your bag of goodies in the car, then you need to stand over there, where there's a gap in the dust that's Jack-shaped.' He points at the front door of Amberley Cottage.

I walk down the path, dreading the re-instatement of time, as this will be my last chance to forge my own destiny.

'Any questions before I zip back upstairs and have to explain why I broke the damned rules and helped your ass again?'

I chuckle at the thought of God, Odin, the Three Fates, or whoever's going to dare give Will Smith a hard time, then thank him once again for his help. For the final time, I take a deep breath, and depress the three stones, leaping over the hedge and out of harm's way as I do. A second clone is instantly born as I do this which takes me totally by surprise, I hadn't figured on another one, but it makes perfect sense, I've changed my natural life path once again. This is certainly going to get a little hectic.

I cower in the bushes as I hear my clone tripping over his tongue, just as I had done whilst stood on the doorstep. The real Victoria is also at the door, but looks around briefly before closing it again. I can hear the clone Victoria, (Christ! There's another one of her now, how am I ever going to keep track?) telling my second clone to just leave her alone. The door slams and the dejected clone walks away with the stooped posture I had so recently dissolved. Viewing my form of only moments before I cannot believe the transformation a pep talk and some new clothes can make. I feel on top of the world, whereas the recently born clone looks as if he is carrying it squarely upon his shoulders.

I think I've got off lightly until the owner of the house, whose hedge I am resting in, bursts out of the front door, and in a Dublin accent squawks; 'Get up, you blaggard, off my property before I call the law, tykes like you should get yourselves a job, not lay about on well tended gardens that us folk have to care for, g'wan, git will ya.' With that, she begins to beat me with the broom she's carrying, I pray Victoria doesn't hear the kafuffle and beat a hasty retreat.

Once back in the car park, I notice my clone is battling with the roof mechanism of the car; he's standing on the back seat trying to manually pull the roof shut. I smirk at my alter self struggling, and hop in. The steering wheel feels damp, and after a moment I register it's raining. A thumb to the electric roof button only yields a click as the fuse pops once again. All of a sudden I get the urge to clamber onto the rear seat and tug the hood from its cosy home and into the fresh light of day. Mission aborted, I feel it's time to head home for a re-group and a game plan, but the studios beckon, as I need to see what clone one's new show is all about.

*****

I pull up to the gate and wave at the clipboard Nazi in the plastic bubble hut, but the barrier doesn't rise, I wind down my window and raise my eyebrows to the self important thug in a uniform. He looks at me blankly and motions for me to get out of the car and explain myself. I open the door and rise, almost magically triggering a downpour in the process, I curse at the broken open roof and run around to the door of the plastic guard house.

'I'm Jack Todd, you need to let me in.'

'Er... no sir, I've actually had strict instructions *not* to let you in, so if you wouldn't mind moving your vehicle as you're blocking the way.'

'What the hell are you talking about, man! I've been coming here and performing for the last six years, now open the gate you idiot or I'll get Charles Hess to fire you so fast...'

'It was him who told me not to let you in, sir, so if you wouldn't mind.' He gestures to the cars that have formed a queue behind mine. I shrug, defeated and comment; 'Okay, but with the cars behind me you'll have to open the gate to let me turn around in the yard.'

'As you wish, sir, I'll open the exit gate for you as well then. Might I suggest you put your roof up as well, sir.'

I look at the rain with contempt, then the guard, but manage to hold my tongue. I dash to the car, only realising when I get there it was pointless as I have no cover there either, and start the engine. The interior is soaked, and I've no longer got the bin liners to cover the seats, so squelch as I engage the clutch and pass through the gate.

Predictably, I ignore the guard's instructions and head straight for my parking slot, but am shocked at the illusion I find there. A Lotus Elise sits in the space, with the number plate H.4 ZYS. *'What on earth is Hazy's car doing in my slot, I'll get security to move it. Er... No, on second thoughts, best not.'* Then the ghostly illusion of a metallic black Lamborghini Gallardo pulls into the slot, and my clone steps out with Victoria. I'm stunned as I watch them cuddle and kiss under an umbrella before sprinting to the main building. I sit in the soggy Beemer and try to make sense of it all. Failing miserably, I decide to hide the car under the cover of some trees and head to studio twelve where I'd seen them setting up the stage. Security seems tighter than usual, but having walked the halls of Shepperton for many years, I manage to get into the show undetected.

A blur of confusion invades me, the stage is set as previously for *Dangling the Apple* but my vision jitters and loses focus as it fades to the *Trampoline* set, then back to *Dangling* again, back and forth over and over again. I shake my head and close my eyes for a moment, hoping for clarity. When I reopen them it's just the same. I'm getting a headache; it's like watching a 3d movie without the 3d glasses. Brendan, *the git*, appears just off camera and starts with his usual 'And in on five, four, three...' The bands of the two sets strike up and it just adds to the mayhem in my brain. How can they be running *Dangling* without me I wonder, but this is too easily answered as Hazy bounds onto the stage drinking up the applause. At the same time, my clone also appears on stage, but flies through the air, suspended by a steel cable, bouncing impossibly high off a trampoline that's set into the floor. It's all a bit too showbiz for my liking, and I struggle to see clearly what's really going on. The characters cross and blend into one another as the room begins to swirl and I fear I may pass out at any moment. I need to stop this.

I sit in quiet contemplation, eyes closed, trying to block out the real images of the current reality and focusing only on my clone's voice in his new show *Trampoline*. It seems to be working, the more I concentrate on blocking Hazy out, the clearer the clone and his reality becomes. After a minute or two, Hazy is almost faded to silence. I open my eyes and look up to the spectacular show in front of me.

'Welcome, ladies and gentlemen, to this, the first of the brand new series of *Trampoline!*' The crowd go berserk, and as they do so the clone just laps it up, smiling from ear to ear with a smarmy showing of freshly whitened pearly whites.

'And as this is a brand new show, I thought I'd take just a moment to put the game into context.' A screen then bursts into life behind him as he takes a more subdued stance, dipping his head slightly like a priest about to give a sermon. The lights dim and the screen shows the streets of London, focussing on the tramps, homeless and beggars upon it.

'It was on these streets of London that I first became aware of the plight of the homeless. As the tabloids have recently shown with their harsh pictures and cutting reports of me at my most vulnerable, I was far from my best only a few short months ago. This however changed, once I met those who had far less than I could ever have imagined possible. The homeless community welcomed me into their world one damp night when it had all become too much for me to handle. I was staggering, drunk and aimless, around the arches near Waterloo station and truly had the appearance of a down-and-out. I collapsed from exhaustion and fever, then passed out after being ignored by dozens of commuters who were too busy in their daily routines to see if I needed assistance. When I did regain consciousness, it was after I had been moved to a derelict house that served as a meeting place for some of the homeless in the area. This squat was to be my home and hospital for the next few days, and whilst there, with no medical assistance other than a shared bottle of scotch and the stimulation of conversation and camaraderie, I grew in strength both physically and mentally, more than ever before. The generous people I met there, who survive on less than a tenth of the food that you and I consume or waste, were eager and selfless enough to share what little they had. This isn't a sob story, or a charity call. It is to put into context the contestants we have here this evening, and indeed every week for the entire series. These are not actors, they are not regular people dressed up, but they are the people we ignore, the people we walk past without eye contact and the people we complain about that should get a *"proper job."* They have all volunteered from the streets and shelters of our city to be with us here tonight, and in the coming weeks. Each and every one will prove to you, the viewing public, that they are truly worthy of that *"proper job".*'

A burst of applause and cheers raises the roof, I throw my eyes up and wonder if I really *was* this transparent when on stage. The clone makes a calming motion with his hands and continues, 'I also learnt whilst in this community, of the vast wealth of talent so many of these people have, and the reasons they fell into such desperate times were usually only one step removed from our own lives. Daniel, who actually carried me on his own shoulder to the squat was once a city broker, very successful and enjoying the good life. His wife and three children were killed in a taxi on the way to the airport for a trip to Bermuda. The only reason he was not in the taxi was because he had to nip into the office early that morning and was due to meet them at the airport. The twist of fate that saved his life also destroyed it with one hit. Since then a spiralling depression led him into the hands of bankruptcy and into the cardboard beds that line the streets of London. Ladies and gentlemen, Daniel.'

Again the roof is raised, and a surprisingly confident, well dressed man walks out onto the stage.

'Daniel, please, tell the audience a little about yourself.'

The man then clears his throat and runs through a few scripted lines that he reads from the autocue. I wonder where this is going, but don't need to wait too long. A further two contestants are introduced as Mary and Tom, and they take their places behind a large semi circular podium that dominates the stage. The screen then shows three down-and-outs, walking together on the pavement of a city street. They look filthy and rather unhealthy, unemployable is an understatement. They are the three contestants just a fortnight ago. We are then treated to an edited account of how they came to be dressed the way they are now, by way of a peek into the make-up department, and the makeover these three scruffy characters received.

'So, ladies and gentlemen, as you may have grasped, the object of the show is to transform the lives of people less fortunate than ourselves, and give them the opportunity to rejoin the community we live in.' It's then that I notice the light glint off his Rolex, or more importantly my Rolex. Of course, if he was never mugged by the bandits, he never lost the watch. The shoes look rather familiar as well... 'None of the contestants are coerced; they all make a free will decision to be featured, to ensure that those who are happy in the way they live are left be. All the contestants tonight have skills in certain areas, and these will be unravelled as the game gets under way. Right, let's begin. The first round comprises of twenty quick-fire questions, the winner of this section will join the winners of the next three weeks for the shootout round in four weeks' time where you will all get the chance to play for job opportunity number one, which is as a team co-ordinator at London Zoo, so, hands on buzzers…'

The game sets into motion, and I can't bear to watch my smarmy clone any longer. I head out of the studio, but as I stand, my concentration breaks and the stage reverts to reality, and *Dangling the Apple* with Hazy drawing cheers and adoration from the audience. It's just too much, and I head to the exit as quickly as possible.

When I reach the car, I'm a little disappointed to see the bag with my new clothes in tatters as the rain and wind has pelted it for the last hour. My current clothes had just begun to dry, but are re-soaked once out in the elements again. I head home in silent sodden misery to the prospect of a hot bath and a nice cup of tea.

26. Palatial expectations

With summer as distant a memory as sanity, I face this November morning with a sense of optimism. It's been three months since my pep talk with Will, and I've been heeding his advice. Victoria and I are on politely plutonic terms, but the more time we spend in each other's company, the stronger my feelings for her grow.

I've set aside this Saturday afternoon to escort her to Hampton Court Palace for a walk in the grounds and a wander around the maze. I wonder where it will lead, who knows? Home life has settled into as near normality as can be expected, clone 1 shares the master bedroom with clone Victoria 1, clone 2 still resides in the spare room and I have converted the upstairs study into a bedroom for me; the master of the house, not that you'd know it. Clone Victoria 2 hasn't been seen since clone 2 made a hash of things on her doorstep, and he bitterly regrets the event, as witnessed by his continual depressions and binge drinking. I feel like a kind of in-between. Clone 1 has become the most successful presenter on television, his salary is due to rise next year, but the amount is yet to be finalised. He has the girl, the car – did I not mention the new Lamborghini, and the fake tan to match. He's all that I should be, and *would* be were it not for my meddling with destiny, still, little I can do about that now. Then there's clone 2, a mess. He ballsed it up with the girl, lost his fiancée, lost his job and acquired a thirst for alcohol, anti depressants and a dark bedroom twenty hours of the day. Finally there's me, trying to get the girl, trying to get another job and still trying to fix the sodding roof on the Beemer.

The wall clock in the kitchen tells me it's time to make a move, I thank my lucky stars it's a clear day and reverse the decapitated car out of the garage, knocking a plant pot over in the process but not caring. I collect Victoria from York Road and she's looking breathtaking as ever. The drive to Hampton Court is pleasant, if a little chilly, and the conversation sporadic but comfortable. We walk and relax as we take in the scenery, imagining what it might be like to be king or queen, and I muse that at least one former ring bearer was indeed royalty. I wonder if the time is right to pass the ring on to Victoria. First, I believe an explanation is in order, so I suggest we take afternoon tea in the café.

'Let's get a cup of tea and a slice of cake.'

'Sounds good, Mister Jack,' she's started calling me that by the way, I take it as a term of affection and it makes me glow every time I hear it, 'is there somewhere nearby, or should we head out to the café I know just over the bridge – they do a chocolate sponge to die for, and I'd rather have a hot chocolate on a day like today. Wow, look at those beautiful birds.' With that she points at the vast fan of feathered friends racing across the sky, into the cool heights of the clouds. The sun is falling, and I know that dark will be upon us within an hour or so, I sense the car's heater will be working overtime on the way home.

Victoria and I take an outside table, as the tourists have also fled to the warmer climes that the late birds were heading for, and we sit in quiet contemplation. I'm ever mindful of the mess I had formerly made when trying to speak my mind to Victoria, and with the absolute denial shown by Wendy of the ring and all its powers, I decide a tactful approach is appropriate.

'Victoria, I've known you for a while now, and think that we communicate quite well. I have something to tell you that although on the surface might seem quite extraordinary, yet in reality it's rather straightforward.'

'Okay, what's this all about then. Mister Jack?'

'Well, it's hard to explain, but I'll give it a go; I was given this ring by a dying man, he'd been hit by a car.'

'Oooo, did you know him?'

'No, not at all. He gave me it and said it would change my life, my destiny, and it has, massively.'

'Are you sure? You lost your job, your fiancée, and if you could change destinies surely you could have saved Richard? Or at least fixed the roof on your car.'

'No, it's not that simple, how do I begin to explain…'

'I think it's better that you don't. We've had a pleasant afternoon, so I think we should just keep it that way.'

'But, I... I... I suppose you're right. Lemon sponge or chocolate cake?'

'Chocolate cake.'

I leave it at that, frustrated at not only the missed opportunity, but my inability to take control when times demand it, and my quashed emotions for the girl I love once again. I wanted to give her the world, the power to change her destiny, to really live again, yet all I received was a self-defence mechanism that automatically triggers every time the reassurance of my feelings is even hinted at. I'm frustrated beyond belief.

We spend the return journey in near silence. I reach for the stereo to break the agony of it but the fuse has been previously sacrificed to the God of roof closure, so we sit, listening to the sound of turbulence, both mental and physical.

*****

I pull up outside Victoria's house, and with a peck on the cheek she's gone. I have to double take my vision of the front door as the clone Victoria exits the house and walks down the path towards me. She turns left out of the gate and I watch as she walks towards the main Queens Road, turning at the junction once she gets there. I jab the accelerator and head off in her direction, hoping to follow her inconspicuously, yet jump with fright when a figure running across the road

I hadn't noticed is suddenly upon me. I slam the brakes, but my momentum is too much, yet instead of mowing the man down, I simply glide through him. I shudder and shake in convulsions as it registers I have merely run through my second clone. He, however, crouches in the middle of the road, and is also shivering and convulsing as a second car smashes into him, sending him skywards like a rag doll. I brace myself for the impact, but it doesn't come. The car swerves around me with the screech of tyres, and is gone within seconds. I glance to the rear view mirror, noticing that an instant clone of the offending car sits slewn across the road and the clone driver is now giving my departed alter self some hasty but sadly futile attention. I sit in disbelief as I have caused the death of my clone by simply occupying the same space as him, causing him to stall momentarily in the road, therefore altering his timeline and instigating his demise. My brain races with the consequences and scenarios this leads to and I fear complete mental shutdown. I close my eyes and try to stop for just one minute the whirlwind of emotion and thought that spiral out of control in my over populated mind.

'Jack, Jack! Are you alright?' Victoria is at my side, I had passed out and fallen forwards with my head pressing the horn button on the steering wheel. I rouse and shake my head in an effort to clear it.

'Yeah, fine. Sorry, I…'

'What happened, are you hurt?'

'Yeah, I, er… no.' I feel another dizzy spell

coming, and sensing this Victoria grabs my head, turning it towards her face.

'Stay with me, Jack, we'll get you some help, you've banged your head and it's bleeding.'

'I don't er... neeed... annnyyy...' Boom, blackout.

*****

I wake in daylight amongst unfamiliar surroundings. A pine Welsh dresser dominates the brightly decorated room, a few original oil colours sit on the walls, three portrait, female, two abstract; small but colourful. A dining table and four chairs sit in front of a set of closed French doors that seem vaguely familiar. I can smell bacon.

The sofa I'm upon is slightly too small, and my back makes its complaints at the previous night's choice of bed as immediately as I move.

'Ketchup?' comes the familiar voce from the kitchen as the beautiful Victoria appears in her dressing gown.

'Yeah, perfect,' I respond, hazily.

'You don't have sugar do you?'

'No,' I respond, 'not in my bacon sandwiches.' This raises a titter from the kitchen, and I feel we're off on a somewhat better footing than the one on which we left yesterday. I enjoy being pampered by the girl of my dreams, but force an early closure around 10 a.m. to save seeming reliant. A kiss to my cheek lingers that moment longer than it should, meaning the world to me, so I head off back down the path a new man. After all, I can move back into the spare room now the second clone's history. One down, one to go.

27. Santa's clause

The month of December is always a special time of year; the carol singers, the smiles on everybody's faces at the prospect of a couple of weeks off, and the expectation of a little romance under the mistletoe all help make what should be the gloomiest month, fun and exciting. I head into Kingston town centre to find that perfect something for that slightly elusive somebody. I mooch from shop to shop after battling with the endless stream of traffic, a brace of daglo coated Eastern European parking attendants who are yet to grasp the English language and the driving rain that pelts me from a forty-five degree angle. In desperation of the ongoing hood problem, I purchased a hard-top conversion for the Beemer on eBay, although I feel the bargain price might have reflected the colour that I forgot to check whilst happily bidding away; I didn't wonder why the seller neglected to put a photograph on the advert until a metalflake emerald green hood arrived with white and yellow speed stripes over the top. Still, it goes with the mid blue quite well – when it's dark.

A nose around Links of London has me contemplating a silver pendant with a subtle but not insubstantial diamond set in the centre, hung from a white gold chain. The piece is just under six hundred pounds, maybe a little excessive I think, but I keep it in mind. Next is Karen Millen, a look at the dresses is greatly stimulating for the mind, as I fantasise what they will look like sprawled on my bedroom floor whilst I look over Victoria's bare shoulder, but again I resist. Clothes are just too easy to get wrong and the cop-out of gift vouchers should be reserved for those with a blue rinse who are so out of touch with the youth of today they think tank tops are still fashionable. What next, gadgets are pure boys' stuff, household items a little condescending and furniture just awkward. After four hours battling with the last minute shoppers I return to the car, at least the roof's easy to spot in a packed car park. The machine robs me of a fiver, and I sit in the sea of red brake lights, waiting for the opportunity to breathe fresh air once again.

*****

I arrive home around five, and commence the ritual of dinner making. Beef Stroganoff, brown rice with a dash of cinnamon and a side of broccoli, followed by raspberry infused Crème Brûlé and fresh coffee. Despite living on my own (ish, if you don't count the clones) one mustn't let standards slip, especially when it comes to diet. I take my plate and wander into the dining room, the clone has left a mass of ghostly paperwork on the table and I sit to eat whilst nosing through his correspondence. Apart from a rather horrific servicing bill for the Lambo, the only other piece that's of interest is a confirmation letter from our friend Mr. Hobbs at Sunset Travel, confirming four tickets for a flight to Recife, then on to Shambhala

Island Resort, scheduled for departure at a rather civilised 9 p.m. on the fifteenth of January. An envelope I'm unable to move partially obscures the passengers' names, but I presume that two would be himself and Victoria, but remain at a loss as to who else he's taking. I decide there and then what my Christmas gift will be to my Victoria, the real Victoria, a ticket back to finish the holiday we all started nearly a year ago. After a further exploration of the papers I also see a photocopied article from *The Sunday Times* newspaper, whose subject matter is of all things, ballooning:

One of the most famed cluster balloonists is Larry Walters, who, it's reported, in 1982, attached 42 weather balloons to a garden chair, cut the rope that tethered him to the ground, and shot into the sky. Having intended to rise just a few hundred feet, he rose to a dizzying height of nearly 3 miles into the air with only a pellet gun to assist in his descent.

Although cluster ballooning was around long before Mr. Walters brought it to the attention of the world, his amazing feat captured the public imagination and helped to raise the sport's public profile.

Today, it is widely recognised that the highest altitude achieved via cluster ballooning is that of a Brazilian Roman Catholic priest called Adelir Antonio de Carli. Who in the village square of his home town,

339

decided to see how close to God he could truly get, suspending himself by 1000 balloons. Once the tethering chord was released, he launched into the sky at tremendous velocity, with the spectators losing sight of him after only a few moments when he floated out above the ocean.

He was then missing for several days, eventually his body was found by an offshore oil rig support vessel on 5th July 2008. Carli, it is reported, at one point reached the record breaking height of 6,000 metres before he lost radio contact with the coast guard, and no doubt soon made quite firm contact with the God he so keenly wished to meet. His altitude may have indeed been the world record for cluster ballooning, but for this privilege, he paid the ultimate price. His life.

What the hell is my clone up to, I wonder. Cluster ballooning in Shambhala? Surely not.

*****

The following morning, I nose the car into a rather tight corner of the grotty car park's upper level, wincing at the aroma of stale piss as I exit the car and head into the town centre. Sunset Travel looks somewhat unlit, sending a pang of worry through my brain, waking it from its idle state of motor neuron inaction instantly. I go to the door and peer in, closed. It's only when I step back slightly that I see a small notice on the glass informing me of the later opening time on Mondays of 10 a.m. Relieved, I head to the closest *'Star spangled megabucks'* for a double choccy latte mocha thingy without the whipped cream or the flake, costing the equivalent weekly allowance, both monetarily and calorifically, for an average family of four in the Western world. Talking of world, I watch it slowly drift by with hopes, dreams and stuffed bags of Christmas cheer, whilst the ones on the receiving end of the counters, I'm sure, are just beginning to crave their next fag break.

Ten o'clock rolls around soon enough, and I see the familiar cheery face of Mister Hobbs approaching his shop, sidetracking momentarily for a bag of something from the bakers en route, or should that be en croute, no, never mind.

I allow the travel agent a few moments to settle in, and with the staccato flicker of the warming tubes, a welcoming flood of light extends from the poster filled windows.

'Good morning, sir, and how can I be of assistance to you today?' chirps a cheery Mr. Hobbs.

'Yes, fine thanks. Listen, a while ago you arranged a trip for us to Brazil, Recife to be precise, and then on to an island resort called Shambhala.'

'Rrriiigght,' he looks at me a certain amount of caution, probably anticipating a complaint.

'Whilst we were there, some of us were killed, so I'd like to book the same sort of thing again please.'

'Rrriiigght, which bit specifically do you want to book again then, sir?'

'Shambhala, where they got killed.'

'Rrriiigght.' His eyes narrow and his demeanour changes significantly, I sense his hand creeping closer to the telephone, or maybe it's my imagination, so I decide to clarify my intentions a little.

'Sorry, please don't get me wrong. I meant to say, that a couple we met there suffered a bereavement as he got eaten by sharks, but she escaped unhurt so I'm taking her back there again.' He still looks worried. 'To finish the holiday I mean, not to feed her to the sharks,' I joke, but he still looks unconvinced. I get the feeling Mr. Hobbs will be dialling the boys in blue once I leave and have them digging up my patio before lunch time, but I ignore his wariness and prompt him into action.

'So, Shambhala Island, for two, departing for Recife at 9 p.m. on the fifteenth of January sounds good, what have you got around that?' Mr. Hobbs then jabs a few keys, stimulating the panoramic screen into life that occupies most of his desk, then searches his database for available flights.

'Gosh, Look at that! 9 p.m. on the fifteenth is available, with the connecting helicopter flight from the Hotel Paradisio in Recife, where you receive complimentary refreshments before continuing to the island. Will it be a beach pavilion for two then, sir?'

Crikey! I hadn't thought of that, the accommodation is all for lovers and honeymooners, single bedroom pavilions with large double beds. It may seem a little presumptuous if a double bed is presented to Victoria on what is supposed to begin a 'plutonic' holiday (although I *will* do my best for it to end a little more romantically). 'Do you have any with two bedrooms, or a twin room instead of a double?'

A prolonged jabbing of keys and a selection of random eye and lip movements from Mr. Hobbs's face yields nothing of interest.

'Sorry, sir, it appears to just be a romantic escape, so doubles is all they have. You could rent two pavilions, which would be a solution, sir.'

'And how much extra would that be then?' I hesitantly question.

'A surcharge of just eighteen hundred pounds according to their web site, sir.'

'Eighteen what, are you kidding, I want to sleep in it, not buy it.'

'Oops, sorry sir, that's off season. Two thousand three hundred.'

I gulp. 'So the total for one week, with two pavilions iiiis?'

Tap, tap, tap the small plastic calculator goes, I fear the tiny l.e.d. screen he's working on may run out of room with the number of jabs the keys are getting.

'Four thousand eight hundred and twenty-seven pounds.'

'Blimey.'

'Plus the two thousand three hundred pound surcharge makes it, seven thousand one hundred and twenty-seven pounds, *sir*.' He's enjoying watching me squirm, I can tell. 'For just the week?' I question with an upward inflection to my tone and raised eyebrows.

'Yes sir, for the *whole* week.' My stomach turns as I hand him my multi numbered plastic rectangle, and wince when he swipes the card, as if he's cutting my very flesh with Sweeney Todd's razor.

The wait for an authorisation number seems to take forever, I pray I won't give him the satisfaction of returning the card with a DECLINED chit to keep it company in my ever depleting wallet. Being unemployed has its advantages, but they certainly aren't monetary. The little electronic miracle worker chugs out a receipt and I thank Mr. Hobbs for his help, he returns a smarmy smile and I leave, dumbfounded at what I have just done. Seven grand on a Christmas present for a girl who I hardly know, and I was thinking six hundred quid for a pendant was excessive only twenty-four hours ago. Maybe I *should* go and see a doctor; it'd be a lot cheaper.

*****

The days tick by as the anticipation builds, I can't wait until Christmas to present my future angel with her somewhat excessive present, and she calls me a week before the big day to invite me carol singing on the twenty-third. How could I possibly refuse? My clone is also moving out this weekend as he's bought a larger house in a posh private road with the clone Victoria, so I take this as a positive omen and watch in silence as he organises the big move. I'm also thrilled that I will be able to enjoy the house alone with the real Victoria after our romantic, sorry, *plutonic* trip to

Shambhala, and wonder what she will do with her house in York Road once we return. Let it I suppose, people are always looking for renters in this area. I mull this over with quiet confidence. After all, if my clone is an alter version of me, he must contain all of my chemistry, character and behaviours. So, Victoria's clone must be an alter self of her, and therefore should also contain all of her chemistry, character and behaviours. Following this logic, if Victoria's clone self can fall in love with *my* clone self, surely the *real* Victoria can fall in love with the *real* me. I just need to find the right combination of words and actions, then put them into the right order. I decide the best way to do this is to model my clone, do what he does, say what he says, and ultimately mimic his success.

Tuesday the twenty-third of December rolls around faster than I could have possibly imagined, I'm standing on Victoria's doorstep with a modest Christmas card and the tickets to our destiny that lie within. I'm really nervous and find my palms uncomfortably sweaty, clenched inside my jacket pockets. It's drizzling lightly, and like every year there's more chance of a torrential downpour than snow. The door swings open and there she stands, like a true Christmas angel, although thankfully not sat upon the traditional tree.

'Hi, Jack, come in, I won't be a minute.' She disappears back upstairs for a moment and I make myself comfortable on the sofa, looking fondly at the simple rustic décor. A few items are truly girly, the odd splash of Laura Ashley rears its head, but most of the surroundings are more traditional farmhouse, the stripped pine dining table and dark green enamelled Aga stove that emanates a warming glow from the wooden topped kitchen. I notice an original three quarter view portrait of her in oils on the far wall, half life sized and somewhat obscured by the Welsh dresser that sits on the adjacent wall. I stand to take a closer look, but my flow is interrupted by the sound of her descending the stairs once again.

'Right, Jack, we're due at Saint Charles' by six, so we'd better get going, have you got an umbrella? It looks absolutely horrid out there, God! I could do with a holiday.'

'Yes, I've got a holid, er... I mean umbrella in the car, from golf. Enormous it is, should do the pair of us fine. Best wear a coat though.'

We leave by the front door, though noticing as we do, the cute diamond shaped leaded light window set within it, from which hangs a full and welcoming holly wreath. A short sprint to the car, as the drizzle has now evolved into a thunderstorm, and we sit with steamed windows in the dark.

'Victoria, I know it's a day or so early, but I have a little something for you.' I hold out the card, and she looks at me with those 'Stop a herd of charging wildebeest with one blink' eyes and says;

'Oh thank you, Jack, that's so kind.' Then kisses me, almost on the cheek, our lips overlapping by a tiny but incredibly important ten millimetres. I'm now officially in another stratosphere of ecstasy, and she hasn't even commented on the bizarre coloured roof yet.

We arrive at the church after ten minutes of driving rain, and sprint to the foyer, where Father Andrew welcomes us with the news of a rain check, as if we needed it confirming. I look deep into the most perfect pair of baby blues imaginable and suggest we spend the rest of the now postponed evening in a local French restaurant I know, down by the river. I sell it to her with the promise of fresh produce in delicious home cooked sauces and the perfect warming atmosphere of candlelit tables that overlook the Thames, failing to mention of course that the restaurant was in fact ten miles up the road in Putney, but she agrees on the spot and we set our sights for the bright lights of London.

The conversation remains light yet engaging, the subject matter, as ever, enthralling. We dine on rack of lamb for two, perfectly pinked, with potatoes Dauphinoise, yet it's not until we are sat back in the car with a bottle of Merlot seeping slowly into our veins that she opens the card.

'My God, Jack, what's this?'

'I, er… thought with your er…' Christ I sound like a stammering fool, 'I thought it would be good to get away, both of us, in separate bedrooms of course, and what better place than where we met, don't you agree?' She looks confused, her lower lip scrunches up to her upper as a myriad of thoughts fire across her cerebral cortex. A moment passes, although it seems like a year, and she responds;

'Yeah, why not. I have such bad memories of that place, wouldn't it be great to replace them with good ones, let's do it! Let's go and have a laugh, Mister Jack.'

The relief that floods my body is unimaginable, I want to grab her and hold her forever, to let her know that from now on she will always be safe, that everything will turn out just fine and that I will truly be there till the end of time for her. But of course, being the mature well adjusted male that I am, simply reply 'Cool, I'll confirm the booking tomorrow and we're on our way.' Little does she know it's already booked and paid for in full, but best not spoil the moment.

I then suggest the option of a nightcap at a gentleman's club I know just up the road, (no, no, no. Not *that* kind of gentleman's club, the type with a roaring open fire, walls spread with an abundance of bookcases and a butler called Jeeves.) but the evening seems perfect without further stimulation so we head home by eleven. I find myself surrounded by a glow of superhuman positivity, till my head hits the pillow and my vision fades to black, engulfing me in a deep state of sporadically dream-filled sleep sometime after midnight.

*****

Santa comes and goes, leaving little but a full

colour credit card statement and an empty house littered with spiky brown pine needles. I look forward to January with eager anticipation, and Victoria joins me for the New Year celebrations. We decide upon a St. Trinnians party, which has my friend Joe's house bursting at the seams with over two hundred aptly attired twenty and thirty somethings, cavorting in a blend of stretched old school attire and fishnet stockings. I remain relatively sober and behave myself for the whole evening, shocking I know, but I'm just so excited about our holiday I daren't mess it up with a misplaced advance or suggestive comment, something which I'm apparently quite prone to whilst under the affluence of inkerhol. I drop her home around one and receive a swift peck on the cheek, I watch her sway slightly as she heads up the path, giving me a little wave that ignites my heart before disappearing behind the door.

The next fourteen days drag by, each taking at least fifty hours I'm sure. The clone has moved out as predicted, and taken his exotic Italian sports car with him, he's even bought Victoria a new Merc convertible as a run-around. Life appears to be returning to somewhere approaching normal, I'm still unemployed, single and stressed, but that's a whole lot better than where I was a month ago.

Before I know it, I'm packed and dragging my suitcase off the bed, heading for Victoria's house late afternoon on the fifteenth of January. I've never looked forward to a trip away as much as I do today.

Right here, right now, I'm already in paradise and I haven't even left my postcode yet.

I arrive at Amberley Cottage moments latter and Victoria answers the door with a beaming smile, throwing her arms around me exclaiming her absolute joy at our imminent adventure. *'Worth every penny,'* I think to myself as we load the car and head out towards Heathrow.

28. Déjà vu

After checking in at the British Airways desk, the pair of us cruise through the excessive airport security and head airside. The usual temptations abound, thirty quid on a ticket to win a Ferrari, some new aftershave and a Hugo Boss shirt fulfil the boredom quota, Victoria chooses a cream cashmere cardigan and some perfume which is accompanied by a host of complimentary bathing products. I stick my nose into Waterstones as the plane is delayed an hour and mooch around the shelves to find something interesting. *Prank!* by a chap called Hag Hughes finds its way into my hand, a comedy about a couple of lads trying to get rid of Robert DeNiro's corpse; seems like fun, so I join the queue for the till. Victoria joins me as I near the bleeping check-out, and hands me *The Love Machine* by Jacqueline Susann, then goes on to give me the rundown:

'It's about a chap called Robin Stone, famous in the American television network, and all the raunchy goings on backstage, along with the riotous parties and many girlfriends he's had.'

I'm quite taken aback at the overtly sexual nature of her choice, after all she seems quite prim and proper from the outside, and the fact it has a direct link to my (yes alright, *former*) job. Maybe I'll be pleasantly surprised later on, if things fall as perfectly into place as I plan. After a couple of blips and a pin number our books are thrust into a bag by the disinterested and multi studded assistant. As I turn though, the breath is literally taken from my lungs. I almost bump straight into my clone, brushing my arm through his body, and sending a wave of shudders through me. Hazy's clone then follows, walking straight through me as he makes his way up to the counter.

'Jack, Jack! Are you alright Jack?' Victoria stands before me with a furrowed brow of concern, she's holding my arm and I'm in a light daze, the room sounds echoey and I feel I need for a moment to recover.

'Yeah, fine,' I lie, 'let's sit down over there.' I regain my composure and head to the lines of coffee stained blue sofas that rest uniformly in front of the departure screens.

'I'll get us some drinks, coffee?' Victoria enquires.

'Er... yeah. Mocha without cream and a bottle of water please'

'Croissants?'

'Great.' I smile, she disappears into the crowd and I set my beady eye looking for Hazy and my clone, wondering what they're up to. I stand to survey the area properly, but I'm unable to see them. Victoria returns after twenty minutes bearing drinks, and after half an hour of further waiting, the departure gate flashes onto the screen. We walk the equivalent of half a marathon to the exit lounge, I spot the clones sitting near a vending machine, predictably wearing a hand scrawled 'out of order' notice, taped crookedly to the still illuminated full colour front that depicts a burst of ice cold refreshment exploding into the mouth of a waiting teenager, who probably choked on it moments after the shutter had been depressed. My clone sits with Victoria's, Hazy's sits with the clone of a girl I know called Tess, whom I recognise from the special effects department at the studios. I sit and silently wonder how many more clones there are out there in the world, with both my changing of destinies that has created them and those that have used the ring before me. They call the first few rows and the queue forms quickly, I've never understood why people are in such a hurry to board a pre-allocated seat flight. We sit in the comparative luxury of the sofas until our section is called, then we rise, noting that the clones do likewise. I allow them a little distance before joining the line, then follow them down onto the plane.

'Seats thirty-five D and E, enjoy your flight with us this evening.' We take our stubs and head to the mid section of the plane, stopping in my tracks though when I see my clone sat in my seat.

'We can't occupy the same space,' I mutter, a little too loudly.

'What are you talking about, Jack?'

'Er... nothing. Just thinking out loud.' My brain races, searching for a solution that I seem sadly bereft of. If I simply swap seats with Victoria, I'll have a somewhat reduced shuddering sensation, but it will be constant for the whole flight, let alone any incidental contact with my clone. There's nothing for it, we'll have to be moved. Suddenly it hits me, I continue past aisle thirty-five and head back to the wing seats that boast more legroom. Victoria, confused asks; 'Jack, what on earth are you up to, our seats are back there.'

'I need a little space, my hip is playing up and I need to be able to stretch my legs out to alleviate the pain. Couldn't possibly sit on a plane for eleven hours without stretching my legs, so I thought we'd swap with these people in the wing seats next to the emergency exit, what do you think?'

'Why didn't you book these seats at check-in then, Jack?'

'Oops, didn't think to, sorry.' We arrive at the exit seats, and they are occupied by a couple who seem set for the flight.

'Hi, my name is Jack, and this is Victoria. We're booked onto this flight in aisle thirty-five, but I've got a rather bad hip that needs a little extra legroom, so we'd really like to swap seats with you, is that okay?'

'Not really, we booked these seats especially.' The sour faced woman with a Brummie accent answers. 'Go and find somebody else to swap with, these are taken.'

'I'll give you a hundred quid…'
'No.'
'Two hundred?'
'No.'
'Two fifty?'
'No.'

354

'Oh come on, you're being unreasonable.'

'We're not bloody moving so piss off.' That told me.

'Come on, Jack, let's just sit down and see how your hip is a little later on. People are staring and I'm getting embarrassed.'

'No, love, I need these seats.'

'Don't *love* me, Jack, I'll be over there, in our *correct* seats.' With that she turns and leaves. The sour faced woman pulls an even worse look as she scrunches her features at me. I return with a sarcastic smile and head across the body of the plane to tempt the passengers on the other side. This time I have a little more success, and we agree on three hundred and seventy-five pounds for a pair of extra leg room wing sided exit seats. Phew! Victoria joins me, and I'm glad of the resolution to a potentially catastrophic problem.

*****

We arrive in Recife mid morning, taking a cab to the familiar Hotel Paradisio where Naboo greets us once again. Our luggage is taken from the taxi and loaded straight onto the golf buggy that whisks us round to the helicopter pad, upon which sits our transport to the island. We manage to get loaded and airborne just as the clones arrive to climb aboard their clone chopper, that sits waiting for them in the same space vacated by us just moments earlier. Timing, it appears, is of the essence. We remain one step ahead of the clones for the remainder of the journey, and once we arrive safely at the resort, we are, as before, greeted by the florally attired Emma, Robert and Peter, along with a kiss to the hands from Bounty, the little girl, with her usual gift of flowers to both of us.

Across the wooden walkway, and once again I drink in the absolute splendour of what surrounds us, as we arrive in the bar next to the pool for our welcoming glass of Champagne.

'I'd forgotten quite how beautiful paradise can be.' I mention to Victoria, although I'm not sure from her expression if she's entirely comfortable with my decision to return to the scene of her fiancé's death. I choose a seat next to a speaker that gently pours the sound of steel drums from it, a place where I would never normally sit due to my ears' acute sensitivity to noise and the irritation this might cause. I find myself making decisions now that I wouldn't usually make, ensuring my distance from the clones. Sure enough, five minutes later the clones arrive, laughing and joking animatedly, a contrast to our subdued conversation, and they take a seat at the large round table near the bar.

'Are you okay, Jack? You seem lost in your own little world.'

'Yes, sorry, I'm fine. Just tired from the flight I guess. What do you fancy for dinner?'

'We could eat at the restaurant on the beach tonight, it was so beautiful there last time we were here.'

'Perfect, I doubt we need to book a table, but I'll

ask when we're shown to our rooms.'

A white and blue floral shirted man then approaches, and we follow Peter out to our beach-front pavilions, numbers nine and ten.

We arrange to meet for dinner in an hour, so retire to tend to our post travel needs. A shower and a shave has me bright as a brass button, and I wait on the front deck for Victoria to appear. Whilst sat there, enjoying both the warmth of our surroundings and the strange buzzy and croaking noises emanating from the jungle behind us, I see the clones approaching. My clone and Victoria's enter pavilion nine where the real Victoria is, as Hazy and Tess climb the short stairs to number ten, right where I'm sitting. They disappear into the building, as I see Victoria exit her pavilion onto the deck, then down the stairs to the path. We walk in the moonlight to the restaurant, and enjoy a candlelit supper to the soundtrack of lapping waves and whispered music. She looks absolutely perfect, framed by the dancing glow of candlelight that illuminates her face to the backdrop of the inky blue ocean, a simple dress showing her sun deprived shoulders for the first time since September.

'It's strange, Jack, but shortly after you left me to get ready, I felt this great chill that shivered right through me to my bones.' I contemplate the comment for a moment before answering in a non committal, 'Probably just got a bit of a chill from the air-conditioning in the plane, you'll be fine after a good night's sleep.'

'I hope so, it's probably nothing.'

We finish our meal and amble slowly back, bumping into each other occasionally. I manage somehow to resist the incredibly strong urge to thread my arm around her waist, and we peck cheeks, both left and right, before returning to our individual residences for the night.

I sit in the lounge, idly flicking through the brochure, whose contents I already know from my last visit, and think to retire, but the day seems unfinished, and I cannot resist a quick dip in the infinity edged pool that punctuates the front deck of my residence. It's here, whilst relaxing under the stars, that I hear my clone and Hazy discussing something that tweaks the curiosity switch in my mind, a plan, or so it seems. They sit on the deck of Victoria's pavilion and run through the logistics, of what appears to be, abducting two cows. I shake my head and put it down to a bit too much beer and a tired head. I withdraw from the plunge pool and head inside to the warmth of my waiting bed.

*****

A burst of sunlight penetrates the room as I'm rudely awoken by the squawking of a parrot that's perched in the frame of the window I'd neglected to close last night. The turquoise and yellow bugger flaps and creates as I shoo it from the room, leaving feathers floating slowly to the ground in its wake. Boy what a surreal start to what will probably be an equally surreal day in paradise. I go for an early stroll along the beach, mindful of bandits this time, and Victoria wakes around nine. We agree to enjoy a lazy day by the pool, and head over there after sharing a room service breakfast.

Mid morning sees the clones joining us at the pool, but the boys stay for only a moment, before heading off, out of sight for the rest of the day and leaving the girls to bronze their bodies in the tropical sunshine. The afternoon passes pleasantly, and although Victoria and I are getting on extremely well, intimacy is not really in the frame for the moment. To try and enhance the mood, I order a surprise candlelit dinner for us on the beach, taking inspiration from the thought of Jack Vettriano's painting 'Elegy for The Dead Admiral' that depicts a butler serving wine to a lone formally dressed woman, sat at a table on the beach, to the background of two violinists in black tie. The table is fully set with the best silverware, in preparation for a three course meal, and seems strangely apt as I am indeed taking a widow for dinner on the beach. The staff are more than obliging as they set out a table and chairs on the firmer part of the sand, and serve us roasted Cantonese duck in plumb sauce over jasmine rice and crunchy vegetables under the myriad of stars that illuminate the sky. Nowhere else on earth could possibly be more romantic.

With our food devoured and the infusion of a couple of glasses of wine, the conversation leads to our futures, Victoria admits to a feeling of great loss at Richard's demise, but feels ready to move on; it's been nearly a year and it's what he would have wanted. I re-tread the steps that led to the breakdown of my relationship with Wendy, (whilst being rather selective about the fact she thought I'd gone mad) and confirm to Victoria that it's indeed time for me to move on as well. We chink glasses to new beginnings and drink in the beauty of the moment.

'Are you all finished there sir, madam?' *Perfect timing pal* I thought, thankfully not out loud.

'Yes, thank you it was wonderful.'

'Would you like to look at the desert menu?' At this point I would do anything to get rid of the waiter, so I say:

'No, thanks, that'll be all.'

Instantly I think that I should have at least consulted my dining partner, but she seems un-fussed by it all and stifles a yawn.

'I must go to bed, Jack, all this sun has worn me out.'

'Me too, might I escort madam to her pavilion?' I josh.

'That would be wonderful, kind sir,' she replies, and we walk up the beach together, slipping her hand into mine as we go. The closer the pavilion becomes, the harder my heart begins to beat, until I fear for a herd of stampeding elephants who mistake it for jungle drums. We reach the base of the steps to her lodgings, and she turns to kiss me, on the lips, for at least two long seconds. Nothing overly passionate, but enough to send the right signal; catapulting a lightning bolt straight through my heart. Almost dizzy with delight I smile as we lock eyes and I wish her a good night's sleep. She fails to invite me inside, so I take my cue to leave and head back next door.

After twenty minutes of tossing and turning, I decide it's too hot to sleep. I wander out onto the deck and plunge into the small infinity pool that sends steam into the evening air. I dip my head under the water for refreshment, and once above the surface again, I hear a conversation nearby. My clone and Hazy's are talking with great enthusiasm about some imminent adventure they're plotting. I clear my ears but still struggle to hear with any clarity as they are on the next deck. Try as I might, I can't quite hear their conversation, and wonder what on earth the boys are up to. I realise that although I can see them, they cannot see me, so I'm free to walk around them undetected. I decide to towel myself off and head over to eavesdrop their conversation.

The pair of them sit at a rectangular wooden table that lies between the plunge pool on Victoria's deck and the patio doors. The doors are closed and the clones have their backs to the pavilion, so I walk around behind them to see what's going on. They have, sprawled out on the table, a map of the island, folded to show the section of coastline local to us. There are red lines drawn upon the map all over the place, one from an area of what looks like wasteland, over a road and down to a beach. One from a point in the ocean back to a cove, several out to sea, and the resort where we currently are is also circled. There sits, in the middle of the ocean a large cross with a circle around it, then either side of this, probably two or so miles away in opposite directions, a further two crosses; slightly smaller with large circles around them that overlap at the point where they meet the large cross. I also note a pair of black hand-held devices on the table that look vaguely familiar. I stand in the shadows, leaning against the wall of the pavilion to observe.

'Right, so with Victoria and Tess heading safely for the cove, after they've helped you in the field,' my clone continues, 'you will meet me here, at the dive site, once you have finished placing the cows.'

'Right, so will you have begun to sort the weather balloons by then, or will you be waiting for me?'

'Cows, weather balloons,' I think, *'what the hell are they planning?'*

'The balloons are the latter part of the job, as I've told you, and they're in *your* boat. Please pay attention, it's imperative we work together as a team on this to ensure it all goes smoothly this time. I certainly shouldn't need to remind you about the last time we attempted this crazy stunt now should I?'

'Er… no, Jack. Right, so I meet you at the dive site, kit up, then join you at the wreck.'

'Correct, remembering of course to bring with you the un-inflated weather balloons and the rope from the cows we need in order to get the job done. I will have gotten all the cylinders in place by then, so I should be pretty much ready for you.'

Ping! A light bulb illuminates in my mind, alerting me to the fact that they're going back for the gold. How on earth did I not see this coming?

'Right, Hazy, let's programme this new G.P.S. module with the co-ordinates from Richard's old one, so we can convene at the same point; directly above the treasure.' My clone picks up Richard's device and scrolls through the memory for the last entered co-ordinates. He then switches on the new device, and after a moment of warming up, the green glowing screen signals it's ready. He synchronises the two devices and I commit the co-ordinates to memory.

Suddenly, the patio door beside me swings open and I'm taken somewhat by surprise. Luckily, the door opens outwards, and conceals me from Victoria, the real one that is, who walks out into the moonlight wearing just a towel. She enters the plunge pool one step at a time, discarding the towel as she sinks further into the water. I gaze in awe at her breathtaking figure as her naked body's light coating of sweat glints in the ghostly illumination. I'm trapped, the clones continue unaware, and I remain frozen, incapable of forming a solution to this new found problem. My ears are hearing a jumble of voices as the details of the plan evolves, yet my eyes remain fixed on my object of affection, as she slowly becomes fully submerged in the small pool. A moment later her head breaks the surface once again, sending a flow of concentric ripples out to its edges. She leans back as if stretching under the water, arching her body rearward, her firm breasts punctuating the otherwise calming water. I stand in awe, caught like a naughty schoolboy between the conundrum of right and wrong, action or inaction, lust and guilt.

A gust of wind catches the door, slamming it violently, breaking both my trance and jolting the relaxed Victoria back to reality. She swivels around instantly to see where the banging noise came from to see me, devoid of any cover, cringing at the thought of being caught in the act, so to speak. I grab the ring, and with a swift *'Please!'* to the heavens, I depress the three stones. Nothing, I press them again repeatedly as Victoria leaps from the pool gathering her towel in front of her.

'Jack, you pervert! I never thought you were like this, get off my property and never come back.' The door slams again, this time with her on the inside.

'No, Victoria, you've got it all wrong, it's not like that at all, I was just…'

'Go away, Jack, I'm calling reception to see if they can remove you.'

'No, please, it's all a mistake. I can explain…'

'No, go away. NOW!'

I know I'm in deep trouble here; I can't explain the clones for fear she thinks I'm mad, I have little other excuse for being on her deck in the middle of the night and I really don't know where to begin explaining. I decide it's best to scarper and think about it in the morning. Why does this stuff always happen to me?

*****

I rise around nine, but a fitful and interrupted night's sleep has left me feeling tired. I have, however, had a brainwave. I realise that any further communication with Victoria for the time being would be futile, so decide to write her a note, explaining that it was all a misunderstanding and I'll talk to her tonight over dinner, allowing her the day to relax without thinking about it too much. This I slip under her door on my way down the beach.

I follow the curve of the bay around, patting my top pocket to ensure I have my passport, and set my sights once again for the shack of a locals' bar that still sits out on the peninsula, obviously they haven't had any hurricanes since my last visit. Again I find the distance deceptive as I trudge through the golden sand, filling my shoes and causing friction between my toes, rubbing them raw.

The familiar rocky outcrop shows itself once more as I round the bay, expecting to see my golden toothed friend at any moment. I reach the outcrop safely, and decide to wait a few moments to see if he will appear. I'm not disappointed, and after probably only half an hour's relaxing I see him walking along the beach towards me, large cutlass blade by his side. I wave, something I doubt he expects, and he picks up the pace to jog towards me.

'What you doin' here off the resort, white boy?'

'I need your assistance with something, and as you are wearing my watch,' I point to his arm, causing his smile to drop and blade to be pulled, 'I figure you owe me.'

'Don't owe you nothin'. Gimme your wallet.'

'I'm not so stupid this time, all I have on me is a guarantee of my goodwill.' I hold my hand out bearing my passport. 'Now as you know, without this I have no way of leaving your beautiful country, and *you* no doubt have a rife black market that will reward you handsomely for it. It is, however of more value to me than your black market friends, so I have come here to propose a deal. I will give you double the black market value for the safe return of my passport, provided you can supply me with some items I need for first thing tomorrow.'

'What dem items be, white boy?'

I smile, knowing I've caught his attention. 'I need enough dynamite to blow a piece of rock, say thirty foot square, and some underwater timed fuses. Now I know you guys use it to illegally blow the reefs and harvest the fish, filling your boats and taking it to the mainland because I saw it on the National Geographic channel one time.

'Da what?'

'Doesn't matter, can you do this for me or not?'

'Yeah, I can do explosives real easy. Meet me back here with the money in an hour.'

'Not that simple, my friend, I'll have your money once I've completed my task.'

'No deal, get outta my face.' He brings the blade up to my throat and says through gritted teeth, 'You gimme that passport and get your white ass off my beach, or you be shark food in minutes.'

'Ten thousand U.S. Dollars worth of gold,' I croak, the blade pressed hard against my oesophagus. Suddenly the tension dispels, he stands back and eyes me suspiciously.

'Where you getting ten thousand Dollars worth o' gold from?'

'Dynamite, do we have a deal, yes or no?'

'We got a deal, one hour, then the gold by sundown tomorrow, or...'

He draws the large blade across his own throat, smiling.

Oh shit! I fear I've just made a deal with the devil himself.

29. The depths of despair

Morning breaks again, this time the closed window ensures my feathered friend badgers somebody else this morning, as I have work to do. Victoria ignored my request for dinner last night, and refused to leave her pavilion; preferring room service and silence over illuminating conversation and mental stimulation. To be honest, I can't blame her after how it all looked. I have a few more days to set the record straight though, so *no worries*, as they say in Aus.

Hazy and my clone are busy ferrying stuff from their pavilions down to the jetty, they load several gas tanks into the Rib and run through the procedure once again when loaded. I'm not sure exactly what they're up to, but I manage to swipe a hand-held G.P.S. off of another moored boat and plot the remembered co-ordinates. Things are looking good, Hazy and my clone part company, and I decide to follow Hazy, for no better reason than to find out what the whole *'cow'* thing is all about. Hazy arrives back at the pool to collect the waiting Tess and (clone) Victoria, then the three of them walk out the front gate and head away from the resort.

After fifteen minutes walking in blaringly hot sunshine, we reach the field. Hazy drops his blue sports bag to the floor, and withdraws a loop of heavy gauge rope, and a further loop of lighter gauge, which has a lasso end to it. The girls take the heavy rope, and grab one end each, Hazy then approaches a grazing cow with a little trepidation. The animal seems perfectly calm, and after a couple of strokes, Hazy slips the lasso easily over its neck. The girls then spring into action, looping the thicker rope around the back of the animal, and pulling it tight, causing the cow's legs to shuffle forward and it begins to walk, directed by Hazy at the front. Any time the cow thinks it's time to resume eating, the girls give it another little reminder with the rope, and off it goes again. I'm amazed that even a clone of the cow is created once its destiny is altered, this really is becoming just too confusing.

I follow the procession out of the field, across the road, and down onto the beach, it's a section sheltered from prying eyes as it appears to be a deserted cove where a second boat is anchored in the shallows. This whole fiasco takes over half an hour, and once there, the troupe coerce the reluctant cow into the water, marching it out to about three feet deep, then tether it to the waiting boat. I realise at this point, that I will lose sight of Hazy once the second cow is attached as he departs by water, so I jog back to the resort, heading straight for my pavilion in order to grab the bag of dynamite and some diving gear on my way to the jetty. I still can't see what the hell they're going to do with a couple of cows, but best get a boat so as I can find out.

'The Rib, at the end of the jetty,' I interrupt, as the rather overweight florally clothed man speaks to some other guests on the pontoon 'I need it for a few minutes, is that okay?'

'No, sir, we have it booked for the rest of the day,' the American resort employee informs me, 'you have to reserve these boats in advance, sir. We have a slot tomorrow for a couple of hours in the afternoon if that's okay?'

Bugger it, I miss good old Richard and his organised attention to detail.

'Where can I get a boat now? I need one immediately.'

'No can do I'm afraid, sir.' He continues in a Texas drawl, 'Tomorrow's the best I have.'

'This is really urgent,' I insist, 'I must take it immediately.'

'Well I'm afraid that's not possible. Check with reception and we'll see what we can arrange tomorrow for you, sir.'

He turns back to the other guests he was speaking to before I interrupted him, and continues to explain the workings of the small sailing boat they are about to head for the horizon in. I take my gear and continue towards the Rib.

'Sir, sir, you can't take it out, sir,' he calls out after me, although *we'll see about that*. I dump my bag into the Rib and note it already has four cylinders on board, I just hope they're full. I then reach behind me for the explosives, but feel a hand on my shoulder that commands attention.

'Sir, I must insist, these folks booked it yesterday,'

he motions to an approaching couple, 'so I suggest you do the same, sir.' Throwing caution to the wind, I swing around and barge the large Texan twit off the pontoon and into the water, casting off immediately and firing up the motor. Thankfully the key is in the ignition, and I race out, into the ocean, to intercept my destiny once again.

*****

I see Hazy up ahead, chugging slowly out to the horizon. Although his boat is larger than mine, he plods along at an extremely sedate pace, the cows in his care have long since given up the will to live and have drowned in the wake of the boat. Now they are just simply being dragged along by the rope around their necks. I draw alongside the ghostly clone of Hazy and still find it difficult to work out what he's doing. He seems relaxed, reclining in a chair behind the wheel that he steers with his foot, soaking up the January sun's warming rays. I remain at a constant pace beside him for the next twenty minutes.

Suddenly his G.P.S. squawks into life, taking him by surprise. He picks it up from the dashboard of the boat, and after checking its screen, kills the engine, allowing him to drift silently in the still water. The rope attaching the cows to the boat is fastened to an electric winch at the back of the vessel, and he operates this by the small keypad on its side, reeling the large animals in. Once the cows are up to the back of the boat, he reaches down with a large knife I hadn't noticed previously, and slits one of their throats, sending a burst of blood gushing from the animal's open wound, spattering Hazy in the process. I think the pressure of blood pumped to the brain of the dying cow was sealed once the rope tightened around its neck, not allowing it to return to the body. He then cuts the rope and leaves the animal to sink down into the depths.

Hazy splashes some water on his face to wash away the blood, then jumps back into the driver's seat after releasing the winch once again, and re-starts the engine. Progress is now somewhat swifter with only half of the drag on Hazy's boat, so we make the second destination in a little over fifteen minutes. Again, the same procedure, wind in the cow, slit its throat, cut it loose. I still fail to see the point of all this until a dorsal fin cuts through the water right past me, heading straight for the cow's carcass. *Ahh,* I think, *bait to keep the sharks away from the dive site, now I get it!*

Hazy again washes the blood from himself, ignoring the shark, then cranks the engine back into life. I deduce that he will shortly be heading to the dive site, so follow the course my G.P.S. plots for me to gain some time on him.

Once at the site, I drop anchor next to the clone's Rib, and begin kitting up for a dive into the deep once again. I check the cylinders, and they are, as hoped, all full. The explosives I inspect once again, just to make sure they are all assembled correctly, then check the time delay on the remote detonator; thirty minutes. I clip it to my belt and think to keep it to hand, so as I can abort the explosion if needs be at any time. With a quick crossing and a high speed *'Our Father'* I plunge backwards into the big blue.

The first thing that strikes me is the bright clarity of the water that I'd forgotten from our last dives nearly a year ago. I marvel at the marine life as brightly coloured friends surround me, inquisitive to this alien in their serene environment. I drop a few metres, then stop for my body to adjust before sinking further. A *'spadoosh'* above me signals Hazy's entry into the water, and I drop to my next equalising point a few metres further before looking up to check his progress. He also has to have the periodic stops for equalising the pressure in his ears, as it's the first dive of the holiday for him too. We race to the bottom in a kind of concertina'd fashion, and I fin towards the wrecked plane once I near the correct depth.

I can see my clone has set to work, cutting the chest with a saw. He's taken the weights from his belt and wrapped them around his ankles, giving him the ability to stand as if on land, not bob horizontally as I do with my buoyancy centred on my body. I stall in the water to observe a moment, he's cutting the padlock with an engineer's metal hacksaw, but obviously finding the sub-aqua task somewhat taxing. The volume of air used in such a task must be tremendous, as he discards his regulator and begins to breathe through the regulator of a loose cylinder next to him. He has a total of twelve cylinders around him for both breathing and inflation purposes, so I doubt he'll run out before the avalanche of rock from my little explosion crushes him and Hazy into the sea bed forever. On that subject, I set about finding a few gaps in the rock of the overhanging ledge in which to plunge my dynamite. I check the clock, twenty-one minutes before detonation, so stop a moment to spectate, feeling re-assured that I have sufficient time to clear the site before the big boom.

Hazy appears with a trail of rope, attached to which is thirty or so limp weather balloons and what looks like a load of postal sacks. He joins my clone at the wreck, and takes over the sawing for a time, using the regulator from a spare cylinder to save the supply he has on his back for re-surfacing and general mobility. I glance to the timer, eighteen minutes to go, I must leave on eight to clear the site without any shock waves taking me unaware, this allows the required five for my decompression stop en route for my three minute rise to the surface. I then synchronise my wrist-mounted dive computer to the detonator for added peace of mind.

After a further four minutes, the pair manage to break the lock from the chest. The lid bursts open with a flood of stale forty-year-old bubbles to reveal what looks like a load of grey cloth, maybe I was right about Hitler's laundry after all! The pair begin to delve inside the open chest, but my view is obscured so I move in for a closer look. Releasing some air from my B.C. allows me to drop to within a couple of feet of the ocean floor and then fin my way over to where the discovery is being made. I glance to the timer to see that I have twelve and a half minutes remaining, which leaves four and a half minutes before I need to evacuate. I pull myself into the wreck, and settle in behind their ghostly figures, but conclude that floating up above them would gain me a better vantage point. A few puffs into my vest has me rising gently, a couple of thrusts with my fins and I drift serenely above the chest. Hazy unwraps one of the rolls of grey cloth, and as he does so there bleeds particles of black oil out into the clear water; it was obviously used to preserve the contents of the chest from damp whilst in storage. As Hazy unravels the cloth, we all marvel at the glow of golden treasures within. Richard appears to have been right with his guess that the mysterious cargo really is the missing Nazi gold. The burst of bubbles from the clones' regulators show me they're shouting with joy at their discovery, yet little do they know of the fate that is about to befall them.

The clones then begin to scoop the rolls of grey cloth into the mail sacks and inflate the balloons to which the sacks are now attached. One by one, the balloons rise to the surface, laden with stolen gold. At one point there must be ten rising together in front of me, all making their way to the surface. Even at a conservative £250,000 per bag that makes a whopping two and a half million quid with just what's on its way up, let alone what's already at the surface and what remains down below. This is only the first flight case as well; there must be at least thirty on board. One hundred million pounds is a crazy figure to contemplate, yet it sits below me and is being harvested by my clone and some joker who set me up on national television. Life just isn't fair sometimes, as they are about to find out.

Suddenly, I become doubtful that I'm doing the right thing. It's time for action though, I look at the timer; nine minutes. Do I pull the plug? After all, I've never killed anyone before and it feels quite wrong, or do I continue with the plan and avert the success of my alter self by destroying him with an explosion as I fin to the surface safely out of the blast zone, claiming the clone's life as my own? Click, eight minutes: Decision time. I drop the timer and fin for the surface, knowing my original plan is the best. The clone will be dead and I can carry on as normal, taking the pre-destined path that was mine in the first place.

As I watch the gadget sink to the floor, I'm suddenly caught; my gas tank has hooked behind me on some jagged metal. After a moment's twisting and shaking, I look to my dive computer; seven minutes, that's one minute too little to safely clear the area before detonation. I frantically thrash my arms and legs, trying to work my way loose, but it's futile. I glance down to see the two clones blissfully unaware, loading more and more sacks, yet I cannot see the remote timed detonation controller, it's fallen from view and its safe retrieval is now becoming my only hope of survival. I glance to the readout again; four minutes to detonation. I have no time to clear the area now, so must break free and terminate the countdown. The only thing for it is to remove my B.C. and my air supply with it. I undo the clasps and slip from my vest, taking a last deep breath from the cylinder as I do. The weights around my belt pull me to the floor easily, despite my full lungs, and I fin swiftly to assist. My search for the detonator is frenzied, causing a swirl of sand that impedes my vision, but I continue in a state of panic. I glance once again to my wrist; one minute thirty seconds and notice blood spewing from my hand as I have suffered a laceration from something sharp. No time to worry about that, and no control device in sight. I frantically search the bed, cringing at the impending blast.

The clones have begun to rise, clear of the wreck and are making their way to the safety of the surface. I see why they have aborted as the menacing predatory figure of a shark becomes clearer as it approaches. Thirty seconds to go, I spy the device in a crevice between two rocks. I jab my fingers into the gap, desperate to retrieve it, fifteen seconds, I try to shuffle the box clear, but it jams against the narrow walls. Five seconds, I retrieve my dive knife from my calf sheath, and jab it down, into the crack in an effort to prise the rocks apart. No luck, they're solid, I push the knife in once again, and manage to manipulate the device so as the keypad faces me, then plunge the tip of the knife onto the abort button, managing to depress it with only two seconds to go.

Elated, I exhale completely, forgetting my lack of cylinder, then frantically fin with no air inside me, back up to the snagged device on the wreck's roof. My lungs scream with pain as I desperately fight the urge to draw a deep breath before air is available. Once there, I grab the regulator and plunge it into my mouth, gasping the dry powdery air it provides. A red cloud emanates from the gash in my hand, so before the shark's interest grows too keenly I set about releasing the snagged rig from the jagged metal, then replace it on my back. I swim down one last time inside the wrecked carcass of the aeroplane, and grab one of the grey cloths, discarding its contents in order to wrap my hand and stem the flow of attention grabbing blood. Once bound, I collect up a second grey cloth and head for the surface with its contents, eyeing the finned predator from a distance as I rise.

The five minute pressure stop is an agonising wait, and after only two long minutes I'm baulked from behind, startling me as I drop my precious gold-lined cloth. I see the lazy glide of a passing turtle who wasn't looking where he was going and feel a wave of relief at the thankful sight of a shell not a shark. Only then, do I realise I have dropped my treasure back to the depths, and although there seems to be only one shark, and he's preoccupied fishing around in the wreck, I'm sure he can still taste my blood and don't wish to give him the opportunity to sample the flesh that goes with it. Sadly I watch my small slice of fortune fade from view, and will the display on my dive computer to show me a green light.

Once back on the surface, I'm concerned to see a growing number of dorsal fins surrounding me. I fin as calmly as I can to my Rib and haul myself over the side, discarding my tank immediately. The clones are frantically fishing out the bobbing domes they're surrounded by; there must be twenty weather balloons, all laden with sacks of gold. I calculate five million pounds worth at least, probably more. A good day at the office for the clone and Hazy, I must say.

Exhausted, I lie flat on my back, absorbing the sun's rays for a while, then rise, light-headed, to stimulate the boat back into life some ten minutes later. I glide the Rib back towards shore, unsure of what I will find there. Assault and theft charges from the resort employee, a displeased Victoria, and angry bandits when I turn out my empty pockets.

BANG!! An avalanche of water hits the boat, accompanied by a mass of black looking rock, a few fish and a couple of gold trinkets. A massive wave erupts from the sea and nearly capsizes the boat, throwing me off balance and into the water. Disoriented, I search around for the Rib, then realise the engine is still running, albeit at idle. Suddenly panicked at the thought of being left alone in the middle of the ocean to drown or be eaten, I start swimming with all my strength towards the boat, but it continues moving at a pace I could never match. Frantically I swim, but in vain. The orange boat chugs away from me at a frustratingly slow but untouchable pace. I scream a stream of obscenities after the bobbing craft, and splash the water in violent frustration. It's only after a minute that I realise the Rib is fitted with a circling system in case of such an event, and wait calmly for it to complete its loop back to collect me. Thankfully the sharks have all either been deafened or blown to pieces by the blast, so I remain somewhat safe and relieved at the lack of company. Once back aboard, I take the helm and set the throttles to full speed ahead, carving my way back to the relative safety of land.

30. Bandits at five o'clock

I stow my diving gear in my bag before I see land, as I think a sharp exit from the jetty is appropriate. The forty minutes I'd spent returning to Shambhala was done in quiet contemplation. The explosion had no doubt buried any further hope of harvesting the gold surreptitiously, it would now be a major excavation to win any of it back, involving specialist machinery and many dive crews. This would be impossible to keep quiet, and I fear for my freedom should I ever go public with it, after all, we should have reported it upon its first discovery. The explosives are also an issue as they've proved somewhat unreliable due to the supposedly terminated detonator, detonating; so I don't fancy even risking a return to the site in case there's some unexploded dynamite down there. I'm left, so it seems, with two small trinkets that the blast launched into the Rib. Both I shall present as offerings of peace; one to Victoria, and the other to the bandit in exchange for my passport. I dock quickly, tie the boat, and then hastily make my way back to the security of my pavilion.

I mount the steps swiftly and enter, only registering once inside that the door was open. Before I realise what's happening, I have the blunt feeling of a gun muzzle pressed into the small of my back. I drop the dive bag to the floor and automatically raise my hands in submission.

'Look, I needed the boat, it was an emergency.'

'Dat won't help you now, white boy.' The feeling of the pit of my stomach dropping is my cue that I'm not even lucky enough to be being arrested.

'You got my ten grand in dat bag have you, boy?'

'Er... no. Things didn't quite go to plan. Your bloody dynamite nearly killed me!'

'You gotta be careful wid dat stuff. It *BITES*.' He laughs as I jump out of my skin.

'Listen, I've got some gold for you, but it's all I have. It's here in my pocket.' I reach down into the pocket of my shorts and bring out one of the two gold chains, this one with a gemstone pressed into a pendant it wears. I reach back over my shoulder to hand it to my assailant.

'Not good enough, white boy.'

There is a flash of light, a searing pain on the top of my head, as the room fades instantly to black.

*****

I come to on the floor, and not the floor of my pavilion I hasten to add. I'm in a bamboo shack, the windows are boarded up but I can see through the small cracks that it's daylight, late morning I'd guess from the temperature and freshness of the air. My head splits with the pain as I run my fingers gently over it, wincing when a large mound on the back confirms that the flash of light I saw before being rendered unconscious was purely internal, a bolt of motor neuron electricity at the shock my brain received before shutting down. I had been struck, presumably with the butt of the gun, and now find myself a prisoner to the bandits. I scour the bare room for an implement, a weapon, but none are obvious.

After a time, probably midday or so, a man I recognise from my initial mugging enters the room with a cup of water and two bananas. He sets them on the floor just inside the door, then retreats, locking me in once again. I eat and drink quickly, realising it may be my last opportunity for some time, then sit in the corner once again to try and plot my escape. I feel dirty, exhausted and weak, and drift off to sleep once the digestion of the food begins.

I wake some time later to the heat of the day, my head painfully reminding me of its strike the past evening. I guess it's the middle of the afternoon by the escalating temperature and mugginess of the jungle residence I'm captive in. I stand at the covered window once again and squint out of the gaps to find some clues as to my location. None are apparent; however I do spy an outbuilding which appears to have several boxes of dynamite visible through the open door. I decide that swiping a few sticks from this shed is my primary goal once I manage to escape. I scour my room for a weakness, a place for me to begin my fight for safety. The walls are all rough plaster, wooden inside though I deduce by knocking one gently. I beat away as quietly as possible at the plaster with the base of the thick ceramic cup my water arrived in. Quickly the wall covering falls away and I manage to get down to the thin plywood centre quite quickly. Here though lies a problem, the echoey sound of the cup on the wood, if beaten with any force, would alert my guard to the fact I was up to no good, and have him in the room and no doubt beating me with a stick in moments. I cease my work, deflated at the lack of progress and sink once again to the floor. I sit in silence, contemplating my fate, and wondering why the bandits have me prisoner. Surely if they were going to kill me it would be best done sooner rather than later, unless they are waiting for the cover of darkness to dispose of my body. If I were in their shoes, which reminds me that one of them *is* surely in mine, I think, I would probably have put me on a boat whilst unconscious and sped out to sea to be fed to the sharks, therefore destroying any evidence. By this token I deduce they need me alive, so although this brings a certain amount of relief, it's not exactly reassuring.

Some time later, several hours at least, I find myself staring at the ceiling. The sun is falling, so I guess it's early evening. Then, all of a sudden, it dawns upon me. The ceiling, and therefore roof, appears as most of the other rough residences in the immediate area do, to be made from tightly woven bamboo poles. The dark brown chord that ties them together seems to be the most vulnerable part of the room, so I think of how I can cut parts of it in order to allow me to shuffle the large bamboo poles along enough to form a gap of sufficient size to let me squeeze out of, and up onto the roof. I scour the area but all I can see is the ceramic mug. With this my only option, I think of how to break it as quietly as possible, therefore affording me a sharp edge to work with. I wrap the mug in my torn and filthy shirt, then with the heel of my hand, lean with all my might onto it, bouncing up and down until a muffled 'pop' tells me my task is complete. I see the edges are truly sharp now, as it's cut through my shirt and punctured my hands, soaking parts of the garment in blood. I rise to my feet, wiping my sweaty brow with the shirt, and feeling the grit of powdered ceramics grind into my forehead, grazing it lightly also. I wipe my bloody hands on my bare chest and climb up onto the window frame, determined now of my escape. I use the sharp edges of the broken cup to slice away, one by one, the threads of the binding twine. As I frantically make my progress, I choose to ignore the further lacerations my hands incur. The blood streams down my arms as I feverishly move the shards back and forth over the twine. The tension is released with a light crack as the first gives way, bursting a pole free. This allows the neighbouring two to be unthreaded easily, and I hope this will be easier than I first anticipated.

I set to work on my second beam, although now having to bind my raw hands with strips torn from my shirt. This hinders progress somewhat, as the blood flows so quickly from my mutilated palms, it makes it difficult to grip the small pieces with adequate purchase to use them efficiently without the added grip the shirt's rags offer. 'Pop' a second pole bursts free, again liberating the ones either side. This allows me to shift six large poles on top of each other, and allow the first burst of deep orange sunlight to enter the room today. One more is all I need, and progress slows as the shards are becoming increasingly blunt. The final chord takes an agonisingly long time to cut, I fear discovery at any moment, as my frustration grows with every stroke of the depleting tool. 'Pop' finally the chord breaks, and I breathe a sigh of relief as I unthread the dark twine that binds the poles together. As this is a corner piece, it allows an even larger space, so I easily pull myself up into the freedom of fresh air, drinking in a lungful of victory. Darkness is descending swiftly, and as the vast orange sphere makes its way to the horizon I sense that time is of the essence. I slide from the roof and land awkwardly on the dirt, twisting my ankle, but thankfully not spraining it.

A short hobbled dash has me into the dynamite store swiftly, and I rifle through the contents in search of another timed fuse, not that I actually trust them now, but as the saying goes; 'best to have and not need, than need and not have.' I stuff a couple of sticks into each pocket of my shorts, then give up looking for the detonators. With what I have planned, there's certainly no time for subtlety.

Back outside, I wonder the best way out of here.

There is a track made by jeeps out in front of the buildings, but I'm looking for something with a little more cover. I scour the surrounding area and spot a footpath, or more accurately a trail, out in the opposite direction. I decide to follow this, keeping a wary eye in the fading light for anything venomous, be it with a scaled skin or eight legs. After less than five minutes, I appear, as I had suspected, near the rocky outcrop where I had first encountered my captors. The tide is out, so I easily pass the rocks and continue back towards the resort, staying on the edge of the jungle, just in case I encounter any unsavoury characters en route.

My plan is simple, so simple in fact, I wonder why I hadn't thought of it before the underwater episode that nearly led to my own demise. If the clone and all his fellow clones are unaware of my presence, then why not plant a few sticks of dynamite directly under his nose, and blow the bastard to oblivion, gifting me the perfect life. It's so simple, it's beautiful.

I march with unbending focus, determined to end this right now. I'm sure as the night creeps upon us that the clone, and hopefully that bastard Hazy, will be in the main restaurant. I set my sights for the resort, and ignore the excruciating pain that my tender ankle screams through my nervous system.

I enter the complex by the pool area;

'Sir, sir, you cannot come in, this is for residents only,' an employee implores, 'Piss off,' I respond as I barge past him, waving my hand with a dismissive swipe that catches the side of his head. I continue unabated towards my final destiny.

The main restaurant is within the building that sits at the head of the resort. I stride in purposefully, although with quite a pronounced limp now as my ankle is swollen and extremely painful. I catch my reflection in one of the large floor to ceiling mirrors that line hallway, and am quite taken aback at my Neanderthal appearance; the blood is streaked across my unshaven face, chest and down both arms. Dirt and bruising abound, and the filthy shorts I wear are scarred with ragged tears and blood. They also, quite worryingly, bulge with the four red sticks of explosives. Wide berth is an understatement, if I saw *me* coming, I'd run a mile, and keep going!

Past reception, sending the staff scurrying, I head towards the open courtyard where 'Restaurante Renascido.' can be found. Upon my bold approach, the *maître d'* disappears quickly, leaving me free to enter unchallenged. I spy towards the back of the open space, a table laid for two, upon which sits my clone and his beloved clone Victoria. I approach, to the disgust of all around me, who rise and scream as I enter the confined space. Unperturbed I also spot the beautiful *'real'* Victoria, dining alone in a secluded spot, and send her a reassuring smile. She, however, looks utterly horrified and stands, with her hands to her face, screaming louder than anyone else. This throws me momentarily from my monumental task, but I re-focus on the oblivious object of my attack and continue relentlessly towards him. I search the immediate area for what can be sacrificed to destroy my alter self. The table they sit at is only feet from the wall of the hotel, so I decide to bring this down on top of them in a crescendo of cascading brickwork, crushing him into the ground, as should have been done in the first place.

I scour the immediate area for an illuminated candle, in order to light the fuse of the first two sticks. As I retrieve the explosives from my pocket, the table to my right is quickly vacated by the lovers that sat there and I plunge the fuses into the open flame of their candle. The fuses immediately explode into a fizzing mass of sparks as the animated flames make their gradual way along the cartoon looking foot-long fuses. I raise the red sticks above my head like a trophy and with a demented grin, shout;

'You're mine, you bastard, all mine! Let this put a stop to all your meddling and destruction in my...'

BANG!

I hear the noise, but fail to feel the pain of the impact until I'm taken from my feet and thrown forward to the floor. I skid to an abrupt halt, face first on the harsh cobbles of the courtyard, and choke violently on the blood that quickly fills my lungs. My vision is only that of the stone floor that faces me, soaked in my own blood. As I lie there dying, a sense of complete tranquillity invades my twitching body that fights for the last ounce of rapidly depleting life. I remain surprisingly aware yet detached from the whirlwind of frenzied action around me, and have the strongest of sensations that I'm being pulled from above; an unrelenting force takes my broken body up and clear of the corpse that lies in my form on the floor. I shudder and convulse like never before as I am lifted miraculously, several feet from my ghostly body. I see now the gaping hole in my back where the bullet entered, smashing my ribs and bursting my lung, as seems to be traditional with ring bearers, so I've learnt. A crimson fan radiates slowly from my dying body, bleeding out the force of life itself.

The higher I rise, the clearer the picture becomes; the bandit stands by the entrance, a smoking gun hangs by his side, and he's being hailed a hero. A guest feverishly stamps at the fuses to dissolve their power as they creep ever closer to their thwarted destiny, a dousing from the iced Champagne bucket confirms their inaction as screams and hysteria engulf the open restaurant.

This is my end, where I die. A tear of sadness fills my eye as I see Victoria simply leave the restaurant, without stopping to give me a second look. *'Is this really how it should end?'* I ask myself. The higher I drift, the less it seems to matter, as a warming glow of white light penetrates the inky blue sky, drawing me up to where I belong. Higher and higher, slowly at first, then ever increasing until the island reduces in size in front of me. My mind floods with the colourful memories that fill my head, those that have sat dormant for decades burst into my consciousness as vividly as if they were happening right now, all at once. The light becomes brighter as the draw upwards strengthens, rising higher, a warm sense of comfort surrounding me. Then suddenly, nothing.

It's like a rope has been cut, the Earth's magnetic draw pulling me relentlessly down towards its core. I'm freefalling out of control, the slightest movement of any limb sends me tumbling and spiralling out of control, with only one thing constant, my trajectory back to planet Earth. Faster and faster, the wind noise whistling through my ears and buffeting my cheeks, my nose fights to draw a breath from the air that seems so pure and clean. Over and over I tumble. Sounds, colours, sensations all serve to confuse. All I know is where I am headed; down. A frightening thought then bursts to life, the former serenity of mind eroded; what if I'm going to Hell? Hell is down, and I grow a fire of fear in the pit of my stomach as I continue to drop, through the light cloud now that causes turbulence and confusion, falling still further, Shambhala in sight now, growing ever closer. My focus regains as I see the resort below me now. The turbulence desists, and my rate of descent eases to a gentle fall. My fears of Hell are dispelled as I see the courtyard below me now, my body missing and the bandit gone. The diners relax as normality prevails, and my focus falls to my clone at his table with Victoria. Falling closer I seal my eyes, not wishing to see the impact of my final moments, then… Silence.

I open my eyes and stare into hers, across the table

where our hands are entwined. I notice my Rolex, returned, or is it just that I have become once again the man I should always have been? A smile grows across my face with the glowing reassurance that this is, indeed, the life of my dreams. I break my hand from its loving embrace, and reach to my finger, removing the ring that has taught me so much. I stare deeply into the beautiful pearls of blue that punctuate the smiling face of the girl who has captured my heart, and slide the ring home, onto the hand of the woman that I love so dearly. 'Victoria, my angel Victoria. With this ring, may I thee wed?'

Prank!

taking the joke just a little too far...

A NOVEL BY
HAG HUGHES

Paul (Hazy) Hayes loves a bit of innocent fun, in fact he spends most of his Alcohol fuelled life plotting the next wind up, the next joke and searching for his next victim. He is cruel.

But what if it all goes wrong and someone gets killed?

Would YOU help him dispose of the body?

This hilarious debut novel is set amongst the colourful and exciting of backdrop of a World Championship motorsport team, where success and inspired invention meets sharply with disaster and desperation. Hazy's tale then threads its way through the curious and usually closed doors of the British film industry in his quest for the ultimate revenge. He is led to battle with friends, foes, lovers and ultimately his own conscience, as he attempts to hold together both his life and his sanity under the crumbling reality of divorce and destitution.

Oh, and Robert DeNiro's corpse in the boot of his car!

Released July 2008.
Available from: www.haghughes.com and all good retailers.

Mr. Right

He's Out There

By
HAG HUGHES

Girls,

What would you say if I told you that there is a system that you could easily learn, that would attract the perfect partner to your life quickly and effortlessly?

I'd have your attention, wouldn't I?

Well now that I have your attention, allow me to elaborate a little. For many years I have dedicated my life to a study of the attraction process between men and women, both out in the field (bars and restaurants, supermarkets, workplaces, parties, etc.) as well as studying with an infinite number of professional coaches in the fields of psychology, physiology, behaviour and attraction. People who are hailed as the best in the world.

And guess what?

I have discovered a fascinating system, blending all of these learnings and skills that is so powerful, it will not only have handsome men vying for your attention wherever you go, but it will also allow you to easily and effortlessly ascertain their suitability as a long-term partner within moments of speaking to them. So if you want to hear all the girls asking:

How come *you* always find the right guys?

Order your copy of **Mr. Right** today!

Released August 2009.
Available from: www.haghughes.com and all good retailers.